DESERVED, CONTORTED RELICS

MOLISIA
BAUSTIC MOUNTAINS
GAROBANSUROV
DEEPV
HOR
RIFTOLEN
INFERTI
DESERT
N
W
E

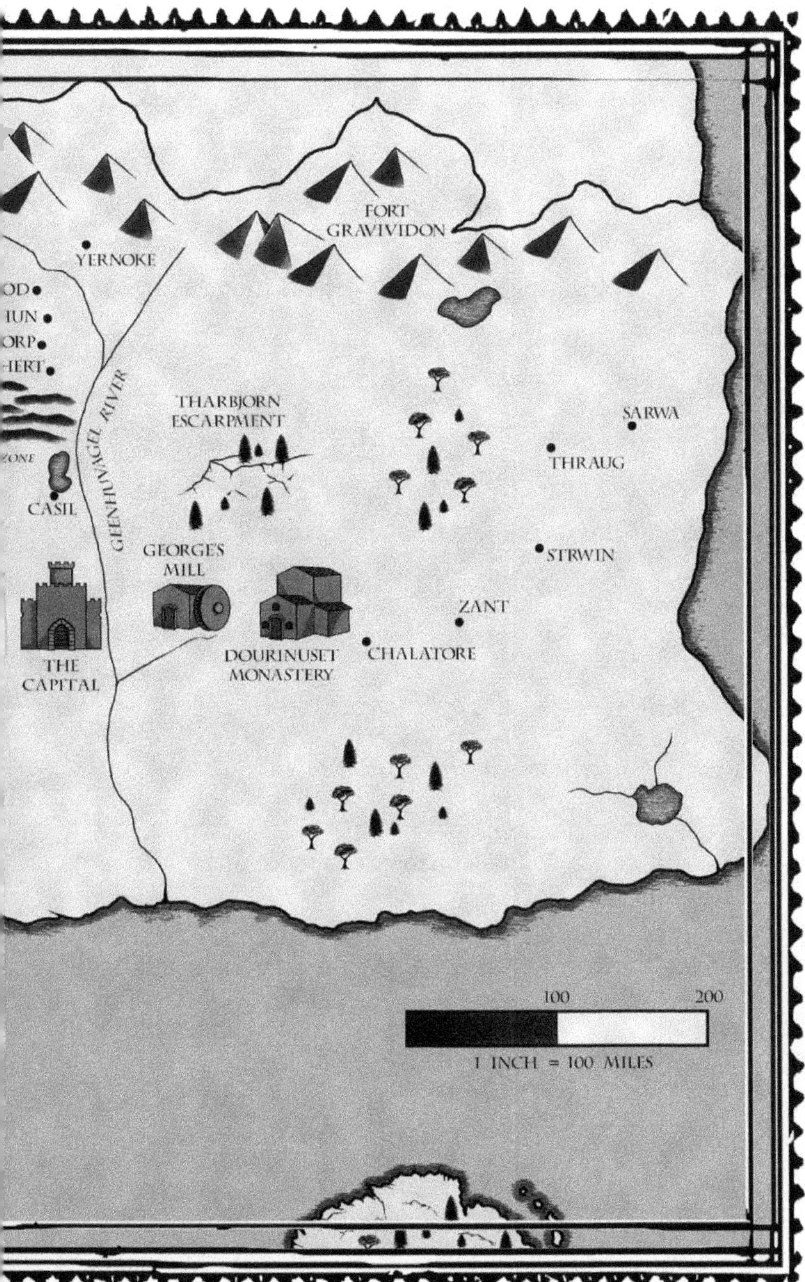

YERNOKE
FORT GRAVIVIDON
OD
IUN
ORP
HERT
ZONE
CASIL
GEENHUVAGEL RIVER
THARBJORN ESCARPMENT
SARWA
THRAUG
GEORGE'S MILL
STRWIN
THE CAPITAL
ZANT
DOURINUSET MONASTERY
CHALATORE
100
200
1 INCH = 100 MILES

ALSO BY NICHOLAS WUDTKE

—NOVELS—

Black Needle, Book One: Parabolic, Magnetic Key

Black Needle, Book Two: Blunt but Imminently Fatal Projectile

Black Needle, Book Three: Deserved, Contorted Relics

—SHORT STORIES—

The Swords, Friendships, and Winds of Far Off Places:
A Collection
~ FREE copy available at website below ~

Find out more, join our list, and purchase your next
great read at www.NicholasWudtke.com.

Black ┃ Needle
Book Three

DESERVED, CONTORTED RELICS

NICHOLAS WUDTKE

BLACK
NEEDLE
BOOKS

For Lifeson

PROLOGUE

One of life's greatest treasures was gazing upon beautiful sights—no great mystery. Some would've adamantly posited that the more you saw, the better. And for others, it was all relative, meaning everyone perceived exactly the same amount of beauty in what they witnessed, accumulated throughout their lifetime. The lead characters in this story hadn't entirely decided how they looked at it. But they did know, for at least in the short term, all the wondrously aesthetic sights they've observed in their travels have had an impact on how they viewed their own homes. Perhaps, if they'd never gone anywhere, their homes would've been lovelier to them, perhaps less so. It was just one buoying question in a sea of questions that may very well turn out to be eternally ensconced in mystery.

CHAPTER 1

ALTHOUGH THEY HADN'T been there much lately, Mick and Dave lived in a little corner of the world, inhabiting opposite ends of a winter-tinged pond, almost large enough to be considered a lake. The pond was no doubt a natural beauty unmistakable by oral description to those familiar with it. Dave and Mick's houses were small, but the scenery was grand.

There was only one other home on the isolated, unnamed body of water. Ironically, the owner of the house was absent even more than Mick and Dave. Technically, the person was gone so often neither Mick nor Dave had ever gotten the chance to ask them to where they constantly ventured. In fact, Mick and Dave didn't even know what he or she looked like.

Dave lived on the deep end of the pond, Mick the wide. Dave had built a sturdy seawall on his side, making for better pond access. Mick's home was identifiable by the far-from-ostentatious pole pavilion, bereft walls, built alongside the pond. He really enjoyed sitting beside the pond, as it rained, devoid getting wet.

It would usually take five minutes of brisk walking to get from Mick's house to Dave's. Mick had just sluggishly done it in six.

He found Dave sitting by his firepit bordering the seawall. A fire was blazing, and cool air was wafting. "I would guess the ice will be unseasonably off the pond by next week."

"That sounds about right," replied Dave. "Winter has been pretty mild this year, thankfully."

"May I be so bold as to say I could make do without long winters?"

"You may."

The two sat by the fire for half an hour, afterwards, they got to work, doing for what it was Mick had come.

The plan was to leave Chalatore again to aid in the war effort. They determined that while they were away, they'd allow some young men they knew to stay in their houses. Someone may as well use them, they thought.

Dave had one last thing to do to make his house ready for the move-in. With Mick's help, they would repair the chimney. It would be an easier job for two, because one on the ground could hand things to the other working up on the chimney. Undeniably, it was a pain in the butt to climb up and down a ladder repeatedly.

Passing an uninteresting stone up to Dave, Mick commented, "Have you ever wondered if Old Man Johnson would like to come to the Capital with us this time? I think he could handle making the trip, plus, I know he's fascinated with the coming of the Icytryxis."

"That he is. He doesn't have many years left, I don't think, for such a journey. I think we should propose the idea to him."

"We should. And I'd envision we could pretty much carry most of his load, which wouldn't be much, I'm sure. He could sleep in one of our tents with us too."

"We'll ask him next time we see him," said Dave, securing the bland stone into its rightful place.

The chimney was completed in an hour, after which they sat by the fire, watching the ice on the pond get thinner and thinner. It wasn't really something that could be seen, only something that could be imagined. The week previous, they'd done the same with the snow. By that point, the snow was almost completely gone and not expected to return, an expectation not unlike the smoke that'd been escaping through the hole in Dave's chimney.

Yet again, Mick and Dave expected to miss the annual armwrestling tournament in town, beckoned by things elsewhere. They felt bad about it, because they knew how much local tourism could've been boosted just by the Knowing Circle recipients entering. The Knowing Circle was the highest award given by the king of their home country, Garobansurov. Nonetheless, there were more important things than tourism stealing their attention.

Though, they were doing their best to help out the tournament's organizers by hosting a fundraising event for new equipment. The tournament's tables, bleachers, tents, and concession stand were getting old, and funds were needed to repair and replace them. So, Mick and

Dave came up with the idea to host a benefit fish fry. They usually didn't icefish much, but they had spent the last month on their pond catching a rather large supply for the event. To keep the fish fresh, they kept them alive in a makeshift pool temporarily thrown together near Mick's house. The water was kept from freezing by the residual heat of the house and the substantial amount of body heat produced by the many fish.

The event was to take place at Chalatore's only park and was scheduled for the morrow. Dave and Mick had event preparations to discuss.

To Dave, Mick stated, "I don't think we'll have to go very far for firewood with which to cook, tomorrow, as there's plenty of it close to the park."

"That should save some time. We still need to peel and cut potatoes, set up tables and chairs, and clean fish, all by nightfall," replied Dave.

Noticing the wind had picked up, Mick said, "I bet we'd have time in the morning to clean some of the fish, if by chance we don't get it all done today."

"Maybe. We'll see how it goes."

Rare for the season, a leaf plummeted towards Mick's face. He flicked it away, and asked, "How many people do you think will come?"

"I think a couple hundred would be a good turnout. If any more were to show up, we wouldn't have enough fish."

"I think we'll be good. We've got three hundred fish—three fillets and a pile of potatoes for each person."

"I still can't believe how well we did fishing," blurted Dave. "It was almost as fruitful as fishing from the Icytryxan sea-ship."

"Yup, almost. We should make plenty of money for the tournament reparations."

The pair worked hard all day and got everything completed, even all the fish cleaning. Basically, all they had to do the next morning was haul all the fish to the park.

An even warmer weather pattern than the previous moved in, as the morning sun ascended.

The event was scheduled for noon, so Mick Thraiker and Dave Ghrere woke up early enough to tote all the fish and start the fire. They also wanted to get a good chunk of it cooked, before the event began. Their good friend, Old Man Johnson, would help out with the cooking. Plus, a few of the local women had volunteered to help serve.

Calculatingly, at 11:00, Mick, Dave, and Mr. Johnson began to light the fire. Usually, it didn't take three people to get a fire going, but the wind that'd picked up the day prior hadn't yet felt like settling, making for a difficult task. Once the flames reached a desirable height, the trio stopped adding wood.

Dave said to Old Man Johnson, "We were actually wondering something yesterday. Would you like to accompany us on our trip to the Capital this time? You aren't getting any younger, and this may be your only opportunity to lay eyes upon the Icytryxan atlytl corp. You wouldn't have to carry anything."

Mick added, "Trust me, seeing the atlytl projectiles in motion would truly be worth the trip. The spectacle is undeniably mystical."

Old Man Johnson threw a handful of filets into one of the pans on the fire and took a few moments to think. "A few days ago, I had the feeling you would propose the idea to me. I pondered on it but came to no conclusion at that time. But for some reason today, it only took a few seconds to decide. As long as you'll go at a pace I can handle, I would very much like to come."

"We can promise you this, no problem. Though, I suppose I should mention there really is no time frame as to how long we'll be there this time."

"That's fine," responded Johnson. "I have plenty of gitis (Garobansurov's currency) for indefinite accommodations."

"I doubt any of us will have to pay much for lodging."

"I imagine. Also, I'd be delighted to see my old buddy, Tim Warmane, again."

"He actually mentioned during the last time we were there that he wished you'd come someday," noted Dave.

"When will be leaving?"

"Probably next week."

"Excellent. By the way, how did you guys catch so many fish?"

Mick chuckled. "It's a secret. I guess it's a proficiency we only recently cultivated."

The first batch of fish and potatoes were ready for consumption. They began the next batch without delay.

"It must be noon," said Mick, "because our first few patrons are heading this way."

"Let the festivities begin," declared Dave.

Mick and Dave's fundraiser turned out to be a great success. Plenty of people came and filled their stomachs. There'd been enough to feed everyone. A lot of the time had ended up being spent by the villagers discussing what crazy shenanigans Mick and Dave might run into on their next trip. At a certain point in their lives, Dave and Mick would come to learn that the villagers had created a wager system, betting on what exactly would happen to them this time. Old Man Johnson had refrained from betting for two reasons: First, he would be a part of the excursion; and second, he'd learned from Mick and Dave's last cross-country journey that he was bad at guessing such things.

Thanks to the fundraiser, they gathered enough money for everything the armwrestling tournament needed. Mick and Dave were happy to contribute, as they loved that tournament.

Seven days after the fish fry, Mick, Dave, and Old Man Johnson found themselves walking the only road directly connecting Chalatore to the Capital. It wasn't straight, but it was more level than most Garobansurovian trails. Nobody liked a path full of ruts, especially while carrying loads. And like always, Mick and Dave had large ones.

They didn't plan on stopping at any locales for an extended amount of time, as they had during the last trip to the Capital. So, the trio anticipated they'd make decent time—at least decent time for an old man and two carrying large packs. Barring unforeseen incident, they were certain the trip would be pleasant.

Their first night of the trek was spent in a meadow. Normally, Dave and Mick didn't like making camp in terrain without wind blocks, but it was a fairly still night, so they were accepting of it.

While lighting the nightly fire, Dave asked Old Man Johnson, "How are your legs holding up? I noticed you were walking with ease for the most part."

"During the first half of the day, it seemed I was walking like I was fifty years younger. The second half wasn't as friction-free, but I still managed to enjoy myself. My legs are a little sore, but I'm sure they'll be good to go by tomorrow."

"Feel free to tell us to slow down whenever you wish—we're not really facing any deadlines."

"Yup, will do," said Old Man Johnson; a man who, although you wouldn't expect, liked his moniker.

"Excellent."

Johnson kicked an annoying rock out from underneath his feet. "I was wondering, what do you guys think are the chances a battle will transpire while we're at the Capital?"

"Good question. I'd say there's maybe a thirty-three percent chance a battle will occur," replied Mick.

Dave added, "I'm going to say a little higher, a forty percent chance perhaps. I just have that feeling. Knowing Gamald is still at large is a rather ominous thought."

"Those are some fairly good odds," admitted Johnson. "Where do civilians go for safety during times of battle at the Capital? I'm not worried or anything. If I were worried, I wouldn't have decided to go."

"We figured that. There are plenty of places for refuge. The King, of course, can take shelter in the castle's bowels. Civilians could do the same, I suppose. Also, many could take sanctuary in the basements of some of the larger buildings. A few of the smaller homes have basements too, but not many, due to a layer of bedrock close to the surface."

"Oh yes, I remember hearing that once."

Dave commented, "I'm hoping this time around, we hear how the western front is holding up. I'm really starting to worry about that. Yes, the western coast is pretty far from the Capital, but it still affects us all."

"It does indeed."

Dave asserted, "I do know I'm not making the same mistake this time in thinking that nothing hazardous is going to happen."

"Right. Something always happens," said Mick. "I'm prepared, as my sword couldn't get any sharper than it is now."

"Who knows," stated Mr. Johnson, "maybe I'll join in on a battle if one happens. I still have the strength to draw back a bowstring."

"Go right ahead. I doubt King Rowlangiv will stop you," said Mick, following the path of a bat with his eyes.

The trio talked of the Capital for another hour and went to bed.

The next few days of the walk were as smooth as the first. Old Man Johnson had only slowed the pace a handful of times. Mick and Dave didn't care in the slightest when he did. They were more than ecstatic their lifelong friend, Old Man Johnson, was there to share in on the memories.

On the fifth day of the journey, they finally ran into a snag. Despite Mick and Dave walking the road to the Capital multiple times before, they'd never encountered a lone child on it.

When they caught up with the kid, Dave asked, "Hello, where are you headed, youngster?"

"Hello. I don't really know. My father left my mom and I at home, while he went off to war for the King. He said he would be back at some point, but he never returned. My mom has since died, and I don't know what to do. So here I am, wandering aimlessly along this road."

Mick looked at Dave and Old Man Johnson in disbelief, and said, "None of the people in your village would help you? Your mom had no friends?"

"The answer to both is no."

Mick told the child their names and learned his name was Will.

Dave spoke: "We are headed to the Capital now. You're welcome to tag along to see what happened to your dad, or you can walk with us to the next village. These are dangerous roads to be walking alone."

Will replied, "I wouldn't know what to do in some random town, so I think I'll come with you to the Capital and see what happened to my dad."

"Sounds good, Will. We have plenty of food, so you won't have to worry about that."

"Where have you been sleeping, Will, while on the road?" asked Mr. Johnson.

"A few times I found sheds to sleep in, and a few times under trees."

"You can sleep in a tent with one of us, until we get there," commented Mick. "It's a little crowded with two people, but it beats getting rained on."

"Thank you so much. I can fight too, if we run into bandits."

"I imagine you could, Will. I won't stop you."

Fortunately, the party wouldn't run into bandits, unlike the last time Mick and Dave had walked to the Capital. They would, however, run into a lot of bad weather.

One night in particular was especially horrendous. Lightning strikes were so close together there was no clear line separating light of day and night sky. Vein-like bolts of electricity thoroughly illuminated the heavens. The rain came down torrentially, the volume of which was immeasurable. Their tents were exposed to a wind so violent the stakes nearly came undone. Despite the strongest winds the handmade tents had ever encountered, they remained faithfully intact through it all.

Will particularly enjoyed the storm from inside the tent, it was a fresh sight for his young eyes.

Having woken to puddles strewn everywhere, Mick said, "The whole thing was rather reminiscent of the huge blizzard that night by Fort Gravividon. You know, Dave, one of these times our tents are going to lose the battle."

"Impossible. They don't know the meaning of the word *lose*."

"Let's hope you're right. I doubt we'll ever find replacement tents half as durable."

The day after the storm, its aftermath made itself known. It may've stopped raining, but the wind was still gusting ferociously, which made for arduous walking.

The trail could've been considered impassable by some that day, because of how muddy it'd gotten. But Mick and Dave's group were of the hardier sort, not paying the trail's condition much attention. In their minds, they could've run into way worse things than a rainstorm and a sloppy trail.

At the halfway point to Myothraces (the formal name of the Capital), the quartet made camp in the most beautiful place yet of the trip.

"I'm surprised we've overlooked this area for camping on every one of our previous trips through these parts."

"Me too, Dave," replied Mick. "I can't even recall ever sojourning here."

"I know we've seen this ravine before, but I don't think we've ever seen this particular area of it."

"It does seem deeper and more scenic than any memories I have of it. Captivating."

Will spent the whole evening playing near the ravine wall, building forts. Old Man Johnson playfully threw rocks at the forts, trying his best to knock them over. They were having a blast, as a bond was beginning to take shape.

Mick and Dave spent time searching the area for black needle pine trees, since the only other one they'd ever found had been in a similar setting. But the mystery of their swords (which had hilts made from the wood of the black needle tree) continued to be a mystery, as a second tree remained undiscovered.

They made their nightly fire close to a stream trickling through the bottom of the gully. They erected tents uphill from the stream, having gotten lucky in locating the one and only patch of grass. Sleeping on grass was far more comfortable than sleeping on rock, which the whole area was nearly nothing but.

"There must've been a battle down here long ago," observed Mick. "I've been seeing a lot of rusty iron fragments. None of the fragments resemble a weapon of any sort, but there's way more than what could be considered natural."

"I've seen a few too," said Dave. "They must be extremely old to have deteriorated this much."

Old Man Johnson joined in. "It's impossible to tell to whom the weapons belonged, but when we get to the Capital, I'll spend some time researching it."

"As if there was any doubt you would," joked Dave.

Mick, Dave, and Johnson chuckled.

"It is my thing, isn't it? I do love the Capital's library," declared Old Man Johnson.

"Don't we all."

They marched onward. The day's second half saw a little slower going than the first. Old legs were taking their toll. Though, steady progress was surely made, while Mick and Dave allowed Johnson every courtesy he required. Will's pain in having not seen either of his parents in a long time lessened, as having company was a nice distraction. Weather started cooperating as well.

Three nights after the campout in the ravine, the quartet decided that a little respite from the wilderness would be agreeable. They paid for a room in one of the small towns along the way. Will especially liked the idea, for it was the first time he'd ever sleep in an actual bed not his own.

Playing in the garden behind the inn, Will met a few other children staying with their families. They ran and played games most of the night. They would've played *all* night had the other youngsters' parents let them.

Old Man Johnson had also spent some time sitting in the lovely garden, an unusually large creation boasting eight thoroughly maintained sections. Anyone renting one of the inn's three rooms really got their money's worth.

Will came into the room and crashed onto one of the two beds. To him, Mick said, "Fun place eh? What games did you play out there?"

"We played hide and seek, tag, and my favorite: kick the can."

"That was my favorite when I was your age too. It's more fun in the dark though," professed Mick.

"In the dark?"

"Yeah, you play it like you normally would in the daytime, but you do it in the dark. It's fun because you can't see as well."

Will's face lit up with excitement. "That does sound fun. It's too bad my friends can't play anymore. I sure would love to try that."

Dave joined the conversation. "I know how you could play."

Will's face lit up even more. "You do? How's that?"

"All of us here could play—that's if Mick and Mr. Johnson want to play too."

"Count me in," said Mick. "I won't give up the opportunity to finally play kick the can again."

"I'll play too," emitted Johnson. "One is never too old for games at least once in a while."

"There you have it. We can even separate into teams."

"I want Mr. Johnson on my team!" erupted Will.

Enthusiastically, the four went to the garden and played youthfully well into the night. Under the circumstances, Will couldn't have had a better day. He played so hard that he fell asleep instantly upon reaching his bed.

Old Man Johnson wiped his brow and said, "I ran more today than I have in the last three years combined. I will sleep well tonight."

Breakfast was decided at the restaurant across the street.

They sat at the restaurant's only open table and began discussing every facet of the previous evening's game. Will could barely keep his mouth empty of words long enough to fill it with food. He never realized there was so much strategy in kick the can. In the end, Will decided the game was definitely better in the dark, just like Mick had said.

The meal turned out to be identical the discussion: excellent.

Well rejuvenated, the quartet left the inn just after breakfast, and continued their journey to the Capital. The rest of the trip would be spent in tents.

A few days before reaching their destination, Old Man Johnson chanced upon a rather beautiful locality. He'd found it while following the sound of trickling water, as he had needed to fill canteens. The locale contained an impressive grove of trees surrounding a crystal-clear spring creek. The majestic trees seemed as if they'd been placed there for a reason. They stood out from the rest of the forest like an oasis in a desert.

After Johnson came upon his discovery, he beckoned Mick, Dave, and Will, who'd been waiting patiently on the trail. To them, Johnson said, "I know we planned on walking another half an hour tonight yet, but you all have to come see this awe-inspiring grove of trees. I claim we make camp within this mystic setting."

"Lead the way."

Upon seeing to what he was led, Dave's eyes shot wide open. "The trees seem to have been manipulated somehow. The limbs match up more symmetrically than they should."

"Maybe they were wrapped with wires to shape them, like a bonsai tree."

"Good find, Old Man. We'll camp here tonight for sure," said Dave. "Call me curious. I'd like to look around for any signs that someone had indeed purposefully done this to the trees."

"Me too," asserted Mick. "We may find some sort of homestead within the vicinity. That'll supply clues."

Post the erection of the tents, they all scanned the area methodically. However, nothing but natural elements were discovered.

"The trees are old, but not so old that if someone did grow them like this, enough topsoil would've accumulated to cover every spec of evidence."

"That was a mouthful. Are you sure you worded that right?" Mick chuckled.

"I think so. You know what I meant if I didn't." Dave laughed.

"I did, and you're probably right. Oh well. I guess it's another thing we'll never know."

"Nevertheless, it's extremely stunning. Great find, Old Man Johnson."

"Thank you," returned Johnson. "The stream is very picturesque as well. I'm going to fish in it."

"Good luck," emitted Mick. "You probably have an hour of daylight left, I'd say."

"I'm joining in on the fishing," Will announced excitedly.

"Terrific," said Johnson.

Daylight waned, and the duo cheerfully returned with morrow's breakfast, which the four ate at sunrise.

They left the mysterious tree grove behind and walked on.

The final days of the voyage had ended up being an undeniably joyful experience. The miles were steady, and the scenery was noteworthy.

Old Man Johnson was extremely proud he'd made it to the Capital without slowing the pace too much. He figured he'd make it but thought his legs would get a lot sorer than they had.

They approached the Capital from the east.

Hawk and Leopard (Mick and Dave's childhood nicknames) were glad to see atlytl projectiles flying over the tree canopy in the distance, which meant the foreign race of the Icytryxis hadn't gone elsewhere. Deep down inside, Dave and Mick wanted to fight a battle alongside the Icytryxis. Being partly responsible for the Garobansurov/Icytryxis alliance, Mick and Dave felt an affinity towards the foreigners.

"It looks like there's an entire platoon of Icytryxis out in the practice field."

"A lovely sight indeed." Dave turned around and closed the gap to Old Man Johnson, who'd been trailing. "You have to come see this."

Johnson followed.

Dave pointed. "Look there, above those trees."

"It's as magnificent a sight as I'd imagined. They're faster than I pictured. Although, it could be an illusion, since I can't see the projectiles' entire flights."

"It could be. As you'd assume, the projectiles are still governed by conventional physics. We'll be to the practice field in an hour, then, you'll be able to see the full arc."

"Excellent. I do have a particular proclivity for admiring weapons in action."

"We know." Widespread chuckles arose.

CHAPTER 2

SUBSEQUENT THE ALLOWING of time for a sizable viewing of soaring projectiles, the quartet finally took the last few steps of the long trek from Chalatore to the Capital. They entered the main gate without hold up. The guards were well aware of whom Mick and Dave were, having allowed them and their guests passage without delay.

The last time Mick and Dave were at the Capital, they stayed at the castle, being Knowing Circle recipients and all. But this time, they had no intentions of doing so, even though King Rowlangiv would probably want them to. Nevertheless, they didn't want to overstay their welcome in the slightest. They hadn't yet thought about where they were going to stay, basically planning to figure things out on the fly.

Upon seeing no further damage to any part of town, Mick and Dave realized they hadn't missed any battles. But that's not to say one hadn't transpired elsewhere.

"I see the place is full of commotion, as much as ever."

"Very true. A rather large building is under construction to our left by the gate, I see," added Mick.

Addressing Will, Dave said, "The first thing we'll do is go ask the soldiers what happened to your father."

"Thank you so much," returned Will.

They quartet headed straight for the barracks, which had doubled in size since Dave and Mick had last seen them.

Having found exactly who they were looking for, Mick blurted, enthusiastically, "There sure has been a lot accomplished since we've been away."

"Mick! Dave! So glad you're back. And Old Man Johnson! You made the trip this time! Great to see you all." Jason Thorncat hugged his friends. "Yes, we have been quite busy. We put up the new barracks, as you see before you, in under a month. All the town's masons and carpenters were enlisted for the job."

"What are they currently assembling over by the main gate?" Mick asked.

"That will be a dual-function building," replied Jason. "The top part is intended to be a new archer platform; the bottom part, an eatery of some kind. I don't know much about it, I just know the eatery's proprietors and Rowlangiv agreed to split the bill."

"That's smart," commented Dave.

"In your absence, we had also built all the raised areas from where the atlytl troops would launch projectiles in defense of the outermost walls."

"I missed those on the way in. My view must've been obscured," said Dave.

"Now who would be this youngster with you?" asked Lieutenant Thorncat.

"Will Shultz," replied Mick. "We ran into him on the way here from Chalatore. His mother passed away, and his father (Harry) went to war and never returned. So, we promised Will we'd take him to the Capital with us, in the hopes of ascertaining what'd become of his dad. Does the name ring a bell?"

"Not to me it doesn't, but I can learn quickly of Harry's whereabouts. Where are you staying? I'll come search you out when I've gathered the information."

"We're actually not sure yet. Any suggestions? We've decided not to do the castle thing again."

"I'm sure you could though."

"Yeah, I'm sure we could too," noted Mick. "Too much castle may soften us up too much."

Jason laughed. "We can't be having that now can we? My suggestion would be the inn a hundred yards to the west of the barracks here. It's inexpensive and nearby all the action. I think it's called the Doze Inn."

Dave chuckled. "Clever name. We'll try it out. I'd hate to sleep in a place with an uninspired name."

"And I'd hate to be away from all the action," joked Old Man Johnson.

Jason laughed once more. "Ain't that the truth. I'll see you guys in a bit then, when I find out the information on Harry Shultz."

The group of four parted from Jason and headed west to the inn. Along the way, they ran into another familiar face: Syryx. It was at her and her family's house where Mick, Dave, Jason, and Yori stayed during their last year's mission far away across the sea.

"Syryx!" cried Mick. "We're back."

Animated, Syryx set down the sword she was sharpening. "I was hoping to see you two again soon. Jason mentioned he thought you'd be returning as soon as the snow disappeared. It looks like he was nearly correct."

"Yup, almost," returned Dave. "We set afoot a little over a week past snowmelt."

"You guys are looking fit as ever."

"You too, young lady," professed Mick, earnestly. "Our companion here is the friend from a few of the stories we'd shared with you: Old Man Johnson. And the kiddo is Will. We met him on the road and are trying to learn the whereabouts of his father. Jason is actually spearheading that mission as we speak."

"Oh yes, I remember the fascinating stories with you in them," said Syryx, as she reached out her hand to Mr. Johnson. "Wonderful to meet you." After Syryx shook Johnson's hand, she turned to Will. "Good to meet you as well, little one. The right person is on the job to find your dad. If anyone can locate him, it'll be Jason. He's the best tracker in the land, from what I've heard, Will."

"Good to meet you too, Ma'am," responded Will, slightly apprehensive about meeting an Icytryxan for the first time. Though, he was happy to hear Syryx's words.

"Where you guys staying? I'll tell the rest of the crew you're back."

"Jason recommended a place west of here called the Doze Inn."

Syryx chuckled. "Clever name. I knew there was an inn over there, but I never actually read the name on the sign."

"I said the same thing about the name," Dave emitted. "We'll probably end up staying there, unless there's no vacancy or something. If that's the case, I'm sure we'll find you sooner or later."

"I'm sure. See you then."

The group walked the relatively short distance to the inn and looked up at the sign. "I can see why Syryx never read the sign, it isn't very discernable."

"I don't think I would've read it either, Dave," said Old Man Johnson. "Judging from the woodwork, however, the place does look quaint. I like the front porch. I can see myself sitting here quite often, watching the sunset. I like it already. The first week is on me."

"We won't complain about that."

The four of them stepped inside the lobby. As expected of an old building, the wooden floorboards creaked with every passing step. "Quaint indeed."

Across the lobby, a man rivaling the age of Old Man Johnson could be seen tending to check-ins. Opposite the check-in counter was a fireplace, within which a fire was blazing, unnecessarily. Unnecessary, since it was a rather warm spring. Atop an oval rug, in front of the fireplace, a few relaxing chairs had been placed. Finishing off the overall cozy ambiance of the lobby, a huge, intricate painting of the ocean hung on the wall.

Old Man Johnson walked across the lobby to the counter. "Hello, sir. Do you have rooms available? Optimally, two with multiple beds each?"

"That we do, my good man," replied Charlie, the salesclerk. "How long are you looking to stay?"

"I'd like to purchase for a week. But I guess I have a question: Do you offer a bargain rate for longer stays?"

"In fact, we do. Compounded, a week is fifteen percent cheaper than a single night, and a month is thirty percent cheaper yet."

"Well, that's a bargain indeed." Old Man Johnson turned to look at Mick and Dave. "What do you guys think? Should we just get a month right away?"

"Might as well."

"We'll take two rooms then, both for a month. We don't yet know how long the child will be accompanying us, but if he happens to depart, we won't complain about the extra bed."

"Excellent," responded Charlie. "Though, you can always change it to a single bedroom, whenever. I'll reimburse you for it."

"Mighty fine establishment, no doubt," said Old Man Johnson.

They collectively paid for the rooms, Johnson's share being a little more, as he'd promised to pay for the first week.

"Your rooms are at the end of the hall, numbers nine and ten. Here are the keys. I'm sure you'll be seeing plenty of me in the next month. I'm practically here every day."

"Do you own the place?"

"My son and I do. He's not here much, though, because he's also a soldier, an archer."

"Fine man, I'm sure."

"That he is. There was one thing I was wondering, before you go to your rooms: Why do you guys look so familiar?" Charlie looked quizzically at Mick and Dave.

"Did you go to the Knowing Circle presentation last year?" asked Dave.

"I did."

"You must've sat in the back."

"Yes. I arrived later than I'd wanted."

"Had you sat in the front, you'd probably be recognizing us now."

A bewildered look sprang onto Charlie's face. After thinking for a few moments, he finally figured it out. "How exciting is this! Thraiker and Ghrere in my motel!"

"For at least a month, barring something unforeseen," added Mick.

"If it's not too much trouble, one of these nights I'd like to hear what it was like on the Icytryxan island."

"Gladly. Any time," responded Dave, as he and the rest began walking the hall to their rooms.

Eleven rooms in total lined the only hall, including a room without a number.

Having reached the end of the hall, they pondered who got what room. Mick and Dave took the room on the right, as Old Man Johnson and Will took the one on the left, having assumed Will wouldn't want to separate from his new pal.

The two rooms were exactly the same, except for the single painting in each room. Both had two beds, a table and chair, a rug, a small side-room for washing and whatnot, a suspended wooden rod with hangers, and a window to the world. "Well worth the price."

"Which bed do you want, Dave?"

"Doesn't matter. Or wait, you take the one by the window, because you tend to rouse better. If a surprise attack on town were to ensue, you'd hear it better than I."

"Good thinking. Beneficial indeed."

Twenty minutes of stowing gear away coincided with Will running back and forth between the rooms in animation.

Jason appeared, followed Will into Mick and Dave's room, and spoke: "So, I figured the General would know best of the whereabouts of Harry Shultz. I was right, he knew. Harry was never a part of Ulfenkerki's army specifically, but he remembered the name. Apparently, Harry and a few others were sent to the western front to ascertain data, since information from that side of the country has been sparse. I guess Harry and his two companions were chosen because they possessed the best endurance amongst the soldiers stationed here at the time. It's a very long trip, requiring a ton of stamina, especially if you're trying to perform it reasonably fast. The Capital actually held a sizable race, and these three were the winners." Jason turned to Will, put his hand on his shoulder, and said, "King Rowlangiv had declared your father's undertaking a special honor. You should be very proud of your dad. He's doing a great thing for us. The mission is taking longer than expected, but there's no reason to believe he's deceased."

"Thank you, sir, for finding that out for me. I am really proud. I never knew Dad was such a good runner. He could always beat me, but I'm just a kid."

"You're welcome, kiddo. I didn't enter the race, but I'm sure he could beat me too," responded Jason.

Mick voiced, "I'm guessing they departed the Capital while we were away on the Icytryxan mainland."

"Yes, they did. Ships had also been dispatched, going the long way around. But they came back with minimal information, having run into trouble at sea. Molisia's navy has been patrolling our western shore, I'm to understand."

"The harbor towns of the western shore have two armies, led by two generals?" inquired Dave.

"Yes," answered Jason. "Generals Dalarginta and Wiotweisten. All we know at this point is that the harbor towns remain intact."

"You'd think Molisia would've at least attempted to capture the harbor towns. I'm sure they have the manpower. They seem to have plenty of it here in our neck of the woods," noted Mick.

"It is quite the enigma," responded Jason. "So, Will, you can either stay here with Mick, Dave, and Old Man Johnson, or you're welcome to temporarily stay at our orphanage."

Will replied without the slightest of hesitations. "Here, with these guys!"

"I don't blame you. They are a rather entertaining bunch." Everyone chuckled, as Jason disappeared into the hallway.

It was getting late, so the quartet played a few card games to relax. There weren't too many activities more suitable than cards to prepare a mind for an easy transition to dreamland.

Mick carried out his morning stretches, and commented to Dave, "I suppose we should make rounds today and greet everyone."

"That's what was on my mind too."

Mick and Dave exited the inn, while Mr. Johnson and Will stayed behind.

The duo barely made it fifty paces past the inn before encountering someone on their greeting list. "Gregg Hogarty!"

"Dave, Mick, you're back!"

"We are," returned Mick. "Back in the thick of things."

"That you are," Gregg emitted. "Tension doesn't get much thicker than what it's been at the Capital lately. Everyone is on edge. Battle looms."

"What about you, Gregg, are you on edge?" asked Dave.

"No more than normal. The soldier's life is just one giant roll of the dice."

"True. Too bad you can't just switch to cards. Then, at least you'd know you'll always get dealt another hand."

Gregg chuckled. "Quite right, Mick. Though, it's too early in the morning for metaphors for me."

"It actually is for me too," noted Mick. "That one just sort of slipped out."

"You'll have that."

"No doubt, a long day is in store for us," Dave uttered.

"Same here, I'm thinking."

Mick said, "We'll see you later, Gregg, I'm sure. The coincidental crossing of paths does seem to be a consistent occurrence here at the Capital."

"The Capital is a place full of un-expectancies, to be sure. Later guys."

Mick and Dave continued their day's task of telling everyone they were back. Walking towards the barracks, the next person upon whom they stumbled was Syryx's brother, Thyxer. Thyxer, along with the rest of his kin, treated Mick, Dave, Jason, and Yori like family while they were on the Icytryxan island of Swyrove.

"Hey, Mick and Dave. Syryx told me you were back. Glad you're here."

"It's good to be here, and good to see you," said Mick.

"It's too bad Yusyta isn't here right now, but I'm sure she'll eventually see you."

"Speaking of whom," stated Dave, "how did things work out with her and Alfonso? When we last parted ways with her, she was on the way up the Dourinuset hill to rekindle her long lost love."

"I'm ecstatic to report that it all went wonderfully. She generally stays here, but for a handful of times per year, she goes and visits him at the monastery. The monks are quite accommodating. She is as happy as she could possibly be. I'm guessing she'll return in a couple weeks."

"Well, that's good to hear. What a happy ending for the couple."

"Indeed. How was Chalatore?"

"Our stay at home was agreeable," replied Mick. "It was undeniably far more uneventful than our time spent abroad, but it undoubtedly supplied us with sufficient renewal."

"Excellent to hear. Where are you staying now?"

"At a quaint little place called the Doze Inn, west of here not far. Stop by whenever, we implore. You can meet Old Man Johnson."

"I'm sure I'll be there plenty of times in the near future, same with the rest of the family."

"Terrific. We have a few more people to visit, so we'll see you later, Thyxer."

"Yup, see you later."

The duo began to search out General Ulfenkerki: the *Black Bear* known to some. They'd formed a pretty solid relationship with the both wise-appearing and wise-in-practice General in the last few years. It took the pair a while to find the General, but they ended up locating him with help from another soldier.

"General, sir! Things, not unlike yourself, are looking sound, I see," exclaimed Mick.

"If it isn't Thraiker and Ghrere! When Jason told me yesterday you were back, I was pleased. Very pleased."

"We were pleased as well, in seeing that the Capital hadn't been attacked yet."

"Day after day, the scouts return with no new intel. In a way, it's good news, but one can't help but be nervous, knowing Gamald is out there somewhere in the wilderness, scheming. Who knows, maybe he went to join the Molisian western forces. The east remains safe, thanks in no small part to you two. Having our entire eastern coast being nothing but cliffs is pretty handy during war-time."

Dave added, "But not so much during peacetime."

"True. Trading would, then, definitely be easier for the eastern villages. Is Chalatore safe and sound?"

"That it is," replied Mick. "Our part of the world has been free from aggression all winter."

"The calm before the storm. There are so many things pointing to this being a long and bloody war, I'm afraid."

"Hopefully, we can contain it to being just long and not bloody," proposed Dave.

"Optimistically, yes."

"See you later, General."

"Hold on a second, before you go," blurted Ulfenkerki. "I would like you to continue being present at important war meetings. Even though you're not officially a part of the army, I feel you're too valuable of assets for Garobansurov to not be in the loop. The officers and I have been meeting every Monday morning at the usual place. Rowlangiv shows up occasionally as well."

"We'll be there," said Mick. "Speaking of the King, we should stop in and say hi."

"You might as well. He should be in the castle. I haven't heard to the contrary."

"See you Monday, General, if not before."

"I'll come with you. I'm heading that way. You may not be able to pop into the castle as easily as you used to, since there are a bunch of new guards who might not recognize you."

"Much appreciated."

Luckily, Ulfenkerki had accompanied Dave and Mick, as without him, they wouldn't have gotten into the castle without delay. After the three had gained entrance, Mick and Dave began searching for the King, while Ulfenkerki had business elsewhere in the castle.

King Rowlangiv was sitting in the main dining hall in solitude when Mick and Dave approached him from the rear.

"I don't think I've ever seen you just sitting here in this room doing nothing," announced Mick.

Having immediately recognized the voice, the king turned his neck half-way around in obvious pain, and replied, "Hey guys. I think I ate something bad, my stomach is killing me. I ate supper, and I've been sitting here ever since, wishing it would pass."

"Maybe you ate some bad meat."

"Could be. It happens. Can you help me to my room?"

Dave placed Rowlangiv's arm around his shoulder and began helping him up the stairs to his chambers.

"Where are you guys staying?" asked Rowlangiv.

"At the Doze Inn."

"I imagine you'd already assumed you were welcome to stay here again."

"Oh yes, we figured we would be. Though, we also figured a change of scenery would do us good." Dave smiled, and said, "Plus, we might risk turning soft, being around so much luxury here."

Rowlangiv chuckled as best he could. "I must be really soft then, since I've lived here my whole life."

"You're exempt from that, of course."

Dave walked the King into his room and lowered him onto his bed.

Rowlangiv voiced, "I'm glad you're here and hope to talk more when I'm feeling better."

"Before we go, is Yori around?" asked Mick.

"She and I talked this afternoon, and I'm pretty sure she went home afterwards."

"Thanks, sir. I hope you feel better soon."

Dave and Mick left their king to relax and exited the castle.

The last person they needed to visit that day was the King's most trusted advisor, Yori Rothlin. She was a lady with whom (along with Jason) Mick and Dave had gone to the Icytryxan mainland. They'd made the trip last year in an attempt to persuade the Icytryxan army to align with

Garobansurov's. A success of which Mick and Dave were still proud to this day.

Yori's house wasn't exactly close to the castle, being slightly over a mile away. But for a person who walked as much as Mick and Dave, a mile walk was considered nothing more than a hop, skip, and a jump.

Having reached the north end of town in no time, Mick and Dave began searching out Yori's home, to which they'd never actually been. Yori had once given them a good description of it and how to get there, so finding her house turned out to be relatively easy.

"Her assortment of wind sockets billowing in the wind, coupled with the melody of her wind chimes," noted Dave, "is rather hypnotic."

"Definitely. Pleasant."

Mick knocked on Yori's door. It opened, and a bewildered face appeared.

Once Yori's eyes focused, and she realized who was at her door, her face lit up. "There's a sight I was hoping to see more sooner than later! Come in, please."

Mick and Dave took a seat in her brightly lit (too bright for some) living room.

"Is my house how you imagined?"

Mick replied, "Mostly, except for your lawn ornaments. I can't say I recall you having such a wonderful collection in any of your past home descriptions."

"I must've left that part out. Though, I don't know why I would've. How silly of me. When did you arrive?"

Dave answered, "Yesterday. Our old friend, Old Man Johnson, made the trip with us too. Along the way, we'd also encountered a destitute child wandering aimlessly down the road. We brought him with to help find his dad. His mother is deceased. His father turned out to be one of the three that'd been dispatched to ascertain intel from the western front."

"Oh yes, I remember that. That was a while ago. No wonder the child was helpless and worried."

"His name is Will, and he's back at the inn now with Mr. Johnson."

"Poor thing. I bet all this is really hard on him."

I'm sure it is. He found a pretty good friend in Old Man, so he's been pretty occupied."

"Would it be okay if I stopped by and helped out with keeping him company?"

"Oh sure," replied Mick, "anytime. We're staying at the Doze Inn: room numbers nine and ten. Stop by whenever."

"Thank you. It's the least I can do. I hope his father is alright and makes it back soon."

"One other thing, Yori, before I forget. Rowlangiv is a tad under the weather. We think he ate something bad."

"Thanks for telling me," replied Yori. "I'll check on him in the morning. Other than that, though, he's been rather upbeat. Having both Ulfenkerki's army and the Icytryxan army here at the Capital has really set his mind at ease. War takes a lot out of him. I see it."

"I could imagine," noted Dave. "Have you been doing anything exciting lately, yourself? Even a king's advisor needs to enjoy herself, once in a while."

"That she does. I guess, to be honest, the most enjoyable part of my life recently has been getting to know the Icytryxans further. I've really grown to appreciate their way of life—it's no doubt fascinating."

"Does that mean at some point in the future you would advise the king to emulate their philosophies?" Mick asked Yori.

"I do think about that a lot. But I'm pretty sure I wouldn't. A concept such as having no politics or money is something that could take a society thousands—or maybe even tens of thousands—of years to get used to and see the value in. This way of conceptual thinking couldn't just be dumped onto the masses."

"I agree," stated Mick. "It even took the Icytryxans that long to evolve into such thinking."

"We do have individuals here in Garobansurov who live like the Icytryxans, and they seemed pretty happy."

Mick instantly knew exactly about whom Dave was talking. "That they did. During our entire time at the Dourinuset Monastery, we hardly seen a depressed face."

"Except for a few times on Alfonso Alardo, but that has since been remedied," remarked Dave.

"Monks truly do have a heightened sense of discipline," proclaimed Mick. "Not everyone is as religious, but that doesn't mean they can't have focus in their lives."

"Who knows, though, maybe if we did stay longer at Dourinuset, we would've noticed an underlying political hierarchy."

"Maybe," replied Yori. "The same could be said for the Icytryxans. It's possible that it's so faint it takes years to witness."

"Quite possible. Maybe even decades. Time may tell. I know that during my time with the Icytryxans, I saw nothing of the sort," emitted Dave.

"Me neither," stated Yori. "And I've been with them longer. I hope we never see any sign of politics amongst them; it'd be disappointing."

"Yes, it would be. It really is interesting thinking about our differences."

Yori agreed, "It is. Garobansurov and the Icytryxis are so different, but yet so alike."

"Indeed. Time for us to leave, but stop by at the inn anytime, Yori," said Mick.

"Will do. I'll probably come by tomorrow."

A checkmark had now been placed on every line of Hawk and Leopard's list of people to see that day, they therefore went back to the inn for the night. They met up with Mr. Johnson and Will and hung out in the lobby for a few hours, meeting a few of the other people staying at the inn.

After a great night's sleep, Mick and Dave left the inn to go mingle with the armies. They knew many of the soldiers in both Ulfenkerki's and the Icytryxan army.

The pair enjoyed reconnecting.

By afternoon, Dave and Mick were back at the inn.

Like she said she would, Yori stopped by and did her best to comfort Will. She told him all about the mission his father had undertaken, kindheartedly omitting the scary parts.

Digressing, Yori spoke to Mick, Dave, and Johnson. "I went to see the King this morning, and he was doing better. He'd surmised that he caught a bug, as opposed to eating something bad, as no one else had gotten sick from eating the same meal. He figured he had caught the sickness from someone outside the castle."

"That's really good to hear," said Dave. "I guess Mick and I are going to catch it now, though. I practically carried him up the stairs, so I couldn't have been any closer to him. Oh well."

"I probably will too. I was standing pretty near to him this morning," emitted Yori.

"Well, when we all get sick, we might as well hang out together and entertain each other."

"Sounds good, Mr. Johnson," said Yori. "Plus, it would be best to avoid the armies and not let them catch it all at once."

"They'll all inevitably catch it sooner or later; but, yes, it's best for them to not all have it at once. You never know when a battle could ensue."

"Correct, Mick," replied Dave. "There was that time last year, when the Molisian squadron without warning infiltrated town via the tunnel."

"Yup, that was quite unexpected." Yori said, "Sicknesses spreading this far from winter is a rare occurrence. I don't like it. But I'm not going to lose any sleep over it."

"Me neither," said Johnson.

Jason stopped by to visit. Now, six were sitting and standing in Johnson's room—plenty of elbow room amongst friends.

They all talked productively for an hour, before Yori and Jason departed.

Out of sheer restlessness, Dave woke early and walked aimlessly through town. He ended up creating a two-mile loop. By the time he got back to the inn, everyone else was awake and hanging out with Charlie in the lobby eating baked goods for breakfast.

"Charlie had told me how delectable the bakery across the street is, so I had to go check it out. Here you go, Dave, try this."

Dave took a few bites out of the sweet treat Mick handed him. "You're right; this hits the spot."

"They're reasonably priced too. I do believe we'll be going there quite often. Did you wake up sick at all?"

"No. Did you?"

"Thankfully, no."

"Good. On a different note, as I was walking, I got the feeling maybe we're here at the Capital for no reason this time. General Gamald and the Molisian armies would have to have a long arm indeed, if they think they can reach us here. The battle force currently stationed here is very overwhelming."

"You're right, Dave. Maybe the Molisians know how large the force is and aim to implement some other type of war tactic."

"It's possible. We have that war meeting with Ulfenkerki in a few days. There, we can find out if anything like this is on anyone else's mind."

"True," responded Mick. "It doesn't seem like the Molisians are raiding smaller villages either, otherwise we'd know."

"Gamald is very sly. He could be doing anything and be doing it anywhere. It just seems too quiet."

"I agree. I thought for sure when we got here to the Capital, someone would know at least somewhat what was going on in the west."

"We'll have to wait it out," recommended Dave.

"Watch, now that we talked about this, we'll go to the war meeting, and we'll learn things are uttermost dire."

"That does seem to be how jinxes work."

For the rest of the day, Mick and Dave practiced swordcraft with the armies, as Will and Old Man Johnson spent time at the park.

Like they had thought might happen, Mick and Dave woke up sick.

"It seems I've got the same stomach pain Rowlangiv had."

"I've got the same thing, Dave. I don't think we're going anywhere today."

"I wonder if Yori feels the same way."

"We'll find out soon, if she does in fact show up here."

"Maybe she won't feel like making the walk, if she does feel really bad."

"That's possible. Sometimes a person doesn't even feel like walking to the next room when they're under the weather."

"If she does come," said Dave, "I have an idea on what we can all do to pass the time."

"Surprise us."

Old Man Johnson went across the street to pick up breakfasts—lighter fare for Mick and Dave. He also grabbed something for Yori if in case she came.

The quartet wasn't two bites into the meal, when Yori hobbled into the room.

"That walk was rough," emitted Yori, "but I know time spent with you guys would be much more enjoyable than time spent alone. I assumed you were sick too?"

"You assumed correctly. Both Dave and I have the bug. Make yourself comfortable, young lady. Old Man Johnson picked up a light breakfast for you, thinking you might show up."

"Well, thank you so much. I knew it would be worth the shuffle here. I doubt I'll be able to eat much, but I'm sure at some point I'll want to try to digest something."

"Here's the good news, Yori: Dave said he has an idea on what we can all do while we sit here and suffer together."

"That's good, I never came up with any ideas myself."

"I told him to surprise us."

"Neat."

Dave emitted, "In order for us to perform my idea, I'm going to have to run next door to pick up a few supplies."

"Good thing there's a shop there."

"Right. I wouldn't want to walk much further. Give me ten/fifteen minutes, and I'll be back with what we need. I'll tell you then what it is we're doing. Trust me, you'll like it."

Dave left the room, and Yori put forth, "Do you guys have any guesses as to what he'll come back with?"

"I think he'll return with something the kid can also do. I doubt he plans to leave him out."

"Oh, I doubt it too."

With a noticeably slow gait, Dave entered the small general store two buildings down from the inn. He got what he needed by using as few steps as he could. Fortunately, most of the materials he'd required were in the same area and not in the store's rear.

He arrived back to the room, where Mick, Old Man Johnson, Will, and Yori were sitting easily.

Presenting his purchases, Dave said, "Today, we are going to teach a young child and an old man how to play Fantysy-Escape—the favorite Icytryxan pastime. I picked up some rudimentary gear for the mini-version of the game."

"It definitely looks like you got everything a person would need for it," stated Yori. "What a great idea you had, Dave. I'm glad tenfold I stumbled here this morning."

Mick began explaining the overview of the board game. "Essentially, it's a story telling game. A huge chunk of your points will be gained by telling a better story than your fellow competitors. Each player listens to the other stories and then chooses which yarn of which they want to hear the ending. The more people who choose your ending, the more points you get. Further points are accumulated through the navigation of the game board, which we must first construct before we can begin to play."

"That sounds fun," said Will.

Old Man Johnson commented, "I remember you explaining the game to me over the winter. It came across then as being intriguing. I'll be pleased to play."

"Excellent." Mick went over the rest of the rules and overall game play.

Having taken a couple hours, the five had put together all the requisite parts, during which time those who were sick began ignoring the fact they were sick—at least to a degree they weren't in agony.

Once everything was set up, they started the actual game. The jovial experience would last the rest of the day. Will enjoyed the game thoroughly. In fact, he played so hard that he ended up falling asleep before the game was finished.

At the end of the night, Mick asked Yori, "By your opinion, would you say the Icytryxis army and our army fit together seamlessly? I've been thinking about that for a while now."

"That's a good question. At first glance, they do appear to mesh very well. Neither party is very irritated by the other. There have been no serious fights from what I've noticed. But when you really spend the time to sit down and focus, you begin to see the little things. I can't actually put words to what those things are, I'm not quite that philosophically astute to do so. But I can see it from at least a sub-conscious level."

Mick replied, "It would definitely be something for Dave and me to pay attention to."

"Yes," added Dave, "there are many complicated things to look at. It's definitely worth studying. Having the two cultures' armies work as one would be highly favorable."

"It's very interesting stuff."

Not wanting to walk home, since she was still feeling sick, Yori slept in Dave's bed, while Dave slept on the floor. He deployed the same sleeping pad he used for camping.

The day spent in sickness had turned out to be not that bad.

In the morning, they all woke up feeling better. On Mick and Dave's schedule was the war meeting with Ulfenkerki and crew, so that's where they headed after breakfast.

They learned the meeting locale had been changed. It was to be held in the new Icytryxis barracks, as opposed to the old barracks, where Mick and Dave had last attended a war meeting.

The old barracks were stone structures, appearing as old as they actually were. The new barracks were wooden fabrications, made by hundreds of workers in the matter of weeks.

Mick and Dave entered the vast meeting room in the new barracks. It was already occupied by Jason Thorncat, Gregg Hogarty, a handful of Capital Guard and Army officers, and half a dozen Icytryxan soldiers. Since the Icytryxan army divvied no ranks, Icytryxan soldiers took turns attending the war meetings. Mick and Dave knew everyone in the room.

With his normal punctuality and stoic countenance, Ulfenkerki walked into the room. "Good morning squad. I'm glad to see not everyone got sick. This will be a short gathering, for nothing new has come into the fold. Construction of all the various war machines and apparatus is coming along nicely. I've been seeing a lot of hard work being done. I'd sent a new batch of scouts out this morning, since a bunch came in last night. Unfortunately, they had nothing to report. All told, I have almost fifty scouts out in the wild as we speak searching for Molisian threats. That's about all I have. Does anyone else have anything to add?"

Everyone shook their heads no.

"That'll be all, then. Same time, same place, next week."

Before leaving the room, Mick and Dave approached Jason. "Dave, Yori, and I did end up getting sick yesterday. I take it many soldiers caught it too?"

"They did. Thankfully, it has passed for most of them. For a while there, the General was worried the army would be weakened by the sickness. You never know when an attack may occur. Such a rarity, a summer illness is."

"That it is. Good thing it was merely a twenty-four-hour bug."

"Yup," replied Jason. "What do the two of you have planned for the rest of the day?"

Realizing they were the last three in the room, Dave untucked his shirt, and replied, "Probably nothing identifiable as very important, maybe some drills."

"Sounds good. Same here."

Subsequent the gathering, Mick joined the Icytryxans in their training. Although he wasn't very proficient with one, nor did he plan on using one in battle often, Mick practiced on the atlytl. It really was a fascinating weapon, he thought.

Meanwhile, Dave went to one of the exercise yards to work up a good sweat.

At the end of the day, Mick met back up with Dave in Old Man Johnson's room.

Mick asked Dave, "Did you get the chance to study any Icytryxan and Garobansurovian interactions today?"

"Not yet, but I certainly intend to. It's going to be an important aspect of the war," acknowledged Dave.

"It is. One thing I saw today was an Icytryxan soldier walk away from a group obsessively talking about a certain person in town here. I didn't know whom it was they were talking about, but I'm assuming it was someone those of the group deemed important."

"Exactly," commented Dave. "The Icytryxan soldier probably felt the Garobansurovians were overly adulating this person and didn't want to be a part."

"Oh yes, for sure. Sometimes people will go on and on about an individual, like what this person says and does is so important compared with everyone else."

"It's something of which to take note," stated Dave.

"Too bad we're not still setting up our battle scenarios, like we did in Swyrove," mentioned Mick. "We could watch how the two races actually battle with one another."

"That would be useful. But I believe only during a real battle, could we truly see how they respond to each other. A mock combat situation just wouldn't be decisive enough to actually go through with it—at any rate, not during war-time."

"Yeah, I suppose. When we did it in the Icytryxan homeland, it wasn't a period of war for them."

"Everything is more hectic during wartime."

"Undeniably true."

Chapter 3

A SMALL PEBBLE rolled down a mountain deep inside the Baustic Range. The pebble had been dislodged by vibrations emanating from within the mountain.

There were so many Molisian soldiers rallying within the mountain's caves that their cumulative movements had caused measurable tremors.

Gamald's new army had reached critical mass. It was now time for the unleashing.

Sitting in his office, surrounded by officers, General Gamald spoke: "I know we're all sick of being in this cave, hiding like the animals at the bottom of the food chain. But our patience has paid off. Thousands of our countrymen have answered the call. Molisians are sick and tired of these Garobansurovians having better lives.

Their farmland is superior, their resources are more plentiful, their weather is better, for crying out loud, even their damn women are prettier! This ends now! Today, we leave here with the ultimate goal of conquering the Capital, and any other city and small village along the way. Steal their money, rape their women, drink their beer, I don't care. Do what you wish, but don't burn the buildings down, our civilians will eventually live in them."

Standing near General Gamald was his next in command, Major Leedle, who'd been given a promotion. Gamald usually didn't hand out very many promotions, which was why Leedle had been a lieutenant for so long. Garobansurov didn't bestow the rank of major (among other specific ranks), military hierarchy going straight from first lieutenant to general.

Leedle asked, "When we infiltrate the smaller cities along the way to the Capital, do you plan on leaving garrisons behind, in case the enemy tries to seize them back as we resume marching south?"

"I do. That was one of the reasons I've waited this long to go on the offensive. We've now swelled enough to defend the cities we'd conquer. Furthermore, our scouts have reported that the number of soldiers has somehow doubled at the Capital in the last six months. But this won't be a problem. Even with us leaving garrisons behind, we will be invading the Capital with nearly three times as many soldiers as they have defending it. But it will take a while for us to get there, that's for sure. The journey will be an exciting one. We will completely dominate everything in our path. The soldiers will enjoy it, trust me."

Leedle gauged everyone's faces in the room and liked what he saw. "That's right. We will enjoy this."

"In finality, fight well, stay alive, never surrender, and take no prisoners. We will begin leaving this cave immediately."

Called the Southern Molisian Army by the political leaders of Molisia, they began to funnel out of their hidey-hole nestled in the Baustics. Seventy-five hundred strong, it was one of the largest armies the continent of Taraosk had ever seen. However, it lacked a substantial supply of war machines, since such lumbering contraptions were hard to conceal. Stealth was their greatest ally; without it, they would have never been able to reach such a size. If Ulfenkerki had been aware of Gamald's location, he would've cherry picked the Molisian army to pieces. Gamald recognized this and had taken every measure to avoid it.

The Molisian soldiers were glad they didn't have to clean up after themselves, because it would've taken forever. The place would be left a putrid mess. Animal carcasses were strewn everywhere, urine soaked the floors, flies infested the garbage, and sweat soaked the bedding. The thousands had no regard for hygiene. They weren't there to keep house, they were there only to conquer. Someone else could worry about the mess, they thought.

The cave exodus had reached climax by midday, and with the first step southward the raiding had officially begun. Garobansurovians nearby had no idea what was coming.

Having marched a few days, the Molisian horde reached the first mountain town. Instead of dying by the hands of the Molisians, the inhabitants had wisely fled. They had just enough time to get away. It wasn't much of a town, so General Gamald decided against leaving soldiers behind to keep it secured. They seized what valuable items they could and began moving on to the next town.

As his next course of action, Gamald dispatched a stealthy advance-platoon. He knew a few of his soldiers had the thirst for blood more than others, and that they yearned for unsavory activities. In other words, Gamald wanted to keep morale high by allowing these soldiers their fun.

TAKING PART IN an army drill, Dave and Mick trained vigorously. Mixed with Icytryxans and Garobansurovians, the drill session incorporated a variety of hand-to-hand combat situations. Ulfenkerki didn't mind if Mick and Dave joined his sanctioned training routines, even though they weren't officially part of the army. There were very few warriors General Ulfenkerki trusted like he did Mick Thraiker and Dave Ghrere.

Sweat emanating from every orifice, Mick said to Dave, "I really worked my muscles hard today. They may even be sore in the morning."

"Same here. When we get back to the room, I have a few things to share with you."

"Alright. I hope it's not about that time I swung my sword and pathetically missed at what I was aiming."

"It's not." Dave Chuckled. "But I did see that."

"A gnat flew into my eye."

"Are you sure your anchor foot didn't get impregnated by the seed of momentary clumsiness?"

Mick laughed. "Good one. Yes, I'm sure."

The pair returned to their room at the Doze Inn.

After popping in to say hello to Old Man Johnson and Will, Dave began speaking about what he had mentioned to Mick earlier. "It is definitely true that the two races get along well, some could even say very well. I'm almost positive that the alliance is going exceptionally smooth and will last indefinitely. But a big part of me says there is more that can be done to improve how affectively we work together and excel at warfare. If I look closely, I can see separation amongst them, even though for the most part the Icytryxans and Garobansurovians comingle fairly well."

"You're right. If I really sit down and scrutinize the situation, I can see they are friendly with each other, but for some reason, the bonds just aren't seamless."

"Exactly, Mick. How this will affect our war capabilities remains to be seen. One can only speculate."

"There are many differences in our cultures, bound to influence personal relationships."

"It's worth watching, and very interesting stuff. I won't trouble you with naming any names, but during training today, I'd witnessed specific circumstances of individuals being less enthusiastic when communicating with the other race."

"Yes, it is noticeable, at least to someone looking for it. The formation of social circles in every society is evident, and our case here is no different. Some circles include members from both races, that much is clear, but what isn't clear is why exactly are some circles, like the ones you witnessed, less neutral? What governs this? Are philosophical differences therein that persuasive?"

Dave kicked off his shoes, and returned, "It could be so many things. We might as well keep studying it, for it surely affects our homeland. In my gut, I feel we can help in the long run."

"Oh, great! Does that mean there's going to be another monumental, far-off undertaking for us?" Mick chuckled. "I was starting to grow fond of just hanging out at the Doze Inn here."

"We shall see, my good man. We shall see."

Supplying a refreshing change of course, Old Man Johnson and Will entered the room and divulged their eventful day.

SHE HAD OTHER talents, skills considered by most to be valuable enough to earn a living. But for the time being, Anna found herself waitressing at the only bar/restaurant in the area—an area not exactly labeled near the Capital.

She was beautiful enough to flirt her way into large tips, wise enough to not let it go to her head, and serene enough to enjoy the smaller things in life. She was very likable and respected, as she more times than not supplied the initial like and respect.

A married couple decided one night after school they'd treat their two children to a meal at Anna's workplace. The kids had performed their chores without complaint for a span, which in their parent's eyes merited an enjoyable evening.

To kick off the fun evening, the family played a game while walking to the restaurant, fittingly named Guess

What I'm Thinking About. The conclusion of the game coincided with them being shown to their table.

They were in a great mood all night, right up until the youngest child realized she'd lost something. "Dad, I lost my giti that you gave me for my birthday last week!"

"Where did you last have it?"

"It was in my pocket, I remember. I checked just before I went to the bathroom."

The family members all looked for the giti. They searched all around their table, in the bathroom, and on the path that she would've taken to and from it. After searching for a time, they began to lose hope.

Anna was waitressing a table nearby and noticed the family pursuing the lost item. As soon as her task at hand was finished, Anna approached the family, and said, "I can't help but notice you looking for something. Can I help at all?"

"My daughter lost a giti apparently. She had it just before going to the bathroom, which was the only place she went while here."

Anna smiled at the little girl. "I'll inform the staff to keep an eye out for it. I'm sure it'll show up."

"Thank you so much," returned the child.

Faithfully on a mission, Anna told everyone about the girl's missing giti and began searching herself.

Anna had gone outside to search the bathroom once before but decided to go and look again. Once inside, she realized that because of the grotesquerie of it, she never looked into the pit the first time. This time, with bravery on her side, she held her breath, cringed, and peered in. Sure enough, there it was—the unmistakable corner of a giti was just within view. However, Anna was in no mood to go fishing through the waste that lurked below.

I hope I never have to immerse myself into a putrid situation.

So, instead of telling the little girl where her giti was, and allowing her to dig it out herself, she just reached into her pocket and pulled out one of her own.

Smiling, Anna approached the family, giti in hand. "Look what I found, sweetie. It was hiding in the grass, about thirty feet from the outhouse. The wind must've blown it away a little."

"Oh, thank you so much! I wonder how it fell out of my pocket."

"What were you planning to spend it on?" asked Anna.

The little girl thought about it for a moment. "I think a board game that my brother and I could play."

"That will be a lot of fun. Well, I hope you and your family enjoy the rest of your evening."

The father smiled, and said, "Thanks, Anna."

Anna was happy to see the little girl and her family get back to enjoying their evening. Everyone's good moods lasted well into the night.

Late in the evening, a few hours past sunset, the last patron left the establishment. Anna locked the main entrance and began closing the kitchen.

The kitchen window was usually left open for ventilation during business hours. But after business hours, it needed to get closed in order to make it harder for any would-be thieves to break in. Anna couldn't reach the window, so she always pulled a chair up to it to stand on. Standing on the chair, with her hands on the window, she heard a commotion outdoors. She peered out the window and gasped with terror at what she saw. Some of the townsfolk were trying to run away, but they weren't getting very far. An entire regiment of soldiers was slaughtering everyone in Anna's village.

Horrific screams were coming from all corners of town. Bodies began to pile up in the streets, Anna noticed. Women were being bound, gagged, and corralled.

I must act fast.

Fortunately, behind the bar, there was a shoot that led to a pit. It was basically nothing more than a garbage pit, put there out of conveniency for the bartender, so they wouldn't have to leave their post to dispose of refuse. Anna had no other option. If she ran, even though she was a good runner, she would succumb to the same demise as everyone else who ran before her. Additionally, she wasn't the sort of fighter who could take on multiple foes. And if she were to hide anywhere other than in the pit, she was certain she'd be found. The pit was her only option.

So much for my hopes of never having to immerse myself into a putrid situation.

Anna was lucky in the fact that she had already locked the main entrance. It bought her some time. Just as she heard pounding at the door, she began to lower herself into the pit.

The pit was roughly ten feet deep and at first glance not as dark as she'd imagined. It was large enough that she could advantageously keep to a side, just out of view from anyone who'd decide to look down the chute.

She hit the ground with a thump and was confounded by how big in actuality the pit was. Plus, there was more moisture than she would've pictured.

Soon after she finished her quick scrutiny of her surroundings, she could hear five or six soldiers scoping out her place of employment. She could even hear what a few of them were saying.

"Look everywhere. We don't need anyone slitting our throats in the night," said a soldier.

"We hit the jackpot. There's enough alcohol here to last us a month. Thank you so much General Gamald for allowing this to happen," said another.

"I can't wait to have my turn at the women we found. There were some really good ones in the lot, I saw," said a third.

"Not until I have my turn first," said a fourth.

Anna's mind was full of dread. Those were her friends they were talking about. Terrified, she began to freeze.

I must snap out of it. I must keep my focus. It's a matter of life or death.

The soldiers above searched every nook and cranny. One of them discovered the shoot and looked down. But he didn't see Anna hiding off to the side.

Eventually, more soldiers came into the bar/restaurant. Anna realized it was the largest building in town, other than the church, and the place with the most alcohol. So, it was bound to draw a crowd.

She hunkered down in the corner, drowning in the frightful assumption she was going to be there a while.

CHAPTER 4

OLD MAN JOHNSON spent the day visiting with folks he knew from his past, while Will went with Yori on a tour of the castle. Most children of town were not afforded this privilege, but Will's case was special. Everyone knew his father was on a very important mission, and that his mother had since passed. Plus, you could say he had friends in high places. He could've even met the King if he wanted to, but timidly, he didn't.

Mick and Dave continued studying the foundational philosophy regarding the comingling of soldiers from different walks of life. It consumed them. As long as nothing more important popped into their lives, they would sustain doing so. Along with the studying, they maintained training, exercising, and attending

Ulfenkerki's war meetings. They also made sure to not neglect the here and there activity of leisure.

After having been at the Capital for almost a month, Dave and Mick were finally going to see their friend, Yusyta. She was an Icytryxan and the younger sister of Thyxer and Syryx. Yusyta had recently reunited with the love of her life, the couple having been separated due to unusual circumstances. She'd just arrived back at the Capital, having been away visiting this love at the Dourinuset Monastery.

Mick and Dave were in their room when Yusyta knocked.

Dave answered the door, and exclaimed, "Yusyta! Come in, please. I'm glad to see you had a safe trip back from Dourinuset."

"I did. It was safe and jubilant."

"Between the two of them, Thyxer and Syryx had told us all about your successful reunification with Alfonso," emitted Mick. "We were rapturous at hearing this news. All winter long, you were on our minds. We couldn't wait to hear how the whole thing went."

"It couldn't have gone better. Our ending is carved in stone with the word *together*." Saying these words to her great friends brought immense emotion to Yusyta. "You two were on my mind as well. I thought of fantastical ways of letting you know how it all went. There was a time when I'd almost decided to walk all the way to Chalatore to inform you."

"That certainly is a long walk. Just think of it this way: If you'd made the walk then, we wouldn't be having this exciting rendezvous now," noted Dave. "But it would've definitely been a pleasant surprise seeing you show up unexpectedly."

"So, what shall we do to make this rendezvous as exhilarating as possible?"

"Good question, Yusyta. Let me think here." Mick pondered. "We could get the whole crew together and eat at the best restaurant in town? Assuming Thyxer, Syryx, Jason, and Yori are all free tonight."

"I would be delighted. I can ask my kin if they'd be available, easy enough—probably Jason too, since I see him frequently at the barracks."

"And Dave and I can walk over to Yori's house to ask her. Before we part to do that, let me introduce you to our friend from Chalatore, Old Man Johnson. I'm sure you remember him from many of our stories. Plus, this is Will, whom we met along the way."

Introductions were carried out through smiles, as Mick began telling Will's story to Yusyta.

After the story, Yusyta separated from the group, having arranged to meet back up at the barracks.

Hawk and Leopard were successful at pinpointing Yori. She wasn't going to be busy, so she joined up with Mick and Dave, elatedly.

Yusyta had been just as fruitful, having gotten her family and Jason to join in on the evening.

"Now for the tricky part," commented Mick, standing in a circle at the barracks with the rest.

"What's that?" voiced Yusyta.

"Agreeing as to what the best restaurant in town is," answered Mick.

The party chuckled and decided, having not taken up too much time in the process. Most agreed the Cedars was the finest, all except for Jason. Though, he proclaimed it didn't matter to him where they went.

Together again, the seven headed to the northwestern sector of town—the fancier, more expensive district. It was a good thing they were all dressed the part.

The Cedars was named so, because of the five large red cedars ornamenting the front lawn, majestically. The seven stood and admired the towering beauties before entering the eatery.

After perusing the menu, the group ordered their food: some the signature dish, some the special, and some something new.

"I do believe the last time we all ate together was on championship night of Fantysy-Escape, before leaving the island," said Yori.

"That sounds right," replied Syryx. "I hope there are many more nights to come of us eating together."

After the group shared many pleasantries, and admired the taxidermy on the walls thoroughly, Dave began talking on a more serious note. "Yusyta, from your perspective, how has the colliding of the two cultures been? I remember you said you were going to focus on the implementation of a smooth transitional paradigm for the amalgamation. I ask because Mick and I have begun studying the cultural differences from a military perspective."

"Yes, it certainly is unprecedented knowledge, never before delved into from a firsthand vantage point. And it needs to be studied, thoroughly." Yusyta continued, "I won't bore you with the details, but through my research thus far, I can tell you the fusion from a social standpoint is definitely not without flaws. But as a whole it's working. I'm not seeing any reason to believe the alliance was a mistake. We definitely share common goals and generally look at morals through the same window."

Mick added, "The unification of our philosophies—Garobansurov and Icytryxis—is definitively prone for resistance. The philosophies are so principally different. One of us believes in both politics and money—fundamental quests for power. The other believes in neither—making the acquisition of power for the Icytryxis a manifestation that can only be obtained from within. They are two poles apart mindsets. Like oil and water, the philosophical blending will never be perfect. But with a little help, the two can coexist in a place."

Yori spoke next on the issue. "Rowlangiv is definitely fortunate to have multiple minds going at this. His greatest concern is keeping as many of us alive as possible. And I, as his adviser, am pleased when productive work is being performed. Innovation is on the forefront of Rowlangiv's platform. I've always appreciated the old adage: *Work smarter, not harder.* I'll inform the King we are studying this with great purpose, and I'm sure he will be eternally grateful. For in his eyes, if just one life is saved by an effort, the effort's value is astronomical."

Jason added, "I'll be sure to keep an eye on social interactions as well and let you all know if I see anything of interest. I doubt I'll give much thought to the philosophical side of things myself, but I can certainly help you to do yours."

"Thank you so much, Jason," noted Mick. "On a more personal note, how are you enjoying it here, Thyxer, Syryx, and Yusyta?"

"I'm sincerely having the time of my life," replied Yusyta, "but my circumstance is different. I'm pretty sure, though, that without my reunion with Alfonso, I would still be enjoying Garobansurov. It's rather lovely, and the people are as nice as I remembered them to be."

"I agree," Thyxer added, "the landscape is beautiful, and the people are very agreeable. I haven't second-guessed myself once about enthusiastically siding for an alliance. I entirely believe the whole is greater than the sum of both our parts."

"I wholeheartedly feel more at ease knowing my country has such a great partner to the north. Our people are safer now, and will be for a very long time," proclaimed Syryx. "I know I especially have taken pleasure in being here. I've made some great friends, people with whom I've earnestly enjoyed spending training sessions. And of course, it's been great being here with each and every one of you."

"Same to you, Syryx. And I am so glad to hear that from all of you," said Mick. "I would have a heavy heart if I knew you didn't like it here."

"Well, please know that we really are fond of being here," returned Syryx.

"Just the same as it was about being in your homeland," remarked Yori, genuinely.

After they finished eating, the group sat in the restaurant's foyer, and conversed for another hour—discussing, as you'd think, topics they thought were interesting.

A few days after the dinner, Mick, Dave, Jason, and Thyxer (Thyxer's turn in the rotation) found themselves at one of Ulfenkerki's morning war meetings. The four of them had gone in thinking it was going to be an uneventful meeting, since most of them had been lately. But they knew something was going to be different when the General came into the room many minutes early, for he was habitually as prompt as the sun.

There were 15 in the room, and they all could see Ulfenkerki's stern expression. They wasted no time to sit and listen attentively.

The Black Bear looked around the room to make sure everyone important was present. He saw that they were and began to speak. "Late last night, I received a couple scouts, who'd been on assignment patrolling the northern region. They had traveled far rather quickly, so I knew they had something important to report. What we all were afraid was going to happen, did happen. Gamald came out of hiding and is on the move, toting a massive army—one more immense than before. He is raiding villages and heading in our direction. My scouts informed me the Molisians already have two northern villages under their control. Rowlangiv is aware of these events and has informed me the battle plan will be whatever I and the Icytryxis collectively fashion. Normally, I'd be the one to generate the plan; though, favorably, things are different now. The Icytryxis must be in on battleplan constructions, for we are an equal partnership. How would you, Icytryxis representatives, like to proceed?"

Thyxer looked at his compatriots and saw they weren't jumping to speak. So, he stood tall, and said to Ulfenkerki, "From our side of the table, we'll have you discuss strategy with the Icytryxis individuals we regard as having the best mind for war tactics. These four have no first-hand experience in warfare, but they have applied themselves to the studying of the craft with the utmost concentration."

"Excellent, Thyxer. I will look forward to talking with them. Hopefully, we talk this afternoon yet. I won't discourse here too long, so we can all get our balls rolling. It has been estimated the Molisian army is 7,000 to 7,500 strong, which is considerably more than we have here—three times more. I have no idea from where Molisia is getting this many soldiers. It's not like Molisia is that much more populated than us. I would bet that many of their soldiers are very young. Suffice it to say, this would be a shame. I wish the diplomats Rowlangiv sent to Molisia had been successful, as we would've welcomed any immigrants with open arms. But, no, the Molisians just want the easy way out. In their eyes, it's easier to attack than to work. I do know that if this Molisian army intends to attack the Capital, it will take them at least three weeks to reach us. So, we have time yet to prepare.

"Even being outnumbered so greatly, I feel we can win this. But I will say this: All would be lost if the Icytryxis hadn't decided to align with us. My 1,000 soldiers coupled with the 500 Capital Guard and Archer Corp wouldn't have been enough. The Kingdom would've surely fallen. But thankfully, that's not the case. We have a very dynamic army here, consisting of fully trained soldiers. Moreover, we boast a strong defensive position, barring we deliberately fight on the field. But I know I will highly recommend to the four Icytryxis war specialists against relinquishing the protection of the city walls. That will be all for now. We will reconvene later today, if the Icytryxis and I devise a plan before nightfall. Regardless, we all will assemble again soon."

The room emptied quickly.

Mick and Dave spent the rest of the morning and afternoon honing swords and swordcraft.

When they arrived back to the inn, they caught up on lost meals and received a courier message sent by Ulfenkerki. War council was to reconvene at 7:00.

Having found seats at the war meeting, Dave and Mick saw King Rowlangiv was now present.

Back to his usual promptness, Ulfenkerki walked in and immediately began to speak. "As I'm sure you've all assumed, the Icytryxis strategy team and I had successfully held discussion. Together, we decided on our best course of action, which I will share with you all now without delay. Foremost, we did indeed decide to keep the advantages fighting within the Capital walls provide. The walls, the elevated platforms for atlytl usage, the archer towers, the nearly indefinite supply of resources, even the castle itself all supply a greater possibility of victory. The Molisians will have to face an unmeasurable number of arrows and atlytl projectiles even before reaching the city walls' outer shadows. Optimistically, their numbers will be greatly diminished before our walls are breached.

"It has also been concluded we'll wait to recapture our cities in the north. We'll need all the soldiers we've got to defend the Capital. However, we *will* man three of our four forward bases with archers for cherry picking. These will be the fastest runners among the Archer Corp. They will have the leg speed to go on the offensive and get back behind the Capital's walls, before being attacked themselves.

"We've still heard nothing from the far western front. We can only hope Gamald hasn't coordinated his assault with Molisian regiments from the west. My western scouts so far haven't reported any unfriendly movement, fortunately.

"Now to discuss the Capital's interior. I have discussed this matter with Rowlangiv, and we agree. He will be informing the townspeople tomorrow that all civilian-based tasks are to be put on hold. Every person in town—young, old, rich, poor, man, woman—is to help with the constructing of war machines, defensive structures, and traps. For the next three to four weeks, all of town, including the soldiers, will be helping in the manufacturing side of the war effort. Those who refuse will face consequences. To all you soldiers in this room, I'm afraid you'll be pulling double-time—training and construction both. Our lives depend on it. Don't worry though, you'll get your sleep; a tired soldier is a much less useful one. The Icytryxans have a design team working as we speak, devising schematics for various warfare apparatus. I've already seen some of these schematics— they're top notch.

"We will be having these war meetings every morning from now until this mobilized Molisian army is eradicated. So, I will see you all tomorrow morning, same time as normal."

Any questions anyone may've had had surely dissipated under Ulfenkerki's uneasy state. The asking of questions would be best suited for the morning when the General had had the chance to let his troubles permeate.

Everyone vacated the room and spent the rest of the day burdened by heavy thought.

King Rowlangiv, again, attended the morning meeting. Even though most of the decisions were ran through him first, he still felt it was important to be present.

Since they'd arrived early, Mick and Dave talked with the King for a bit before things started rolling. It was mainly small talk.

Ulfenkerki stepped to the front looking more relaxed. Upon detecting a refreshed General, the rest of the room eased their posture.

The reinvigorated man facing the crowd began his address: "Good morning, fine people. As far as inventory goes, we will have plenty of ammunition—projectiles and arrows galore. Plus, there will be plenty of Thorncat Missiles, which will be fired first, obviously. Armor and weapons are also sufficient—no worries there. The food stores are plump full; we definitely won't have to worry about a siege, as we can outlast anything they attempt. Like always, our greatest deficiency is our supply of metals. The Icytryxan design team, combined with the Garobansurovian, is currently formulating our approach to how we can best allocate the metal we do have into various combat devices. We want as many war machines and traps as possible. There is also a plan to disassemble many public erections to provide for the military project."

King Rowlangiv added, "During my announcement to the community today, I will also ask for personal metal contributions. I'm pretty sure they will comply without delay."

"I'm sure they will too." The Black Bear stretched his tight back before continuing. "Last night, we dispatched messengers to the northern towns, instructing all those in danger to come take refuge at the Capital. Here, they will be given beds, food, supplies, and anything else needed for comfort. Anyone desiring to stay in their village and fight would also be given permission to do so. Though, I informed the messengers to urge them to come to the Capital to make their stand. There's a much better chance of survival for them here. If the Capital falls, we all fall."

"I'm sure a lot of the rural areas will have no idea what's going on—such is the way of things. They will have to weather the storm in isolation. There just isn't time for the messengers to reach everyone. Ultimately, we want to win this war and, in the process, keep as many Garobansurovians alive as possible."

"Throughout history, there've been very few concepts less pleasant than the one known as war. But war is something that cannot be escaped. Like many times in the past, we will labor hard to persist."

Speaking next, King Rowlangiv followed the man he personally chose as general. "Thank you, General. It's a good preparatory plan. I hope to see all of you at the main square to listen to my address. You probably won't hear anything new, but your presences will go a long way in keeping morale high and hope alive."

Everyone in the room expressed they'd be there.

The King continued, "Do any of you have any questions?"

After a brief pause, Jason inquired, "Did the scouts mention what the Molisians had for assault towables?"

"The data was minimal regarding that, but it was mentioned that what the Molisians had as towable war machines wasn't impressive."

"We will put more focus into defending from infantry attack then," declared Thorncat. "I envision they will attempt to breach our walls in every place imaginable, like a river trying to find and punch its way through a damming landslide."

"True," responded Ulfenkerki. "It isn't easy to hold back a river, but with the right plugs, it can be done."

Mick also had a question: "Other than those designated for the forward bases, will there be any soldiers defending the anterior of the main wall, or will the whole of our force be stationed behind the wall?"

"Everyone will be positioned either behind or on top of the wall," replied the General. "It'd be a suicide mission to protect the wall with bodies. Yes, with enough warriors, sometimes guarding the wall from the front is practical. But unfortunately, we don't have that benefit. Throughout Garobansurov's history, I don't think we ever have."

"You read my mind," Mick reciprocated. "I don't recall ever reading about it either."

Ulfenkerki talked of lesser articles for a bit, and once he realized there were no further questions, he dismissed the meeting.

Seeing as Rowlangiv's address to the community was scheduled to commence in an hour, everyone in the room headed straight to the main square for it. Along the way, Jason said to Mick and Dave, "Don't either of you get any ideas of fighting in solitude on the other side of the wall. I know you're reckless like that sometimes."

The pair chuckled. "Oh, don't worry, old friend; it never crossed our minds."

The Capital's main square was starting to fill up. Some who were of the more perceptive nature were already guessing at why the King was about to make a public address. Though, most of the civilians had no idea a Molisian army was nearing.

Mick sat by Jason, while Dave found an empty chair next to Old Man Johnson and Will.

The laborious moving of chairs from storage to the main square's assembly area was a job coveted by many. The crown never had to pay anyone to do it, civilians just volunteered. It was no different than everything else that needed to be done for the crown's affairs—truly considered an honor.

In perfect harmony with the assembly area becoming completely filled, King Rowlangiv approached the podium. The crowd became silent as close to instantaneously as one could visualize.

Using the loudest version of his voice, Rowlangiv began: "Thank you all for coming on such short notice. It's imperative you, my citizens, hear this news from me first, even though I'm sure some of you have already guessed at why we're all here. Reconnoiters have recently revealed to me that a massive opposing army has been mobilized in the north, near the Baustic Mountains. We have reasons to believe it's being fronted by General Gamald—the escapee who'd spearheaded Molisia's Sarwa campaign. Our decision—General Ulfenkerki's, the Icytryxan war-strategy committee's and mine—is to defend from within the walls of the Capital. We've recommended to the Garobansurovian populace of the northern towns to fall back to the Capital, where we'll all reap in the tactical benefits it provides. Given a victorious outcome here, we will, then, retake those towns in the north that were lost. The Molisian army is much larger than ours, but I assure you, I believe we can win. Our alliance with the Icytryxis is unconquerable. Our battle dichotomy is one that has never been witnessed by any living Molisian soldier. They've no idea what they're about to face and will be overwhelmed by that with which they're unfamiliar. Our two armies have been trained with precision for many years, while the Molisian army is built on soldiers with barely enough experience to understand the mere concept of vigorous training. Yes, I assure you, we are going to win.

"Up until the battle, I am ordering a hold on everything not military-related. We will all participate in the construction of fortifications. Our deficiency of metal is our greatest weakness, therefore, we'll be disassembling many communal structures and reallocating the metal. I'm sure, for many of you, I don't even have to ask, but it would be greatly appreciated if you would donate your own metallic articles, big or small, to the Defense Fortification Project—*DFP* for short. Whatever you can bestow will go a long way. You can start contributing as soon as I'm through speaking, as the construction project will commence immediately.

"I know some of you are thinking that it may be wise to leave the Capital before the Molisians get here. I won't stop you. But you must remember, if the Capital falls, Garobansurov falls. Unspeakable things at the hands of the Molisians will happen in the countryside and cities alike. Events leading up to the Battle of Sarwa was evidence of this, as the Molisian hordes did unthinkable things. I'm sure some of you here can personally testify to this, having been in the area at the time. Anyone who wants refuge during the battle itself is welcome in the fortress of the castle. It is strongly defended, and where we'd make our last stand if need be. No invading mass has ever made it across the causeway and into the castle doors.

"I would strongly suggest to anyone who can wield a weapon to fight with us. The honor you'd receive from such a noble deed would be immeasurable.

"There's never been a better military partnership. Garobansurov and the Icytryxis WILL be the ones left standing in the end."

The King took a step back. Without hesitation, every man, woman, and child of the audience showed their king they were behind him by cheering louder than they'd ever cheered before. The cheers progressed into rally cries.

Rowlangiv never loved his subjects more.

After their throats were too sore to cheer anymore, Mick, Dave, and Yori walked back to the Doze Inn. They sat in the lobby and discussed what'd transpired in the main square.

"Yori, did you write that speech?"

"Nope, Mick, he usually writes his own. It practically took him since we learned of the Molisian army to memorize it."

"It was very moving," noted Dave. "So, Yori, will we be seeing those deadly throwing stars of yours in action again?"

"You bet."

"If Rowlangiv lets his most trusted advisor out onto the battlefield that is," added Mick.

"Oh, he will. We've discussed it."

"You can put his mind at ease," said Dave, "by telling him you'll be fighting near us. That is, if you wish."

"Well, thank you guys. I'm sure he'll appreciate that, as will I. We've made a pretty good team in the past."

"Yes, we have. I'm not sure yet though where we'll place ourselves during the battle. We have plenty of time to think about it," remarked Mick, before smiling and nodding at another resident of the inn who'd passed by.

Dave asked Yori, "Are you in agreement with the King? Do *you* believe we will win the battle?"

"That's actually a hard question, because there are no battles in the history books comparable at all. No documentation of the atlytl paradigm in war survives. Regardless, the paradigm will undoubtedly better our odds of victory. We will have other advantages too—the walls, the castle, the high ground, the mind of Ulfenkerki, and of course last year's Knowing Circle recipients."

"Oh you," interjected Dave.

Yori grinned and continued. "Our loyal citizens will work hard in the upcoming weeks. Their level of industry will be unprecedented. Additionally, I know your humble souls won't want to hear this, but I put a lot of stock into having you two on our side. I am personally acquainted with no finer warriors. My answer to your question is thus: I'd give us an eighty to ninety percent chance of winning—forty to fifty percent chance of doing so with manageable casualties."

Mick replied, "Correct, we're too modest to think of our skills as being significant enough to alter battle statistics. I do like your odds, though."

"It's going to be a hectic few weeks for all of us," inserted Dave.

"Time for me to get the chaos started. See you later, guys," emitted Yori.

"Have fun. And we'd better go make sure our sword-muscles get a thorough workout," noted Dave.

After Yori had left, Mick and Dave grabbed a snack and went to train.

At the end of the day, because they'd never done it before and were feeling inquisitive, Thraiker and Ghrere went out of their way to examine the army's official weapons cache. Most folks weren't allowed into the military storehouse, but being Mick Thraiker and Dave Ghrere came with privileges.

The cache was impressive they thought. It had a large supply of maces, battleaxes, spears, bows (long, short, and cross), slings, war hammers, sickles, recently added atlytls, and a plethora of different-sized swords. Some of the swords had serrated edges, some had barbs, some had ornate crosspieces, but all were sharp.

"On a sad note, this storehouse is tinged with the unmistakable appearance of death."

"One would have to assume it would be before going in," Dave said to Mick.

"No doubt. I have to swing one of these war hammers before we leave. I don't think I've ever done so with one so high-quality."

"Knock yourself out, Dave, but not literally. I want to further scrutinize the spears."

Once the pair had finished running their hands over all the weapons that'd caught their attentions, they headed back to the inn for sleep.

Through a satisfying morning yawn, Mick commented, "Well, are you ready to build?"

Dave finished tying his boot. "As ready as ever."

Will and Old Man Johnson joined up, and the quartet began strolling to the nearest building-station, knowing they didn't have to travel far. All of town was bustling with commotion. Almost every soul in town was or would be proudly working. The only ones who wouldn't be working on fortifications were those physically incapable of doing so.

The task at hand for the quartet was the disassembling of park benches. The benches contained a fair amount of metal that could be made into militarily useful articles. The benches could be refabricated at any time after the war.

It took the crew half a day to isolate all the desired material. The latter half of the day was spent hauling all the metal to the proper locales with carts.

Since everyone in town worked out of loyalty, there was no designated stoppage time. Everyone basically worked until they were sore. This architype was not much unlike that which the Icytryxis deployed daily in their homeland.

Mick and Dave made it well into the night the first day, having continued working even after attending a generous segment of army drills. A sweaty King Rowlangiv was also spotted handling a maul, swinging away laboriously.

ANNA HAD NOTHING to do but think. Her prison of the garbage chute couldn't have been more stifling. By this point, most would've taken a foolish risk, attempting a low chance for success escape; not Anna, she was witty and patient. And alive . . .

If I have to listen to that annoying laugh one more time, I'm going to jump out of this pit and strangle him with his own intestines. I've heard cats hacking up hairballs that sounded better. I can't believe his compatriots haven't stopped him yet. Spineless Molisians.

The booze has to be running out soon—they sure have been going at it a long time. I know we didn't have THAT much in stock . . .

There doesn't seem to be too many of them anymore. The main army must've moved on, leaving these simples here to hold the city. If only they would all leave the bar for a mere hour, I could escape. But, no, there always has to be someone in the bar. And they all sleep at different times. I can't win.

I am glad though I don't have to listen to them rape my friends. Either they do that in another building, or the main army took them with.

I hope they don't find the nearby Halisk farm, where a lot of beer is brewed. They would then have an almost endless supply. The agonizing laughter would never end then. Please don't go a mile east, you spineless Molisian simples.

I wonder if the King has become aware of this army yet. His scouts could've reached him by now, I'm sure. The Capital itself is more than likely going to be attacked. Oh God, I hope they win.

What should I do today to pass the time in this hellscape? Let me think. Yesterday, I guessed at which drunks would fight first. Boy, was I wrong. You'd think by now I would be better at guessing that. They sure brawl for the dumbest of reasons. I mean really! Beating each other bloody over losing at cards, that's just ridiculous. That game killed some time, but I'll try something else today. I will try to determine which one ends up pissing himself first. That'll surely kill some time. I'll do that, along with guessing which one burns himself first on the grill today.

I hold in high esteem the person who will come in here and stuff that annoying laugh down his annoying throat. They'd be the hero among heroes.

Unfortunately for her, half the Molisian garrison was planning a raid of the countryside dwellings for supplies—especially for more liquor.

The man with the egregious laugh would lead the way.

CHAPTER 5

HAVING WORKED PAINSTAKINGLY on fortifications for the last couple of weeks made for aching muscles. But for Mick and Dave, sore was a good thing. It meant renewed strength.

"The last two weeks went by pretty fast," said Mick.

"They did," agreed Dave.

The duo stretched and went to Ulfenkerki's morning strategy meeting.

Looking fresh and upbeat, the General began his soliloquy: "Things have been going incredibly well for these last couple of weeks. All of town has been working very hard. The soldiers are doing great with double time—drills and fortifications assembly. I ask all of you here at some point today to take a tour of town and examine everything that'd just been built. Mainly stick to the outer wall defenses, which is where the most time has been spent building."

The Black Bear talked for another ten minutes, before adjourning the meeting.

After the summit, Jason asked Mick and Dave, "When were you guys planning to carry out your observational excursion of the ramparts? I'll accompany you if I'm free during that time?"

"We can go any time. Does in an hour work for you?"

"It does. I'll meet you back here then."

Mick went for breakfast, and Dave a run. Afterwards, they met back up with Jason at the barracks.

"Where shall we begin?"

"We might as well start at the nearest spot of the wall," Dave replied to Jason.

The three walked two hundred yards from the barracks to the wall.

"Here's one of the new installations, an impressive ballistae battery," stated Jason. "Fine craftsmanship."

Dave voiced, "This should handily annihilate at least a couple of their war machines. It's too bad these apparatus take up a lot of metal. I doubt we made many more."

"Jason, does the army have ballista specialists within the ranks?" asked Mick.

"Actually, we do, and there are also a few Icytryxans quite proficient. They can all hit their mark with the minutest of error."

"Exceptional," said Mick. "Good thing this ballistae battery is facing north."

"There always seems to be enemies to the north," voiced Jason.

"That's because there's mainly ocean to the south," joked Dave.

The trio resumed the tour and came upon the next point of interest.

"Although there are already plenty of catapult emplacements," said Mick, "it never hurts to have a few more."

"I think the Molisians know the Capital boasts a lot of catapults, which is why they aren't bringing many towables themselves. They know that since we have the high ground, we can destroy their machinery easily. They're no doubt banking on their overpowering number of soldiers," commented Jason.

Neighboring the catapult station was one of the new atlytl launching platforms, built upon the Icytryxis arrival. A person could walk all the way down it for nearly two hundred yards, peering over the nearby parapet on tiptoes. The platform ran parallel the rampart, and removable access points connected the two. It was all designed so Icytryxans could fire their atlytls over the archers lined up along the top of the wall.

Dave climbed to the top of the platform, hopped across one of the connections, and stood on the main wall. He yelled down below, "I wonder how long this pile of rocks have been sitting up here, they look pretty undisturbed."

Jason and Mick followed Dave to the wall. Jason looked at the rock pile, and replied, "I know they've been here quite a while. I also know we're bringing up even more to help eradicate ladder infantry. As I'm sure you know, you can never have too many rocks to heave down a wall during battle."

"Oh yes, we learned that a couple years ago at the Battle of Strwin."

"Yes, we did," reminisced Jason. "That does seem like a long time ago. Optimistically, the upcoming battle will go as well as that one."

Dave responded, "It will. If you haven't noticed, the three of us have won every skirmish we've ever fought in together."

"We have haven't we." Jason scratched his chin. "Interesting."

The trio reached the last access point and the end of the atlytl platform and climbed down.

Eying the old archer towers along the way, the trio continued to the next point of interest: the site where all the traps were being fashioned.

Atop dozens of tables, sat many different varieties of metallic traps. The majority of them were spring loaded and ominous.

As the trio ogled the traps, a soldier approached. "Good to see you Jason, sir. You as well, Mick, Dave. Would you guys like to see the map depicting where on the battlefield all these traps will be set?"

"Definitely."

The soldier pointed. "In that building there. They'll show it to you."

After concluding their admiring of the devices, they went to the building at which the young soldier had pointed.

"Impressive," noted Mick, looking at the blueprints. "The layout will present quite the perilous labyrinth for an invading mass."

"I know I wouldn't want to get my leg clamped by one, especially while also trying to evade arrows and projectiles from above."

"Me neither, Jason."

"It's a good thing Gamald didn't have an abundant supply of traps to lay out for the Battle of Sarwa."

"Definitely. There were some, but not a whole lot."

Dave said, "I hope the trap setup/take-down team is dependable. There are a lot of traps to be accounted for and picked up. I'd hate for a single one to be left behind after the battle. We wouldn't want a child or anybody to stumble upon one and lose a limb, or worse, their life."

One of the soldiers in the building overheard Dave, and said, "The trap arrangement team meets here often. They seem to be taking the job very seriously, and on some occasions, they're here conversing feverously well into the night."

"It's good to hear the panel is passionate about their important post."

Jason chuckled at Dave's remark. "That's a lot of p's."

Dave returned a laugh. "It wasn't purposely planned, I promise, my pal."

Smiling, the trio left the building and continued the tour. They rounded a ninety-degree corner, and came across another stout atlytl platform, all four sides of the Capital having been equipped with one.

Jason commented, "Only three of the platforms will be lined with Icytryxans during the upcoming battle, which three depend on from which direction the Molisians advance. It'll most likely be from the north, as I doubt they'll circle around and approach from the south. All thousand Icytryxans can fit onto the three platforms and simultaneously launch projectiles effectively. We wanted larger platforms, so more Icytryxans could squeeze onto the one nearest the assault. But we ran out of time."

"What was built seems to be quite adequate," said Mick. "That's just the way of things. There never is enough time and money for everything desired."

"So true."

After the platform and the viewing of another catapult placement, they ventured to the last stop of the tour: outside the city walls to see the new spikes. These wooden devices were used to slow enemy movement, but not prohibit it.

Mick uttered, "I'd hate to be impaled by one of these."

Walking back to the confines of the city, Dave said, "The new defenses all look to be superlative. Combined with the old, they will be quite the solid tool."

"Yes, they will greatly increase our chance of winning," agreed Mick. "Marvelous tour."

"Yori had told me that you two were kind enough to offer to fight alongside her during the battle. Have you decided on your stratagem yet?" asked Jason.

"I know I at least," replied Mick, "yearn to see the atlytls in action up close and personal. So, I'd like to be near the wall. I'm not sure where though."

"Same here," added Dave.

"All the archer towers are already reserved for the eagle eyes. Anything but atop the wall for you two would be a waste of resources, in my opinion. The longer you two are on the ground standing idle, the worse it is for the crown. We need you by the action, the sooner the better. Agree?"

"Sure, but we freelance warriors would hate to take any spots away from the Crown's official soldiers."

"You know perfectly well most of the soldiers would offer you their spot on the wall," pleaded Jason. "They know full too well how capable you are of winning battles."

Dave said, "I suppose. What about Yori though?"

"She is very competent with a bow and those throwing stars of hers," replied Jason. "It'll be fine."

"We'll check with her first if it's alright to battle from the wall."

"Go ahead. You know what she'll say."

A few days later, Mick and Dave were able to ask Yori about Jason's proposal. Just like Jason presumed, she was all for it, as she looked forward to flinging her throwing stars down at the enemy. Her skills had surely progressed since the year previous, and in addition, she now possessed three times as many.

THE WEATHER of northern Garobansurov was being cooperative for an advancing army.

"They aren't making this very much fun for us. All these towns are deserted by the time we get to them," Leedle said to Gamald.

"I'm sure the king told them all that they could make their stand at the Capital," replied Gamald. "On a personal note, I want those two who defeated Grunt and Roar at the Battle of Sarwa to be at the Capital when we get there. I want to see the looks on their faces when we breach the walls and storm the town with our overpowering army. I want to gut those two while they breathe. I really liked Grunt and Roar, they didn't talk much." Gamald swallowed hard, due to the lump that'd just formed in his throat.

"Mick and Dave will be there," returned Leedle, who, as being Gamald's second in command for a reason, knew when to patronize. "They will be there, I'd bet on it, along with Ulfenkerki and Rowlangiv."

"I think this town we are now approaching is the last one of size before the Capital."

"I believe so. We're almost to our final destination."

"I hope there is at least minimal resistance in this next town. The soldiers could stand for a bit of practice before the big fight."

"With any luck, there are women for them too. Farmer's wives and daughters are too few and far between," Leedle said to his general.

"Right. We had more women back in the cave."

The massive Molisian army entered Biask, unopposed. It was a virtual ghost town. All who'd remained behind were those too old to walk to the Capital. On one of his grumpier days, Gamald would've killed the elderly for the heck of it. Luckily, it wasn't one of these days, partially since the townsfolk had wisely left enough liquor behind to appease the raiders. The townsfolk liked the elderly enough for such a courtesy. They could've carted the elderly with them to the Capital, but apparently affection didn't run that deep for non-family members. There was always a line.

The soldiers ransacked every house in Biask. Since it was one of the larger towns along the warpath, Gamald would leave behind an occupying force. Combined, all garrisons left behind on the great march totaled a little over five hundred head, which in itself was a pretty formidable force with which to reckon. At some point, if the Capital had happened to survive Gamald's assault, Garobansurov would have to reconquer its towns.

"We'll sleep here tonight," Gamald told Leedle. "The troops have reached their threshold for walking today."

"Plenty of beds and booze." Of no real importance to anyone but himself, Leedle switched his body weight to the other leg. "Do you think, General, the age factor of our soldiers will diminish our chances of winning?"

"Maybe a hair, but I believe once they cross over the wall, it won't matter how young they are. No matter the age, the instant an invading soldier smells blood, loot, and women, they switch into a zone of pure adrenalin. They'll fight on impulse and without fear."

"Good point. I remember those days."

"Me too. I'm going to commandeer that house for the night." Gamald pointed.

"I'll tell everyone to not bother you."

HIGHLIGHTED BY A SUPERB training session with the black needle swords, Mick and Dave had reaped a productive day.

Everyone at the Capital now knew how close the Molisians were, so battle preparations had begun ramping up. Rowlangiv was pleased in what'd been accomplished to date and was sure to come up with a reward deserving of such effort.

Rowlangiv had no heir. If he happened to pass, while the Capital persevered, a new line would be chosen. The crown had been in the Rowlangiv family for over three hundred years. He'd planned to rear children, but it was something that thus far hadn't materialized. The king wasn't all that old, as his parents had died unnaturally young.

The King planned on joining the battle, but he didn't intend on rolling the bones in any attempt at heroic feats. He'd work a bow at distance with experienced king's guards for protection.

Mick and Dave rounded out the day by spending it with Old Man Johnson and Will at the park nearest their inn.

Johnson said, "I've been thinking about this for a while now. Do you think it'd be alright if I shot arrows over the wall with the volley crew? And then when it comes to melee fighting, I'd take refuge with the rest. I can still draw back a fairly heavy bow, but my sword swinging days are over. My arc is just too slow."

"An extra archer would be a nice asset. And you're right, there's no use handing the enemy an easy target, as an old man with a weak hip sticks out like a sore thumb. To be sure, I'll ask Jason tomorrow if it's okay for you to join the volley crew."

"Thanks, Dave. I guess my hip is feeble, but my back is sturdy yet."

Will asked if he could do the same, but he was told he didn't have enough experience. Boys will be boys.

Early the next day, Jason gave confirmation that Mr. Johnson could do as he wished. Johnson went to work straight away strengthening his drawback muscles even further. Mick and Dave helped out with pointers. Although his arrows couldn't fly as far as those of some of the more proficient archers, Johnson's could certainly clear the wall with authority. The same couldn't be said for some of the others on the volley team.

A few days had elapsed; Mick and Dave sat attentively at the morning war meeting.

General Ulfenkerki, with his usual get-to-business attitude, discoursed, "As we speak, the Molisians are three, maybe two, days march from here. Most of the fortifications we wanted to get done, are now done. I have my ranged guerilla teams selected for the forward bases—quite the capable bunch of hard asses. I will have the traps deployed the day after tomorrow. And please help to remind all the townsfolk to stay behind the wall once the traps are operational. It's vital. They'll get amputated or killed if they leave the city and step in the wrong spot. Also, from this point on, there'll be an hour-long period in the mornings when we'll be going live with ballistae, catapults, bows, and atlytls. It's imperative the townsfolk stay vigilant while we practice. Of course, we'll have a team on the lookout for strays, but it's better to be safe than sorry.

"Rowlangiv asked me to repeat to those who don't plan to fight that they can make haven in the castle. The castle is the best sanctuary, they'll be safest there. So, please share this information. If it ultimately comes to it, we will also make our last stand there. The causeway is exceptionally defensible. No army has ever made it into the castle. The Capital's whole defensive layout was designed by a master engineer, whose name I can't recall. I've always thought the ingenious part of the design is how tower archers can reach most parts of town with arrows, thus eliminating the possibility of a siege. The Molisians marched all this way to *fight*, not siege.

"We will attempt diplomacy, obviously. Rowlangiv has selected his diplomats—a team including an Icytryxan—who'll be deployed soon, I think tomorrow. Odds are against it working. Nevertheless, we must try. I personally think the diplomats are bravely foolish. They're more likely to lose their heads than prevent the battle. But I suppose they know what they're doing. Godspeed to those daring souls.

"Tomorrow, we will discuss in detail the synchronization of all military divisions. Are there any questions?"

A few insignificant questions were put forth, and the room emptied in procession.

For exercise, Mick executed a run. In the meantime, Dave spent some time with Thyxer and Syryx at the practice launch field. Thyxer and Syryx were fine-tuning their atlytls, aiming to get the best performance out of their equipment.

Dave asked them, "Where on the body precisely do you aim with the atlytls for the best chance of lethality? I know I can downright tell you where the blunt ones hurt the most. Aah, memories."

Thyxer answered, "The terminal hits are the ones that enter the head, neck, heart, or lungs. And occasionally a strike to the stomach, kidneys, or intestines can be deadly. Sometimes it's instant death, while sometimes they'll bleed to their demise. Leg and back hits frequently immobilize, rendering the target useless on the battlefield. Back home, while hunting, I once hit my quarry in the spine, paralyzing it. I just had to walk up and slit its throat."

"What species was it?"

"A svig," replied Thyxer. "You don't have them here, and I doubt you saw any while you were by us. They're pretty rare and sly."

"I had read about the stunning animal, while on Swyrove. I have one more question. Are the atlytls more fatal at close range or long range?"

"That's actually an interesting inquiry. It would defy the laws of physics for a projectile to have less velocity upon leaving the weapon than it does later in its flight. But there are other aspects introduced into the equation. Can we aim better at long range? Our examinations have verified that the answer is no. However, once you get too close with an atlytl, melee weapons are far superior, since they don't require reloading."

"Intriguing," said Dave. "I'd assume there is also a point when a plunging projectile reaches terminal velocity, gaining no further momentum, due to air resistance."

"Yes, you're right. There are graphs showcasing that very principle back on Swyrove."

"I'm sure there are some here somewhere too, depicting the same principle with arrows. Maybe at the library. So, in theory, would it be sensible mathematically to start unleashing the atlytls with no reserve when the Molisians are just within range?"

"Correct," responded Syryx. "There are plenty of projectiles to go around, so the plan is to launch as fast as possible when the enemy is within the kill zone. It's unlikely we'd run out of projectiles. If they were limited, we'd go at things differently."

"I imagine. It's undoubtedly advantageous that the projectiles are reusable. Though, I'd hate to be the one retrieving them all after the battle, all hundreds of thousands of them."

Thyxer and Syryx chuckled at Dave's comical declaration. "Yes, hundreds of thousands of little, metallic balls will be strewn everywhere on the battlefield, needing to be recovered. But there'll be hundreds of us on the salvage crew, so gathering them all won't be as arduous as you'd think," said Thyxer.

"We'll reclaim all of our arrows too," added Dave. "If we win."

NEVER HAVING BEEN anywhere near a hostile army before, Frytytz was fairly apprehensive about the situation. He'd methodically studied treaties and diplomatic courses for nearly a hundred years back home, so if ever there was a chance for all his effort to pay off, now was the time. Brittle, ancient texts from faraway lands had been available for him to read in Swyrove. It was his only way to learn the subject, seeing as there never was much call for diplomacy in a world free from war and politics. He didn't know why, but the topic fascinated him. Frytytz wasn't young, so if he hadn't jumped at the opportunity now (however perilous he was informed it may be), there may never be another chance for him again.

Joining Frytytz on the mission to treat with Gamald were Capital natives, Nina and Paula—young, ambitious women with adventurous spirits. They knew it was possible Gamald would capture them before diplomatic conversation began and add them to the soldier's album of rape victims. But they too were students of the craft, desiring to make names for themselves. This was the only way. Given they survived the upcoming encounter with Gamald, they figured if future ambassadorial missions were to emerge, they'd be called upon by virtue of their experience. High risk, high reward, they thought. Successful or not, they might never get another chance.

The Molisian army was a day's march from the Capital—Frytytz, Nina, and Paula were half a mile from them.

"Well team," said Frytytz, "it's almost time."

"It's possible that soldiers snatch us before Gamald even knows we're coming."

"True, Paula. They might do that and not even tell him about us."

"It'd be easy for them to do," noted Frytytz, "since they'd just have to impersonate him, as we don't know exactly what Gamald looks like."

"Right. Artist's renditions can only be so accurate."

"All we can do is cross our fingers," said Nina, "and walk headfirst into the storm."

With the Molisian army now directly in front of them, the diplomats slowed their pace. Latched onto a healthy fear of the unknown, the three pushed forward. They held their solid green flags up high, hoping the Molisians would honor the continent's one and only symbol of treaty.

The Molisian lead group spotted the Garobansurovian diplomats and their flags, halted, and looked at each other in bewilderment. They were surprised to see diplomats so soon, having figured none would appear until they were practically on top of the Capital. Molisia usually didn't put as much effort into pre-battle mediation, so the lead group was staggered. Nevertheless, they notified Gamald of the development. It had, however, popped into the soldiers' minds to rape first and notify later.

The entire army parted, creating a path for Gamald, Leedle, and Gamald's personal guard team. Led by the personal guard (the four best fighters of Gamald's army) the General's party approached the Garobansurovian diplomats. Seven thousand soldiers stood still, waiting for the affair to unfold.

"I am the general of the army before you. To whom am I speaking?"

"General, sir, my name is Frytytz. This is Nina, and this is Paula. We have been chosen by King Rowlangiv to come to terms. If a bargain can't be struck, we'll be on our way, as there's no point in wasting either of our times."

Nina added, "Plain and simple, we have an offer to present. This war has been costly for both sides, the deaths of those we hold dear never forgotten. If we can come to an agreement, many lives may be saved. There is no need for any more bloodshed."

Gamald scratched his jaw, searching for words. "Correct. I could do without further loss of family and friends. Let's hear the proposal you've been instructed to put forward."

Paula swallowed hard and spoke. "The King is willing to bestow farmland on any Molisian who so wishes for it. It's a valuable proposition, since Garobansurovian citizens pay dearly for it. But the citizens have since expressed willingness in allowing you the land. War is more costly.

"Those individuals where farmland isn't to their liking can choose a tract of land more suitable to their needs. Some like a more scenic parcel. I know I do. All the King asks in return is for your armed masses to stay on your side of the border."

Gamald pondered and produced, "There are two points to bring up. First, your country has already proposed this arrangement to our governing body, to which they've already refused. Second, I don't really have the authority to approve the terms for all of Molisia. I couldn't accept even if I wanted to. And I'm not about to go all the way back across the border to confer your bid, which I know has already been declined."

Frytytz said boldly, "What may I ask could the offer have been to persuade you away from battle. I'm just curious. Do you have a counteroffer perhaps?"

"We are here for power. Power is only good to hold over people, not land. Give us your people, and we will have no need to band together, brandishing destructive weapons."

"I understand. Your men want women, and your women want men."

"That, and the elimination of the fear that'd inevitably surface in worrying about your retaliation. Real power."

Frytytz was taken aback. "I must say, sir, nobody can accuse you of not aiming high, that's for sure. You certainly go right for the jugular. But you're right—all the wealth in the world isn't worth anything, if you know at some point those who gave it to you are eventually going to take it back by force."

"You're getting it. Furthermore, the King can give us the land to produce crops, which, in turn, can be traded for money. With this money, one can go to the brothel. At first, everything seems legit. But it's a facade. In the end, it's valueless, because all the king has to do is print more money, or the equivalency of, and give it to his allies. Eventually, our crop money won't be worth anything. So, it all comes down to this: You give us exactly what we want, we take our spoils back with us to our own fortresses, and the balance of power shifts. Otherwise, my massive army will take down your government."

Paula asked, "Can't you acquire what you desire in Molisia?"

"The wealthy and powerful in our own country have stolen far more than their fair share. We are the young and powerless," answered Gamald. "Either we gang up and defeat the mercenaries hired by the nobles of Molisia, or we invade the country to the south. We made our decision, as we can't defeat the aristocracies."

"So, Garobansurov's war is only with part of Molisia?"

"Basically, yes. The wealthy of Molisia also have the upper class of the country of Norvic backing them."

Nina joined in, "Which leads us to this question: You, General Gamald, are renowned, probably rich, and visibly not young. Why would you lead such an escapade?"

"Glad you asked. True, I am all of those. I have no problems acquiring everything I desire. Basically, it stems down to the fact I'd rather see foreigners die than my own countrymen. My soldiers would raid Garobansurov with or without me, I just make them better through experienced leadership. I am loyal to those who've been loyal to me. Countless underprivileged Molisians had exhibited utmost loyalty to me in my youth, the most difficult times of my life. It's a debt of gratitude I must repay."

"I couldn't be more grateful for your honesty," said Frytytz. "My companions and I will relay your counteroffer to the King and let you know as soon as possible his response. Though, it is a lot you're asking, and I doubt he will comply."

"Don't wait too long to convey and return; things are going to get ugly here awfully soon."

"Noted."

AS SOON AS the diplomats arrived back to the Capital, an urgent war meeting was called by Rowlangiv and Ulfenkerki. Mick and Dave were to attend, along with all of the other regulars.

In one of the larger rooms of the castle, every sentence of the diplomat's exchange with Gamald was relayed to the King.

Rowlangiv shook his head in disbelief. "Well, at least we've learned things about the Molisian infrastructure that'd previously been unfamiliar to us. Gamald gets right to the point, that's for certain. I suppose sometimes only war can alter the dynamics of supremacy. We will battle soon, no doubt, as I can't counter his terms with anything even close to what he wants."

Yori proclaimed, "We're behind you, sir, one hundred percent."

One and all in the room had let it be known Yori was correct in momentarily speaking for them.

Ulfenkerki spoke next: "We will fight within the next thirty to forty hours, I'm thinking. The army is ready. I must confess, I'd like to talk further upon the Molisian political framework."

Rowlangiv shuffled in his chair and cracked his back. "I do too. Go on with discussion, Kermoy Ulfenkerki."

"It is rather daunting, knowing we're fighting only a part of the country. I can't help but imagine how hard it'd be to repel both the nobles and the provincials if they ever decided to join forces. Plus, it's even more daunting, thinking about warding off the Molisians and the Norvics combined."

Ulfenkerki continued, "I wonder if there is a tangible land division amongst the Molisians. It's hard to grasp the wealthy even allow the deprived to run around raiding foreign villages. You'd think the nobles would fear the Molisian underprivileged and us teaming up and coming after them."

Ulfenkerki sighed. "Things have undeniably gotten more complicated."

Jason stated, "Molisia is a larger country than ours, north to south. It takes a long time to walk from the northern end to the southern. I think the soldiers invading us mostly live on the southern side of the country, and the nobles live more to the north. It's a circumstance that probably makes it difficult for the wealthy to regulate the actions of the poor."

"Possibly," said Ulfenkerki. "The more populated cities are to Molisia's north, which is where the affluent are prone to congregate. It's definitely advantageous that there are so many miles between us, and that no faster mode of land transportation than walking exists. We'd have a lot more to worry about if their ships were faster."

Rowlangiv commented, "Plus, we still don't know what's going on in the western side of our own country. I'm hoping that gets remedied soon."

"Maybe we'll send more scouts in that direction, after the battle," the general suggested.

"Yes. And even though they did a commendable job, I'm not sending the diplomats back to Gamald," asserted Rowlangiv. "It would be an unnecessary risk to their lives. I'm sure Gamald knows perfectly well we weren't going to agree to his absurd proposal."

"Good thinking," agreed Ulfenkerki.

The war meeting had lasted a few more minutes and was adjourned.

The hours leading up to the battle were hectic. Mick and Dave carried out training sessions with Yori to enhance their teamwork. Old Man Johnson fine-tuned his archery. Will worried about his dad. Old women prayed. Drunks kept on drinking.

As soon as the assaulting army was spotted on the horizon, all of those who intended to fight got into position. The guerilla fighters arming the forward bases had already been in their stations for a while.

Mick, Dave, and Yori got into position on the wall, right in front of one of the atlytl platforms. They'd have projectiles screaming over their heads shortly.

Mick commented, "Now is when we can really observe the chemistry between Garobansurovians and the Icytryxans."

"This is going to be a very interesting conflict," returned Dave.

"I'd guess the Molisians have no idea they're about to be bombarded by both arrows and pointy, metal projectiles," voiced Mick.

"I'd guess that too," replied Dave, "unless I knew they had spies in town."

"Possible, but unlikely. Rowlangiv has really ramped up gate screening since the last time the Capital was infiltrated."

"Very true," said Yori. "The Knowing Circle day assassination attempt had surely persuaded the King to prioritize the screening of the Capital's comers and goers."

"It takes just one spy to slip through the cracks. We'll have to wait and see if the Molisians have any sort of defensive tactic for the projectiles," stated Mick.

"They may have constructed oversized shields to protect from above. This would help them a bit, but it'd also slow their sprint to the wall and increase their time under our catapult fire."

"Right, Dave. And carrying larger shields than normal would steal some focus from avoiding traps."

"We will know shortly what preparations they took, if any."

All the traps and war machines were ready. All those intending to fight were stationed nervously. All those not intending to fight either had taken refuge or were too old to care.

Will and Yusyta had gone to the castle with the other villagers who desired a place of safety.

Determined, Old Man Johnson stood amongst the archer volley team. He was by far the oldest but definitely not the ineptest.

As the overseer, General Ulfenkerki felt he could see the events unfold best from the heights of an archer tower. He'd strategically positioned his next in command, Jason Thorncat, on the other end of town. This way, experience was on both ends of town.

Thyxer and Syryx were situated on different atlytl platforms, both itching to start the barrage. They'd intentionally separated for their first-ever battle, because they were both regarded as being militarily astute, and them splitting up would benefit more soldiers.

Gregg Hogarty and his aptitude to throw knives was atop a wall—not the same wall as Mick, Dave, and Yori. He and his barrel of knives took up a lot of room, but nobody minded, as they knew exactly how proficient he was with those knives. The soldiers all knew how many Molisians Gregg could put out of action.

There wasn't a soul in the Capital over the age of ten who didn't know what lurked on the horizon. Some couldn't handle the pressure and panicked. However, most knew it was imperative to remain calm, cool, and collected in order to stay alive. Remaining calm kept a person's sense of awareness keen.

Chapter 6

AS EXPECTED, the Molisian army would only pass by one of the forward bases on the way to attacking the Capital. The occupiers of the bases nowhere near the action headed back behind the shielding city wall. The ranged guerilla unit in the active base was attentive. A few paced nervously back and forth, amidst the looming threat. A total of twenty Garobansurovian archers waited, bow in hand.

The base itself was made of stone, having two tiers that included parapets, ten archers for each tier. A couple thousand arrows lined the fort's innards, ready for utilization. If at least one-fourth of these arrows were to find the body of an enemy, the base would be considered successful.

The ranking officer of the forward base waited patiently, watching for a large portion of the opposing army to be within range. When it was, she gave the signal, yelling loud enough so everyone in the base could hear: "Fire away!"

Swiftly and rhythmically, the archers shot arrows into the opposing mass, to the point of heavy breathing. The more arrows they unleashed, the better—grab, notch, draw back, release, repeat.

Eventually, there was return fire, but the parapets sheltered effectively. One of the archers caught an arrow in the arm, but it wasn't a serious enough wound to keep him from continuing his duty.

While discharging arrows, the officer paid attention to how close the adversary was getting. Once they were too close, it would be time for the next phase.

Having seen it was time, she shouted, "Last arrow!"

Each soldier launched their last arrow, dropped their bow, and displaying great organization filed out of the base. All twenty ran as fast as they could back to the protection of Myothraces.

For the first few moments of the run, they had to worry about incoming arrows. One soldier was struck in the leg, forcing a debilitating limp. A nearby warrior draped the wounded's arm over his own shoulders and would benevolently aid his compatriot all the way back to the confines of the city.

Once the runners reached the ominous trap zone, they had to pay more attention to their footing. Three of the soldiers had perfectly put the trap placements to memory. The rest followed them.

The archers of the forward base successfully navigated the convoluted trap field and made it inside the wall. They didn't know exactly how many Molisians they immobilized with their undertaking, but they did get the sense it was enough to justify the risk. The twenty took a quick breather, then, dutifully joined the rest of the archers stationed in their various locales.

Shortly subsequent the guerilla team reaching their new posts, the vast Molisian army was within range of the Icytryxans' atlytls. Thyxer and Syryx's long, strong arm muscles were full of energy, just waiting to erupt, like a poorly built dam. Armed with the new Thorncat Missiles Jason had designed on the mission in Swyrove, the Icytryxans began their salvo. The projectiles were airborne far before the arrows of the Garobansurovian archers stationed on the wall. Simply speaking, the arrows couldn't go as far, neither could catapult and ballistae fire.

The torrent of projectiles flew from the platforms, over those on the wall, and out past the trap field with a certain kind of grace and beauty that very few had ever seen before. Virtually every Icytryxan who'd made the trip to the Capital were swinging their atlytls and doing so fluently.

Mick, Dave, and Yori were awestruck at seeing all the projectiles flying overhead, risking sore necks as they ogled the sky.

"You could say," offered Dave, "that a huge factor in the grandeur is the imposing thumping sounds the projectiles compose as they hit the Molisian shields."

"And their skulls," added Mick. "You wouldn't think you could hear such a thing happening so far away, but I suppose with their being so many, the sound gets augmented."

Yori pointed out, "The army has advanced far enough that you can now see the devastation the projectiles are causing."

"Oh wow," returned Dave. "There are bodies strewn everywhere. Most are motionless, while some are crawling inch by inch to get away. The atlytl: a powerful weapon indeed."

"Good thing last year we faced the blunt projectiles during the exercise in Swyrove, and not these."

"For sure, Mick. We'd be pretty holy."

The Molisian host was now within range of the catapults and ballistae. The ammunition from the impressive war machines joined the fray alongside the projectiles. Thick thumping sounds now joined the thin ones made by the projectiles—a veritable orchestra. Carnage was everywhere.

Not so coincidentally, the Molisian army was within Garobansurovian archer range when it reached the trap field. Mick, Dave, and Yori finally saw some action. They loosed arrows along with their compatriots. Bows were not Mick and Dave's primary weapons, still, they manipulated them well.

Shortly after those on high ground could liberate their arrows, those of the ground volley squads could follow suit—including Old Man Johnson. *What a rush*, he thought, as he endeavored to move quicker than he had in years.

Incoming catapult fire began, followed by arrows. Those on the wall made sure to peripherally watch the Molisian catapults, as there weren't many things more deadly than getting leveled by a catapult stone.

Dave commented, "Some, not all, of the traps in the trap field are making connection. You can hear them snapping shut."

"I could do without the screams of agony though," replied Mick. "It is rather heartrending."

"True," agreed Dave. "It could very well be us in one of those traps."

The first cluster of Molisian ladder troops reached the top of the wall, followed by many more. One could tell they'd practiced ladder ascension, for they were getting to the top in three blinks of an eye.

It'd taken a while for a Molisian to reach the top of the wall at Mick, Dave, and Yori's post. The trio had been quite proficient at keeping them at bay, through black needle and throwing star usage. Mick went to work on those who'd reached the top, while Dave and Yori continued clearing the ladder, demonstrating utmost urgency.

Standing at a strategic vantage point, Yori precisely flung her throwing stars with both hands, content with how many Molisians she was hitting. Dave used his bow for foes lower on the ladder, and his sword for foes higher up. It was a successful stratagem for the pair.

Having gone through hell, another soldier made it through Dave and Yori's gauntlet. But once on the wall, Mick wasn't the greatest obstacle the inexperienced Molisian would face; it'd be his own impatience. The young Molisian had high hopes that he was going to storm the entire length of the Capital and be the one to capture the King's head. In his mind, if he didn't hurry, someone else would get to it first. A poke and a stab from

Mick's sword were all it took to end the dreams of glory of an ill-prepared Molisian.

Eventually too many troops had broken the imaginary plane separating relative safety from imminent danger, as the Molisian wave had crashed ashore, aiming to crush everything in its way. Dave and Yori were forced to abandon the ladder and switch into survival mode.

Yori was nowhere near as adept with a sword as Mick and Dave, so she stood in the middle of the two to fight from a secure position.

In the meantime, Jason, Ulfenkerki, and Gregg were also trying to keep their heads above water. The Molisian wave had engulfed the entire city.

Gregg held out a long time before having to switch to his melee weapon; he'd really done a number on the ladder troops with his knife throwing skills. He'd almost run out of knives, having had to reach all the way to the bottom of the barrel (literally) for new ones to throw.

Jason collided with one of the Molisian army's better fighters right from the get-go. Which was surprising, since usually the adroit soldiers were allowed the privilege of not having to man the front lines. At first, the head to head battle was evenly matched. In the end, Jason got lucky. Thyxer was nearby and had seen Jason's predicament. He momentarily stopped firing projectiles over the wall and launched one directly at Jason's adversary. Theoretically, it was a risky maneuver; he could have just as easily hit Jason or another ally close by. Nonetheless, the sharp projectile drove home into the spine, instantly paralyzing the Molisian. Jason was grateful for the service and wasted no time finishing off the opponent.

General Ulfenkerki had taken down a couple of soldiers fast enough to swell his confidence. When things got hectic in his tower, he retreated across a plank bridge to the atlytl platform, where he operated his bow and studied. The army was better off if he didn't play hero, staying alive to direct, organize, and scheme. At the time, he was arguably the best plotter in the land.

Thraiker/Ghrere were meanwhile trying to figure out how they were going to get across to the atlytl platform. The bridge nearest them had been destroyed by a tandem of very heavy Molisians crashing through it. Yes, they could jump all the way down and re-climb the stairs back up to the platform, but that would squander precious seconds. In battles such as these, seconds meant everything.

Fortunately, Mick and Dave had time to resolve the problem, since they—and Yori—were defending their part of the rampart extremely well. It was no surprise really, as they *were* Knowing Circle recipients.

Dave was met by a brute of a man and his war axe— a fine-looking axe at that. It was no basic wood axe. A lot of time had been put into its construction. Dave spent a second thinking about to whom he could give the war axe after the battle. He was getting too far ahead of himself, though, and shook the thought to concentrate on the task at hand.

The axe crashed down on every spot near Dave, except on Dave himself. Seeing such tremendous power was overwhelming. Dave waited for the right moment to counter-attack. Once the Molisian swung his monstrous weapon too hard for his balance to handle, Dave made his move. Not hesitating in the slightest, he sliced off two of the fingers holding the axe. Without all ten fingers holding it firmly, the axe was no longer menacing. Dave blitzed at his opposer's body, something he wouldn't have been able to do hadn't the fingers been chopped off. A few jabs of the sword and the fight was over, the ornate axe falling to the ground with a clang.

Wisely, Dave refrained from thinking whom he wanted to tell first about the available axe, deciding instead to glance at his nearby friends to make sure they were alright. Yori was fine—sweating profusely, but fine. And Mick looked to be in top form, dancing on his toes with exactitude.

Dave picked the next Molisian with whom to collide.

Mick was currently pitted against a mediocre opponent, so he strived to conserve energy by winning the fight without any over-exertion. The battle for the Capital was nowhere near over, so any energy he could bank would be worth tenfold in the end.

Mick side-stepped an oncoming pounce from his next opponent with poise. Having gone in for the kill, the tip of Mick's sword found his enemy's artery. Blood spilled copiously. The Molisian's last breath was taken, as he for an unidentified reason jumped over the wall. Mick was legitimately surprised by the odd action.

Having first made sure his little group was out of harm's way, Mick hunted for a new target amongst the approaching swarm.

The cadre of atlytl handlers nearest Mick, Dave, and Yori had assisted in solving the dilemma of the missing bridge. An improvised one had been handed up by someone below. It was last thing Old Man Johnson contributed to the battle before retreating to the castle.

Things were now dangerous throughout every city street, especially for old men lacking agility.

Mick, Yori, and Dave made great effort to hold out as long as possible before withdrawing across the newly placed bridge to join the Icytryxans.

Stealing a few breaths, Mick watched his countrymen cross, and quickly said to Dave, "Notice something?"

"I do. We'll definitely discuss it later."

The next stage of the battle violently began, as the bridge was kicked down for obvious reasons. The time for the long-range purposed atlytl was over, since the whole of the Molisian army was now either over the wall or just about to be. Though, some Icytryxans continued using their atlytls, picking off adversaries at the apex of their ladder ascension. The atlytl platform was an excellent perch from which to do this.

Yori had a few throwing stars left, while Mick and Dave had a few arrows. First, they zeroed in on targets atop the rampart, then, they switched to the Molisians that'd reached the ground.

Ultimately, too many Molisians reached ground level, so Mick and Dave exchanged archery equipment for black needles and jumped down. Yori stayed on the atlytl platform and used Dave's bow. She would be safe there for the time being.

As Yori worked the bow, she was dumfounded that the Molisians were so occupied with getting into town that they were forgetting to cherry pick. They just blindly followed the person ahead of them, like sheep. She said to herself, "War is and always will be a thinking man's game."

Mick was confronted by an opponent who truly felt invulnerable to pain. The Molisian had felt this way his whole life and went into battle thinking it was going to be more of an advantage than it really was. A person couldn't simply ignore a blade sent through the neck. The pain you could ignore, sure, but this ignorance was irrelevant to who lived to fight again.

Meanwhile, Dave's adversary wasn't as naïve, and one of only a few dozen female Molisian soldiers at the battle. She put up a good fight, firmly believing she could win. Her self-assurance was attributed to many years of practice alongside her brother. The same brother had convinced her to go to war alongside him, promising her glory. It was a promise he could not keep, for that glory was never realized, as her life ended by the loss of her leg. Tragically, the wound bled out, as her brother died beside her.

Combat was also intense at General Ulfenkerki's position of town. Striving for vigilance, the General had previously climbed down from the atlytl platform to take part in ground fighting. Despite marvelous sword work by himself and those around him, Ulfenkerki recognized the bevy of foes would soon be too much to handle—at least at the current location.

Having just defeated an opponent through great effort, the General shouted, "That's all we can do from here. Fall back to the castle. The defensive installations there will aid us."

Conferrer of organization, Ulfenkerki knew if the soldiers retreated to the castle, the Molisians would have free reign to go about the city. However, they would have to contend with the archer towers guarding the causeway to the castle. Archers from this high ground reaped a target zone encompassing half the city. The Molisians could loot the area the tower archers couldn't reach—a loss Ulfenkerki was prepared to endure, given that the King would have a better chance for survival. Ulfenkerki wasn't going to command the Icytryxans to do the same—for their decisions in battle were their own—but he assumed they would. And they did.

Luckily, most of the non-military personnel were already taking refuge in the castle. Yes, there were some civilians who'd foolishly remained in their homes—as Garobansurov, like everywhere else, saw no shortage of hardheaded folks. They would be left stranded, as battle plans could not be designed to accommodate irrationality at the expense of rationality.

The good news for Garobansurov/Icytryxis was they now had roughly the same number of combatants as Molisia: 1,500. The atlytl wielders in collaboration with the wall defenders had diminished the Molisian military significantly. Of great importance, they'd also managed to annihilate every Molisian catapult with their own catapults. Ulfenkerki wouldn't have ordered a retreat to the castle if the Molisians still possessed catapults with which to bring it down.

Gamald hadn't played his best card yet, though. He waited patiently to unleash it.

Messengers were dispatched in every direction by Ulfenkerki, telling the rest of the soldiers scattered about the wall to recoil to the castle. Mick, Dave, and Yori received the news, and pondered their next move.

Mick suggested, "Yori, I think you should hurry up and run with the mob to the castle. Dave and I will probably hold back to cover the retreat."

She replied, "Will do. You guys don't do anything fancy now. Promise me you'll do what you have to do, then take great effort to make haste to the castle."

"We promise," said Dave, looking at her Yori with honest eyes.

Yori joined the rest of the Garobansurov soldiers in the sprint to the castle, while Dave and Mick hung back.

Mick yelled up to the last few Icytryxans on the platform, "Collect all remaining projectiles before you head to the castle, you may yet need them."

Covering the retreat of the last batch of Icytryxans, Thraiker and Ghrere smoothly defeated all of the enemies present.

The pair jogged behind their compatriots, and with eyes in the back of their heads, they demonstrated hyper-alertness. Any Molisian soldier trying to attack the rear would have to face Dave and Mick first.

Many arrows were shot into the retreating mass. Dave blocked one of these arrows with his shield, a quick move that would impress a good number.

Once they reached the castle, Mick and Dave learned two-fifths of the King's army had been killed. None of the deceased happened to be Mick and Dave's close friends. Although, the duo had known many of them on a personal level. Sadness befell them.

GAMALD CORRALLED his warriors, pleased to be at the interior of the Capital. Only one thing remained: defeat the King. He gathered together his officers to discuss the next step.

Within the walls of a clothing store, Gamald remarked, "First things first, go ahead and inform the soldiers they can loot anything they want. Just don't burn the buildings. We intend to keep the place intact to utilize for our own base of operations. Just stay out of range of those archer towers. Ulfenkerki withdrew his army to the castle to take advantage of the archer towers guarding it. Of course, it will be a problem to charge across the causeway to get to the King—not an easy thing to do. It's a good thing we won't have to do it."

The officers looked at each other, dumbfounded.

"Later, I'll tell you all how I intend to accomplish this," stated Gamald. "Changing the subject, I'm sure they've already disengaged them all, but make sure you check on the status of their catapults. I'm almost certain they designed each one to contain a removable mechanism capable of rendering the machine inoperable—like a key. They'd be really stupid if they hadn't."

One of the officers pondered and spoke. "Couldn't we just duplicate the mechanisms required to reactivate the catapults at one of the forges in town?"

"They would've made those inoperable as well."

"How do you make a forge inoperable?"

Gamald responded, "By making sure they were all built in a heavily guarded locale. I'd be surprised if the forges weren't right next the archer towers. Besides, even if we did have a working catapult, their mini-catapults mounted on the castle would have no difficulty destroying ours."

"I understand, sir."

The room became quiet in purposefulness thought.

HAVING CHECKED on all their friends, Dave and Mick took a nap on random couches, though sleeping all the way through the night wasn't going to be an option. They figured the Molisians would use the cover of darkness to make their move. It'd be much harder for the tower archers to aim in the dark, creating a better path for the Molisians to assault the castle.

Satisfied their naps were sufficient, Dave and Mick filled their stomachs with the jerky that'd been in their pockets. They had too much adrenalin flowing for sizable meals, even though meals would be prepared for all by the kitchen staff.

Mick stepped out of the castle to assess the situation. He noticed there were others doing the same. Mick walked to the end of the causeway (confident the tower archers recognized him and wouldn't shoot) and glanced around. He couldn't see the Molisian army, but he could hear them at the other end of town. It was an ominous sound, knowing at any moment they could strike.

Mick looked down at his feet and noticed the greasy causeway. He couldn't help but think how it was his and Dave's idea last time to grease the causeway, and how well it worked.

In the meantime, with the castle being pretty crowded, Dave squeezed in by Thyxer and Syryx.

Syryx stated to her companions, "The civilians are all waiting it out in the catacombs. It will be no doubt safer down there, if and when the fight reaches the castle."

"True," agreed Dave. "If the Molisians get inside the doors, there will certainly be havoc."

With a cheerful countenance, Thyxer said, "I'm pleased how the battle is going. As I was launching projectiles earlier, I told myself that the alliance feels right in every way. It really was a powerful feeling. I was in euphoria, capturing the sensation of how much safer we Icytryxans are in protecting ourselves in tandem with Garobansurov. I couldn't help but picture all of those back home safe and sound. I have no doubt, the Molisians—if not them, certainly someone else just as aggressive—wouldn't just stop with your capital. They would extend their tentacles out as far as they could reach and seize everything within grasp, including Swyrove."

"That's a beautiful sentiment, my friend," said Dave. "I had a similar feeling during the battle as well. Being on the rampart, and seeing the countless projectiles sail overhead, I felt so small. I was in awe at being on the same team with such an honorable and potent civilization."

Mick joined the group, and the four talked more on the alliance and of the battle: past, present, and future.

Influenced by realizing how much daylight was left, Mick and Dave snapped out of pleasant conversation modes and into alert modes. They slipped back into all their combat adornments. As in most prior battles, they opted for light armor. There were, however, many soldiers donning heavy armor, especially the King's Guard. Finalizing the act of becoming battle-ready, Dave and Mick strapped the *black needles* and their scabbards onto their wastes.

As many of the soldiers ate the meal prepared by the kitchen staff, aided by volunteer servers, Hawk and

Leopard peered out one of the castle windows. From the heights of the castle, they could see the congregation of Molisian soldiers off in the distance. Large groups encircled large campfires.

Since sound traveled well in thick evening air, Mick and Dave could hear the distant conversations—not the words themselves, but the underlying theme of pure aggression and determination. Mick and Dave's hairs stood on end.

Jason saw Mick and Dave by the window and stole a few moments from the responsibility of his military position to say a few words: "Do you think they'll attack tonight?"

Mick responded, "I would say the odds are in favor of it. They don't stand to gain much by just hanging out. It's not like they can put us under siege or anything."

"That's true," agreed Dave. "I'm sure they're well aware that the castle's food storage is overflowing. Otherwise, they know we wouldn't have retreated here."

"I believe you're right," said Jason. "Ulfenkerki thinks it'll happen tonight too. The soldiers are pretty nervous. Those who aren't overly nervous are eating right now. As for myself, I guess I'm not relaxed enough to eat. I've never been the exceedingly calm type."

"I hear that," noted Mick.

"Well, back to duty," shrugged Jason. "Yori was looking for you guys earlier. If I see her, I'll inform her of your location."

"Okay. I'll go look for her now too," said Dave, standing up.

As Jason went back to his rounds, Dave began searching for Yori. He found her on the third floor. The pair cemented battle plans, Yori resolving to continue to fight alongside Mick and Dave. Being the King's most trusted adviser, she definitely wasn't obligated to be a combatant. But she had grit, courage, and venom in the form of throwing stars. Admittedly, she had a little more courage knowing her back would be covered by Mick and Dave.

Dave rendezvoused with Mick back at the window, and said, "Well, that's been solidified: The beautiful throwing star tempest, Yori, will fight with us again."

"Good," stated Mick. "Also, I've been seeing increased action from the congregated Molisians."

"I wouldn't be surprised if Gamald had some other plan than simply raiding the castle head-on. Assaulting the castle via the causeway would practically be a suicide mission. He's not that stupid from what I've gathered."

"I know we've plenty of sentries watching every facet of the castle, in case the Molisians opt for the hook and rope method. So, that would be just as dumb of them."

"We would have the advantage in a catapult exchange," put forth Dave, "since our castle-mounted catapults reap the high ground. So, I don't think Gamald will put any effort into bringing down the castle walls."

"I'm sure Gamald has a version of castle onslaught in mind in which he's confident."

"And I'm sure he'll implement it soon. The version of castle onslaught he'll deploy will remain a mystery for now."

"Cards while we wait?"

"Cards indeed."

Dave and Mick played, each knowing the other had the ability to count cards. It made for some rather interesting games.

As cards were counted, the rest of the Garobansurovian personnel went about their comings and goings, each trying to lock down their own adaptation of fear ignorance.

Surrounded by guards, Rowlangiv was the most worrisome. He truly felt a strong affection for his subjects, having every intention of dying with a sword in his hand, if it came down to it. He'd fight on the front lines if his citizens allowed him to. Alas, it was something for which the people would never bestow their blessings. They'd give it more of a thought if their king actually were good with a sword.

Dave had just won the third poker hand in a row when he was startled by a child's scream. Galvanized, he and Mick jumped up from their table and quickly glanced out the window. However, they saw nothing out of the ordinary. They heard another scream and learned the sounds were coming from within the castle.

A flight down, they found a child standing above what appeared to be her mother out cold and spread out across the floor. There were others present, conversing speculatively.

A nearby soldier said frantically to Mick and Dave, "Everyone is thinking it's poison. I don't know what else it could be. She isn't showing any signs of physical trauma."

"Yes, possibly poison," responded Dave. "But from where? Poison isn't exactly common around here."

The soldier said, "You're right. I can't recall hearing about a case of poisoning in a long time."

"The law of parsimony would suggest the culprit is our Molisian adversary," remarked Mick.

"Precisely. The simplest explanation is usually the right one," added Dave.

Mick emitted, "How they would've gotten inside the castle, though, I have no idea."

Dave blurted, "We must hurry to the King to make sure he doesn't eat anything. The latest meal could have been poisoned. I'll run directly to the King now, while, Mick, you make haste to the kitchen to warn them there."

"Will do. This could be a very serious incident indeed, all planned by Gamald."

The lady's lifeless body was carried to the medics, as Dave dashed to where he'd last heard Rowlangiv was situated. Luckily, the King was still there.

Approaching his King, Dave projected, "Sire, there was what seems to be a poisoning just now. Don't eat anything."

"I never eat anything during wartime that hasn't first passed through my food testers. Actually, I've unintentionally evaded food all day, due to my apprehension."

"Okay, good." Dave sighed in relief.

The King rose from his chair. "Come with me, Mr. Ghrere; we'll investigate the occurrence."

The pair went straight to the dining area and was stricken with dread. Complete chaos was strewn everywhere. Bodies lying motionless, the moans of the dying, and the shrieks of the hysterical were just some of the frightful things into which the King and Dave walked. Mick was present, already helping to carry people off to the physicians.

Incapacitated with grief, the King begged, "How could this have happened? We've painstakingly kept track of every single person who'd come into the castle in the last month or so. There hasn't been so much as a fly that's gotten in without my permission."

"We must act," said Dave. "I will locate General Ulfenkerki immediately. I have no doubt the Molisians will use this as a springboard to strike."

"Right," noted Rowlangiv, completely distraught over the realization his people were dying. "I'll see to it that nobody eats anything else. I'll also spearhead a committee in charge of getting to the bottom of this all."

Dave began sprinting through the castle looking for the Black Bear, performing a mental count of the dead along the way. The number in his head was increasing quickly.

He found Ulfenkerki, realized the General already knew about the situation, and said, "I just came from the King—He knows. I told him I'd search you out in case you were unaware."

"I'm assuming the saboteur or saboteurs acted on Gamald's command, having infiltrated the castle— possibly the kitchen staff—a while ago. We've been too cautious lately for it to have happened recently, having scrutinized everyone as of late. We must hold war council as soon as possible. Dave, you and Mick please come to the usual meeting room in twenty minutes. I'll get word to everyone else. Guided by some bizarre coincidence, most of my officers are already nearby."

"Will do."

Dave located Mick, who was still assisting with bodies, and told him about the emergency conference.

The pair spent a moment comforting the family of one of the deceased, and hurried to the meeting room in the barracks. Rowlangiv, Jason, Ulfenkerki, a handful of Icytryxans, and most of Ulfenkerki's officers were present.

Ulfenkerki faced the assemblage and began, "Unfortunately, we don't yet know who precisely had all succumbed to the poison and how many. We'll know shortly. I'm assuming this plan to poison was conceived a long time ago. The assassin has probably been within our midst for a while. Gamald correctly assumed there'd be a point during the battle when we'd retreat to the castle, where it'd be much easier to poison a multitude."

"Food was handed out without reserve," Ulfenkerki continued. "The situation is dire. We have sustained a massive hit to our armies, and we are now outnumbered. Which brings us now to the discussion of what we should do next. I've thought it over, and my proposal would be to take advantage of the element of surprise and implement an unorthodox battle strategy."

Those in the room pondered what strategy to which the General could be referring. They all came up empty.

The audience perked up their ears, as the Black Bear resumed, "I suggest the Icytryxans fire their projectiles at the horde. Fatalities won't be numerous at the onset, since they'll promptly run and hide. But what they won't expect is that the Icytryxans who'd fired weren't the real

Icytryxans. Our infantry and archers will have been the ones who'd fired the atlytls. The real Icytryxans with their capacity to launch projectiles much further will have tactically gotten into position before any launching commences. A few seconds after the decoy projectiles are launched, the Icytryxans will fire not at where the horde *is*, but at where the horde *will* be as they try to take cover. The Molisians will be surprised by the new angles of incoming fire and will get hit just before reaching their sanctuary. It's all a matter of perfect timing. If we can get it just right, a huge portion of their army will fall. Hopefully, it'll be a larger portion than what the poisoning did to us tonight."

After hearing the Black Bear's plan, the overall consensus in the room was positive.

One of the Icytryxans said, "We practice timing maneuvers like this often—shooting not where an enemy *is*, but where they *will* be. I'm confident we can pull it off."

Jason commented, "Then, after all the survivors have reached shelter, is the plan to attack building-to-building, or will we wait them out?"

Ulfenkerki replied, "We won't attack immediately. It'll still be dark when we deploy my atlytl plan, and us going from building-to-building in the dark would benefit them more than us. They'd be able to lurk in the dark and hear us coming. Yet, we won't have the advantage of getting to wait them out, because the poisoner is still at large and can strike again at any time. We will have to hunt down the soldiers relatively soon after the projectile launch." The General paused. "It is disappointing that we can no longer reap benefit from our advantageous causeway. Woe, unavoidable is the waywardness of war."

The General paused again, taking a few seconds for thought before recommencing. "I'd like to deploy the atlytls immediately, before the Molisians learn of their success with the poison. But first, we must inconspicuously replace the archers in the towers with dummy personnel. I'd say *Operation Retaliation* will commence in an hour, barring the Icytryxis as a whole aren't okay with the plan."

Everyone left the meeting. The Icytryxans directly reported the plan to the rest of their community. It was a go.

The soldiers within the castle instantly took to action fulfilling the steps in Ulfenkerki's scheme. Everyone who could fire an atlytl with enough force to reach the target zone was instructed to report. Old Man Johnson and Yori couldn't launch as far as the plan specified, so they didn't present themselves. Dave and Mick could, so they did.

Waiting for command on the castle's main level, Mick and Dave were confronted by a noticeably distressed Syryx. "I don't think you know this yet, but tragically, Thyxer was one of the poison victims."

"No, we didn't! How is he doing?"

"He didn't survive. He ate the food, while Yusyta and I didn't."

Both Mick and Dave's faces turned white as snow. Dave gave Syryx a massive hug, and said, "I am so sorry."

Syryx emitted, "His last words to me were, *I die with honor, knowing in my heart our people are protected.*"

Mick gave Syryx the next hug. "That they will be. These invaders will meet their demise, if it's the last thing we do."

Syryx let a single tear roll down her cheek, and replied, "It shall be done. We will rain projectiles upon them with the force of a thousand thunderstorms. I want to tell you how much Thyxer cared for you two, along with Jason and Yori. He thought of you all as family. He personally told me that having you four at our home last year was one of the most enjoyable times of his life."

"It was for us too."

"I have to go now, but we'll talk more after the battle."

Syryx left the company of Mick and Dave and joined her kinfolk in getting into position. One by one, the Icytryxans slipped out of the castle in the dark and found a place of concealment. It was a good thing it was a starless night with only a quarter moon, otherwise they may have been spotted.

Just after the last tower archer was replaced, all the participating Garobansurovians grabbed an atlytl and waited for Ulfenkerki's signal to begin Operation Retaliation. Ulfenkerki grabbed an atlytl and lead the five hundred members of the diversion team down the causeway in a silent jog. They got just close enough that their ammunition when launched could reach the gathered Molisians.

The one thing that was going to be tricky for the Icytryxans was knowing in the dark when the diversion team would commence their launch, so in turn they could begin theirs. This would be potentially remedied by positioning a signaler in a particular castle window, instructed to hold up a candle as soon as the diversion team began their offensive. Not all the Icytryxans were equidistant from the target, so each one had to keep track of their own math.

Waiting for the signal seemed like an eternity for Syryx. She couldn't help but be impatient, yearning so much to avenge the loss of her older brother. Her eyes were fixed on the key window with the utmost of focus. The gaze was so limitlessly intense she could feel her heart beating in her chest. There were even a few times when she forgot to breathe. Resolutely, she told herself to relax, otherwise she'd pass out and miss her chance.

Finally, the infinite pause in time ceased, and she saw the signal-light pop up in the window. *One, two, three,* she counted, as was her math. With a burst of pure energy, Syryx emerged from her hiding spot, and shot projectiles as fast as she could at where the mob of Molisians would soon be. It didn't matter if she forgot to breathe at this point, since pure adrenalin would keep her oxygen-deprived brain from shutting off. Adrenalin was no doubt powerful stuff.

Shimmering like meteorites in reflective light, so many projectiles took to the night sky that it was said they could be seen from the castle.

The offensive had lasted five minutes. Any longer and it would've wasted projectiles, commodities that weren't exactly inexhaustible.

They'd have to wait an hour for the sun to come up to gauge the effectiveness of the plan. To accomplish this, they'd stand high on the castle and count body-shaped silhouettes lying on the ground in the distance.

As expected, the sun came up. The body count was made and reported to Ulfenkerki, who then called for a war meeting, which was also expected.

Mick and Dave joined the usual crowd.

The Black Bear spoke: "I just received the body count, and it's very good news indeed. We wiped out one third of them—500. Now, we outnumber them, roughly 1,200 to 1,000. I wish we could just keep launching projectiles at them, but we'd run out eventually. Also, there's the poisoner we have to worry about. We do have kilns within our proximity to forge more projectiles, but the looming threat of a repeat poisoning weighs too heavily."

Ulfenkerki scratched his chin. "With the King's permission—for there'll most likely be collateral damage—I say we smoke them out. We'll construct smoke torches and lob them into buildings suspected to harbor Molisians. Some of the torches will inadvertently burn buildings down. But far fewer buildings will turn to ash this way than if we were to burn them out or if we were defeated."

Ulfenkerki looked to King Rowlangiv.

The King acknowledged, "We can sustain a few burnt buildings. Go ahead and smoke them out—the sooner the better. I know we have all completely stopped eating, something that can't go on for long."

Ulfenkerki resumed, "The torches won't take long to craft, as they're pretty simple devices. We'll start the assault in the matter of a couple hours. All soldiers will be deployed in the assault, except for a few dozen to be perched on buildings serving as a ranged support group.

Furthermore, there will be sub-strategy requiring flexibility, for which I'll provide instruction on the field."

The plan was set. Mick and Dave, yet again, were to go to battle with no promise for reward. The pair surely weren't the type who didn't care one way or the other about staying alive—*survival* was top priority; truth was second. There were many answers to life's greatest questions that could only be revealed from within the eye of the hurricane. Seeking knowledge, Mick and Dave bravely faced the eye with steadfast passion.

The fuel for smoke torches was made from a blend of organic materials. The exact recipe for the concoction was stumbled upon hundreds of years previous by accident. The story goes that there was once a great forest fire requiring prompt extinguishing. After several days of fighting it, most was subdued—all but one pesky section. They couldn't get at it with water, since the smoke billowed too profusely. The intoxicating fumes were unbearable. Eventually, officials decided to let it burn itself out. They would just focus on containing it.

When all the dust had settled, out of curiosity the firefighters inspected the nuisance zone to learn what'd caused it to smoke so much. What they discovered was astonishing. Apparently, they found residue from a species of shrubbery that up to that day had never been catalogued in the plant archives. They collected some of the shrubs' unburnt seeds lying underground and planted them out of spite. Advantageous for Garobansurov's current situation, the shrub species was aesthetically pleasing, so it became widespread, while awareness of the shrub species' smoke capabilities endured.

The dozens on the torch construction team hastily ran through the safe zones of town, gathering specimens of the fabled shrub. Most parts of the shrub were utilized and combined with a few other materials for the smoke torches. They made hundreds.

Yori had eaten a small portion of the poisoned food—which, out of the process of elimination, was later confirmed to be the pies. She'd be too sick to again fight alongside Mick and Dave. However fortunate, she wasn't ailing enough to feel her life was in danger. She would remain in the castle with Old Man Johnson, Will, and the rest of the villagers who weren't going to fight.

CHAPTER 7

TWELVE HUNDRED Garobansurovian and Icytryxan soldiers burst out the castle door for battle. Ulfenkerki led them down the causeway and to the danger zone.

Immediately, arrows came hurtling at them from many directions. The Garobansurov/Icytryxis alliance returned fire, essentially creating a stalemate. It was now party time.

Smoke torches were lit and thrown into the first few buildings. The Molisians tried to escape by slipping into adjacent buildings. Some made it, some were stopped in their tracks by the infantry. Ulfenkerki quickly adapted to the pattern and ordered the army to split up. A quarter stayed where they were, while the other three quarters sprinted through arrowshot to the other three corners of the battlefield. This way, as was Ulfenkerki's plan, the

Molisians would have to retreat inward, eventually meeting in the middle and being surrounded. The Molisians were too afraid to escape to open ground, as there they'd again be fired upon by the atlytl juggernaut.

Assuring to not make the same blunder as at the Battle of Sarwa, the General sent contingents to all the city's exits to ensure Gamald wouldn't escape all over again. Gamald was the glue keeping Eastern Molisia's forces unified. He needed to be captured.

The historical success of Mick and Dave fighting side-by-side spoke for itself. The pair knew exactly how to complement each other and what the other was thinking militarily. Without giving it a second thought, the two rushed to action with shields and alertness fully drawn.

Holding their shields overhead protecting vital areas from arrows, Leopard and Hawk ran with their platoon to their designated quadrant. Torches were lit and tossed into target buildings. As smoke began to form, Thraiker and Ghrere readied the black needles—sharp, old friends. They gave the handles a squeeze for good luck.

As anticipated, young Molisians came running out of the smoke—some were coughing. Mick's first course of action was to help an Icytryxan defeat an exposed enemy. Since there weren't many adversaries at the onset of this stage of the battle, Dave's sword remained unblemished. He spent a few moments studying.

ANXIOUSLY CLINGING to hope, a bulk of the Molisian army sat in the town's largest church with Gamald and Leedle. (Mick and Dave had toured the same church the year previous.) Gamald perceived his side was about to lose. His mind desperately clawed for a strategy to turn the tide. No ideas were coming, so he toggled into survival mode.

The enemy was closing in around General Gamald. Virtually anyone else would've lost the ability to think effectively and submitted to the pressure. Gamald, however, contemplated more efficiently when in danger. He knew Ulfenkerki was too smart to fall for the same mistake he'd made at Sarwa, as this time there'd be soldiers guarding the exits. After ten minutes of intense focus and kicking over a religious statue for the heck of it, he found his idea.

DAVE WAS FINALLY able to get his sword dirty again as a horde of soldiers rushed directly at his crew.

Dave put a challenger to rest with an impressive fake and follow through, while Mick eliminated a foe with an equal bout of impressiveness. They'd be the last soldierly accomplishments the pair would achieve that day, as the battle was nearing its end.

The four fronts of the Garobansurov/Icytryxan army closed in on each other. Victory was at hand. Then, as unexpected as a storm cloud on a clear day, Gamald and Leedle emerged from the church, surrendering. They were unarmed and had their hands in the air. The rest of the Molisian army followed suit.

All in all, 300 Molisians stood awkwardly with their hands held high.

Ulfenkerki had no intention of breaking protocol: The capitulation would be honored. He personally approached Gamald and put him in restraints. The same was done with the rest. Some may've considered taking someone as cunning as Gamald prisoner to be a foolish move, but to Ulfenkerki, Garobansurovian ethical code surpassed all.

As procedure dictated, the Molisians were brought to the holding cells near the barracks. In the olden days, they would've been led to the dungeons below the castle. However, these cells had long since decayed. The barrack cells would be a little cramped seeing 300 new arrivals. To prevent inhumane conditions, the cells would have to be expanded. King Rowlangiv would never subject a fellow man to cruelty. He had a heart. But he'd no doubt keep them locked up until the war was over.

When news of the surrender reached the civilians in the castle, cheers wisped through the lofty halls. The citizens were ecstatic to be alive, though they were well aware the war wasn't over.

A few of the Capital's most extravagant buildings had been ignited by the smoke torches and burnt to the ground. No one cared too much, even the buildings' owners, as they knew their properties would get rebuilt.

All the food of the castle was thrown out, and everyone suspected of the poisoning was detained for intense questioning. It wasn't easy to sort out the possible suspects, but they did the best they could.

King Rowlangiv received the news of victory and of the surrender. He knew immediately what he wanted to do next—question Gamald himself.

In another part of the castle, Yori, Old Man Johnson, and Will embraced joyfully, having themselves just learned of the battle's triumphant outcome. In fact, there weren't many in the castle who hadn't embraced joyfully at hearing the outcome.

IT'S NOT AN EASY thing to do, trekking a great distance after witnessing firsthand the deaths of your traveling companions. Beholding death by the sword was never a calm experience. Though, Harry Shultz had great reasons to persevere. He had a wife and son back home, both whom he loved dearly.

Little did he know his wife was dead and his son was at the Capital holding on with all his might to the hope his father was alive and would soon return.

An impenetrable desert stood between himself and the Capital, around which he'd have to travel. He clung to vital information, which needed to be brought to the King without delay. His information regarded the war on the western front. Up to this point, it was data that'd been clouded in mystery to all those at the Capital. It was unquestionably an important post Harry held.

As he traveled towards the Capital, he couldn't help but recall the memories of all the joyous times he'd spent with his family. One in particular went as such:

Two years prior his mission in the west, Harry wanted to take his son to a scenic area of which he knew. It'd be a multiple days' journey, so they intended to camp a few nights. As it would be Will's first camping trip, they both were thrilled and couldn't wait to spend so much time together.

They said goodbye to a worrisome mother and started the exhilarating trip.

As they walked, Harry explained to Will how beautiful the place they were going was. Harry had visited the locale in his youth and was excited to share the same experience with his son.

When they reached the destination, their hearts sank. The scenic wonder they trekked so far to see was no longer there. Apparently, within the last couple of decades, all the old, majestic trees had been logged off. Plus, the monolithic stone formation giving the impression of magically guarding the trees had toppled to the ground and shattered.

They stood in the area in utter disappointment. Discontent lingered for an eternity. Harry couldn't help but feel it was all his fault. He was heartbroken. So badly, he wanted his son to have the same amazing experience he had as a child.

Will was just about to cry, when his father said, "It'll be alright son. I have an idea of something else fun we can do instead."

Will perked up a tad. "What's that, Dad?"

"Come with me, I'll show you."

Hand-in-hand, the pair ventured the dirt trail dissecting the sea of stumps. The trail was a frequently traveled connection between two rather active villages.

Harry plopped himself onto one of the massive stumps adjacent the trail. Will followed.

"Here's what we're going to do, son: Every time someone goes past, you and I will question them about who it was exactly that callously chopped down all these trees. There are plenty of trees in Garobansurov, there's no need to heartlessly harvest the most beautiful ones."

Will's eyes lit up. "That is a great idea, Dad!"

The duo sat on the stumps and played wondrous games, until the first travelers appeared. They questioned them with great fervor but got no answers.

"That was fun, Dad. I can't wait until the next group comes."

Father and son sat in that very same spot, performing the very same routine for the entirety of the day. Some of the people had been friendly about the questioning, just glad at having someone with whom to talk. Others were not so friendly, clearly not wanting to be bothered. But each inquisition had been spent in the same amount of zeal as the last. The routine had lasted right up until the final minute of daylight.

Radiating bliss, they made camp and discussed the day's events.

Will, barely without a smile all day, said, "I'm so excited that we have one more day and night here."

"Me too, son."

The pair woke and spent the whole day doing the very same thing as the last. And even though they never figured out who had harvested the trees, they were happy as ever, having spent quality time together. They did, however, learn something interesting. They learned that when the gigantic stone formation struck the ground it was heard in the nearest village, ten miles away.

Will and Harry camped out one more time and left for home in the morning. In many ways, they were glad that what they got out of the voyage wasn't what they expected.

When he reached the end of his memory, Harry realized he exuded a silly smile. He couldn't wait to make more memories with his family. He just had to make it back to the Capital safely with his vital intel.

Harry couldn't help but feel empathy for the families of the other two with whom he started the journey. Resolutely, he told himself he'd be the one to explain the deaths to them.

Visualizing a map of Garobansurov, he estimated it would take a couple more weeks of arduous journeying to reach the Capital. Subsequent to that and relaying his information, he'd begin the much easier walk home.

Dangerous trails still lay ahead, so far from civilization. He remained vigilant.

BY A THOROUGH search of every home of the kitchen staff, the poisoner's identity was discovered. Everything added up. This individual had begun kitchen duty a month before the battle. Rowlangiv was impressed how the culprit never indicated he was following Gamald's orders—loyal to the end.

The King passed a sentence of life imprisonment for sadistic war practice.

The reconstruction of town began. All the traps on the battlefield were collected, and all the dead were properly buried.

Mick, Dave, and Yori spent the whole day after the battle with Syryx and Yusyta, consoling them. They reflected upon great memories of Thyxer. Jason came and went, as he had many respects to pay, spending time comforting the families of many other fallen soldiers.

King Rowlangiv began to painstakingly visit with all the families of the fallen, including those of the Icytryxis. It would take him all week to visit every single one.

Thyxer's funeral was three days after the battle and was rather lovely—full of reminiscence. At the funeral, a dozen spoke beautiful words about him, including Mick, Dave, Yori, and Jason. Sorrowfully, the four shared a few memories of their time across the sea.

All had great faith Thyxer was securely stationed in the haven the Icytryxis deity (Infinitum) provided for the deceased.

It'd taken a while, due to post-battle disorder, but Mick and Dave were finally able to discuss what they'd learned at the battle. They talked about peculiarities involving Garobansurov and Icytryxis fighting together.

In their room at the Doze Inn, Mick said to Dave, "Whenever our two armies came together, they stuck with their own race for the most part. There was never an even combination in the amalgamation."

"Was that rhyme on purpose?"

Mick chuckled. "I can't say that it was."

"You're right, though. I noticed the same thing—in both the wall blitz and the building to building phase. Though, of course, even with the union of different stereotypes within our own culture, you're going to see in traumatic situations the same sort of banding together."

"Affirmative. Regardless, I think it's safe to say the diversification we gained by aligning with the Icytryxans greatly enhanced our war capability. Having multiple core battle stratagems is very advantageous. It's imperative we keep both tools sharp."

"I agree wholeheartedly. Like in our speech last year, the advantages of fighting *side-by-side* are boundless. We're one step closer in achieving grand multifariousness."

"We must avoid allowing either part of the dichotomy becoming less than the other," said Mick.

"True. Not necessarily agreeing with each other's philosophies but understanding and respecting them will yield great results."

"One balanced unit."

Dave suggested, "Maybe we should share our views with the King."

"I agree. In light of the fact the army is inopportunely diminished, I'm sure he would appreciate any helpful input."

"We'll arrange a summit."

King Rowlangiv and one of his personally appointed generals (the other two, Dalarginta and Wiotweisten, were stationed on the western front) met near the castle's front gate. It was an important day.

"Well, General Ulfenkerki, do you think we'll get any more information out of him than the diplomats?"

"I have high hopes we'll learn a bit more about Molisian political infrastructure, but I doubt we'll gain anything that'll help us win the war."

"Possibly. Just knowing more about the enemy's political framework will be of use to us in the future."

Ulfenkerki emitted, "A part of me believes Gamald has something hidden up his sleeve yet—he always does."

"Too true."

General and King walked the passageway, a long corridor connecting the cells containing the captured

Molisians. They came to a small room barely large enough for a spit, stepped inside, and waited patiently.

A few moments passed, and Gamald was escorted into the little room by two prison guards. The door was shut and locked, while the two guards remained in the room.

After taking a seat in the available chair, Gamald looked Ulfenkerki in the eyes, and said, "We meet at last, General. Good to see you too, King Rowlangiv. Sarwa was quite the battle, wasn't it?"

"You could say that," replied the Black Bear. "The tides definitely turned many times."

"The tides had no idea what they wanted. Plus, to say the least, you certainly surprised me here," declared Gamald. "I don't know how you did it, but recruiting the Icytryxans to align with you, nothing short of a miracle. I've heard stories of how they embrace completely different beliefs than anyone else, and how they rarely go to war."

"All true. It wasn't easy. We'd sent diplomats to Swyrove last year to establish a relationship."

"Ah yeah, the fabled unreachable island. It's true it exists then. May I ask, who were your diplomats?"

"You may," replied Ulfenkerki. "There were four. One of the King's advisors, Yori Rothlin. And the other three you may've confronted on the battlefield: Jason Thorncat—my next in command, Mick Thraiker, and Dave Ghrere. The latter two are recipients of our highest award, the Knowing Circle."

Gamald curled his lip and exhaled. "Ah yes, Mick and Dave, the two who'd defeated my best soldiers, Grunt and Roar, at Sarwa. Did they participate in this battle? I didn't see them."

"Yes, they were here."

"Interesting. I'm surprised you didn't send your diplomatic negotiators—Nina, Paula, Frytytz—to come speak with me now."

Rowlangiv joined the conversation. "Even though I don't agree with your tyrannical ways, I feel you at least deserve the courtesy of being questioned by a Garobansurov person of significance—you being as important in the political world as you are."

"That is courteous of you. What would you like to know?" put forth Gamald, before preparing for what he thought was sure to be a well-thought-out interrogation.

Ulfenkerki opted for a relaxed stance. "I have no intention of beating around the bush. How can we end this war?"

Gamald replied, "So much for a well-thought-out interrogation." Gamald scratched his head. "I don't want this war to continue, same as you. I want to see my compatriots alive and well. The young and poor of Molisia are certainly fewer in number today than they were yesterday. Despite my yearnings, I wouldn't be able to convince anyone to end this war."

Ulfenkerki looked deep within himself. "For the sake of conversation, would you ever consider joining with us and waging war on the other head of Molisia—the head identified as the rich?" Ulfenkerki knew Rowlangiv well and that the King would assume this line of questioning to be purely theoretical. Unless at some point the King felt the option was practical.

"Interesting concept, General. However, even with your new alliance with the Icytryxans, the three of us wouldn't stand a chance against the wealthy Molisians and their Norvic allies."

"What I don't get is how does it benefit them to allow you to run around killing yourselves in war? Doesn't that mean less tax money for them? And if they're so rich and powerful, why don't they invade us themselves?"

"Both good questions. The only answer I really have for the latter is, *because we thought of it first*. And as for the former: they're not exactly condoning our actions. We're just doing it anyways."

"You're risking civil war with them then, aren't you?"

"Indeed, we are. I have no idea what the future holds. I turned my back on the wealthy and chose to help out the less fortunate with their endeavor here."

Rowlangiv asked, "Why are you so righteous with your fellow countrymen, but such a tyrant with our people? You've done nothing but murder, rape, and steal ever since you've stepped foot in Garobansurov."

"I haven't done so personally. I can't really prevent any of that from happening from my soldiers. You have to understand, my men have been the whipping post of Molisia all their lives, and now that they have a bit of freedom, they're addicted to doing what they want. I don't exactly control them. Yes, I'm their general, but it's not like you imagine. If I don't let them have their fun, they are just as likely to turn around and kill me. Without me, though, they all would've died a long time ago. I heard about your poisoning. I knew about it, but I wasn't the one who instigated or planned it."

Ulfenkerki stated, "So, if it were up to you, how would you like to proceed from here? Respond wisely, for it very well may happen."

Gamald thought for a few seconds, sub-vocalized a few things, and replied, "I think it would best if you kept us detained until the war is over. I know I couldn't convince you otherwise. I guess the only request I would have is for you to make our stay as pleasant as possible—maybe a little beer once in a while."

Ulfenkerki looked at Rowlangiv, received an unspoken signal, and said, "Granted."

Gamald was led back to his cell by the soldiers who'd brought him. Rowlangiv and Ulfenkerki remained behind to talk.

Rowlangiv looked out the door to double-check that Gamald was gone and out of earshot. "Do you believe him?"

"Maybe parts. I definitely know we can't revolve our war strategy around what he said about the political system of Molisia. It may be true, it may not be—who knows? We don't even know what's going on in the western side of our own country. I think it's about time we send a fleet with new messengers all the way around to the Riftolen harbor to ascertain what's going on. I think the foot messengers are a lost cause."

"We might as well. Sending a fleet is extremely risky and will take a long time to organize, but it's better than waiting on those who may never return. Though, I really do hope the foot messengers show up. I'd hate the thought of knowing we'd sent them to their deaths. Plus, I don't think I could bear not knowing about the west for another few months. In the meantime, I have another important plan to activate."

Rowlangiv told Ulfenkerki the plan, and the two of them discussed it for a time. Ulfenkerki liked the plan and had no objections. They both hoped the party to be involved would agree to it.

ANNA WAS GETTING better at being perceptive from her prison. She could now determine by ambient light if it was a day under the sun's dominion or one for the clouds. She knew which of the soldiers despised which, and which shared man-crushes—It was funny how some of them followed others around like lost puppies in the woods. However, she couldn't tell when the tavern was completely empty, since some of the soldiers had the tendency to lie around all day doing nothing and not making a sound while doing it.

Having worked in a bar for many years, you'd think I would've known the human capacity for alcohol toleration. I was dead wrong, these drunkards are on a whole new level. They're drinking so much they must've found every stash of booze within a ten-mile radius of here. If I ever get out of here, I don't think I'll be able to be around alcohol again.

Anna lost count of what day it was. At first, she knew how many days she'd been trapped, but after being in the chute for as long as she'd been, she no longer cared.

If Anna hadn't heard the soldiers talking about the other women from her village they'd raped and/or murdered, she would've attempted an escape by then. It'd be a failed escape, no doubt. She had a strong will to survive and a patience to match.

If only there was something small and reflective down here that I could set over the chute-hatch to use in peering out into the bar. I doubt they would notice something small. If I were extremely brave, I'd stick my head out and look around. But alas, I'm only moderately brave. I should just do some pushups. Maybe then I could get strong enough to defeat them with my bare hands when they're in one of their drunken stupors.

One, two, three, four, five pushups.

The Molisian soldiers above Anna had no idea their army had just lost at the capital, and that the assaulting force was all but wiped out. They carried on, nevertheless. With utmost resolve, they continued to defend the town that was conquered. The same was true for the other contingents left behind by Gamald at the other various northern Garobansurovian villages.

CHAPTER 8

T HE MEETING WITH the King that Mick and Dave had requested was scheduled for later that day. In the interim, they remained true to form and trained, trying to elicit an even further understanding of swordplay.

The time for the meeting came around, and Mick and Dave met Rowlangiv at the castle in one of its more formal rooms upstairs.

Rowlangiv shook Hawk and Leopard's hands, and said, "Good to see guys. Thanks again for helping at the battle."

"No thanks are necessary, sir," returned Dave.

"Yori told me a little about why you requested this meeting, and that you were studying battle tendencies of the alliance. I feel this is definitely something that needs to be studied. I'm to understand that you discovered something important during the battle?"

Mick answered, "We became aware, on multiple firsthand occasions, that our two cultures had fought well as a team. Though, there is room for improvement. For instance, the Garobansurovians fought largely beside the Garobansurovians, and the Icytryxans fought largely beside the Icytryxans. There wasn't a great mixing of the two. Why does it matter, you ask?"

Dave took over in the discourse, "It matters, because eventually, as more battles ensue, the separation will cause one army to become greater in number than the other. Therefore, we would risk losing this great advantage we've achieved in creating a double-edged sword. The exceptional melee capacity of the Garobansurovians is one edge of the sword, and the venomous projectile attack of the Icytryxans is the other edge. It's a two-pronged attack if you will. It all boils down to the law of averages, or more specifically, the law of large numbers."

"I get it," remarked Rowlangiv. "It's like if you flip a coin so many times: Sooner or later, both sides will land face up the same number of times. Ultimately, if the two cultures are evenly intermingled during the battles, it'd be unlikely for one side to outlast the other, given all other variables are equal."

Exactly," noted Mick. "As you know, sir, the same phenomenon occurs with practically every stereotype. Everyone wants to stick with their own group. And it's certainly exaggerated with our situation."

Dave retook the baton. "The silver lining is there were a reasonable number of soldiers who in unifying manner fought alongside the other culture. They didn't give it a second thought. The mindsets of these particular soldiers are commendable."

"Bolstering our army with further individuals exhibiting this trait would be a lofty and worthwhile goal," stated Rowlangiv, "one in which the two of you could apply to a mission of utmost importance. It's a mission I conceived earlier, and one I discussed with General Ulfenkerki this morning, just after our engagement with Gamald. Ulfenkerki concurred that the plan was achievable, especially achievable by the two of you. It's a fairly massive undertaking, I'm afraid, but it's one geared precisely for your skillsets."

"Is it an undertaking as massive as our last year's crossing of the sea to persuade a peaceful culture to go to war?" asked Mick, with a slight undertone of humor.

"Well, at least you won't have to cross the sea," responded Rowlangiv, grinning. "I know you two have already done more than enough for the Crown, and for that I am thankful. But you must understand that what I'm about to propose, I trust in the hands of no one else."

"You undeniably have me intrigued," emitted Mick. "You might as well spit it out, sir."

The King divulged, "This last battle, which I'm sure you know, has greatly diminished our forces. If we are to survive, we mustn't continue to operate with a skeleton crew. Normally, in times like these, I would send an army through the countryside to recruit, and to recapture the northern towns. But I don't have an army to send, we need what soldiers we have left to guard the Capital."

"There is good news," the King continued. "For many years, I've been squirreling away a large sum of gold for a rainy day. And it hasn't rained any harder than what it's doing now. Standing in front of me are those who I can trust with this gold to go out into the countryside to procure an army. Add personnel as you see fit, finding soldiers you can trust. You can kill two birds with one stone, recruiting as you recapture the northern towns. It's a lot of gold, so you'll be able to acquire a sizable force. There are many potential warriors in Garobansurov that can be bought for the right price. This will also give you the opportunity to implement your newfound strategy of recruiting soldiers that you think stand a better chance at fighting alongside the Icytryxans. And like I said before, Ulfenkerki is wholeheartedly on board with this."

Rowlangiv took a deep breath then resumed, "I know you guys are on this great inner quest to discover what exactly is the most significant facet of life. What better channel than this? You can learn a great deal by studying the creation and organization of an entire army from scratch. Not many people in the history of the world have ever been afforded this opportunity. I'm not promising you that you'll find your answers, but I am promising you that you'll have an experience unlike any other."

Smiling, Mick replied, "Well said, specifically that last paragraph. I can tell that you aimed at choosing just the right words."

The King chuckled. "I did indeed. I admittingly tailored them to your liking."

"You know us well," Dave added. "I imagine with the kind of gold of which you're speaking, our first acquisition would have to be for hiring someone to help carry it all."

"You'd think, but pound-for-pound, gold is far more valuable than gitis, so it doesn't weigh as much as you're suspecting. All told, it probably weighs fifty pounds. It'll be a heavy load at first, true, but what I remember from some of your stories is that you're used to heavy loads."

"That we are," said Mick. "The heavy pack certainly wouldn't be the thing that'd dissuade us from your mission."

"I'd want only the two of you to set forth from the Capital," inserted Rowlangiv, "as I'd want this undertaking to be solely in your hands. If I were to send any other volunteers with you, I'd feel they'd get in the way of your overall control over the situation."

"True. Is there a timetable involved with this mission, sir?" asked Dave.

"Not a finite one, but time is of the essence. The longer our army is diminished, the more vulnerable we are."

"In that case," stated Dave, "we won't take long to come to our decision."

"Excellent. And believe me, your decision is completely up to you. If you decline, you won't lose any respect from me."

"We appreciate that," replied Mick. "We'll come back tonight with our verdict."

"Sounds good. I'll inform the guards you'll be stopping by later."

The best place to brainstorm at the Capital, according to Mick and Dave, was anywhere not at the Capital. So, that's where the pair headed after taking leave of the King. They exited the city's main gate, as a walk through the countryside was conducive for clear thinking.

Desiring to remain secretive about the mission, Mick and Dave steered away from anyone but themselves.

A few hundred yards from the wall, Mick said to Dave, "So, what are your thoughts?"

"Well, he is right about the mission being favorable for the study of life. If we were to participate, there'd be many philosophical riddles at which we'd get a crack."

"I agree. Though, it would definitely delay considerably our return to Chalatore. Our homes may not be there when we return."

"That's a stretch, but a possibility, I guess," remarked Dave. "I can honestly say that the endeavor sounded thrilling to me when the King first presented it."

"It did to me as well. The only deterrent of which I can think is how dangerous it is. Once certain people become aware of how much gold we'll have in our possession, they'll stop at nothing to get their hands on it, including murder."

"Right. And that is why we would need the perfect strategy."

"Perfect strategy is truly our specialty," noted Mick. "It seems as if we've decided to partake in this massive undertaking."

"It does, and massive undertakings appear to be our secondary specialty."

Mick laughed. "I guess with us, perfect strategies and massive undertakings go hand in hand."

"That they do. We might as well go inform Rowlangiv of our decision, without delay. Plus, I'm positive he'll be fine with it, but we'll have to tell Old Man Johnson he'll have to sojourn a while yet."

"True, he'll understand the importance of this assignment, plus, he still has Will to watch after."

Clearly nervous, Rowlangiv paced back and forth in a long hallway of the castle. When Mick and Dave appeared at the far end of the hallway, the King couldn't help but hold his breath.

The King restarted breathing and the three met in the middle of the hall.

Seeing Rowlangiv was tense, Mick got right to the point. "We would be honored to comply with your request, our King."

The King smiled. "I couldn't be more pleased. You guys are the epitome of class, you know that?"

"Epitome is such a strong word," Mick replied lightheartedly. "When would you like us to begin this expedition?"

"The sooner the better."

Dave emitted, "Well then, I see no reason why we couldn't leave tomorrow."

"Splendid," stated Rowlangiv. "I'll give you a list of the villages more than likely still under Molisian occupation. We've many refugees here at the Capital from those villages."

"One thing I was wondering," Mick made known, "is that what if the Molisian occupiers could be monetarily persuaded to join our military. Would that be something of which you'd approve, sir?"

"Good question. My response is that I'll leave it entirely up to you. Every aspect of this enterprise will be managed by you."

"Very well," noted Dave. "We will be back with an army."

Rowlangiv specified, "Stop by in the morning to get the list of villages, the gold coins, and further gratitude from me."

"Will do, sir. Although, we wouldn't necessarily need any more of that last one."

"You'll probably get it anyways," the King chuckled.

Dave and Mick left the castle and went to the Doze Inn to inform Old Man Johnson of the quest. Just like they expected, he was completely supportive. Will was upset Mick and Dave would be leaving, but was comforted by the fact his buddy, Old Man Johnson, would remain behind to continue watching over him.

Will said to Mick and Dave, "While you guys are gone, can you look for my father?"

Dave replied, "We will look with both eyes, and as hard as we can. If we see him, we'll tell him exactly where you are, and I'm sure he'll come rushing to be with you."

Having been additionally comforted, Will replied, "Thank you so much. I hope you see him."

At dusk, Mick and Dave made a point to search out Yori, Jason, Syryx, and Yusyta to tell them they'd be gone for a while on a mission. Heaping piles of luck were dumped on Mick and Dave by their friends for their assignment.

In the morning, the pair began to fill their backpacks with provisions but quickly realized the gold would have to go on the bottom. So, they decided to get the gold first, then, pack.

Dave noted, "With the gold, our pack weights will be almost the same as normally, because we won't have to bring much food."

"Right. You and I will just eat with the soldiers that we recruit, as hunting among other things will become easier. We'll only need a little bit for the first few days when it's just us."

Mick and Dave hoisted their tried-and-true backpacks onto their backs and went to the castle for the list, gold, and gratitude.

Rowlangiv greeted Dave and Mick, led them to a certain closet of the imperial wing, toggled a certain secret lever, and pushed open a certain secret door.

Mick blurted, "And here I thought we'd seen every part of the castle, Dave."

"Apparently not. I wouldn't have guessed there to be a hidden door inside this closet. Are there any other hidden passageways, sir?"

"Nope, this is the only one. For many years, I've been telling the maids that I like to get dressed in this closet, as I have to somehow explain why I disappear into it so much. I tell them I like the lighting in it, it makes me look less fat."

Mick and Dave chuckled. "Clever. I suppose then, you'd actually have to come out wearing a different set of clothes."

"Yes, most of the time."

Having come to the end of a passageway, King Rowlangiv removed an odd painting from the wall, revealing a metal contraption inside a cavity. "You'll never guess who made this lockbox for me. Actually, I'm sure you can."

"Tim Warmane," uttered Dave, confidentially.

"That's right. He has skills other than constructing swords."

"He's good at cards and chess too," added Mick. "We played quite a bit, while we were here for his constructing of the black needles."

Rowlangiv pulled a peculiar key out of his pocket and opened the contraption. "I think I have even played cards with him a time or two in my youth. And lost a time or two."

The King ran his fingers through the contents of the lockbox. "Most of these coins were given to me throughout the years for my own personal use. But you know me, I rarely walk the path of extravagance. So, instead of spending them myself, I just brought them here, a handful at a time. They will now help us win this war."

"Is each coin the same?"

"Nope. There are two kinds. The smaller ones are worth 200 gitis, and the larger ones 500. Gold is pretty valuable these days, which is another reason why I decided that now would be a good time to cash them in."

Mick responded, "Good thinking. You might as well put half in my pack and the other half in Dave's."

Dave put forward, "I've the feeling many potential soldiers won't know the value of the coins, nor the means to find out. I know if I were to sell my services, I'd want proof that what I'm being paid is worth what I'm being told it's worth."

"You bring up a good point," noted the King, dumping coins into Dave's backpack, "but I've already thought that part through. You will be given something

I've never before given anyone during my reign: my official wax seal. With it, you can draw up official contracts of the Crown, therein stipulating that if the coins aren't worth what you say, they can be brought before the Crown to be sold at the contracted price. It'll all be certified."

"You weren't kidding, you really have thought it through. Excellent plan, sir. It should work."

Rowlangiv poured the last of the coins into Mick's pack. "Next, we'll have to stop by my bedroom for the seal, which is in another Warmane lockbox."

"I have never seen anything like these lockboxes," said Mick. "The metal work is extraordinary. I didn't even know a person could forge such intricate pieces."

"Neither did I, until it was brought to my attention by an advisor. I think the only other two Tim had ever constructed were sold to a couple of the wealthier families in town. I know he likes making weapons more."

"Good thing he mainly sticks with weapons," commented Dave, "otherwise, the black needles may never have existed."

Mick and Dave began helping Rowlangiv pick the coins off the floor that'd dribbled out during the transfer process. After every last one was picked up and in the backpacks, the three headed out of the secret passageway to get the seal.

While in the bedroom, along with the seal, Rowlangiv handed over a sufficient amount of wax, and said, "You don't have to write up the contracts too eloquently, just short and to the point would suffice."

"No problem, sir."

"Please remember, this operation is wholly in your hands. Perform this task your way. And I hope you find the answers you seek along the way."

"Thank you, sir. We'll let you know if we logicize any," remarked Mick.

"One more thing: Don't trade your lives for the gold. You guys have been worth more to me than the gold could ever be."

Mick and Dave bowed to their King and left the castle, fifty-two pounds heavier. Rowlangiv had been a little off on his estimation of the weight. Plus, the seal and wax weighed a smidge.

After finishing packing, saying final farewells to Old Man Johnson and Will at the Doze Inn, and receiving a briefing about the captured northern towns from Ulfenkerki, the duo left the Capital. Animatedly heading northward, they laid claim to the anticipation of new experiences.

For a few miles, they essentially followed the ruts and flattened grass made by the Molisians on their southward war-march.

"One thing I know," stated Dave, "is that for these first few days, we shouldn't let anyone at all know about the gold."

"I agree. This initial step is vital. Have you given any thought yet to the hiring of Molisians as soldiers?"

"Not really."

"I guess we'll have plenty of time to deliberate before coming across any Molisian-held towns."

A couple days had passed before Mick and Dave approached a place for potential recruitment. Up to that point, they'd come across nothing but small, family-run farms. Farmers didn't typically endeavor to uproot their farms. Some did, but not enough to justify Mick and Dave spending time recruiting so close to the Capital.

Their current locale wasn't quite populated enough to be considered a town. But there were enough homesteads congregated in the small area to allow Mick and Dave the opportunity to begin the mission.

A hundred years previous, the setting was attached to a much denser population, due to a nearby mine. But the mine had since suffered loss of prosperity, effectively driving the workers elsewhere. Though, a few remained, whose descendants owned the houses before Mick and Dave.

Mick said, "Let's not start too fancy."

"Right. It would be best for now to keep anyone from knowing about the gold in our packs. I highly doubt our ownership of it would survive long in the intense theatre of competition that'd arise from countless vagrants, unscrupulous folks, and bored individuals all trying to get at it at once."

"I see no reason for that not to be true."

Mick and Dave walked up the first house and knocked on the door. The gentleman who answered voiced, "What can I do for you?"

Dave replied, "Hello. I'm Dave and this is Mick. We are here per request of the King to scour the land for new army recruits. As I'm sure you've heard, we lost many soldiers during the battle at the Capital. Resultantly, we need to replenish."

The homeowner stated, "Yes, I've heard. But at least the King was victorious."

"That he was," commented Mick.

"Why wouldn't army personnel be sent to recruit? You two aren't wearing soldiers' garb, so I assume you aren't a part of the army."

"Under normal circumstances," replied Dave, "military personnel would be dispatched for such a task, but because of the danger still present at the Capital, the King insists all soldiers remain. Instead, he sent us, mainly by virtue of our past deeds."

"And what may I ask are these deeds?"

Realizing he couldn't make up a story on the spot to keep from sounding supercilious, Mick responded with the truth. "Two years ago, we re-captured Fort Gravividon and turned the tide at the Battle of Sarwa, grossing Knowing Circles. Last year, the two of us, alongside two others, were the diplomats responsible for aligning the Icytryxis with Garobansurov. Plus, we'd participated in other successful battles of the war, not only as fighters preserving freedom, but as students of thought."

"You could've just said you were Mick Thraiker and Dave Ghrere. I would've known your past deeds then."

"I should have, I guess," asserted Mick. "I forget news travels far and quickly."

The gentleman smiled. "And here you are now, taking part in yet another noble deed."

"That we are," remarked Dave.

"Unfortunately," declared the homeowner, "I am not soldier material—bad hip—but I can point you in the direction of some who may be."

"That would help us out a lot. Thank you."

"In that house, where you see the chickens under the bush, lives an old friend of mine. He and I go way back, we used to log together. He has two sons who he tells me are lazier than an old pig but as strong as a river. He says he wishes they'd join the army, instead of doing nothing at the tavern all day. Up to this point, he has yet not been able to persuade them to become soldiers, but maybe with your help, he can. I can personally vouch for their idleness but also their strength. I once seen them pull the large cart of a stranger in need out of the mud and sit at the saloon for the rest of the day bragging about it. Tell Butch—their father—that Harry sent you."

"We are very appreciative of your assistance. Have yourself a fine day."

"You too, Thraiker and Ghrere."

By the time they got there, the chickens were no longer under the bush, now grazing closer to the front door. They were in the way, so Mick and Dave parted the lackadaisical birds by shouting, "Stupid chickens."

Mick knocked on the door, and to the man who'd opened it—having learned the lesson the first time around—said, "Good day, sir, I'm Mick Thraiker and this is Dave Ghrere. We are here in service to the crown."

Butch nodded his head. "I've heard of you. The Knowing Circle, am I right?"

"You are, indeed."

"What brings you to my doorstep?"

Actually, in a manner of speaking, your friend across the way—Harry—brought us, having mentioned you'd be a good candidate for our inquiry. We are hunting recruits for the army, and he had revealed you longed this for your sons."

"He would be right. I've pleaded to them in the past, but those two are pretty stubborn. You can try, I suppose. I'm not sure where they are currently, but they can't be far, since they usually sleep here after a day of carousing. More than likely, they're at the nearby tavern; if not, they're probably at one of the not-so nearby ones."

"Much obliged."

"I hope you're successful or else—I'm sure—they'll die of liver poisoning soon. Vern and Gus are their names. You'll know them when you see them, because they're the largest men in the area—genetics they got from their mother, certainly not me. She was a beast of a lady."

"Thanks again."

Mick and Dave walked back through the chickens and off the beaten path for private conversation.

"Well, Mick, do we want to go into a bar and risk a horde gaining knowledge of our cache?"

"It would be easier if we could stash it before going in. Though, I'd be more afraid of it being discovered that way, than by going into a bar."

"I agree. Maybe if we went in and held back for a while to first see with what we'd be dealing?"

"Sound plan."

The nearest tavern could be seen in the distance. It went by the name The Lantern, fittingly ornamented by a colorful sign depicting a well-painted mining lantern.

The pair walked past the sign, went inside, and trying their best at not drawing attention, sat at the bar. There were a handful of patrons lined up on stools in front of a reasonably attractive female bartender—including a pair of colossal men.

Mick peripherally observed the colossal pair, looked at Dave, raised his brows, and said, "Yup."

"Yup," reciprocated Dave, knowing exactly to what Mick was referring.

"Where's the lantern after which this establishment is named?"

"I haven't seen it. Maybe it broke," replied Dave.

The attractive bartender brought the drinks Mick and Dave had ordered, and asked, "Where are you from? I can't say I recognize you."

"Chalatore, east of here."

"I've heard of it, but I've never been there. I do recall some of the guys talking about going to the big armwrestling tournament held there."

"Yup, that's the place," remarked Mick.

"Do you two participate in it?"

"If we are in town during it, we do. It really is a fabulous festivity. The organizers love having people come from far and wide to compete," declared Dave, doing his best to promote an event dear to his heart.

Mick shot the lady a question before she went back to the crew of regulars. "I was wondering, where is the lantern shown on the sign out front?"

Wielding her hypnotically irresistible emerald eyes—the reason most came to The Lantern in the first place—she replied, "Almost everyone asks that question. It's down the stairs over there to your left, situated within the original site of the tavern. What you see here was built in addition many years ago."

"Is that section still in use?"

"We typically only activate it during the larger functions we hold, such as when we hire a band, organize a tournament, or anything of the sort. It's an actual mining lamp that was used during the olden days. We replace the fuel in it every so often, so we can use it to showcase our namesake."

"Intriguing," responded Dave. "I hope to be here one day for one of the events you'd mentioned."

"Me too," the woman said, just before walking away to check on the status of the other patrons' beer mugs.

Dave whispered, "Mick, I just heard someone say *Gus*, so I'm now positive those are our guys."

"I agree. Let's give it some more time before we confront them. Maybe they'll become isolated at some point."

"We can't wait too long though, otherwise we'll seem odd by having not approached sooner."

"True. Also, now that I think of it, maybe the other guys at the bar want in on the action," said Mick, optimistically.

"I suggest we listen in for a couple more minutes before making a decision. It's possible that inside this timeframe, we can gauge their vocations."

"Alright."

Subsequent five minutes of inconspicuous detective work, Dave softly voiced to Mick, "I think most, if not all, are shady. They keep talking about suspicious jobs they'd pulled."

"I've come to the same conclusion. The question is do we proceed, or do we not risk the robbing of us to be something they disclose in future conversations?"

"If we do nothing, they may rob us anyways, as their father will ask them if we had talked to them."

"True," stated Mick. "Their little bandit group could assume we have a stash of money for the recruitment and catch up with us in the middle of the night to steal it."

"I believe everyone deserves a chance. Besides, we've defeated much larger groups than this. I doubt there are many more lurking about."

"True. Alright, we'll attempt to enlist them all."

Mick and Dave walked up to the group of five, who were all obviously trying to bed the bartender.

Mick emitted, "Hello, friends. Are you gentlemen familiar with the recent Molisian attempt to conquer the Capital?"

Having a hard time peeling his eyes away from the scintillating woman filling his mug, Gus replied, "Yeah, we've heard."

"I'm Mick Thraiker and this is Dave Ghrere. We have been sent north to conscript soldiers. This settlement is honestly our first stop. Eventually, we hope to have enough soldiers to take back the towns that were lost. And afterwards, new recruits will infiltrate into Ulfenkerki's army."

Quizzically, Gus looked at his friends, then, responded, "What's in it for us? We haven't joined the army in the past, why would we now?"

Dave replied, "We are giving out signing bonuses now, which will be added to the normal pay you would receive."

Butch's other large son, Vern, joined in on the discussion. "You guys are bold, proclaiming you carry enough money to give signing bonuses to a force large enough to take back the northern towns. Anyone could rob you. But then again, if you are who you say you are, it fits. Can you prove it? They say the Knowing Circle recipients carry swords that come across as being magical. Present them."

Mick and Dave knew better than to hand over both of the swords at once. Mick held onto his, in case something went awry, as Dave gave his black-needle to Vern, and said, "The key is in the grip. We found a one-in-a-million tree a while back with extraordinary gripping capabilities, the wood of which we converted into the sword handles. Take a swing. You'll see it'll cling to your hand much tighter than would an ordinary grip."

First, Vern swung the sword at the air, then, at a stick protruding from a piece of firewood lying on the ground by the fireplace. He chopped off the stick with nary an effort, walked up to Dave, and gave the sword back. "That proves that. I've never before experienced such a thing. What did this tree look like?"

"It was a stunted pine tree with black needles."

"You're right: one-in-a-million. Astonishing. I've on no account heard of such a thing," stated Gus. "Well, you certainly are Mick Thraiker and Dave Ghrere."

"So, what kind of signing bonus are we talking about here?" asked Vern. "I suppose I could be swayed, if the price is right, and certain other criteria is met."

Mick replied, "The bonus you'll receive, immediately after slotting in your signature, will be a gold coin worth five hundred gitis. Thereafter, you'll receive a smaller gold coin every week worth two hundred gitis. But remember, if you sign and run, you will be branded a traitor, and will have to answer to the Crown. Along with standard contract vernacular, it'll stipulate the coins are worth at minimum what we say they're worth."

Dave jumped in. "So, what would these other criteria be?"

Vern answered, "Simple: enough free time for drinking and other various activities."

Dave responded, "Drinking will be allowed or denied on a day-to-day basis, depending on the degree of danger present. There will be plenty of free time, while you're with us, especially during the nightly campout. We won't be assigning many mandatory chores, like you'd see while surrounded by the normal army. And even then, General Ulfenkerki isn't too demanding. Basically, the main thing Mick and I will require of you is to be ready for battle when the need calls for it. Other specialized duties providing opportunity for higher pay will more than likely arise. Performance of these duties won't be made compulsory."

"So, we will be allowed tavern privileges once in a while?"

"That's right, Vern," answered Mick. "Taverns need patronage like every business does."

Noticing that only Vern and Gus seemed interested, Dave focused his attention on them. "You would be doing your father proud. We ran into Butch earlier."

"How many Molisians hold the northern towns, and do you expect further large battles, like the one that just happened at the Capital?" inquired Gus.

"General Ulfenkerki briefed us before we left. And although he had no evidence as to exactly how many, his presumption was that some of the larger cities have hundreds guarding them. And the smaller ones, maybe dozens," replied Mick, catching himself gazing at the bartender. He realized he liked emerald eyes. "There hasn't been anything leading us to believe there are other large conflicts looming. But we aren't acquainted with much about the western front at this point—anything could be going on over there. Luckily, we aren't headed that way."

"And you expect to enlist hundreds in the near future to confront the Molisians?"

"That's the plan."

Gus, Vern, and their crew talked it over for a bit, while Mick and Dave went back by their drinks. Sadly, they were now lukewarm. Nevertheless, they guzzled them down, then, they each ordered one more. These, they would carry back to the potential recruits, so they wouldn't have to eventually drink another tepid beverage.

Vern said to Mick and Dave, "I speak for myself and for my brother when I say we've decided to join you. The rest of these guys barely know how to handle a sword, and they would be the first to admit it."

Mick and Dave looked to Gus and Vern's crew, who shyly nodded their heads in agreement.

Vern continued, "One of the main reasons we decided to join is that we're well aware of your reputation as being smart in battle. We know you wouldn't order us to risk our lives needlessly."

"You're right," said Mick, "we wouldn't. Every battle is a series of precise calculations, and in order to win, you must not waste resources."

"We won't let you down."

The contracts for the standard two-year service enlistment were written up, signed, and sealed. As promised, the signing bonuses were given to Vern and Gus.

Dave said, "You might have to wait a while before cashing it in, as I don't know if there are any folks in this settlement who buy gold."

Gus responded, "No, there aren't. But that's fine, we can wait until the next town."

Together, the four checked the remaining homesteads of the settlement for recruits. They also checked The Lantern again to see if anyone new dropped by. Nope, same ole, same ole.

Having come up empty-handed, they moved on, but not before Vern and Gus told their father the news. Butch was extremely proud of his sons that day, and from that point on he sat taller on The Lantern's barstools.

Mick, Dave, Vern, and Gus spent their first night as a group in the Garobansurovian wilderness. Vern and Gus had been told to bring tents, otherwise they'd be sleeping under the stars. Mick and Dave were nice, but not nice enough to let other grown men sleep in their tents with them. Fortunately, Vern and Gus owned tents.

At midday the next day, Gus said, "Just a suggestion, but Vern and I know the owners of the inn—the brothel—at the next settlement. We always get our rooms half-off, and I'm positive yours would be, too. It would be a good place to recruit, as tons of able-bodied men come and go at a place like this."

"You know the owner of a brothel really well, do you?" said Dave, with a cheesy grin. "Been having a bit of fun, eh?"

"We've known the owners for a long time, but I guess you could say it's been an acquaintance that has yielded much benefit." Vern matched Dave's cheesy grin.

"You'll get no judgment from me," declared Dave. "You do make a strong case, though. From the basepoint of a brothel, we could communicate with many prospects. I doubt Mick and I will reap the benefits of the pleasures within, but if you two want to, go ahead. It won't impede the mission any. Enjoy yourselves. Just be ready by early morning."

"I'm already glad I signed on with you guys," said Vern, beaming.

The inn/brothel wasn't much of a secret. It was a large building with a steep roof, and all the locals knew exactly what happened therein. To be fair, half the people of the area lived within. The place was a magnet, as the prices were low, and the skirts were high.

The Molisians surely would've commandeered the place, if they'd taken that route, for Molisia practically invented the brothel.

Post the quartet walking through the brothel's front door, Vern got the attention of a young lady and asked to speak with Brian or Vicky.

A few moments later, one of the proprietors, Vicky, met with Vern and Gus, while Mick and Dave waited in the small, smoke-filled lobby. The lobby was an intriguing niche, because none of the colors of the furniture matched. It almost seemed as if it was done on purpose, seeing as that the colors clashed that badly. Regardless, the chairs were still comfortable.

Vern and Gus accomplished what they said they would, and they all paid half price for bedrooms. It ended up costing not much more than a meal.

The quartet brought their gear to the two rooms containing two beds each. Afterwards, Vern and Gus went straight to the entertainment. Mick and Dave decided that it'd be foolish to leave the gold unattended in the room, so they resolved to go out recruiting only one at a time. Mick stayed back initially, while Dave set forth.

Dave noticed it wasn't easy to speak with any of the men inside the brothel, since they were preoccupied and all. So, he went outside to speak with those coming and going—a much easier task.

By the end of the night, Mick and Dave had recruited three more soldiers, plus another in the morning.

While exiting the brothel/inn, Mick said to Vern and Gus, "You guys were right; it was a good idea to draft here."

"You can say that again," noted Vern. "We both were even able to cash in the signing bonus coins."

"I hope you didn't spend it all already."

"Oh, heck no. Like the room rates, the women were inexpensive. Plus, we're not greedy; we know how to pace ourselves," said Gus through a beam.

The four new soldiers—Aaron, Horace, Albert, and Seth—had already grabbed their traveling gear from their homes, so they were all ready to journey.

Eight armed men were a pretty intimidating force.

Mick and Dave were vulnerable; the six together could've ganged up on them at any time to steal the gold. There was no way around the danger for the time being. Mick and Dave anticipated the susceptibility and were prepared for many possibilities.

Other than having gained the single new recruit that morning, the day turned out unfruitful, except for the covering of many miles. They all made camp together, and half secured supper for all, via hunting. So far it seemed everyone was getting along. It was a good start.

It was a peaceful, starless night, dark as a shadow. Like the surrounding trees, the positioning of the eight tents resembled no pattern.

CHAPTER 9

EVERYONE HAD BEEN inside for a few hours when a slight rustling in one of the tents arose. A menacing face emerged out of a tent, followed by two more. Aaron, Albert, and Seth had dishonorably plotted to steal the gold. They waited until they thought the rest were asleep to make their move. Their plan was to kill the rest, by stabbing them through the tents.

Clutching their swords, the trio crept silently towards the target tents. Their hearts raced, as they were already dreaming about what they could buy with so much money. Two of them even pictured purchasing a fleet of ships.

The plan would've worked too, if it hadn't been for Mick and Dave's ingenuity and experience. Ever since they were accompanied by Vern and Gus the first night, Mick and Dave took shifts watching for thievery. One slept, while the other pretended to. They both lost half a night's sleep every night, but it was better than being dead.

Mick was fast asleep, while Dave heard footsteps and saw movement, peering through a small opening in his tent. A moment elapsed and he could see murder in the trio's eyes. But he waited until he was absolutely certain to strike.

As the would-be thieves wound up their sword arms, Dave vigorously flew out of his tent, yelling, "Wake up!"

Dave's first move was to get in-between the tents and the thieves, so they couldn't poke their swords through the tents. Initially, Dave was strictly in defensive mode. In the matter of seconds from when Dave yelled, Mick joined the fray. And a few moments after that, Gus and Vern even energetically sprung out of their tents to help Mick and Dave.

As the battle ensued, Mick noticed Horace staring out of his tent, frozen, too cowardice to help.

The battle was over in less than a minute. The villainous three stood no chance at victory; they lay dead in the darkest of nights. Dreams of their ship fleet had disappeared faster than a snowball thrown into a roaring fire.

Mick and Dave thanked Vern and Gus, and then approached Horace. "Explain yourself!"

Horace came out from his tent, and nervously replied, "I will admit I froze, but you must believe me, it all happened so fast that I couldn't respond. I know with all my heart that if a few more moments had elapsed, I would've found my bravery and come to your aid. It was honestly the first sword fight I have ever seen."

After Mick and Dave talked it over, the latter said to Horace, "Consider this your last warning. If it happens again, we'll brand you a traitor, and you'll have to answer to the King. As we have no way of knowing you weren't aligned with the offenders and that you backed out the second you saw them losing."

"I promise next time will be different."

"Very well."

The next day, after burying the defectors, the five of them continued on. So much for their good start.

It took a while, but Mick and Dave finally got the opportunity to talk to Vern and Gus alone, without Horace around, who was currently off in the woods hunting.

"Please keep this conversation a secret," said Dave. "Remember when we told you there may be elective responsibilities through which to earn more gitis?"

"I most certainly remember," replied Gus."

Dave continued, "Last night, the two of you earned our trust enough to be offered one of these tasks. As I'm sure you've guessed, you seeing how quickly the robbery was foiled, Mick and I have been splitting nighttime guard duty, which isn't a particularly pleasant commission. Sleep is vital for strong sword muscles, of course. So, here is what we're offering: an extra 75 gitis to each of you per week for you to be added to the guard rotation; or an extra 100 to each for you both to take the two middle shifts, allowing Mick and I the bookends. Or, you could decline all together. You can choose any option."

Mick added, "We may eventually add others to the rotation, but if you decide to do this now, your salary will never decrease until we reach the Capital. And even then, our recommendation will go a long way in securing officer positions for you. Dave and I never forget loyalty."

Gus and Vern discussed the offer between themselves. After a short dialog, Vern said to Dave and Mick, "We will take the middle shifts, the extra 100 gitis being very appetizing. It actually was a no-brainer."

"We aim to earn even more of your confidence," said Gus, self-assuredly.

"For that, we are appreciative," stated Dave. "We'll initiate your enhanced pay this week, even though it's almost over. It's the least we can do for your considerable help last night."

"I hope we find another brothel soon then," said Gus, jokingly.

Horace returned to the fold, so the conversation terminated.

Gus and Vern would prove to be reliable guards in the weeks to come. They would pass all the tests Mick and Dave threw at them designed to determine if they were actually guarding and not sleeping through their shifts. Money well spent.

The day after the robbery attempt, the party reached a settlement built around an ancient river crossing. The existing serviceable bridge was undeniably old, but the crossing point itself was far older. Vestiges of some of the older bridges were still visible, but you'd have to squint just right in order to distinguish them. The primordial structures were camouflaged, blending in well with the surrounding natural rocks.

The setting had been used as a prominent crossing for ages, since the river was narrowest here for miles around, due to a bottleneck. Some called it the Gateway to the North. Others just called it Phil's Crossing, which was also the name of the immediate settlement.

Mick made a point to tell himself to find out who Phil was, planning to ask the locals. It was something he always wondered, having never gotten around to finding out, as every time he'd previously gone through, he was in a hurry for some reason or other. Dave and the others didn't know either.

Like always, once camp was made, the soldiers could do as they wished, as long as they stayed near, in case something drastic happened.

They all decided to visit the Tavern of Phil's Crossing. The ceiling was high, and the situation was busy. It was so busy in fact that condensation from everyone breathing had accrued quite noticeably on the colder surfaces. Practically everyone from the area was there it seemed, which was a good thing, since it made recruiting easier. Going from house to house was tedious.

In the matter of an hour, they'd replaced the previous night's criminals, plus one.

It took a while, but Mick finally found someone who knew who Phil was, and what significance he held. An older gentleman at the end of the bar told the tale:

> "A hundred years ago or so, the settlement here had a different name. I

can't recall what that name was, though. I guess there's always been some sort of settlement situated here. Apparently, the inhabitants of the settlement, before Phil came into the picture, charged people to use the bridge. People complained, but they didn't do anything about it. The king of the time had been informed of the situation, but didn't intervene, because it was said he drank too much to care about much.

"So, one winter's day, along came Phil, trying to cross the bridge. And like everyone else, he ran into the band almost large enough to be considered an army guarding the bridge and was told of the crossing fee. He thought it was absurd but paid the fee, nevertheless. Though, he was determined to do something about the appalling misuse of power, especially after he learned all the money was unfairly pocketed by the area's wealthier individuals.

"What Phil ended up doing about the atrocity was ingenious. He figured if they were going to charge people for using something that wasn't technically theirs, he'd arrange a way to charge the wrongdoers exorbitantly for something of relatively no value. An eye for an eye.

"He gathered together a small crew, and in the middle of the night, they snuck into all the homes of the wealthy responsible for the injustice. Phil had learned of a certain shrub that when burned emitted an enormous amount of smoke. Apparently, it was some new-fangled technology of the time. So, what he and his crew did after collecting a bunch of these shrubs from the countryside, was take the potent part, the sap I guess, and smear it all over the objectives' supply of firewood.

"When the wealthy started their fires, their homes became engulfed by suffocating smoke. The smoke was released so profusely that nearly none could escape out the chimney. 'Twas similar to when a giant tree falls into a creek; some of the raging water will flow over the tree, but much will flood the adjacent banks. There was nothing they could do but leave their homes and search for some other warm place to spend the night.

"Phase Two of Phil's plan was to begin.

"Since everyone wanted to cooperate with him, Phil easily arranged for every single lumberjack of the area to only sell firewood coated with the smoke-inducing resin to those responsible for the bridge fees.

"The homes of the wealthy kept filling up with smoke, and there was nothing they could do about it.

"Then one day out of the blue, a man many didn't recognize—Phil in a costume—entered town and went into the tavern as a salesman. He discoursed about how there were many homes scattered across Garobansurov having smoke issues with their wood. He then presented an elixir to the crowd that he touted would cure the problem. Those in on the ruse paid the enormous price for the elixir, but later got their money back. The wealthy folks of town fell for it, every one of them paying the expensive price for the fake elixir.

"Time went on, and the lumberjacks stopped supplying tainted firewood, as many more elixirs were sold. The wealthy wholeheartedly believed the smoke problem was remedied because of the elixir.

"Phil took all the money and hired his own mercenaries to militarily stop the bridge fees. Only equal force can stop a force.

"Henceforth, the settlers always knew how to impede the unjust. To honor this newly-gained knowledge, they renamed the settlement Phil's Crossing. And to this day, the crossing of the bridge has remained charge-free.

Very appreciatively, Mick replied, "Thank you. That was quite the story. I'm surprised no one else in here knows it."

"They're probably too young. My late grandfather was one of the lumberjacks in the story and passed it down to me."

"That's fascinating," noted Mick. "Here's something that may interest you: At the battle that'd just occurred at the Capital, we used what probably was the very same tree sap in your story to smoke out the Molisians from the buildings. We made tons of smoke torches, which worked very well."

"Captivating," remarked the older gentleman. "What a small world. The resin must still be a pretty tightly kept secret."

"It must be. See you around, old timer," said Mick. "Much obliged to your grandfather for his assistance in making my bridge crossing free of charge."

"You're welcome, and I hope you guys are successful with your mission."

Now thicker in number, the party sat around the campfire, as Mick relayed to everyone the story of Phil and his scheme. The new soldiers (who were from the area) admitted they'd never heard the telling before.

Everyone went to sleep, the charter members of the group having not soon forgotten the events of the night before. They were on high alert.

It ended up being a much more peaceful night, however. Gus and Vern saw no failure in diligently performing their new duty.

The new group was nine strong and operational, but there was a long way to go.

Leading the group northward, Mick said to Dave, "As our numbers increase, I think it'll get easier to recruit. A potential soldier is more likely to join a larger force, since the paradigm will seem less perilous to them. As the old adage states, *There's safety in numbers.*"

"We will see, but I think you're right. I recall Ulfenkerki once saying that too, how the larger his army is, the more incoming volunteers he gets."

Walking briskly with anticipation, the group knew they were coming up on one of the more beautiful places of Garobansurov. They wanted to make it there by evening, so they could camp by the Temple of Old. There were many aged temples in the country, but this one was one of the largest and best preserved, even though a large fraction of it was underground.

The brisk pace paid off, for they arrived at the temple in the time slot they favored. They decided to not only camp by the stone temple, but within it.

Sometimes vagabonds would make refuge in such places. If Mick and Dave's company came across any of these, they'd more than likely just share the shelter. It was rare for overly large dodgy bands to be present, but it was a possibility. Mick and Dave approached the innards with caution.

They descended into the temple's second level, second from the top, and immediately saw firelight. They stopped and listened to get a head count. Having ascertained there weren't many sitting around the fire, they proceeded.

In case it was a trap, Mick and Dave strategically positioned a few of the soldiers in the rear to cover their backsides. The odds were very high, though, it was a group of drifters just trying to survive—perfect candidates for recruitment.

As non-threateningly as possible, Mick walked up to the group huddled around the fire, and said, "Hello folks. What's the news for the day?"

The eldest of the group replied, "Hi friend. We are but simple nomads, biding our time and living off the land. We're alive, so you could say we're successful nomads."

"Indeed. We are soldiers of the King, attempting to increase in number, and take back the northern towns."

The eldest remarked, "We walked near one of the occupied towns a few weeks ago. We kept our distance, but we were close enough to see that you're going to need a much larger force than the one you're exhibiting here in order to retake the town."

"How much larger?"

"Hundreds."

"Unfortunately, we figured that was the case," emitted Mick.

A burly man with a hoarse voice commented, "How do you intend to gain such a contingent?"

Dave answered by running through the usual recruitment speech. The quartet of addressees listened patiently.

When Dave was finished, the burly man (Zed) stated, "Under different circumstances, I'm sure I—along with Nate and/or Charles here—would think long and hard about joining. But as things stand, I must decline. If we able-bodied were to enroll, we'd be abandoning our older friend, Silas, here. He was unquestionably proficient with a weapon a decade ago—awe, you should've seen him—but those days are past. We're a tightly-knit group, and none of us would turn our backs on each other."

Nate and Charles both nodded in agreement. Silas couldn't help but be humbled by such words. If ever he had true friends, these were them.

Mick scratched his chin, and said, "Hold on a second, though. Silas, do you possess any extraordinary assets?"

"I'd say my forte in battle has always been archery. My eyes are very astute, in fact, they still are. It's too bad I can't really draw a bow back like I used to. I was always good with my sword too, but no longer. Plus, this may not count for much, but I'm the best chef amongst our merry little band here."

Mick scratched his chin even harder. "I have an idea. I'll be right back."

While Mick was gone, Charles impatiently said, "Do you have any guesses as to his intention?"

Dave responded, "Not really."

Mick went to the entrance of the temple, where they had dropped most of their traveling gear. He rummaged through it and found what he wanted—both parts.

Having returned to the group, Mick said, "This is the primary weapon of our new ally. If you haven't heard yet, we have aligned with the fabled foreign race of the Icytryxis. They have longer arms and better eyesight, which enables them to use a weapon like this. It's called an atlytl. I was thinking, perhaps, with your good eyesight you may be able to wield one. You may yet be strong enough to have venom behind your throw. That is, if you're willing. I look at the four of you and see the loyalty you have for each other. I'm not about to relinquish the chance of having this loyalty added to our battalion. It's a valuable commodity." Mick extended the atlytl, hoping Silas would reach for it.

"Well, I can still cast a fishing pole, maybe I can this," said Silas, grasping the atlytl with interest.

"The bowels of this long-forgotten temple are spacious enough for the launching of an atlytl," noticed Dave. "Fire away."

Silas backed up, hooked a projectile, and launched it as far as he could. It wasn't exactly an impressive showing of athleticism. The projectile barely made it halfway to the other wall, a mere 100 yards.

Not giving up hope, Mick said, "Now try this. I'm going to set this rock—conveniently the size of a head—over here, and now let's see how many times you can hit it out of twenty. Your eyesight may allow you to prevail here."

Standing beside Mick, Silas eyed up his target, and loosed the first projectile. He missed, but figured he would, as he wanted to focus on using the first throw to gauge the trajectory of all proceeding ones. For the next launch he'd concentrate more on hitting the rock, instead of establishing a benchmark.

Silas lit the fires trapped in his eyes and hurled the second projectile. Right on target.

Out of the next 18 throws, he ended up connecting on 15. So, in total he was successful at 16 out of 20.

"Excellent," said Mick. "Head shots at 80 percent from 40 yards in a battle would be a great asset to the team. It's not quite as accurate as the Icytryxis, but this is your very first time. You could practice along the way."

Dave added, "Plus, you said you're good at cooking."

"So, now that we are offering positions to all of you, would you reconsider joining us?" asked Mick.

Zed replied, "We'll talk it over. You're sleeping here tonight I take it?"

"Correct."

"We will have your answer by morning, maybe sooner. You might as well join us; you won't have to construct another fire that way. We'll have some food ready shortly."

"We will do that," proclaimed Dave. "It's been a while since I've been here. Are the lower levels still intact?"

"Yes, you won't find navigating them to be overly difficult," answered Zed. "Don't forget to bring plenty of torches, though. A few days ago, I climbed down there, and foolishly only brought one torch. It went out, and I could've easily gotten lost in the darkness had I not been close enough to yell for help. I could've staggered around for weeks down there."

"It's a good thing I can hear well," said Nate, "otherwise, we may not have heard you, and you'd still be down there."

"Possibly. Bless your owl-like hearing."

"Speaking of nocturnal animals," remarked Charles, "you'll see plenty of bats down there—just watch out for guano."

"Oh yes, no deep, dark place would be the same without it," said Mick.

Mick, Dave, and their squad carried all their stuff to the second level near the roaring fire. They didn't bother setting up tents, since there were plenty of stone recesses available, compliments of an extinct culture from long ago. It was a culture that apparently knew how to expertly fashion temples that could impressively withstand the elements, including multiple ice ages.

While the nomads mulled over the proposition, Mick and Dave explored the bottom echelons, having remembered to bring plenty of torches and torch fuel. Gus and Vern accompanied them on the trek through the substructure, also bringing plenty of torches—the more the better. Even though they'd seen much of it before, Mick and Dave had never seen the entire underside and were eager to see the parts they missed. A person would actually need a whole day to explore every possible nook and cranny—two days, if they wanted to take their time and enjoy themselves.

The quartet slogged through the mysterious environment, wide-eyed. As they trekked, they imagined all the things that could've taken place there so long ago, which was pretty hard to do, since it was a setting far removed from their own. For all they knew, sacrifices and tortures could've transpired, although thankfully, there was no evidence of that.

The walk had them transitioning from wide-open chamber to tight quarters repeatedly. "No one can say this setting lacks diversity," blurted Dave.

An odd sound resembling wind eerily echoed from some far-off place deep within. They didn't have the time to ascertain what exactly it was—perhaps a mission for another day.

Satisfied they saw most of the main parts of the underworld, the foursome found their way back up and searched for the others. They were easy to find, as they were all sitting around the fire, either eating or preparing to.

Silas commented, "When a person spends most of their day walking, they usually take every chance they get to cook a large, appetizing meal."

"Too true," agreed Mick. "Dave and I are no strangers to that statement."

Mick and Dave integrated some of their meat with the meat-cornucopia already sizzling over the fire. The place smelled fantastic, as long as you weren't a vegetarian.

With the exception of no one, they loaded their stomachs until lethargy took hold.

Not enough sunlight would find its way into the temple for anyone to tell when morning came. So, going to bed, they all knew they'd have to take their best guess at when to wake up.

Their guesses were spot on.

Having slept on it, the nomads felt they came to the best decision possible. Silas said to Mick and Dave, "We've been wandering aimlessly for so long through the countryside that we forgot what it feels like to trust someone other than ourselves. Such things can truly develop into dangerous business. Which is why we've decided to take you up on your offer. You all definitely seem the honorable sort. Participating in your endeavor seems like something that could progress into a further understanding of human virtue."

"We can't promise you glory, wealth, or a better position in life," proclaimed Mick, "but we can promise you knowledge. It's precisely the reason why Dave and I agreed to the mission King Rowlangiv so kindly bequeathed to us."

"Spoken like an honest man," said Nate. "And honest men are who you want covering your back, in war and in the journey called life."

"Wise men are second," added Dave.

STILL TRAPPED in her foul prison, Anna persevered. Her health was starting to deteriorate, due to the unorthodox diet the garbage chute provided. Moldy bread was the primary source of sustenance available. It was just a miracle she remained free of bacteria-related infections. Water was a little easier to come by, since a sufficient amount of condensation accumulated on the surfaces of the cold, damp environment. Anna was grateful at least it wasn't the dead of winter.

I wonder if I could outsprint them when they're all drunk. I doubt it. There was that one day last year when an out-of-towner was caught cheating at cards and tried to run. He would've gotten away too, if it hadn't been for the unexpected speed of a pursuing drunk named Bill. I know Bill was drunk, because I remember bringing him a dozen beers that day. I only remember it because I always thought he was cute and wished he'd buy me a drink someday. Nevertheless, drunken Bill ran down the cheater, who even had a head start. There's always a Bill in every crowd of drinkers, someone drunk who could outsprint me, as I'm not entirely that fast at short distances, although anything over a mile and things would be utterly different.

No, I won't risk it. Although the way it's looking I'm going to have to take a risk at some point.

Now that I think of it, hypothetically one of two things is going to have to happen soon: Either the King defeats the advancing Molisians and sends a battalion to retake the towns lost, or the King loses and the populace of Molisia starts to trickle down into Garobansurov. Let's hope it's the former.

This is another thing that's troubling me: Why in tarnation do these idiots feel that just because this is a bar it's the only place where they can drink? There's nothing magical or glamorous that transpires in a dingy tavern that couldn't also transpire at any other locale.

Anyways, I must be patient. Something advantageous has to happen sooner or later. You can do it, Anna. Do it for your friends who were mercilessly raped and murdered. Bastards.

IT WAS PAYDAY. To keep morale high, Mick and Dave wanted to reach civilization so the troops had something on which to spend their money. Most weren't the type to squirrel away gold for a rainy day. Unfortunately, they didn't know if the next town up the road was under Molisian occupation.

They proceeded with caution, sticking to the hills.

Gus said to those near him, "The next town is just over that next hill, probably another hour of walking. It's not a large town, but I know it has a tavern and restaurant—or maybe they are one in the same, I can't recall."

"I don't remember either," replied Dave.

Keeping low and steering clear from twigs small enough to snap under the weight of a body, Mick and Dave stealthily led their platoon.

Having crested the ridge just before town, they looked down into the village, like birds of prey mindfully scanning the field. Methodically, they spied the area for movement. Silas, Dave, and especially Mick (his nickname wasn't Hawk for no reason) had the best eyes of the party and looked the hardest. Those with poor vision lay in the grass, unmoving and silent.

Silas said to Mick and Dave, "What do you make of it?"

"I see a couple armed men, but I can't tell if they are Garobansurovian or not," answered Mick. "We'll wait patiently and see what happens."

"If we don't see any women and children, I'm almost positive it's under Molisian control," said Dave. "Molisians would have the women locked up for purposes I care not to say out loud. It's what they do."

After watching for twenty minutes, Mick said, "That settles that: no women or children, just a handful of soldiers."

Dave agreed, "Right. That's all I've seen. They seem to go into, what I'm assuming to be, the bar a lot."

"They do. I presume it's where the booze is," voiced Silas.

Dave stated, "It seems the town is held by between eight and twelve Molisians—probably drunk."

"Are any of them stationed in highly strategic places?" asked Silas.

"None are perched advantageously at the moment, no," responded Mick. "Contrary to what they think, exiting the bar once in a while to look around isn't exactly militarily useful."

"What do you think," remarked Dave, "can we defeat them?"

"Possibly. Despite the risk of being noticed, I'd like to institute an overnight stakeout to learn their idiosyncrasies."

"Alright Mick. The spy team can stay up here," Dave put forth, "while the rest of the crew can go back down the hill, where they'll be much more out of the way, posing less of a chance of being spotted."

"Agreed," stated Mick. "You can spearhead that, Leopard, while Silas and I stay up here on the hill for recon. We'll probably just sleep up here too."

"Okay. See you in the morning."

Dave led his team down the hill, as Mick and Silas remained at the observation point. Together, the two watched the town below for hours, before falling asleep in the tall grass. Luckily, it didn't rain.

In the morning, Mick rejoined Dave and supplied the intelligence report. "They are definitely Molisians, I saw their flag. They do have a lookout sentry posted, watching for approaching forces. But it's always a lone observer. Each partakes in four-hour shifts atop the hill on the other side of town. Since our hill is higher than theirs, I'm pretty sure we saw them, without them seeing us. There are twelve Molisians in total, and they mainly stick to the tavern—an advantageous bottleneck for us. Some have bows, but none are waiting on high ground to snipe. I think we can defeat them with hardly any casualties. But the main problem is once we capture the town, there won't be anyone around to hold it. I suggest we attempt the offensive anyways and take a chance that no Molisians are nearby to reclaim it. I think the news will spread fast enough that our fellow Garobansurov citizens will return and defend it themselves."

"I've no objections," affirmed Dave. "I bet we can silently dispose of their sentry, then, work on any other soldiers outside the bar. We could actually just burn the bar to the ground and catch them off-guard."

"We probably could. The King did leave everything, including weighing collateral damage, to our judgment. I don't think the loss of a tavern will be mourned too much," stated Mick.

"Now to go inform the soldiers it's action time."

"I'll go dispose of their sentry on the hill, while you do that," said Mick. "I'll rally with you in an hour."

Dave assembled the troops and to them said, "We are confronted with our first militarized enterprise. We've decided we are going to liberate the town. With proper strategy, we should be able to do it without any of your deaths. Mick and I specialize in missions like these. Get your battle gear on and be ready in an hour."

Demonstrating complete discipline, the unit went right to action.

Inconspicuously gliding from one tree to another, Mick slithered around town and up the hill on which the lone Molisian patrol was situated. When within eyeshot of the sentry, Mick waited patiently, only aiming to switch trees at the most opportune moment. He wanted to get close enough that his arrow had at least a 90 percent chance of hitting its mark. Which for Mick was about fifty yards in moderate wind.

Just ahead, he spotted the perfect tree from which to shoot. It was wide at the bottom and came to a crotch at just right height perfect through which to shoot. Now to see if he could reach it without being seen.

Intensively, he watched the gaze of the sentry. When it was directed away, Mick stealthily slipped 25 paces to the crotched tree. Flawless.

Mick wasn't adept enough with a bow to try for a headshot. He just wanted a clean shot at the back. An arrow in the back wouldn't necessarily kill, but it would demobilize just enough to allow Mick an easy run-up. Furthermore, it was a good thing the sentry wasn't near enough town that he could alert the rest by yelling. If he had been near enough, Mick would've had to employ an entirely different tactic, since a person could still yell with an arrow stuck in their back.

Mick notched his arrow and loosed it when the Molisian was standing still and with his back turned. Flawless again.

The man let out a cry of pain but foolishly forgot to start moving towards his sword. Mick had covered half the distance, before the Molisian even realized what was happening. The wound wasn't paralyzing, but it greatly limited the Molisian's range of motion. He could barely reach down to grab his sword. By the time his arm was fully extended, Mick was already on top of him.

Mick gave the man a few moments to surrender.

Seeing the Molisian had no intentions of yielding, Mick sighed and swung his *black needle* fluidly, supplying the man a quick, clean death.

For a second, Mick wondered why some people didn't value their lives enough to surrender. It was as if they didn't fear death, as if they were certain a better place waited for them. Even though Mick knew he and Dave had come very close to death a few times in the past, he was absolutely sure he wanted to remain in the current realm, having seen no proof there was another.

Since things were about to get dangerous, Mick forced himself to snap out of his death ruminations, as continuing this line of thought while risking his life would be unhealthily counterproductive.

Before reuniting with Dave and the rest, Hawk quickly searched the area to see if there was anything that could help in the forthcoming fight. He found nothing but useless discarded chicken bones.

Mick began rushing back by the team, knowing they would lose the element of surprise if the man he'd just killed was discovered.

The squad was all ready and waiting when Mick approached. Seeing eagerness in their eyes, Mick couldn't help but feel they'd so far selected commendable soldiers.

Mick addressed the team, "We must act quickly. Their lookout is dead, and we have to attack before they find out. Dave and I have been given complete autonomy, which is good news for you, since we really don't care if you drink all of the available booze after we win. I'm sure there's plenty of it. Plus, I highly doubt I have to actually say this, but no raping or thievery other than drinking the townsfolks' liquor. If there are any women, and they're okay with being paid for the service, knock yourselves out. Better yet, work your charm, maybe you won't have to pay."

"There's no shortage of charm here," announced Gus buoyantly.

Needless to say, the soldiers' morale remained high after Mick's favorable address.

As the party skulked through the bushes to get to town, Mick spoke softly to Dave. "I hope there's some sort of flammable agent somewhere convenient in town that we can use to easily ignite the saloon."

"There might be some tar, pitch, grease, or animal fat stored handily in a barrel somewhere."

"I hope so."

The platoon successfully reached the village-fringe and hid behind a shed. Mick peered down the main avenue for adversaries. There was one on high ground and three pacing in front of the tavern. "I doubt we can shoot down the guy on the roof, without him alarming the rest."

"Probably not, Mick," said Dave. "Maybe those loitering around in front of the tavern will go back inside soon, leaving behind just the one on the roof for conventional disposal."

"Good plan, but let's not wait too long, otherwise we risk them discovering their dead scout, therefore eliminating any chance at a preemptive strike."

"Definitely."

The team waited patiently and received only partly good news: Some had gone back inside the tavern, but not all.

"I think if we do it right," stated Dave, "we can still do this. But we have to act quickly. We'll split up to form a quad of teams and perform tasks simultaneously. The biggest group can take out the soldiers in front of the bar. Another team can eliminate the guy on the roof. The third will be in charge of procuring a fuel source for the burning of the bar. While the last directive will be peeking inside the bar to make sure there aren't any civilians who could get burnt by the fire."

Without hesitation, the squad split up—Mick, Dave, Gus, and Vern comprising the larger group in charge of eradicating the soldiers in front of the bar. There were only two to eradicate, so the four of them knew they could handle the task relatively easily. The other three groups were equally confident.

The timing had to be perfect for the plan to work— especially the timing of the two groups facing combat. These two groups were particularly twitchy and ready for action. They felt alive and when it came down to it, wouldn't be elsewhere if they could.

Having relinquished their edge-of-town cover, Hawk and Leopard's team got into position as close to their target as practicable. Mick and Dave would begin their onslaught when the best moment struck, which'd be the cue for the rest of the teams to begin theirs.

Mick noticed the adversarial pair were as far away from the tavern's egress as they were going to be—too close and they'd be able to alert those in the bar. Having begun their pounce, Mick and Gus strove to flank one opponent, while Dave and Vern the other.

During the encounter, one of the Molisians cried for help, but to no avail. Those in the bar were too inattentive to take notice.

When reaping the benefits of a two-on-one confrontation, Mick and Dave never lost—this time being no exception.

As soon as Mick and Dave had begun their charge, the other three teams had followed suit.

The scout on the roof was shot by arrows and tumbled to the ground. A sword to the head and he was dead.

The fuel party ran around town, searching. It took them longer than they wanted, because the first few buildings they entered looked like shops but were actually homes—unusual looking homes bereft fuel. They finally located a supply of coal and oil in a blacksmith shop. The three grabbed the heaviest loads they could and lugged them to the bar.

Meanwhile, the pair responsible for inspecting the saloon for civilians began performing their commission. They looked in the window and saw nothing but soldiers drinking rowdily. There were no signs of innocent bystanders. If there were any in concealment, now would be the time for them to abandon their hiding place and escape, since the place was moments from being torched. Satisfied the coast was clear, the inspection pair gave the thumbs up.

Everyone proficient with either a bow or atlytl got into position near the bar's two exits. From what was gathered, these two were the only ways out.

The coal and oil were scattered on and near the walls of the tavern and lit. The fire erupted nearly as quickly as sunlight could enter the opened door of a dark room.

Half the Molisians panicked uncontrollably when they saw the flames. The other half-fumbled towards the door. All of them were drunk.

The first of the Molisians emerged from the front door and were hit by a barrage of arrows, including a projectile from Silas's atlytl. Instinctively, Mick and Dave spotted those not holding weapons and targeted them for close combat, as they'd be easy kills.

The last two heading out of the tavern had been smart enough to perceive what was happening. They came out with their hands in the air, surrendering. Their lives would be spared, though at the moment, Mick and Dave didn't exactly know what they were going to do with them. They'd worry about that later.

When the dust had settled, Mick noted, "The first village is officially reclaimed, and it's been done without a single loss of Garobansurovian life. A fine victory it was. Unfortunately, there may not be any alcoholic spoils; it probably all went up in the flames."

The soldiers moaned.

The next morning, Mick and Dave searched through the rubble and ashes for closure. They wanted to make certain no civilians were inside during the fire. They didn't find any bones or anything of the sort, but there was a lot of debris, and it wasn't physically possible to check every nook and cranny. They were still satisfied to the best of their discretion. However, they did find a bottle of booze that'd survived. From it, the soldiers all took what they called *victory chugs*.

"The town's inhabitants can start moving back now," stated Dave, putting on his pack in preparation for departure.

"Indeed," said Mick. "I'm sure the news will get to the Capital soon enough. However, it'll be a dead town for a while."

"What should we do with the prisoners? I'd hate to drag them all over the place with us."

"Good question," remarked Mick. "I think we need to locate some better restraints and perhaps a crew of travelers going to the Capital willing to contract with us and escort the captives."

"That won't be easy. There aren't too many folks who trek that far regularly. We'll think of something," said Dave, seeing everyone was ready to go. "Shall we depart?"

"Yup," replied Mick, just before the platoon went mobile. "I was really glad to see that this time Horace had found his courage and engaged the conflict."

"I'm sure he knew he was being scrutinized during the fight and found a little bravery and energy because of it. Regardless, who cares where it came from, as long as it's there."

"Precisely. Another thing I was pondering—as we seek to become a force with which to be reckoned—was how imperative it truly is to determine the trustworthiness of our soldiers. Whom can we trust the most?"

"Certainly," agreed Dave, walking backwards in front of Mick to make eye contact. "Of course, so far we have Gus and Vern. They've been proving their worth, no doubt, and can potentially take on further responsibilities receiving even larger stipends."

"Possibly. Just something we need to keep our eyes on, as things move along."

CHAPTER 10

To AVOID HAVING to climb over rocky terrain, Harry Shultz followed a trail going through the semi-arid fringe of the desert. The quicker he could reach the King with his information the better. There was just enough plant life available to keep him from being concerned about lack of water. He did have a lot of water with him, but the wise man always considers from where the next replenishment will come. Where there were plants there was water, or at least that's what his subconscious was telling him.

Meandering through only sporadic pockets of greenery, the cutoff trail that Harry was traveling wasn't very stimulating, except for the occasional vulture. He knew as long as he kept a certain rock outcrop within view, he wouldn't get lost. Garobansurov was full of shortcut paths allowing for the avoidance of landscape hurdles. Though, if Harry's path veered any further into the desert, he'd have to recalculate and head back to the rocky topography.

Nighttime was fast approaching, for which Harry was glad. He hoped the powers that be would grant him the privilege of spending the night in pleasant weather. Yet, Harry was grateful the periphery of the desert offered better conditions than its interior. Plus, he was happy the surroundings would allow him a great view of the stellar picture. It was a sight often limited in the typical forested environments of the rest of the country.

Harry wasn't able to carry as much weight as some of the other great trekkers of the land, but he did at least have a lightweight tent just tall enough for sleeping.

After he finished setting up his tent, Harry snapped his fingers in delight, pointed to his comfortable temporary abode, and grinned.

Before the sun completely set, he scanned the area for threats. Finding none, he lay in the sand watching the multi-hued sunset.

The sun disappeared and the beauty of the night sky enveloped him. He thought about all the times he and his family had spent gazing at the exact same constellations. He couldn't wait to see Will and his wife again. Harry wondered what they were doing at that exact moment. Perhaps, Will was getting ready for bed, begging his mom for a story, as he so often did; or maybe he was mischievously running around outside, forcing his mom to look all over, as it was time for bed. Will really was good at hiding. Harry couldn't wait until he was the one telling the story, or the one playfully searching for his elusive son all over the farmstead.

Early morning half-light was upon Harry. He was still fast asleep when danger approached. He'd foolishly forgotten to burn, bury, or throw far away what was left of his supper. Uneaten meat still sat beside the fire. Its scent had the ability to draw in ravenous carnivores from far off. Most were basically harmless, but unfortunately for Harry, the ones being lured in that night were members of an extremely dangerous pack of verids. These four-legged mammals had razor-sharp teeth, powerful forelegs, and claws the size of pinecones. Most people never saw one in their lifetime, since they typically kept to the barren places of the world—like deserts.

The verids fought over the small amount of meat by the fire, and greedily wanted more. They could smell prey nearby, but they couldn't see it. It didn't take long for them to figure out why. They ripped through Harry's favorite tent easily, sadly ruining it forever, and burst inside. Two of them, as wild animals inherently do, targeted Harry's vulnerable neck veins. Harry woke up disorientated. It took him a few moments to realize what exactly was happening. Instinctively, he reached for his sword on the left and stumbled out of the tent on his right.

He hacked and slashed with as much strength and speed as he could muster, but it wasn't enough. There were so many verids attacking him that he got overwhelmed. Bleeding profusely, his arms and legs were covered with bite and claw marks.

The only chance for survival in his mind was to go deeper into the desert. Maybe then they'd lose interest in him and stay at the campsite to scavenge. Resolved, he began to walk briskly away from his campsite, trying his best to keep the beasts off with desperate swings of his sword. He managed to slay one, but it barely phased the pack's intensity.

Further and further into the desert he went, becoming more and more surrounded by inhospitable wilderness. He lost his sense of direction, and eventually had no idea where he was.

Finally, one of the verids abandoned the pursuit and went back to the campsite. Harry thought maybe he'd survive the ordeal after all.

It took what seemed like a mile of walking, before the last verid turned away. By then, the sun was completely over the horizon.

He waited patiently, before attempting to return to his campsite, allowing the verids plenty of time to rummage and mosey off. While he waited, Harry tried his best to wrap his wounds with available herbage. But it wasn't working very well, as it kept breaking.

After a few hours, he began to retrace his footprints back to familiar territory. At first, it was easy, as the tracks were quite discernible. However, after a while they started becoming indistinguishable due to the sandy ground being transformed by the wind. Eventually, both his and the creatures' tracks were not detectable at all, having been completely wiped away. Panic set in. He couldn't detect at all where he was. Recognizable landmarks were nowhere to be found, even the massive rocky tor that could be seen towering over the horizon at his campsite had vanished.

Harry took his best guess at which direction to head, but things began getting even worse. For some unexplained reason, his vision became blurry, and he manifested dizziness. Was it a loss of blood? No, he'd lost the same amount in the past without getting dizzy. It had to be something else. Every step he took was excruciating. Even if the tracks reappeared, they'd be almost impossible to spot, due to his disorientated state.

Despondently, he slogged through a maelstrom of emotions. Harry couldn't help but feel he'd never see his beloved family again.

A HANDFUL OF DAYS after the village was recaptured and having spent an effort in vigorous recruitment, Mick and Dave's squadron had more than doubled in size. However, they still had the prisoners in tow, who all required 24/7 constant watch.

Bisecting a patch of yearling pine trees in the path, Mick said to Dave, "I hope the data we received a few days ago turns out being correct, that the next town on our route, Casil, hasn't been captured by the Molisians. I feel bad about last week, how the soldiers lost out on a night of revelry on payday, because of the skirmish."

"We'll know tomorrow. I'd bet the data is right, though."

"Let's hope."

"I have more hope for that than I do for these little pine trees here in the path surviving much longer."

"The Molisian army definitely didn't come south this way, judging by the trees' continued prosperity," noted Mick.

"Keep on fighting, you little pine bastards."

Post having successfully sidestepped all the pines and post lunchtime proceedings, Dave said to Mick, "My gut is going to explode. I'm pretty sure I ate more than my stomach lining cares to hold in."

"I heard once that our gastrointestinal systems contain within itself a second brain."

"That's interesting. I did not know that. Mine seems to be pissed at the moment," said Dave, looking back to make sure all of the crew was present for no reason other than habit."

"Speaking of eating, I recall Casil being the home of a renowned fine dining establishment suspended over a lake."

"Oh yeah, that's right. Old Man Johnson had once said that the behemoth cedar trees used as its stilts had come from a place near Chalatore. I forgot who it was, though, that told him, or if they in fact worked on the project."

"That's a long way to haul lumber," stated Mick. "They must be some pretty remarkable logs."

"I do know that I'm going to eat there for the experience of it and all."

"Me too. Sounds like a good place to bring dates. Do you think we can scrounge up some lovely ladies, while we're there tomorrow?"

"Does Ulfenkerki have an enormous amount of back hair?"

Mick chuckled. "They don't call him the Black Bear for nothing."

Taking into account how many soldiers were in Mick and Dave's unit, they were fairly orderly, having set up camp quickly and in systematic fashion. Organization breeds organization.

Atop a tall wooden pole, a well-loved flag waved in the wind. Along the way, Mick had acquired a large Garobansurov flag to mount at camp. It was always the first thing to go up, and the last thing to come down. A little patriotism goes a long way.

Sitting around the fire, Dave shared the potential good news with everyone. "Pending its status, on the day the morrow (payday) we'll sojourn in Casil for the night. Feel free to revel in any legal applications you'd like. For those of you who don't know, the town has a well-known restaurant that sits atop the water."

Most expressed amusement and made known they were going to patronize the restaurant, as none had ever been to one hovering over a lake before.

Daydreams of beautiful women in fancy dresses spread through camp that night.

At daybreak, Hawk and Leopard discussed between themselves the methodology of recruitment they'd employ in Casil.

Satisfied in their plan, they ordered the evacuation of camp, and the day's walk began.

They didn't even have to wait until Casil to enlarge the company, as they'd gained a few along the way, including the outfit's first woman.

From atop a hill, Mick and Dave could see the sparkling lake beside which Casil sat. "A few miles to go. We should be there in an hour."

"Sounds good," replied Dave, looking curiously at the trees around him. "You know, Mick, on a different note, I can't help but notice that trees are masters of balance. We'd be wise to strive for such athleticism."

Mick responded, "True. It's certainly impressive how they can remain upright in the harshest of conditions. As swordsmen, emulating this attribute would be worth the effort a hundred times over."

"Without a doubt. Adept balance does beget strong swordplay."

"It sure is an interesting topic you spontaneously threw at us, Dave. Keep'm coming."

"I'll try my best."

Just prior suppertime, they all came upon Casil. Half envisioned setting up camp on the outskirts of town, whereas the other half intended to stay at the inn, desiring to spend a bit of their well-deserved pay. Hopefully, there'd be vacancy. Mick and Dave accompanied those aspiring to camp and found a level, out of the way spot.

Subsequent tent erection, Dave and Mick went into town and learned there'd been plenty of rooms available for their soldiers.

Before they began recruitment, Mick and Dave handed out the weekly stipends. The soldiers would have no problems in Casil exchanging the gold coins for gitis, as the town had a bustling economy.

After a strong exertion in enlisting at one of the local taverns, Mick and Dave switched plans of attack. They began their attempt at finding dates for the evening, still wishing to patronize the platformed restaurant.

Not too many women ended up coming into the bar, so they had to try elsewhere. The pair split up, Mick heading south, and Dave heading north.

With a head full of optimism, Dave walked into a shop and scanned the scene for his type. At first glance he saw a few elderly women and a teenager stocking shelves. He walked deeper into the store and saw an attractive woman eying up yarn. He approached her, semi-nervously, and said, "Hello there. I'm Dave."

"Hello, Dave. I'm Liza."

"Nice to meet you, Liza. That is a pretty thread there. It would make a beautiful dress."

"It's my husband's favorite color, and he'd be thrilled if I were to fashion a dress out of it for our upcoming event."

"I'm positive he would be. What kind of event will you be attending if you don't mind me asking?"

"A retirement party at the Moonlight's Reflection. I have an 80-year-old aunt who is finally calling it quits as a teacher."

"She must've really liked teaching, having continued doing it into such an advanced age," responded Dave.

"That she did. The future generations of Casil will surely miss out on a great teacher."

"I'm sure they will. Is the Moonlight's Reflection the name of the restaurant on the water at the edge of town?"

"It is," replied Liza. "You've never been?"

"Nope, but I plan to tonight. I'm really looking forward to it. It seems absolutely breathtaking."

"Oh, it is. You'll love it. My favorite dish is their seafood pasta. Hopefully, the moon will be out, and like the name suggests, you'll get to see its reflection as you eat."

"That would be exhilarating," voiced Dave. "Well, Liza, I hope you find the right thread for your dress and have a wonderful time at the retirement party with your husband."

"Thank you, Dave. And I hope you have a wonderful time tonight as well. Goodbye." Liza looked back to the yarns, as Dave began walking away, but she realized she had something else to say. "Wait Dave! At the expense of me sounding awkward, I feel I must tell you something. I have a beautiful sister who happens to be single and would hate me if I didn't tell you she loves going to the Moonlight's Reflection. I assume you had approached me for the purpose of finding a date for tonight, am I right?"

"Is it that obvious?" Dave chuckled. "I really have to work on my technique."

"Oh no. It was flattering."

"Well, thank you." Dave blushed. "I would love to meet your sister and ask her to accompany me tonight."

"Excellent. I'll take you to her, as soon as I purchase this thread that you said would make a beautiful dress."

"It really will."

MEANWHILE, MICK had tried his luck twice already, but failed—one had ended up being married, and the other had a personality too abrasive to pursue. He wasn't losing hope, though.

He walked away from the main thoroughfare and into Casil's only lakeside park. Halfway through, he spotted a lady sitting on a bench watching the ducks. Mick instantly noticed she was the type of lady who could make a man's heart flutter. First, he removed the annoying rock in his shoe, then, he approached the lady and her bench as naturally and non-threateningly as he could.

Mick cleared his throat, and said, "I think the duck closest is the loveliest."

The lady eyed up Mick to see if she knew him. Having realized she didn't, she replied, "I'm partial to the one just behind it. I like how it has that white spot on its wing."

"Oh yeah, I can see the spot. You're right, that one is pretty. Nice to meet you, I'm Mick."

"Hi, Mick. I'm Lisa."

"Do you ever feed them?"

"I have a couple times. I've brought bread for them in the past. Most of the time they hang out on the other, quieter, side of the lake."

"I would too if I was a duck." The two chuckled. "Do you usually come watch the ducks alone?" asked Mick, hoping to fish her relationship status out of her without having to actually ask.

"Sometimes my sister comes with me. She was busy shopping today, though."

"It's nice to have company sometimes."

"Definitely, Mick." Lisa revealed, "If you look just off to the right, you can see the Moonlight's Reflection."

Mick was perplexed. "The moon is out already? I guess I missed it."

Lisa giggled. "You must be from out of town. That's the name of the restaurant sitting over the lake. I love it there. The ambiance is unforgettable. Unfortunately, I haven't gone in a while."

Mick smiled flirtatiously. "Oh, there it is. Yes, you would be right, I'm from Chalatore, many miles from here."

"I've heard of it. I've never been there, though."

"It's a quaint place to live." Mick noted, "I had actually considered going to the Moonlight's Reflection, thanks to you I now know its name, while here visiting Casil. But I was leaning towards not going, because I'm normally too shy to go to places like that alone. It's a pretty fancy place isn't it?"

"It's the fanciest place I've ever been to."

"But now that I think of it, if a beautiful lady such as yourself wouldn't mind being treated to dinner tonight, I could go without the discomfiture of being alone?"

Turning red as a tomato, Lisa replied, "I've never been asked on a date while sitting on a park bench before. I like it. Yes, that sounds lovely. Can I have an hour to get ready?"

"Absolutely. Take whatever time you need. I'll walk you to your house."

After walking Lisa home, Mick went back to camp to get ready. He would meet her back at her house in an hour.

THE FRISKIER INDIVIDUALS of Mick and Dave's troop wasted no time—they had a pocketful of a gold and the willingness to spend it all. Though unfortunately for them, there wasn't a single brothel in Casil, as it was a town striving for reputation. But there were plenty of elegant courtesans. The guys would have to settle for quality over quantity.

The randy soldiers found their quarry lingering about at the Moonlight's Reflection in alluring, form-fitting dresses.

Morale was high.

Those of the crew who didn't currently have coitus on their mind, but still wanted some action, met at the tavern on the main boulevard, where they intended to not only drink, but drink so much they wouldn't have a care in the world.

DAVE STRUTTED BACK into camp, saw his friend, and said, "I see success has smiled upon you, Mick."

"It has. How did you know?"

"Easy. It isn't every day you put your good pants on."

"Oh yeah, I forgot I did that already. Time to get fancy," responded Mick. "Well, did you have any sincerely edifying experiences in town as well?"

"I genuinely did. I'm going to have to put on my good pants too. I met an extremely beautiful girl at a shop and learned she was married."

Mick chuckled and interrupted, "I'm hoping there's more to this story."

"Funny. So, I was just about to part ways with her, but she beckoned my attention before I did and told me she had an available sister. I went to their house and was blown away by the fact her sister was even more beautiful than she was. I honest to God did a double-take and pinched myself. It was the kind of moment you only dream about. She was wearing a skirt so shiny I could practically see my reflection in it. I didn't even know such a fabric existed. I don't know how I did it, but I managed to get through the conversation and set up the date without sounding too stupid. This is going to be quite the unforgettable evening, my friend. I actually don't think I have pants fancy enough for this."

Mick laughed. "That brings back memories. Remember that time when we were teenagers, and you somehow got Wendy Joyner to go to the dance with you? When you had put your good pants on, you discovered a hole had somehow gotten in the crotch. Since you didn't have the time to fix it, you ran over by me to borrow a pair."

Laughing hysterically, Dave finished the story. "Yes, how could I forget. A week previous to that, I played a prank on you at school, and for retaliation you specifically gave me pants with a small hole in the butt—small enough that I didn't notice it when I put them on, but large enough that Wendy sure did. By the end of the night, she was comically sticking things in the hole."

"Well, at least she had to virtually touch your butt in order to insert things."

"Yeah, that part was nice. She certainly had a good laugh about it, though. I guess it was all worth it."

"To this day," Mick declared, "people still bring that up to me."

"Really? That's hilarious. I honestly didn't intend for the news of your misfortune to spread through town like it did."

"Sure you didn't."

"Anyways," said Dave, as dusk continued to descend, "tell me about your date."

"With pleasure. From the way you described yours, she isn't as life-altering, but she definitely has curves in all the right places and the kind of smile that makes a man truly feel alive. I met her at the park while she was admiring the ducks."

"She sounds lovely, Mick. We both will have a great night."

"We won't have any kind of enjoyable night, if we don't get going here."

"Indeed."

Mick and Dave finished getting ready, walked into town, and parted ways, both fully prepared for an influx of new memories.

IT WAS ONE of those nights where the air was so fresh and cool that it seemed to have a love affair with the lungs. Thankfully, the moon was out, and there wasn't a cloud in the sky, so those going to the water-top restaurant could enjoy the enchantingly romantic sight its name implied.

Mick found Lisa adorned in a black dress augmented by translucent sections in all the right places. The dress accentuated her femininity to a degree even more striking than Mick had the privilege of appreciating earlier. In looking at his date, standing there in her overly colorful living room, Mick realized he wouldn't have rather serendipitously stumbled into anyone else.

After pleasantries, emitting her customarily spellbinding dimpled smile, Lisa asked, "Do you like my living room?"

Too kind to tell her it needed more earth tones, Mick fibbed as best he could. "I love it. That chair in the corner looks very comfortable."

"It is. Why don't you go try it out?"

"Sure." Sitting in the chair, Mick commented, "It's as relaxing as it looks."

"When my husband died a handful of years ago, I almost got rid of it. It sorrowfully reminded me of him, as it was his favorite chair. But I decided not to, because I really do like its color and how it looks here in my living room. Besides, they just don't make very many bright red chairs."

"You're right, they don't. Wise decision keeping it, it is incredibly snug."

"I thought so too. Well, I'm ready when you are."

Having stood up from the chair, Mick responded, "Lead the way, beautiful."

Mick couldn't help but think the living room bore a striking resemblance to the lobby of the bordello that the squad had visited a few days ago. He threw the silly thought away and smiled at Lisa, as she grabbed her contour-fitting black and grey jacket—the icing on the cake of loveliness.

The two exited the house and started the walk to the restaurant, hand in hand.

IN THE MEANTIME, across town, Dave found himself to be quite nervous. For his date that evening was quite possibly the most attractive woman he had ever seen. He pondered, *Maybe protocol was different for perfect tens.* He shrugged the nonsense away, inhaled, and walked up to Liza and her husband's house, where his date, Verona, was temporarily living.

Liza answered the door. "Hi Dave. Come on in. Verona is almost ready, she'll be out in a bit. This is my husband, Steve."

Shaking the man's hand, Dave said, "Good to meet you, Steve."

"Likewise," returned Steve. "Have a seat if you wish. Would you like anything to drink?"

"I'll take a beer. Thank you."

Liza got the beverage for Dave and grabbed one for her husband as well. She knew her husband was always courteous enough to never allow a guest to suffer having to drink alone. It was a politeness quite typical of the area.

Steve said, "Forgive me if I'm wrong, but you're with the crown's soldiers presently in town, right? I've talked to a few of them."

"You are correct. My friend and I are forming a squadron for King Rowlangiv."

"You must be a high-ranking officer then, eh?" asked Steve, hoping for a prosperous match for his dear sister-in-law.

"Technically, no, we aren't actually soldiers of the army. I guess I could just explain it quicker by saying that I'm Dave Ghrere and my friend is Mick Thraiker."

"Really! Fascinating. Does Verona know of your importance?"

"I don't think so," replied Dave. "When I told her my name, she didn't react."

"Well, I'm certainly honored to be drinking a beer with you. I wish all the luck in the world to you on your mission. Have a fine evening with Verona. Speaking of, here she comes."

Having a particular proclivity for wearing enticing skirts it seemed, Verona approached Dave, this time wearing a double-layered one. The seductive, multi-hued garment emphasized her powerful, perfect legs. Verona faced Dave and crossed her legs—a subtlety of hers representing interest.

With a flirtatious tone, Verona said, "Sorry I'm late, I hope it's okay."

"Definitely. I was just getting to know your brother-in-law."

"Verona," blurted Steve, "do you know with whom exactly you're going out tonight?"

"Judging by the way you said that, I'm thinking it's a trick question. Dave. Dave Gear, I think he said his name was."

"No, adorable girl, not Gear, it's Ghrere," said Steve. "You know, Dave Ghrere and Mick Thraiker of Knowing Circle fame."

Verona looked at Dave wide-eyed, and then turned to her sister. "Did you know?"

"I admit I did not. Steve had just learned, as you were finishing getting ready."

Verona found herself getting weak at the knees. Even the most beautiful of women can be humbled by that which is unexpected. She calibrated quickly and pivoted back to Dave. "I guess I get to dine tonight with a hero."

"Well, I am modest, so I probably wouldn't call myself that," emitted Dave.

"I've heard of that modesty too," professed Verona. "Shall we proceed? Otherwise, Steve here will monopolize the situation and talk battle stuff with you all night."

"Now that I would probably do," admitted Steve.

"Under different circumstances, we would certainly do that," added Dave. "Yes, Verona, I'm ready."

Stationary positions were broken, and Dave and Verona followed the lot's hedge line to the lane leading to the lake.

The moon and stars were still favorably unobscured by clouds.

MICK AND LISA had reached the boardwalk one had to traverse to get to the Moonlight's Reflection. Before stepping onto it, Mick saw Gus and Verne, who seemed to be waiting for someone or something. "Hey guys, you look to be anticipating something?"

"Not really. Just admiring the view."

Mick muttered to Gus and Vern, while handing them each a gold coin, "Consider this a bonus. Dave and I chose you two as our right-hand men. We'll draw up contracts later, which will include even more of a stipend than what you've been already receiving. You've been doing an excellent job at night watch. I couldn't be happier with your performances. Come eat with us at the restaurant. Just don't sit at our table." Mick produced a laugh.

"Yes, we proudly take on this new responsibility," said Gus. "And as for eating, we will come do that too."

"Dave is here as well, or will be. Watch our backs. Anything can happen at a place like this."

"No problem."

Mick faced Lisa, exhibiting an apologetical demeanor. "Sorry for the delay. Just a couple guys in the crew."

"Crew?" remarked Lisa, with a quizzical countenance.

"My partner and I are forming a military band for the King. We've just decided those two to be our next in command."

"You know the King?"

"Yes. We've a strong rapport."

"Are you generals, or something of that nature?"

"Nope," replied Mick. "I guess over the years the King has gained a great trust for us."

"What did you say your name was again?"

"Mick Thraiker."

"It sounds familiar, but I can't say I know why."

"We'll talk more about that later. For now, let's enjoy this walk we're about take on."

"Sounds good to me."

The couple stepped onto the boardwalk that almost seemed to defy the laws of physics, hovering over the water mystically, as the poles holding it up had been cleverly positioned out of view. In pairs bookending the width, lighted candles were evenly dispersed along the floor of the boardwalk spanning its entire length. It no doubt added to the romantic atmosphere.

Halfway out to the restaurant, the twosome stopped to take a look at the water below and back at the gorgeous setting they left behind. The lanterns of town seemed to harmoniously match the stars of the night sky.

The restaurant itself was oval-shaped and without many walls. It was designed that way so patrons could freely view, smell, and hear the sounds of the lake.

Exuding savoir faire, the maître d' showed Lisa and Mick to their table. Mick looked around and saw Dave hadn't arrived yet, though he did see a handful of other crew members, some having very attractive dates of their own. Gus and Vern came in a few moments later and sat a few tables over.

Mick got comfortable and took his best shot at untangling the mystery that was the woman sitting in front of him.

Being her favorite part of the whole Moonlight's Reflection experience, Verona walked with Dave across the crescent-shaped boardwalk. Like Mick and Lisa before them, they also stopped halfway to look at the water and back at the beach and city.

"One time when I was here," voiced Verona, "I looked out at the lake and saw a giant fish gulp down a baby duck. It was one of the saddest things I've ever seen."

"That is sad. Poor duck."

"Needless to say, I've never ordered the duck. It *is* on the menu here."

"I wouldn't either after seeing that."

The flamboyant maître d' brought them to their table, which was coincidentally triangulated with Mick/Lisa's and Gus/Vern's. They all waved at each other.

PHYSICALITY BEGAN sooner for Dave than it had for Mick, as Verona was a sensual person, taking every opportunity to brush up on Dave. Dave took the hint with much glee and reciprocated without delay.

AFTER ORDERING their food, Mick and Lisa found themselves being drawn like magnets to the conversation at the table next to them. They couldn't help but halt their own discussion and listen in.

"You know, Nicole, I really don't like that you did that."

"You never said anything before about it," voiced the woman, Nicole.

"That's because I haven't had the courage to, up until this very moment," uttered the man. "Every time you invite your best friend out with us, I feel like a fifth wheel. You guys have inside jokes stemming all the way back to grade school, of which I have no understanding. Half the time, you get so drunk I have to carry you from place to place. You both ignore me. When I say something to the two of you, it's never important enough to garner attention. So, yes, Nicole, I am displeased that you invited her here, especially on our anniversary."

The woman responded, obviously dismayed by the turn of events, "Well, I am positively not going to send her home when she gets here. If you think I'm doing that, you got another thing coming, mister."

Mick and Lisa resisted further urge and stopped paying attention to the nearby kerfuffle, at least enough to talk to each other. "I can't wait," whispered Lisa, "until the friend gets here so we can see what happens next."

"Same here. We have to drag out our meal to prevent ourselves from being done before the friend arrives."

"Good idea. Do you think the lady will tell her friend about what the man said, or maybe do you think she'll try to terminate the evening as quickly as possible?"

"My guess is she'll tell the friend, but we shall see."

"Exciting to be sure," expressed Lisa, eyeballing Mick, experiencing a sense of connectivity.

ALAS, DAVE and Verona didn't get to partake in the entertainment amusing Mick and Lisa, as the domestic quarrel was happening on Mick and Lisa's other side. However, Dave and Verona were by no means starving for amusement—theirs was more of the sheer carnal sort.

Instead of waiting for their food at the table, they walked to the end of the restaurant to look out into the lake. Technically, it was just an excuse to get away and make out.

After the erotic kissing event, Dave confessed, "I'm really glad to be here tonight with you, you're are a very beautiful woman."

"I'm grateful my sister hooked us up too. What a gal!"

"We'll toast to her when we get back to the table. It surely is incredible, the image of the moon reflected on the water. The ripples create 10,000 wondrous points of shimmering light—truly a vision to behold."

"Yes, absolutely awe-inspiring," agreed Verona, licking her lips in preparation for round two of libidinous smooching. She didn't care if her food got cold. Neither did Dave.

SUSPENSE WAS ramping up, as Mick and Lisa swiveled their heads towards the squabbling couple and their unignorable drama. The friend had just arrived.

There was a moment when they thought they'd been bagged for spying. But all was good. They both made a mental note to be more discreet and to especially not turn their heads in such pronounced manners.

Enthralled, Mick and Lisa watched on with low profiles. It was a real bonding experience.

"Hi, Nicole, Phillip," said the friend.

"Hey, Justine."

"Are you ready to have a wild night? I know I am. I've been waiting all day for this."

"Well, Justine, maybe let's not get so wild tonight. It is in fact Phillip's and my anniversary tonight. I was thinking we could do something Phillip wants to do."

"Why didn't you tell me it was your anniversary before?" asked Justine, dumbfounded.

"I guess it slipped my mind."

"I'm a little upset. I could've made plans with someone else, but now I'm stuck."

"I'm sorry," emphasized Nicole. "You can still enjoy the night with us. Dinner is on Phillip and I."

Justine groaned quite audibly, sunk into her chair, and replied, "I suppose. I was looking forward to some fun, though."

Out of nowhere, Vern sauntered up to the table, full of charisma and confidence. He looked at Justine with the king of smiles. "I couldn't help but notice there being a pretty but distraught lady over here, so I took it upon myself to get her a drink. I'm Vern and who might you be?"

"Justine," she replied, graciously accepting the glass of cherry wine.

Vern looked at the couple, and said, "Would the two of you mind if I joined? I would be delighted to pay for all your meals if you extended me this courtesy."

Phillip and Nicole looked at each other, flummoxed. After a few awkward seconds, Phillip replied, "You may, but if it's not too much trouble, can my wife and I have the rest of the night to ourselves, after we eat?"

"Of course," responded Vern. "As we eat, I'll think of something else this lovely woman and I can do afterwards. If It's okay with her?"

Justine answered, "I'd be delighted."

"Have a seat then, Vern." Phillip was ecstatic, as his evening had just been saved.

"Thank you."

"Well, I'll be darned," said Mick, finally taking his attention completely away from the nearby table. "I wouldn't have guessed at that turn of event in a million years."

"It seems your next in command, one of them at least, is by no means a shy character," stated Lisa.

"Ain't that the truth? I like that *no messing around* attitude in him. What an exceptionally uncommon go-getter—a breath of fresh air. Rigid adherence to prototypical disposition can sure get mundane after a while."

"Speaking of not being mundane, our chance meeting definitely wasn't mundane, that much I know. I can't say I've ever had anyone approach me at the park before."

"How often are you there, though?"

"I'd say often enough to get noticed," replied Lisa.

"Well, I certainly took notice. Your beauty definitely drew me in from afar."

"I'm glad I remembered to bring my beauty with me that day then. I tend to leave it at home sometimes."

The pair shared a laugh, and Mick finally saw the opportunity to go in for a kiss—her eyes were practically begging for it.

Mick declared to himself the kiss was magnificent, brimming with chemistry. What a perfect moment, he thought.

After they ate the sensational meal, they went to the restaurant's edge to gaze out into the lake at the moon's reflection—a romantic precipice like none other.

Another couple was nearby jabbering about some nonsense involving their busy schedules. Mick and Lisa ignored them, as their dialogue was nowhere near as interesting as that of the squabbling couple's. However, they were an attractive couple adorned in their evening wear. Both Mick and Lisa couldn't help but steal a look.

Mick got back on track, by telling Lisa, "Your beauty definitely belongs among the stars."

"Well, thank you. It's afraid of heights, though." The pair shared another laugh.

DAVE AND VERONA couldn't hold in their lustful urges any longer, the tugging was too strong. They rapidly finished their entrees and hightailed it out of there—straight to Verona's bedroom. They could have gone to Dave's tent, but Verona's place was closer, plus roomier.

FINISHING UP their desserts, an indulgence Dave and Verona had voluntarily skipped, Mick and Lisa were enjoying each other's company considerably.

Mick commented, "I wonder what they do here on windy, rainy days. You'd think if it were windy enough, the rain would get blown in here, getting everyone wet."

"I'm pretty sure the restaurant just closes during those times."

"Ah, makes sense," remarked Mick. "I'm having a really wonderful time, Lisa. You are excellent company."

"I concur. I'm glad you found me today, by the ducks."

"Me too."

As Vern and Justine walked past Mick, he got their attentions, and said, "Hey Vern, how was your meal?"

"It ended up being spectacular. I met this lovely lady here. Now, we're going to go sit at the bar, and savor some spirits."

Accompanied by two thumbs up, Mick communicated, "A fine evening to you two. Enjoy those refreshments."

After Vern and Justine walked away, Lisa asked Mick, "Are there any members of your crew in the restaurant anymore?"

Mick looked around. "Nope. I guess we win the coveted *last ones standing* award."

"Die-hards we are."

The moon's image had traveled far on the lake's surface in the amount of time Mick and Lisa were at the restaurant. It was undoubtedly time well spent.

Having finally left the charm of the lake and restaurant behind, they returned to her place, where Mick once again found himself surrounded by colorful furniture. Enthusiastically, Lisa sat down beside him, and the pair followed in Dave and Verona's footsteps of desire.

Neither Mick nor Dave slept in their tents that night. As you would figure, a good time was had by all.

Forming a world enriched by luminosity, the sun ascended, ensuring that life goes on as it always had.

Having woken with satisfied libidos, Mick and Dave met up at camp and discussed the cavalcade of bygone events.

CHAPTER 11

SOMETHING was all wrong. Not that Anna slept very soundly in her prison, she unexpectedly woke in a cold sweat. She looked around in a panic but saw nothing at first glance. She craned her neck to listen if anything out of the ordinary was occurring up in the bar. There was a commotion, but there were always commotions.

She looked up through the chute, and saw smoke, but no more than usual. The only thing Molisian soldiers did as profusely as drink was smoke.

Ultimately, she channeled her panic into concentration, and realized it was just a nightmare that'd startled her in her slumber.

Anna resumed normality. Or what could be considered under her circumstances the closest to it.

She'd spent her first week of confinement looking for a writing utensil of some sort (a vital tool with which to pass copious time), but after searching every nook and cranny, she gave up. Instead, she'd devised an ingenious system to be able to play a solitary math game her grandfather had taught her.

Surely, the one thing her surroundings were in no short supply of was pebble-sized rocks. They mainly fell out of the dirt walls and accumulated in clump-like masses on the ground. She'd gathered hundreds of them in all sizes ranging from the miniscule to nearly fist-sized.

The next step to prepare for the game had taken her weeks to perform. She'd separated the multiple-sized rocks into ten different groups, each consisting of equally-sized specimens. She then denoted each group with a single digit, numbered zero through nine. The group with the smallest pebbles represented zero, the largest represented nine, and every number in between. There were also rocks that represented mathematical operations: addition, subtraction, multiplication, and division. She used irregular-shaped rocks for these. But all that was the easy part of this step.

The next phase of the step was memorizing exactly which rock size symbolized which number, so that when they were all mixed together, she could randomly withdraw one and know exactly for what number it stood, plus operations. Her game called for quick recognition. She had to be able to gauge the rocks at speed. As a matter of preference, it'd taken two weeks for her powers of rock identification to be at a satisfying level, enough for the game to commence.

The parameters of the game, as handed down by her dear grandfather, had been implanted indelibly in her mind.

The first thing she had to do was construct numerical templates with her rocks. Each consisted of interweaving horizontal and vertical lines of correct math equations. She made patterns with two, three, and even four single- and double-digit numbers vertically and horizontally. Ultimately, each grid had exactly four, nine, or sixteen minuends, subtrahends, dividends, divisors, factors, and/or addends. Once a template was finished, she removed the central mathematical expressions, leaving only the outer expressions. The rocks that'd been removed were put into a pile of complete randomness. The object of the game was to then insert the numbers and operations from the jumble back into position to line up with the answers. She couldn't just think back and remember what belonged where, as she spent an entire week only making the patterns, eliminating any chance of cheating. She lacked an eidetic memory, so it sufficed.

The entire floor of the garbage chute was lined with strategically placed rocks—a chaotic array that only she could interpret.

It was a difficult game, especially when there were sixteen calculations to figure out, but Anna had all the time in the world to play. The game made her prison experience as close to tolerable as she knew possible.

I wish I had the opportunity to truly thank you grandfather for the game you so cleverly invented, that and so many other things. The game has been an adequate distraction. I even like the name you gave it: Slot'em'in. Rolls right off the tongue.

I need your company, guidance, and love now more than ever, grandfather.

I move as if every step is a year down here. It's so hard.

But maybe by the end of this ordeal, I'll be as good at Slot'em'in as you were. No doubt, my ability to fight boredom is attributable to your genes. Thanks for the priceless inheritance, it's really coming in handy.

For as grueling as these past weeks have been, for the unimaginable cruelty I've witnessed, I resolve to survive and cherish all that's been given to me. If I make it out alive, I vow to never take life for granted.

There's a sound I've never before heard while down here. An owl must be nearby. I hope you stick around madam owl; I get so sick of listening to only drunks.

I wonder what a drunk owl sounds like.

ONE DAY, as Anna was playing her mathematical pastime, she came upon a particular number that had a significance in her past. A powerful memory was brought to the forefront of her mind. The number was 400 and the answer to the line consisting of the product of a couple 2s and a couple 10s in her game. She recalled the memory's entirety.

It was the *summer of freedom*, she called it. She had just purchased her first home and was relishing an emotional high, due to the exciting experiences she anticipated her new home would provide. There were many great memories attached to the home itself, but the recalling of those were for another day.

The house was a block from the carnival grounds in town, which Anna thought was delightful. She also really liked the vacant field adjacent her property. But she mostly liked how she could have anyone she wanted come over to visit at any time. The last people with whom she lived by no means granted her that privilege. They weren't exactly mean, but it was just human nature to be picky about visitors. Not everyone likes everyone.

Carnival time was approaching and with it really great news. Anna's favorite musical group since she was a child was called Thrill—one word, short and sweet. Thrill consisted of three members, all masters of their respective string instrument. The organizers of the carnival had fronted enough gitis to bring Thrill to its mainstage, thanks in part to a sizeable donation from a local business. Seeing that Thrill would perform so close to home was a dreamlike occurrence for Anna.

Blessed with living next to an empty field, Anna envisioned a pre-concert scenario where her friends and family—and maybe even a few enemies—gathered together and camped in the field. She fell in love with the vision so much that she resolved to see it through to fruition. She invited everyone she knew to participate. She didn't care how many showed up. It was to be a glorious weekend of remembrance.

Carnival time rolled around, and Anna's eyes sparkled with eagerness. She woke up early, set up her own tent in the field, and waited patiently for someone to come. And come they did. Her closest friends were the first to arrive, followed by dozens of other folks craving a good time. The entire field eventually became 3/4 full of tents and sleeping carts. Anna didn't even know half of them. She didn't care.

The time leading up to the show was as exciting as Anna predicted it would be, overflowing with comradery and good spirits.

Seeing her favorite band perform live at the carnival turned out to be even more momentous than she forecasted. She'd heard them twice before, but nothing beats hearing your favorite band in your hometown.

After the show, the party continued at the field. Even more people than before showed up at this point. Nobody wanted to go home, and Anna's field was the perfect place to go and drink.

Anna found herself sitting around one of the fires with a couple people she knew, and a couple she didn't. The two she didn't know were rather interesting characters, so overall it was a jovial assemblage.

The two strangers had suntanned skin, perfect teeth, and told really interesting stories about their travels. One of these yarns involved a situation where they'd bet another person that he couldn't run a certain distance in a certain amount of time. The context of why the bet happened in the first place was another story in and of itself. In the end, the interesting strangers had made quite a bit of money by winning the bet, as the time criteria was not met by the other party.

Anna threw a log on the fire, and said, "So how far of a distance are we talking about here, and in what amount of time?"

One of the interesting strangers replied, "It was a mile and a half, and the time was 400 seconds."

Intrigued, Anna replied, "Was the course uphill or downhill?"

"It was a flat course, of which we stepped off the distance."

The other interesting stranger chimed in. "Everyone said the guy was the fastest endurance runner in all the land, and that if he couldn't perform the feet, no one could."

After doing a few mental calculations, Anna blurted out, confidently, "I could do it!"

The two interesting strangers were taken aback by the astonishing proclamation. Skeptically, they analyzed Anna for a moment. "What makes you think that?"

"I'm an avid runner and have come close to running that distance in that amount of time before. If the stakes were high, I think I could possibly do it. Plus, I'm on an emotional high right now, seeing as that I've just seen Thrill, my favorite band."

The strangers looked at each other and agreed on the next course of action. "If you're serious, let's wager then?"

"Sure, if I can afford the terms, I'm in."

"We won't make the bet unreasonable. How about a mere 200 gitis? And since we're humble guests at the gathering that you yourself organized, we will graciously throw a bonus prize into the pot if you should win."

"I like it," responded Anna. "That bonus prize sounds rather enchanting. I can afford that. Let's do it! I'll go to my house and get my wager money."

"After that, we'll step off the course together."

Anna returned and the party created the mile-and-a-half course, making sure it was flat, as it was for the previous runner.

The exact timing of a given activity was always difficult. Common practice for that region was to say the number of the count, followed by saying, "Garobansurov" in accompaniment. *One Garobansurov, two Garobansurov, three Garobansurov*, for example. It was as close to a second as possible.

By this time, a boisterous crowd had gathered for the running event, as it was a rather interesting nighttime affair for all. Many knew Anna was a good a runner, as she'd run speedily past their homes many times in the past. Some even thought she could accomplish the seemingly impossible feat. They cheered her on fervently.

Anna took to the starting line, accepted heartfelt encouragement from her friends, and when the interesting strangers said, "Go!" she bolted away gracefully. Many spectators audibly participated in the count: *One Garobansurov, two Garobansurov, three Garobansurov.*

Most cheered for her success, as opposed to her failure.

Anna ran as fast as her lungs allowed, digging deep into her storage chamber of sheer will. That which clung to the bottom was especially arduous to get at. She could feel the alcohol that she'd consumed affecting her, but the miniscule disturbance of her mental state didn't alter her confidence. Her persistent sense of self-assurance was substantiated by how fast everything was whizzing past.

Her eyes became a picture of perfect focus, her legs one of fluid motion. Her arms sliced through the air elegantly. Her heartbeat was as rhythmic as the ocean tide. She was driven by passion.

On the homestretch, she could hear the congregation yelling out numbers—*350 Garobansurov, 351 Garobansurov, 352 Garobansurov.*

Almost there, less than a minute to close out the remaining distance, she said to herself before all thought dissipated.

For the last leg, she switched from running aerobically to anaerobically, a finishing kick, or so she called it.

She released an adrenalizing holler and lunged for the imaginary transverse line representing the finishing point. The interesting strangers were standing near the line and dropped their jaws.

The assemblage became thunderous. They knew exactly what'd happened.

With a stentorian voice, one of the interesting strangers said, "Not in a million years did I think our challenge could be fulfilled. That was the greatest run I've ever witnessed! You've achieved the unachievable. The winnings are yours."

After catching her breath, Anna pronounced, "Now that was a good time!"

The other interesting stranger maintained, "As promised, when you're ready, we'll deliver you to your surprise reward."

Anna was rushed by suspense, her emotions surged unrestrainedly. "I'm as ready as I'll ever be. Can I bring a friend?"

"Of course."

Accompanied by the friend who held the pot money while the run transpired, Anna followed the men back through the carnival grounds, a place now empty of everything but refuse.

"I'm sure they are still awake. They always stay awake for a few hours after the show."

Anna became perplexed. "Who is 'they'?"

Beaming his perfect smile, the interesting stranger answered, "We figured that since you'd organized the entire campout, you're one of Thrill's biggest fans, and that you'd get a thrill out of meeting Thrill."

Anna had no idea the surprise was going to be so grand. Flooded by disbelief, she stood there in frozen paleness for many moments before replying, "That would be fantastic! Nice play on words there, by the way. Do you know the band or something?"

"We are their managers. Being as nationally recognized as Thrill doesn't come without the necessity for the hiring of managers. We're in charge of marketing, promoting, contracts, organization, and even some heavy lifting."

"Makes sense. And I'm guessing you don't tell many people this, so that way you don't get hounded by fans for autographs and such?"

"Exactly. We assume the band will want to meet you, since you're such a big fan. Plus, I'm sure they'll be intrigued by your run, as they had also thought the exploit wasn't accomplishable."

Anna and her friend were led to the inn near the carnival grounds and introduced to Thrill. Anna was ecstatic to learn that her favorite performers in all the world were genuine and personable. They talked of the running endeavor, amongst other things, for over an hour. She knew the experience was something she would remember forever.

Ann loved thinking about that memory.

I still can't believe I ran a mile and a half in 400 seconds. I highly doubt I could do it again. The stars must've been aligned. The calculus behind the human body, and when it wants to perform at maximum capacity will always bewilder me. Nobody will ever know exactly how our complicated internal systems work. I know I'll never quantify it. Though, one thing I do know is if the King's armies ever do get around to reclaiming this town, I hope they don't burn the tavern to kill the Molisian soldiers within. I doubt I could outrun a fire.

LETTING MORE of the day soak in before departing, Dave and Mick spent some time brushing dirt off their tents. Dave vocalized, "I was disappointed this morning, Mick."

"And why might that be? Having relations with a beautiful girl just isn't enough for you anymore, eh?"

A comical chill shot through Dave's spine. "Oh no, that was more than adequate. The disappointment arose when I woke up and yet again discovered the physics of the world were all still the same."

"I didn't know that was something you hoped would be reformed." Mick chuckled.

"If we were to witness an alteration in the paradigm of physics, proof in the existence of magic would be definitively revealed. I guess the whimsical side of me always wants the world to be more magical."

"Perhaps, a rearrangement in the archetype of physics would demonstrate that we're just hallucinating everything," suggested Mick. "Or that we don't even exist at all."

"It's too early in the day for *that* much philosophy. Let's just go see if everyone is ready to depart."

"Good idea."

Everyone was in fact ready, and in no time the platoon left the idleness of town behind.

Along the walk, Mick and Dave wrote up new contracts for Gus and Vern, around which the establishment of *next-in-commands* revolved. Gus and Vern would be the next tier down from Mick and Dave. Gus and Vern were ecstatic to gain so much trust.

After the formalities, Mick asked Vern, "How did the night with Justine end up? My date and I couldn't help but overhear the little domestic dispute that'd transpired. You really saved their day. I couldn't believe my eyes when you showed up out of nowhere like that."

"Yeah, she told me all about her friend's husband being sick of fifth-wheel status. I don't blame him. Who *would* want to sit there and be ignored? Anyways, Justine and I stayed at the restaurant until it closed and followed through on the evening back at her place. Gus took the easy way out and purchased a lady. I on the other hand am resuming our journey a little wealthier than he, avarice getting the best of me sometimes."

"That it does, my brother," asserted Gus. "I'm more rested than you, however. My activities wrapped up at a reasonable hour, unlike yours."

"We'll see how tired I get as the day wanes," commented Vern. "Then, we shall see who was more productive."

Mick added, "I think it's safe to say the stopover went well for everyone."

Mick and Dave spent the next few miles discussing the details of Gus and Vern's promotion with them. There was more to it than just being labeled with a fancy new title, obviously. Gus and Vern paid utmost attention to Dave and Mick. They didn't want to disappoint two of the very few people who'd ever given them a chance to be somebody. Many had designated them lazy in their hometown, but to Gus and Vern it was done by those who didn't fully understand them. Both Gus and Vern were the type who couldn't pretend to work, like most people could, so they were often seen doing nothing. In reality, they finished their designated tasks quickly and intelligently, and had plenty of time leftover for screwing around. Finally, they had run into people, Mick and Dave, smart enough to realize they weren't slothful at all.

Gus and Vern were enjoying life in Mick and Dave's squadron; in fact, there weren't many complaints all around.

The next couple of days were mainly spent meandering northward through the countryside. Ghrere and Thraiker tried their best to recruit amongst the local population, which consisted of predominantly farmers. They weren't very successful, like usual with farmers. In two days, they only gained three soldiers.

On the third day after leaving Casil, Mick and Dave came to a fairly isolated section of Garobansurov. Towns and villages of any size were rather scarce. The area was known as the Infertile Zone. Geologists were prone to say the area was sterile due to glacial till. There were scattered pockets of farmable land, but they were quite infrequent. The King didn't even tax the land within the

Infertile Zone. Those who desired to homestead therein were given free rein to set up wherever they wanted, free of any charge. Garobansurov's most skilled farmers, nomads, and hunter/fisherman/gatherers were known to occupy the land. They say half of the nation's folk heroes had lived in the Infertile Zone at one point or another. Many songs had been written about this citizenry.

Realizing where they were, the crew merrily sang one of these songs, a melodic chantey about Grizzled Jim, a legend who'd lived in solitude for 30 years and ate only meat derived from animals killed by his bare hands. Mick and Dave wished they could recruit Grizzled Jim. It was too bad he'd been deceased for nearly a century.

Subsequent the convivial tune singing, Mick said to Dave, "Undeniably, we won't accomplish much enlisting these next few days, as we navigate the Infertile Zone."

"True. Inhospitable desert reaches up from the west, and untraversable swampland resides in the east. So, there's no avoiding it."

"There's quite the amalgamation of divergent ecosystems in this area, though, that's for sure."

"Yes. Maybe it has some cosmic significance."

Mick chuckled. "I doubt that."

SOMEWHERE IN-BETWEEN the unpreventable thoughts of never seeing Will and his beautiful wife again, Harry somehow managed to cling onto hope. He wanted to at least find refuge and a water source, as he'd since given up on finding his way back to the campsite. He concluded that the more he searched for that, the further into the desert he strayed. Harry resolved to stick to the area familiar to him, and to fan out from there.

If he could at minimum find shelter, he was confident panic would dissipate, which in turn would make coping with the nausea and dizzy spells much easier.

He made sure to always keep a fixed high point in his line of sight, as he radiated out, which was a certain unmistakable tree miraculously succeeding in desert survival. Its canopy was high enough in the air that it could be seen for almost a mile in every direction, thanks in part to it growing on a hill.

It had taken him two days at practically a crawl, but Harry had already gone north, south, and east of the tree, finding nothing but sand and sparse vegetation. Only west remained.

Thankfully, it wasn't as hot for his westerly trek. It was an omen, perhaps.

With the gnarly branches of his new favorite tree at his back, Harry ventured into the unknown. Unlike the previous two days, he began to see wildlife: vultures, lizards, and scorpions—anything to keep his mind from depressing notions of doom.

What I wouldn't give to find a friendly wild animal for a companion.

He hated when a hill came into his path, because it meant the guide-tree wouldn't be observable for an amount of time. The farther away he got, the more daunting the hills became.

Awe crap, another hill.

Aiming for the summit and trying to quell his newfound hatred for hills, he slowly started to climb the loose sand of the hill. He was losing hope, for he was already a good distance away from his guide-tree. He was certain he wouldn't be able to continue west very much longer.

Harry reached the apex of the hill, scanned the new horizon, and unexpectedly felt a tear of joy roll down his cheek. For in his scan, he'd seen the tops of manmade structures nestled beside a dried-up riverbed.

Shelter at last!

Quickened by both the magical sight and the downhill grade, Harry beelined towards the buildings. Only a few hundred more steps would tell if it was a lifegiving oasis, or some iniquitous mirage cruelly playing tricks on his scrambled mind.

BAD NEWS had sprung up for Mick and Dave's party. Almost half had contracted an infectious agent of some sort, probably from Casil. There must've been a virus circulating amongst the prostitutes, tavern regulars, and restaurant patrons. It was a rare occurrence because it wasn't winter, though summer bugs did occasionally show their ugly faces.

Trying to fulfill a need to get through the Infertile Zone in one piece, the group trudged along, reluctantly.

Hoarsely, Dave said to Mick, "You always seem to be lucky when it comes to avoiding sicknesses."

"I can't argue with that."

"You're lucky I like you, otherwise I wouldn't be keeping my distance," uttered Dave, endeavoring to uphold his comical nature, even when miserable. He thought it might ease suffering just a bit, as laughter was sometimes stated as being the best medicine.

Mick chuckled. "Yes, good thing. How bad is it?"

"It's not the worst illness in the world. Walking with it is tolerable, but if it gets worse, or some other compounding calamity presents itself, I would recommend discontinuing the walk."

"Alright. I'm glad the troops haven't complained too much yet."

Slogging a dozen paces behind Mick and Dave, an unhealthy Vern said to a healthy Gus, "It seems you got the better end of the deal by getting more sleep. My lack of sleep probably weakened my immune system."

"That's probably true, but you still ended up a winner, as I'm sure you enjoyed better conversation with your lady. Mine was nothing more than a business transaction—greatly lacking in congenial company."

"Good point," replied Vern. "Justine and I sure had a charming time."

"But at least we now make enough money to purchase women who specialize in being both attractive and personable," observed Gus, with a large smile."

"I like the way you think, brother!"

"Me too."

Mick and Dave decided to make camp a little early due to the illness, wishing the new morning would bring better health. One thing they knew was that the beauty of their chosen campsite definitely wasn't going to make anyone feel better. It was a pretty nondescript place. Even the limited trees seemed plain. The only positive feature was a solitary flat-topped stone, the perfect size to set the evening meal atop.

Mick and Dave deliberately pitched their tents in moderate seclusion, so they could discuss the private matters of the platoon before going to bed.

Dave said, "We're almost up to forty soldiers now. We've got a long way to go. Good thing the gold supply is plenty adequate."

"I concur," voiced Mick. "There are many settlements for recruitment north of the Infertile Zone and south of the impassable stretches of the Baustic mountains. I think we'll have a sizable army eventually, barring tragedy."

"Same here. And I'm glad we haven't had any deserters yet."

"Definitely. We must be doing something right," said Mick, as he went into his tent for the night.

At daybreak, Mick asked Dave, "How are you feeling?"

"The good news is I'm not any worse, the bad news is I'm not any better."

"I'll go ask the rest how they're feeling."

Mick received a unanimous response to his inquiry: No better, no worse. As expected from folks under the weather, it took longer than normal to set down camp. But once it was finished, the moderately sick troop resumed walking with minimal objection, mainly because they all desired to be free of the Infertile Zone. It just wasn't a very invigorating place.

The gang was moving along at a satisfactory pace when a verbal dispute occurred amongst the ranks.

Acting directly on the behalf of solidarity, Mick and Dave rushed to intervene in an attempt to keep the quarrel from escalating. After much discussion, the altercation was successfully pacified. There was no way of preventing such incidences, especially in close quarters. Mick and Dave hoped future disagreements were insignificant, and the overall harmony of the squad continued to be as commendable as it was before the dispute.

Mick gulped down a massive swallow of water, and said to Dave, "That incident would've never happened on the condition that people didn't believe practically everything they hear."

"Indeed. It's human nature to believe what you hope to be true."

"That it is. Just like the other day when you informed me that I was a better swordsman than you. I wanted to believe you, so I did."

Dave nearly choked on his immune system's phlegm when his laughter escaped. "I would've believed I said that, provided you had changed the word *better* to *equal*."

"You must've been daydreaming as you let it slip."

"Yup, yup."

Mick looked to the west. "I actually hope I'm daydreaming now, as those clouds off in the distance look pretty dark."

"Sorry," communicated Dave, "you're not."

FOR THE MOST PART, General Gamald was behaving himself while in lockup. As promised, he and his men were allowed the comfort of alcohol and smoke on occasion in reward for good behavior. These accommodations weren't special, as this particular policy was granted to all of Garobansurov's prisoners. Why mess with something that worked? In the event that Gamald or his soldiers ever tried to escape, these privileges would've been revoked indefinitely. The King's prison system wasn't cheap on the surface, but it saved money in the long run.

General Ulfenkerki hadn't given up hope in trying to end the war through Gamald. A few times a week he paid the opposing General a visit. Gamald was a definitive power player of Molisia—at least the half with which they were at war.

There were no intentions of relocating Gamald to anything other than the securest of cells. However, in the last few weeks Gamald had earned certain upgrades: better bedding, more foods from which to choose, personal comforts along with the alcohol and smoke, and more time in the yard. Ulfenkerki couldn't help but think Gamald had something sneaky planned. Nonetheless, Gamald received what he deserved.

His morning was free, so the Black Bear headed to the cells to check in with Gamald.

Ulfenkerki nodded to one of the soldiers on guard, and said to the prisoner in the cell, "How's constraint treating you this morning, Gamald?"

"Better than death." Gamald moved from the far end of his cell to the near. "I haven't asked in a while, how's the rebuilding coming along?"

"As you know, the battle destroyed a huge portion of town, but we're resourceful, and reconstruction has seen substantial progress."

"You may not believe this, but I'm glad to hear that. I have no reason to want the people of your country to suffer."

"You know just the right things to say, don't you," noted Ulfenkerki.

Gamald chuckled in his typical supercilious way. "They teach us that at *How to be a General* school, but you obviously know that."

"I do. I graduated with honors."

Gamald sat on his bed, while Ulfenkerki matched the tension-easing gesture by sitting on a wooden, three-legged stool situated just outside the cell. Ulfenkerki was surprised the stool still supported his weight, as it was old, having been in that exact same spot for as long as he could remember—decades.

Gamald stated, "You may not think it, judging by the youthful appearance of my soldiers, but many of them are very practiced in carpentry, stonework, and a myriad of other expertise. Many problems arose on our march here that required knowledgeable hands, problems easily remedied by the young soldiers in the adjoining cells."

"I've talked with a few of them, and you're right, many do seem to speak with the nomenclature associated with ability," agreed Ulfenkerki.

"I propose to you," voiced Gamald, "that my soldiers help you with the necessary overhaul of your city, and in that assistance we could be compensated with a larger supply of liquor and smoke, maybe an occasional conjugal visit."

"I didn't know your soldiers' significant others were in the area for conjugal visitation."

"They're not." Gamald chuckled. "I guess in Molisia we refer to a conjugal visit as a sexual visit from any individual. You have prostitutes here, don't you?"

Ulfenkerki returned the laugh. "Whether the King wants to admit to ignominious prostitution or not, we have plenty. You can find ladies of the evening at most of the Capital's drinking establishments."

"I guess you Garobansurovians aren't all boring twats."

"Unfortunately," blurted Ulfenkerki, "I highly doubt the King will fall for that trick and let you and your soldiers out of confinement and onto the streets for repair work. He knows how crafty you are. However, I will bring it up to him, and maybe we can come up with some other sort of arrangement."

"Very well. But if that arrangement has anything to do with ending the war, I unequivocally meant what I said when I said I don't have much influence over that."

"Right. So how about you, General, do you have any aptitudes other than military leadership?"

Gamald stood up and reached for something under his bed. "In matter of fact, I do. I'm not half bad at intricate carvings." Gamald handed Ulfenkerki a little wooden sculpture resembling a woman's silhouette.

Perusing the sculpture, Ulfenkerki said, "She's got the makings of quite the ravishing woman. Someone you know?"

"Once, long ago."

"How may I ask are you carving it? We certainly haven't allowed prisoners knives of any kind."

Gamald showed Ulfenkerki the backside of his dominant hand. "I have razor sharp fingernails—keen enough to chip wood. The matrix I found in the yard. I'm pretty sure it's oak."

"It is. I can tell oaks by the aroma. Well then, enjoy your hobby," stated Ulfenkerki, handing the carving back. "I'll get back to you about your proposal as soon as I speak with Rowlangiv."

"I'll be here."

"I guess the old adage might be true, maybe the wise man does learn more from his enemies than a fool learns from his friends."

Gamald laughed. "In the whole scheme of things, we're not really enemies."

Later that day, Ulfenkerki met up with King Rowlangiv at the castle to discuss Gamald's proposition, among other things.

Rowlangiv suggested, "I'm on my way downstairs to the recreation wing, if you don't mind accompanying me there for our discussion."

"Are you pondering any mode of amusement in particular?"

"I think anything that involves running, as I've been pretty uncharacteristically lethargic these last few days, regrettably."

The King and his General engaged in a few Garobansurovian leisure activities, breaking sweats and breathing hard, while discussing recent developments. Ulfenkerki told Rowlangiv all about the proposed repairs, the liquor and smoke compensation, the carving of the lady, and even the conjugal visits. Rowlangiv mulled it all over until the last point was scored in their competition.

Taking his shoes off, so his feet could breathe, Rowlangiv said, "I'm not about to give Gamald and his soldiers any special treatment compared to the rest of our prisoners. I don't trust him or like him, nor am I empathetic to his plight. Who knows what machinations he's menacingly brewing? However, we normally allow prisoners certain in-house work privileges, as it's not easy passing up on cheap labor. I think it would be feasible to allow them to repair mobile apparatus from within their cells. Plus, I think it'd be achievable for them to spearhead a project creating various artistic displays for the city."

"That's an insightful idea," voiced Ulfenkerki. "Since transportable repair work would be limited, having them also do aesthetic arrangements would give them plenty on which to toil."

Exactly," remarked Rowlangiv. "Under no circumstances are they allowed out of the confines of the jailhouse. I can't stress that enough. For their work, we can pay them in extra liquor and materials for smoking. As for conjugal visits, have we been allowing that for our other prisoners?"

"Not usually. I think only in rare circumstances. Mainly only when the head count is low."

"It's definitely not low now. I think more fights than normal would breakout if one person is having relations within view of another who is not."

"Yes, good point. Such a scenario would also be true for even those not currently incarcerated," stated

Ulfenkerki. "We'll keep conjugal visits off the table, figuratively and literally."

"It's settled then, General. In other news, I know I'm satisfied that my heart was put through a good workout. I don't feel so lazy now," declared Rowlangiv, grabbing a towel to wipe off sweat. "Actually, thinking further, I'm not seeing any reasons why the Molisian prisoners couldn't start this enterprise post haste."

"Sounds good. I'll form a committee in charge of overseeing it all—probably tomorrow. As for right now, unlike you, my heart isn't done receiving workouts. I have a conjugal visit of my own to attend to."

Rowlangiv chuckled. "Have fun with that. Don't forget to wash off your sweat first."

The Black Bear satisfyingly popped his shoulder while stretching and returning a chuckle. "I didn't need to break a sweat to beat you."

The King laughed wholeheartedly. It was something he really needed.

UNLUCKILY, THE RAIN cloud spotted earlier had engulfed Mick and Dave's party with unsympathetic wet drudgery. The sun's warm, cheery glow had dissipated completely.

Surrounded by the Infertile Zone, and having walked in a heavy downpour for a couple hours, Mick said to Dave, "This may seem weird, please don't think I'm loony, but that point a few hours ago when the rain started feels further back in time than it really was."

Dave pondered Mick's off-the-wall statement a few moments before replying. "You know, though, nothing about the mechanics of time has really been proven. It's very well possible that things occurring further back in time actually happen sooner than things occurring recently."

"I have no mathematical formula to disprove that possibility. It sure is interesting to ruminate upon such alternative conjecture."

"I agree. Notwithstanding, I've always thought you to be a bit on the loony side, Mick."

Mick laughed harmoniously. "I wouldn't have it any other way."

The group trudged in the rain for another half an hour. Having realized something, Mick voiced to Dave, "I can't help but notice how laborious your walking gait has been of late. Is it the sickness?"

"Usually I'm too proud to speak up, you know me, but I actually was just about to do so. Yes, this cold rain—at least it feels cold to me—coupled with the illness has truly been insufferable. I imagine the rest of the crew accompanying me in the sickness are feeling the same way."

"For starters, you are like that—stubborn till the very end. I guess I am too," emitted Mick. "Yeah, I was starting to see the pain in your eyes and the struggle in your steps. I feel much empathy for you and the rest. I'm sure there won't be any objections if we call it a day. We'll stop for recuperation the next chance we get. I'm positive a suitable campsite will present itself soon, optimistically, one that offers reasonable protection from the elements. This wind is tumultuous today, getting out of it will be my primary concern."

"I'll go inform the others of the plan," announced Dave.

"You just want to be the good guy," said Mick, chuckling.

Dave turned around to shoot back a beaming smile. "Oh, my friend, I already am the good guy."

"Sure, sure. You keep telling yourself that."

CHAPTER 12

FORGED BY YEARS—maybe even decades—of wind, the sand dunes Harry had to traverse to reach his destination were endless. The rooftops he'd spotted from the heights of the hill were further away than they originally appeared. But, thankfully, when he'd gotten halfway, he realized that what he saw were indeed buildings, and not something deceptively looking like them. If he could run, he would've, but all forms of tenacity had long since vacated his legs. The ailment negatively affecting him, whatever it was, had no intentions of going away.

His perseverance having paid off, Harry approached the building complex. He could tell immediately the compound was abandoned, as there were no signs of life, no footprints, no motion, and no sound other than the wind. But there was a well!

He beelined to the sight-for-sore-eyes and lowered the weighted bucket into its depths. When it reached the bottom, he closed his eyes and muttered a wordless prayer. With eyes still shut, he began to crank the bucket back up. He grabbed the rope with his other hand and tugged slightly. Never in his life was he so happy to feel the normally cumbersome presence of added weight.

Surprisingly, the bucket was bereft holes and practically filled to the top with water. At that sight, he wondered why the homestead exhibited nary a soul. He also noticed the buildings were old but not ridiculously decayed and unlivable. Farm fields no doubt once vibrant with agriculture could be seen at the compound's periphery, but now it was a place only for the hardiest of weeds. Last but not least, there were enough trees for shade. It wasn't a bad place at all.

He resolved to perform a closer inspection of the place later. For the time being, he was content shoving as much water as he could into his stomach. Water to an extremely parched man was greater than almost anything to anyone at any time.

He set the bucket down, looked at it for a few moments admiringly as if it were gold, and proceeded to the closest building, complemented by a lens of curiosity. He was overcome with the sort of inquisitiveness a person only feels a handful of times per year—maybe even per lifetime in some cases. He just hoped he wouldn't find dead bodies strewn about.

The particular building before him looked like a home, judging by the external latticework. Opening the front door required a strong push. Appreciatively, no dead bodies greeted him immediately. He was correct: it was a home. The interior of the home matched the exterior in level of deterioration—no surprise. Some of the rooms had dilapidated furniture and some had none.

Having stepped over his fair share of fragmented odds and ends, he'd concluded the tour of the home's entirety. But he still didn't know why its former residents had vacated it.

Harry exited the building and carried onto the next.

The next edifice in sequence didn't resemble a home. It had the hallmarks of a storage shed—probably used by the whole community. He went inside and sighed at seeing all the neglected tools. He wished he possessed the non-rusted versions of such a collection at his own home.

Before moving on, Harry became disoriented and had to sit for a spell. His condition was really starting to worry him.

There were four structures left to explore. He determined to save the biggest for the last inspection—the best for last. His next three building explorations were habitations almost identical the first and also lacking corpses. He made a mental note to scan the surrounding area for a cemetery when the building surveys were complete.

Moving on to the last of the six erections, Harry finally became disappointed there weren't any people around, even though he figured there wouldn't be ever since first laying eyes on the place. A tiny part of him thought maybe everyone was waiting patiently in the last building to surprise him. But he dismissed that silly notion rather quickly.

Gaging the innards of the last house, he thought something was odd, but he couldn't place what precisely it was. Solving the riddle was like an unreachable itch he had to scratch. Inquisitively, he pondered, as he stared at a parallelogram on the floor created by light squeezing through the window. Eventually, Harry had to surrender to the unknowing, but he knew it would bother him indefinitely.

Subsequent giving the rest of the abode a walk-through, a bout of nausea and lethargy accosted him. Consequently, he had to abandon previously conceived notions of searching for a cemetery and the rest of the outlying area. He'd have to carry out these intentions some other day, as his unexplainable symptoms won over, forcing him to fall asleep right where he was.

HUNDREDS OF MILES away from Harry, the Thraiker and Ghrere party was taking longer than expected to locate a suitable campsite.

Finally, they found a small settlement where they could drive stake, despite having previously aimed to avoid settlements for the evening. But it was all they could find, as they needed some sort of respite from the wind.

Mick said to Dave, "I'm thinking a closely-knit group resides at this settlement."

"Possibly. Unfortunately, I doubt one of those buildings is a quaint bed and breakfast."

"I doubt it too. Hopefully, our merry band isn't too intimidating for them."

"We'll find out soon enough," voiced Dave. "You can perform the advocatory talking, Mick, since my voice is still pretty hoarse."

"Alright."

The small colony consisted of a dozen buildings, centered amongst prolific farm fields—rare for the Infertile Zone.

As the platoon approached, they unexpectedly saw people working the fields in the rain, moving about the buildings. Rain pounded on the rooftops in unignorable melody.

Just prior initiating oral contact with the strangers, Dave articulated to Mick, "I wonder if they devised a trick of some sort—a fancy fertilizer perhaps—to bolster their crop production, as their farms appear to be surprisingly prosperous in a land with famously defective soil."

"I doubt they invented something extremely innovative, otherwise they'd be selling the technology as we speak and living much more luxuriously than this," logicized Mick. "They're more than likely uncommonly knowledgeable in agronomy."

"Good point. I just hope they don't want to charge us an exorbitant fee to camp here or something."

"I doubt they'll do that, Dave."

"I think your life might be easier, Mick, if you didn't insist on doubting so many things."

"I doubt that too." Hesitating nary a moment, the pair took to laughing.

Wet as a lake, Mick and Dave walked into the heart of the settlement with their armed crew as non-threateningly as possible.

Two of the strangers in particular seemed to be the designated speakers of the outpost, for they were the only ones walking towards them. The rest carried about their business.

As the leaders, Hawk and Leopard walked ahead to greet, while the rest lagged behind.

An older woman with a winning smile and kind eyes shook Mick and Dave's hands, followed by a sluggish man roughly the same age as the lady. She emitted, "Welcome to our corner of the world. I'm Lois and the man beside me exuding tremendous energy is my husband, Gregory. What may we do for such a respectable group of—what I'm presuming to be—soldiers?"

Mick and Dave took note of the woman's sense of humor. They liked her immediately.

Having remembered the easy way to greet people, Mick courteously replied, "Thanks for the warm welcome. I'm Mick Thraiker and this is my friend, Dave Ghrere." Mick paused to see if their names were recognized. Having seen that they weren't—not too surprising since they were in the middle of nowhere—Mick continued, "We are on assignment from the King to reclaim the northern towns taken by the Molisians. Though, bad luck struck, as we've been stricken with illness. This, in combination with the torrential rain, has shepherded our march to a standstill. We've been looking to escape the wind, but since there aren't many forests or rock formations around, your settlement has been our first and only prospect. Would you be so kind as to allow us to make camp in your colony?"

Lois replied, "It shouldn't be a problem, as long as you can offer some sort of proof that you are indeed emissaries from the King, and not Molisians masquerading as such. I would feel much more comfortable."

Mick responded, "I definitely understand. With everything going on lately, you can never be too cautious." Mick slipped off his backpack and reached inside to grab an item. "This is the official seal of King Rowlangiv. He gave it to us just before we departed, so we could manufacture binding contracts for our enlistees. Feel free to compare it to any official documentation you may possess for authenticity."

Gregory joined in the conversation. "We won't have to trouble ourselves with that. After having thoroughly scanned your crew, I recognize a few of them: trustworthy men with whom I did business a couple years back. Drive stake wherever you find room."

"Excellent," noted Mick. "I'll tell the soldiers they can begin their setup. They'll be pleased to escape this miserable weather. Before I forget, about half of the crew are sick, just so you're aware."

"Alright," replied Lois. "Those among us who are uneasy about such things will, I'm sure, maintain their distance. Though, most of us here aren't dictated by minor worries."

The squadron began the ritual of tent erection in an area between all the buildings, the section seeming most out of the wind. The tents were strategically pitched in a side-by-side, oval formation. They and the permanent structures fused together to form a cocoon of comfort. This arrangement would keep as much of the wind and rain out as possible.

To resume the previous conversation, Mick was invited into Lois and Gregory's home. Dave had since retired into his tent to rest.

Gregory brought Mick an overly sugary beverage, and asked, "Why did the King send you and not the actual army?"

"General Ulfenkerki and his army—along with the Icytryxans—are protecting the Capital, while the remaining generals are currently far to the west. The King felt we were perfect to spearhead such a task."

"What is an Icytryxan?" said Lois, through a quizzical countenance.

Mick inhaled a deep breath and began expatiating to the pair, who in their isolation were understandably unaware of distant events. He expounded on the Icytryxans—the mission across the sea to form the alliance, the battle at the Capital, and everything else important that'd transpired along the way.

After the discourse, Lois commented, "I guess we really are cut off from the rest of the world here. But I suppose we like it that way. Though, it's too bad no Icytryxans accompanied you; I would've valued the encounter."

"I'm sure you'll get the chance to associate with an Icytryxan at some point, as they'll be our allies for a long time to come."

"I'm happy to hear that," remarked Lois. "So, how many villages need to be retaken?"

"We're not really sure, but my estimation is a few larger towns and a few smaller towns. Optimistically, we plan to increase the size of our squad by quite a bit yet, as some of the cities we have to reclaim are being held by pretty substantial forces."

"You can try to recruit here if you'd like," voiced Gregory. "Some of our younger residents might want to sign on."

"Much obliged," said Mick. "I'll talk with you two later. I'm going to go see if the crew needs help with anything."

"If you need anything from us, feel free to ask. We aim to assist the King as much as we can."

Mick joined in on the tail end of camp preparations. Looking around and seeing how haggard many looked, he really felt bad for the afflicted. He got to work gathering scrub brush from the nearby countryside for firewood.

By the time Mick was finished with the procurement—having inadvertently placed himself on the precipice of exhaustion—Dave had fallen asleep for the night, completely defunct.

Virtually all of those who were sick had gone inside their waterproof tents right away. Practically everyone else hadn't waited long to follow suit.

Not wanting to sit boringly inside a tent for the rest of the night twiddling thumbs, Mick and Gus found an awning to stand underneath.

Humbly watching the lightning, Gus asked Mick, "Did you learn anything about the history of our gracious hosts?"

"Not really. We didn't get that far, having mainly discussed everything concerning Garobansurov's recent events."

"I imagine being in seclusion comes with a measurable lack of familiarization. It really is a quaint, old-fashioned complex, undoubtedly attached to a reasonable amount of freedom. And hardship."

"Quite accurate, I'm sure," responded Mick. "Lois and Gregory did propose there may be a few of their fellow villagers wanting to join our cause."

"Splendid," said Gus. "I hope we don't get them all sick first."

"True." After witnessing a bolt of lightning crack nearby, Mick erupted, "Wow, that one struck close! Maybe only a few hundred yards away."

"Really gets the ole heart pumping."

Gus and Mick watched the storm from under the awning for an hour longer, then played cards for an hour more under the protection of Mick's tent, activities that were undeniably better than thumb twiddling.

Gus departed Mick's tent, and the two joined the rest in slumberland.

The fast had to be broken in the rain, since the storm hadn't let up one bit during the night. Realizing the rain was still coming down in buckets, and the community sickness was still at full force, Mick and Dave discerned the platoon wasn't going anywhere anytime soon.

By afternoon, Mick and half the soldiers had crafted a solid rapport with mostly everyone in the settlement. They'd been invited into many of their homes to pass the time. Those stricken with the uncooperative illness mainly stuck to their tents to sleep, as it was turning out to be quite the intense malady.

With Dave sidelined, Mick solitarily went about the business of recruitment—a seemingly profitable business, for half a dozen of the villagers appeared interested. Mick just had to close the deal.

FEELING COMPOSED enough in the morning to walk around again, Harry decided to venture outside for exploration, hoping the influx of energy wouldn't cease. As soon as he stepped out, he was unexpectedly blasted by a swarm of gnats. They were everywhere. But they were only gnats, so he appropriately paid them no mind.

Having already discovered water, Harry longed to find food—food of any kind. He thought maybe there would be some in the houses, but after searching, only found a minimal amount therein. Luckily, scattered amongst the weeds of the old farm fields was a fair supply of potato plants. He figured there'd be enough potatoes to keep his stomach from hurting for a week.

He picked what he could find effortlessly and put them in piles. Next, he began carrying them to the house in which he'd slept the night before. A process, however, that was not without humorous incident. Every time he dumped one of the loads, having been transferring them in his shirt, a potato would annoyingly roll away down the steps. By the third batch, and the third time chasing a potato, he couldn't help but laugh at himself. Anything to be optimistic.

After the potato mission was completed, he continued the slow but steady scan of the surroundings. Ultimately, he concluded there wasn't a cemetery. He thought the past residents mustn't have had very many deaths.

Harry found himself engulfed in attempting to discover how long ago the last occupiers of the settlement vacated. There were only insignificant clues, such as the condition of foot trails, the volume of litter (most of which had long since blown away by the wind), wear and tear of the buildings, and rust levels of metallic tools left out in the open. He extrapolated the compound had been free of people for at least half a decade. Unless major renovations transpired, it'd be free of tenants indefinitely. Though, Harry was unquestionably grateful exactly the way it was.

At the end of surveying the adjacent lands, Harry sorted out what his favorite part was. Roughly 200 feet behind the buildings was a grove of deciduous trees that seemingly defied the laws of nature, specifically the law of negative gravitropism. A law that stated, provided no outside influence, a tree's trunk will always grow opposite the pull of gravity. These trees were all growing at a 45-degree angle, and all in the same direction. It was as if someone long ago had deliberately influenced them to grow like this for aesthetic purposes. If that was the case, they did a marvelous job, for the display surely was a sight to behold. Plus, the locale was adorned by an out-of-place rock, superlative for sitting. It was as though the rock had been impeccably placed there for that very reason. The rock was heavy, so it would've been an arduous task.

Post inspection of the location's bygone usage, Harry plopped himself on the *sitting rock*. Absorbing as much fresh air as he could, he contemplated ways in which such a hefty rock could've been placed there. All of them involved great teamwork.

As soon as his affliction got worse, needing to lie back down, he returned to his resting house. But first, he made sure to grab a large supply of water from the well.

That way he'd have some readily available for the nighttime hours—a small convenience to remind himself he was human.

MICK WATCHED SILAS practice on the atlytl, proud of the progress the comparatively old gentleman was making. Hawk spent much time with the healthy soldiers that day in the name of training—a productive but wet enterprise.

At the end of the day, Mick gathered together all those of the settlement thinking about singing on. There were six of them. Most of them were young but old enough to swing a sword and sign a contract.

Mick thanked Lois and Gregory for allowing him to have the meeting in their home, then he addressed the hopefuls: "We appreciate your interest in joining our squad. I had shared with you the general information earlier. I mainly wanted to talk with you all now, so I could answer any questions you may have. Did you get a chance to talk with our soldiers, asking them if they have any regrets about joining up?"

The oldest of the lot, a man by the name of Leon, replied, "I did, and they were admittedly satisfied with their decision to join you."

A lad named Marty uttered, "I got the same. I know I for one am not suited for a life of farm work. I've always wanted something else, given the opportunity. And this is the best one that has presented itself. Count me in."

Leon asked, "The King really gave you enough gold to conscript an entire army?"

"Not an entire army, but one sufficient enough to accomplish our task," replied Mick to the unexpected question. "Though, let's not worry about that right now. I mainly just want to discuss any concerns you may have."

"I guess I'm concerned about how you're going to prevent your gold from getting stolen when your army gets substantially larger?" asked Leon. "And without the gold, you wouldn't be able to pay me every week."

"To answer your question, my collaborator and I promote and pay extra to those we feel valuable in the face of mutiny."

"Can anyone receive these perks?" inquired Leon.

"Certainly, as long as you earn them."

"Very well," responded Leon.

After all questions were asked and answered, Mick was content that most of them would sign contracts before the platoon departed the settlement.

Mick went into Dave's tent to discuss the meeting he'd had with the enlistees and its overall success. Dave was glad at the news and wished he weren't still ill, so he could've helped.

Rain continued to fall copiously, as the sky—though impossible it may seem—became an even darker shade of black. The soldiers wondered, *How dark could the day sky possibly get?*

To pass the time, Gus and Mick visited Lois and Gregory in their home, as many of the soldiers were still closed to reciprocal conversation, having every intention in the world to sleep off their sicknesses.

After the four ate a satisfying meal, Lois posed, "I'm in the mood for a fire. Would you guys like to sit and tell stories around the fireplace tonight?"

"That would be lovely," answered Gus. "Unfortunately, I'm not a very good storyteller, but I am a good listener."

Lois remarked, "Listening is just as important."

Mick and Gus went outback to grab some firewood, which conveniently was dry because it'd been covered under a securely fastened tarp. Securely fastening your tarps was key.

Gus started the fire with ease and sat in an available chair to do his listening.

Mick kicked off the evening of narratives with his telling of the events leading up to that point, beginning with the Molisian attack on the Capital. Gregory and Lois were riveted, as they were thoroughly interested in the occurrences of Garobansurov, the country they loved. They were also dumbstruck by the fact they'd never before realized the walls of their house created an echo effect. These acoustics unquestionably made for an enjoyable storytelling experience.

After Mick's account, Gus stated, "I've actually been curious about what exactly compelled the people of this settlement to sprout roots here in the Infertile Zone, and how long you've been here."

Lois replied, "It's a rather long story. It'll really test those listening skills of yours. Are you up to the challenge?"

"The longer the better," responded Gus, enthusiastically. "But first, let me go grab a couple more logs for the fire and take an extra-long time to water the bushes."

Lois chuckled. "Do what you gotta do. How do you know it's going to be extra-long?"

"They always are," answered Gus, accompanied by an unorthodox sense of accomplishment.

True to his word, Gus returned many minutes later. He threw the logs in the fire, sat in his chair, and leaned back comfortably. Lois cleared her throat and got to business telling her tale:

> "We've been here for a little over half a decade. The charter members of our group have always preferred out-of-the-way places, where we can stake out a peaceful living. The Infertile Zone fits that description splendidly. Lucky for us, we're blessed with a couple adept botanists capable of farming just about anything and teaching the rest of us how. There is also a chemist amongst us, Leon, but it seems he may be joining you. It's okay though, he has passed on to us much of his knowledge already.
>
> "We are happy here—well, most of us anyways. Those leaving with you have always expressed interest in doing so, so it comes as no surprise. I won't trouble you with the extraneous details concerning their reasons for wanting to leave. I wish them well.

"We were also happy at our last habitation, but that came to a dreadful end, and so we packed up and relocated here. The previous residency was in many ways congruent to the one we're at now. It was not an easy place to farm, but we accomplished it, nonetheless. It had only one water source, and huntable game was scarce, along with shade. And I mustn't fail to mention that visitors were no doubt infrequent. All in all, we didn't mind any of that so much. What we did mind was to come.

"The story now takes us a little over five years ago, many miles away, to the setting of our last homestead. I remember it well. It began on an abnormally cold day. I easily recollect those sorts of days because I perpetually don't like them. Like usual, most of us were tending to the fields, tediously performing the various measures required to grow edible flora.

"It was a good thing I was digging with my trusty shovel, for without it in my hand at the exact moment of the attack, I surely would've perished. I wasn't the one to see them first, but I heard the bloodcurdling screams of she who was. The ferocious four-legged creatures sprinted down a hill straight at us with only one thing on their mind: fresh meat. I ran as fast as I could, but I wouldn't have made it to refuge if I hadn't executed the perfect shovel swing. I couldn't do it again if I tried. Miraculously, the business end of my shovel struck the snout of the predator wanting to eat me. The perfect swing gave me just enough time to escape into the nearest house.

"I was close enough to my doom that I remember to this day precisely how bad its breath was. Trust me, you don't want to know that smell.

"My beloved husband was luckily in the opposite field, having been far enough away from the attack to make it to safety unscathed.

"Taking pride in having successfully negotiated a quick fallback, I took a deep, memorable breath. I peered out the window to gauge how the rest were fairing. I wish I could've joined the physically-strong members of the community, rushing out with weapon in hand to help. I could see people running past from my vantage point, but I couldn't see what exactly was transpiring in the fight.

"In the end, I was told one of the creatures was killed, while all our people survived. However, four villagers were badly injured, riddled with bite and claw wounds.

"At first, our injured didn't seem to be in any real danger of not surviving.

But eventually, all four of them became increasingly sick. Nobody knew why. At first guess, one would've postulated that the beasts wielded a venom of some sort. But no animal of that size was known to be venomous, so therefore no anti-venom existed. Fortunately for us, we had a hobby chemist amongst us, Leon, who took it upon himself to examine the dead beast and attempt to create an anti-venom. However, Leon was one of the four victims and was unable to give the task full effort.

"In the days to come, Leon scientifically established that the creatures were in fact toxic. After a thorough investigating, it was discovered that the animals must've recently mutated, having not been poisonous in the past.

"I have since forgotten the actual name of the beasts.

"As time went on, our injured kept getting sicker. To make matters worse, it wasn't the last time we would see the ferocious beasts. Shattering our illusion of safety, they came back repeatedly, unsatisfied in their results.

"We wisely heeded caution at this point, as none of us ventured far out into the fields out of fear of suffering a bite. Thank goodness, no new bite victims arose since the initial attack.

"Our patients were near death, circling the drain, including Leon who no longer had the strength to work on the anti-venom.

"We'd sent someone to the nearest town of size to gather information about our circumstance, but to no avail. Nothing valuable was known of the creatures. To my knowledge, nothing is even known to this day.

"We were growing tired of the beasts and the fear they brought with them and were seriously considering leaving our homes for greener pastures. We held a group meeting to talk of the issue. In the end, we unanimously decided to leave. By doing so, we could also provide for the sick some last beautiful sights before they died, deaths which seemed inevitable at that point.

"The very next morning saw us all loading up our carts with the essentials. We left behind that which wasn't necessary, as the axles of our carts were bereft fancy bearings. Toting an overly heavy load for many miles wasn't in our destiny.

"The four who were dying were lifted onto a cart, which certainly was a hard thing to do, as we loved them all.

"We glanced one last time at what was our treasured home for so many years, and then, stimulated by hope, we bravely began the next chapter of our lives.

"The daily pattern of searching for a new home commenced, and after being on the road for weeks, we were given a surprise. One of our sick started to get better: Leon. However, the rest remained inches from death.

"A day after Leon's turnaround, the first of our patients passed away, followed by the rest the day after. Thankfully, prior to dying, the three got to witness one final, multi-hued sunset from atop a long boardwalk spanning out into a sparkling, picturesque lake. The residents of a nearby town were gracious enough to allow us to bury our fallen in their cemetery.

"Now reduced in number, our closely-knit band of family and friends gathered as much strength as we could and continued our search.

"A few days subsequent the funeral, Leon was able to walk, showing signs he was going to make a full recovery. We asked him why he thought he lived while the others perished. He answered by saying that it must've been the one time in his life when luck was on his side.

"We came upon many potential locales for our new home, but none of them had what we desired most: seclusion. Finally, we heard about this place called the Infertile Zone, where few dared to reside, due to poor soil for farming—plus, it hosted the advantage of being tax-free. Only Garobansurov's hardiest individuals lived therein, we'd heard.

"Being stalwarts, skilled in cultivation, and endurers of adverse conditions, we thought, *Perfect!*

"Finding the area required a little backtracking, though. A minor inconvenience. Once we reached the Infertile Zone, it took a few days to locate just the right setting, but eventually we stumbled on our spot here. Our botanists determined the soil could be transformed into something farmable, and with there being a nearby water source, we declared the journey over. We haven't regretted the location we chose ever since."

"You weren't kidding," said Gus, standing up, stretching, and walking off a sore butt, "that did fully test my listening skills. Quite the robust, extemporaneously told story. I'm certainly glad you found a place that suits your needs."

"Ironically, a few days ago, we were at that lake town of which you spoke and ate at the restaurant on the boardwalk," voiced Mick.

"Lovely place isn't it?" said Lois.

"Indeed."

Gus and Mick hung around for another 20 minutes before going back to their respective tents. They fell asleep, listening, yet again, to the sound of rain hitting their tents. It'd been a pleasing sound at first, but got rather old after a while, as anyone who'd spent multiple rainy days in a tent would tell you. Good thing it wasn't windy as well.

The platoon was especially fortunate that the tents were keeping out water, as there's nothing worse than a wet tent.

Fully renewed after having one of those deep sleeps one can sometimes have while surrounded by fresh air, Mick sprung out of his tent. He was pleased to see the sky wasn't so dark and that Dave was looking spry again.

Mick said to Dave, "I see you've performed the famously arduous task of igniting a fire in the rain."

"Breakfast is halfway cooked as well."

"That's the Dave I know and love!"

"It's the one I love too."

Mick threw a dry log onto Dave's fire, and said, "I hope this morning we find the rest have beaten the virus too."

"I spoke to Vern previously, and he was feeling better. As we speak, he and Gus are helping one of the villagers spread fertilizer."

"Excellent, glad to hear it."

"I haven't spoken with anyone else yet, but I've seen a lot of movement in the tents, so there's potential."

"Maybe this rain will even stop," commented Mick, shaking the accumulated rain off his tent.

"Let's hope."

Fatefully, an hour after Mick had mentioned it, the rain completely stopped. Finally. Mick and Dave also learned that most of the soldiers were feeling better. They decided it was time to move on.

Encapsulating efficiency, all the tents were taken down and everything was picked up. Besides the impressions the tents had left in the grass, it now looked as if nobody had even been there.

Mick went to say goodbye to Lois and Gregory. He thanked them along with the rest of the villagers for their hospitality. He even promised them he'd put in a good word with the King to keep the Infertile Zone tax-free, not that it was in any real jeopardy.

To Mick and Dave's liking, all those previously interested in joining the platoon signed contracts. Four well-equipped soldiers were added to the ranks. The settlement dwellers were sad to see the four go, but they knew it was what their companions desired. The villagers were also a little glum to see the platoon depart from their desolate corner of the world. Human attachment came quickly and without warning to good-hearted folks.

Almost forgetting what it looked like, Mick and Dave navigated the squad into favorable weather. The sojourn no one planned was now officially over.

ANNA FOUND the mornings to be the most tolerable part of the day.

Wow, they're loud! I wonder if it's only men who move around so much and with no obvious reason for doing so. Maybe women do too, I just never noticed, as I've never had nearly as much time to observe the fairer sex. The soldiers definitely aren't as loud in the mornings, thankfully. It's the little soldier, actually, who is the loudest. He and his little feet, back and forth all day long. I know that can't be productive, backtracking usually never is. The pointless patterns never cease. It reminds me of a bunch of squirrels running around aimlessly with nary a nut to gather in sight. Squirrels do it instinctually to be a tougher target for carnivores. Now that I think about it, I wonder if humans hereditarily manifest the same trait. Like the squirrels, maybe at one point in our evolution, we humans were chased around by hungry animals much larger and stronger than ourselves. Moving around for no apparent reason may very well be encoded in our genomes. Interesting theory, Anna.

After her typical morning deep thinking, Anna played a few rounds of her math game to calm her mind. One might think math would overheat a mind just as much as deep thinking, but this wasn't the case for Anna. She was something else, incontestably in a class by herself. A bird of unparalleled beauty stuck in a cage, needing to be set free.

Intending to magnify sound, she cupped her ears with her hands and listened to the soldiers above. The charm of cheap entertainment was too alluring to avoid.

The soldier nearest Anna said, "In reality, I'm starting to get worried. It's been a long time since we've heard anything about the march southward. You'd think by now if we'd been victorious in taking the Capital, General Gamald would've at least sent an emissary with the game plan. It doesn't add up."

"It's possible," voiced the lowest pitched man of the garrison, "our raiding force was utterly dismantled, and that their King is biding his time, hoping we seizers of his country's northern towns will tuck tail and flee back to Molisia."

Another soldier declared, "He can bide his time all he wants, I know I'm not going to abandon our position. Besides, I doubt he'll send too large of an army northward, leaving the Capital relatively undefended."

"Right," agreed the deep-voiced soldier. "If the Garobansurovians did actually end up winning the battle, a mere skeleton crew would now be guarding the King. I think we can handle anything they could afford to send at us. Thanks to our recent plundering of nearby farmhouses, we have more than enough provisions to last a while. Though, we'll have to go on a few more booze heists, as it tends to disappear rather quickly around here."

The man nearest Anna said, "That won't be easy. We've already ransacked every home within a couple mile radius of here."

"Then I guess we extend that radius a couple miles more," blurted the soldier Anna considered to be most obnoxious. "I'm not going without my tasty mead. Has anyone ever actually searched every nook and cranny of this building for more liquor, including down in the garbage chute behind the bar over there? You never know, they may have thrown half empty barrels down there."

The next few moments lasted an eternity for Anna, as she waited for the response.

The serious character Anna labeled the leader spoke up. "You can crawl your fat ass down there if you want, I'm definitely not."

The obnoxious one returned, "I could get down there no problem, but coming back out is where I would run into difficulty."

Anna was relieved nobody ended up volunteering for the job.

She hoped to hear they would create larger looting parties, seeing as though they were now going to travel further for booze. This in turn could leave the bar empty for the first time ever. An empty bar meant an easy escape.

No such luck, as the soldiers mentioned nothing of the sort. Although, she held onto optimism that they may still do it.

It was now the time of night when the alcoholic soldiers slurred their speech too much for anyone to fully understand their conversations. Plus, their asinine nighttime dialogue lacked anything resembling a complete sentence. So, she discontinued listening to them and switched over to her math game.

She played with fervor. There was even a time when she almost forgot she was in her dreadful prison. These were the moments that kept her sane.

Before falling asleep on the far-from-comfortable pile of garbage, she daydreamed of spontaneous cherry pie appearances—her favorite. Maybe she was no longer as sane as she thought.

CHAPTER 13

DESIRING TO BREAK the repetitive subconscious thought sometimes associated with walking, Dave decided to initiate conversation with the nearest person, Leon. "Mick told me all about the story Lois shared involving your group's coming to the Infertile Zone. It was quite the story."

"That it was," returned Leon. "Almost dying is pretty much the scariest thing imaginable."

"You're right about that. I've certainly had my share of experiences under that paradigm," said Dave, trying not to think back. "I understand you know a little about chemistry. How did you acquire such a rare knowledge?"

"Through my father, and him from his father; you know how that goes. Apparently, my great-grandfather was once hired by the Crown to be the official apothecary. He fashioned all sorts of useful potions for the nobles and royals. Some are even still in use to this day."

Dave inquired, "Are you familiar with the formulas for them?"

"Most of them, however, some are so complicated that I have since forgotten."

"Understandable. Have you ever held any aspirations of becoming an official apothecary?"

"I can't say that I have," uttered Leon. "I've only ever looked at it as a hobby. My father was much smarter than I am. I couldn't keep up with him. He was the one who should've followed in his grandfather's footsteps and done it professionally."

"Well, I'm definitely glad you decided to join us," voiced Dave, respectfully.

"Me too."

Still feeling social, Dave walked up to the next group on the road to talk for a bit. Since having been stifled by sickness and inaudibility for so long, Dave was no doubt in the mood to converse. He thought maybe he could catch up on his word count, if that were indeed a real thing of which someone, somewhere kept track.

After being on the road for a few hours, the party came upon a group of travelers. It was a fine encounter, because Mick and Dave managed to recruit every one of them into the ensemble. The company was getting bigger and bigger by the day—a real display of power.

Even more new recruits later, Mick and Dave halted forward progress for the nightly camp. Everyone was excited about camp, because it was going to be the first dry one in days. To add to the high spirits, most took solace in no longer being sick—especially Dave, who was now operating at full capacity.

When they found the time to be relatively alone, Mick and Dave discussed business matters. "I was thinking, Mick, maybe it would be optimum for us to start giving bonuses to not only our most trustworthy soldiers, like we already are now, but also to our most powerful. They are an immeasurable asset to the team and would be a great loss if they decided to abandon."

Mick thought for a second. He became momentarily distracted by a piece of debris that'd flown in with the wind and was now teetering on a rocky precipice. Before committing full attention to the debris' inevitable fall, he said, "In my opinion, I don't know if we should really worry about that. They are all under contract. If they desert us, they'd be marked as traitors and severely punished by the Crown. I think that's more than enough deterrent."

Dave joined Mick in watching the debris of unknown origin plummet off the precipice, before continuing the conversation. "You make a strong case. Maybe you're correct. I just sense it would be a tragedy to lose our best warriors before we start being challenged by the larger battles. I can easily distinguish the most powerful among us, as I'm sure you can too."

"Right, I can tell. There are some strong ones in the bunch. I'm pleased we have them. We have plenty of gold, and I think you're on the right track in thinking we should dish out further bonuses."

"What if we were to hire a camp cook, to relinquish the soldiers of that burden, therefore increasing morale?"

Mick replied, subsequent having walked over to identify the debris, "I really like that idea. At the next town, we'll try to hire one."

"Or maybe we already have a great cook in our midst who wouldn't mind the added task."

"That's possible too. As long as they don't mind diminished rest breaks at our meal stops."

"So, what was the mysterious floating article?" asked Dave, curiously.

"Uninterestingly, just a fragment of a satchel," responded Mick. "We'll ask around tonight about the cook position and leave the discussion regarding additional bonuses open."

"Actually, what we really need is someone gifted in the art of recruitment. Now that would be beneficial."

"Sounds too good to be true. That would definitely be a valuable asset."

It wasn't very hard to pinpoint someone perfect for the cook job. One of the soldiers they'd picked up from the settlement in the Infertile Zone was extremely enthusiastic about the opportunity. He was experienced, having performed all the cooking for the settlement's group outings. The quick marriage was convenient, as Mick and Dave didn't have to waste any additional time searching high and low for their cook.

The next day, having followed a series of ancient cairns, the party finally emerged from the Infertile Zone. Encounters with villages would now be more frequent, though accompanying the increase in villages would be an increase in battle potential. The area north of the Infertile Zone and south of the Baustic mountain range was said to be primarily in Molisian hands. At this point, Dave and Mick's path would no longer resemble a straight line. They would have to start zig-zagging to connect with all the towns. Hopping from town to town would draw unwanted attention, but it was something that couldn't be avoided.

The platoon stopped the march for lunch. It was time for the new cook to prove his worth.

Sitting on a rotten log, praying it would support his weight, Mick said to Dave, "I hope General Ulfenkerki was uncharacteristically wrong with his estimations on how many Molisian soldiers occupy the northern towns. He said some towns may be defended by multiple hundreds, and here we are barely comprised of a hundred combatants."

In the name of whimsy, Dave pretended to hop on Mick's log to see if his buddy would react. Seeing Mick didn't flinch in the slightest, Dave commented, "Although we have plenty of gold left, we just aren't recruiting as many as Rowlangiv had hoped. We're running out of Garobansurovian populace centers from which to recruit."

"I know we haven't really discussed this much yet, but to make up for our shortcomings, how are you feeling now about attempting to enlist Molisians?"

"I don't like it. It just doesn't sit right with me."

I agree," voiced Mick. "It sits even worse than my log here."

"True. I trust our skills in battle. I'd rather liberate the northern towns and tell the King we didn't recruit as many as he'd hoped, than risk having to tell him we foolishly trusted the enemy and weren't able to liberate the northern towns."

"Right. And maybe we can swell our numbers on the march back south. Potentials may be more willing to sign on, knowing they aren't going directly into battle."

"Correct. We'll just have to get creative in winning battles with low numbers. We've done it before."

"Yes," agreed Mick. "Plus, we'll have plenty of Rowlangiv's gold to give back to him if everything stands unchanged. Hopefully, we're pleasantly surprised with more recruits."

Dave sighed. "I know it's become our specialty lately, but after further consideration, I'm really not in the mood for overcoming the impossible odds of having to win fights while attached to inferior numbers. It's best to avoid danger if possible. So, yes, I do hope we gain a few more enlistees."

"Only time will tell."

Just then, Leon from the Infertile Zone settlement emerged from the nearby crowd, approached Mick and Dave, and said, "I would like to thank you guys for hiring the cook. I know he was sad to lose something he loved to do by joining your crew. He utterly enjoyed doing the majority of the cooking whenever we held a formal event or celebration of some sort. His sadness went away instantly through your proposition."

"You're certainly welcome," replied Dave. "A camp cook was something we needed."

"You don't happen to have any more of these compensated commissions available, do you?" asked Leon. "Maybe a chemist by chance?"

"Sorry," stated Mick, "we have no need for a chemist. But as I'm sure you've guessed, military promotions attached to increased stipends are given to trusted individuals. Gus and Vern are our highest ranking officers and correspondingly the highest paid. There are a few others as well who earned promotions."

"I aim to do that then," proclaimed Leon, confidently.

"Excellent. Actually, there is another way," mentioned Dave. "You don't happen to possess the talent of persuasion, do you? We need someone with the endowment of being able to recruit soldiers."

"I wouldn't be able to do better than the two of you," replied Leon. "You guys are both pretty eloquent and concise in your recruitment tactics. I highly doubt I could influence anyone to say yes to signing, when they'd already said no to you."

"Thanks for the compliment," expressed Mick. "I wish we were better, though. Our squad isn't as large as we'd hoped. Gold can't buy everything."

Before walking back to the crowd, Leon announced, "Maybe someone with that attribute will come along unexpectedly."

"That would be the day."

Mick and Dave talked strategy for another half hour, before partaking in the meal prepared by their new cook. They thought the meal was delicious and were immediately pleased in the acquisition of the chef.

A dozen hours elapsed. Since they were now in dangerous territory, Mick and Dave decided to send scouts ahead to see with what they were dealing. They had to conscript a few of their most trusted individuals for the task, because switching sides was an ever-present danger. Mick and Dave had to trust in their decision of whom they decided to trust. Determining whom to trust, as most knew, wasn't the easiest endeavor in the world. This train of thought sparked conversation between Hawk and Leopard, while they hunted.

Dave commented to Mick, "One thing that would be especially handy is having a couple of spies amongst our squad. I'm seeing cliques surface, and I'm sure if any of them were to plan something devious, they'd stop talking about it if you, I, or any of our trusted officers approached."

Mick halted his penetrating gaze into the forest, and replied, "That's a dangerous path. We would be doomed if the soldiers found out we had a spy network. I'm not too sure it would be wise to risk it. But one thing I do know is even though there have been some highlights on this mission, and we're learning a lot about human interactions, I would submit to you that I don't particularly enjoy this lifestyle. I don't like always having to watch my back, protecting this gold. I don't like having to mold my thoughts and actions around keeping a large group together and functioning. It's a game with too many variables, and one that can't be won without an abundance of luck."

"Yes. The politics of it are inelegant," agreed Dave, leaning his bow on the nearest tree. "I sense plots afoot and immoral intentions. Some members of our team are genuinely good-hearted people. But others I can tell operate on a wavelength completely different from our own. Studying them intently would be a force spent wastefully."

"I personally would just like to get this mission over with. I want to conquer the seized towns, bring Rowlangiv a decent number of troops, and go back to not having to run and recruit an army. Every day I feel a group of our soldiers are going to try to steal the gold."

"I'm glad we see eye-to-eye on this," stated Dave. "That doesn't surprise me, though. One thing I feel that makes this task unenjoyable is that if we fail, we let the King down personally. I know in actuality he isn't that way. But it's difficult to not feel like that."

"I concur. So, we're in agreement that we make the best of the situation, do our duty, and then afterwards refrain from any more missions involving the organization of a substantial army?"

"Yes, we are in agreement." Dave and Mick shook hands. "A smaller force, like the one we had after Gravividon, was a peaceful experience, not only because most of them were trustworthy, but because I felt you and I could've convincingly thwarted an uprising by our might alone. A large group, like we have now, you and I couldn't hold back, if they decided to gang up on us."

"Even with the black needles?" asked Mick, humorously.

Dave loosed half a chuckle, and said, "I think once we left the lake town, Casil, we started to accumulate more soldiers than what was comfortable."

"I know what you mean. Up until that point, I felt you and I were in complete control, but after that, it was as if the balance of power shifted. Now, anything can happen."

"True. A large quantity of gold certainly has great impact. I suppose all we can do is try our hardest to get through this task as best as possible.

"I'm definitely seeing why the Icytryxans ran off politics completely," commented Mick. "There's just too much randomness when one tries to keep power using it as their primary tool. I'll stick with sharp metal and well-thought-out strategy for my means of gaining the upper hand."

"Maybe if we had more sharp metal and well-thought-out strategies, we could get ourselves to a point where we wouldn't need any more sharp metal and well-thought-out strategies."

"Intense, Dave. Very intense. I guess for the time being all we can do is keep on keeping on."

"Sounds good. I also noticed that we pretty much abandoned the plan we'd conceived when this mission began of trying to find soldiers that fit like a glove with the Icytryxans."

"You're right, we have. It seems as if we've accumulated many soldiers exhibiting mindsets the complete opposite of the Icytryxans. I can't help but sense people talking behind our backs, politicly scheming."

"We have too much gold."

"That we do. If only we could stash it somewhere, like the King does at the treasury."

"If only."

KING ROWLANGIV, not realizing the cosmic irony, stood within the Capital's treasury, executing a mental count of the wealth. He took solace in knowing how many sentries stood safeguarding the procedure.

Sometimes thoughts would sneak into the King's mind, questions concerning the loyalty of the treasury guards. *What would it take for the majority of them to team up and mutiny the Crown?* Although he understood the basics, Rowlangiv couldn't formulate the exact equation representing what kept the guards loyal. He knew it was a system made strong through many centuries of trial and error. He spent some time thinking about how Mick and Dave would keep their soldiers loyal without the benefit of centuries of trial and error. He understood at that moment how arduous of a mission it really was that he bestowed upon them, though he thought if anyone could orienteer up shit creek without a paddle, it would be Thraiker and Ghrere.

Punctuated by a polite smile, King Rowlangiv made sure to greet all the guards with whom he came in contact on his way out of the treasury. He knew most of them well and trusted them.

Meanwhile, General Ulfenkerki had just left one of his favorite places, the breakfast table, aiming to pay a visit to one of his not-so-favorite people, General Gamald. However, he didn't hate the visits. Even though Gamald was the sworn enemy, not many people could strip away the fact the man was interesting.

Standing in his cell, Gamald saw Ulfenkerki approach out of the corner of his eye, and said over his shoulder, "Before I forget again, I want to tell you how much I enjoy the breakfasts we're given. The eggs aren't bad at all."

Before Ulfenkerki got within arm's reach of the cell, Gamald handed his work tool to the nearby guard—as was customary.

"We have magic, flavor-enhanced chickens here in Garobansurov," said Ulfenkerki, entering Gamald's cell.

"We should go in partnership, breeding your magic chickens with our magic pheasants in Molisia. We'd make a fortune."

"I'll add that endeavor to my bucket list," remarked the Black Bear, instructing the guard to lock the cell door behind him. He didn't mind being in a locked cell with the enemy, because Ulfenkerki was positive he was a much more capable fighter, even if Gamald happened to have a secret shiv stashed somewhere. "I know you haven't seen it in its entirety yet, but I must say all the work you guys have been doing with our city from within your cells is starting to bear fruit. The whole is greater than the sum of all the parts. Many of the townsfolk have been rather impressed by the craftsmanship, declaring the city could even be more beautiful than it was before."

"Impressed enough to come thank us personally?" asked Gamald, donning a funny grin, which, for him, usually only meant one thing: unsavory thoughts.

"I wish I could allow that. Would you extend the same courtesy if the tables were turned?"

Gamald pondered for a moment. "I would allow conjugal visitation for you, only because I'm starting to appreciate you and these entertaining rendezvous."

"How generous of you. Although, I won't be able to reciprocate the gesture, as pandemonium would ensue if one person was receiving conjugal visits, and the rest weren't."

"I'd gladly move to a cell in solitude, if it meant I got a girl sent my way once in a while."

"It doesn't work like that," uttered Ulfenkerki. "Anyways, what are you working on now?"

Gamald handed Ulfenkerki a semi-carved block of wood. "It's the makings of a door handle. I'll be finished by this afternoon."

"It looks splendid—easily passes my scrutiny."

"I have a question." Gamald exhibited a look of seriousness never before seen by Ulfenkerki.

"Ask away."

"You never told me if there were going to be trials for my soldiers who raped your women, during the campaign at Sarwa. Plus, if you were going to hold me accountable for their actions."

"You mean raped *and* murdered. And, yes, there will be trials, but only for the crimes which have witnesses stepping forward to testify. There are three witnesses to two crimes. Luckily for you, no witnesses have made themselves known, willing to attest that you ordered them to commit a serious crime, or that you committed one yourself. The soldier accused of murder had already publicly stated that you had nothing to do with it. I must admit, your soldiers respect you. Also, I remember that you had vehemently claimed innocence in any crimes involving your soldiers—that they were acting only on behalf of themselves. This evidence does hold some weight. So, even though you're stuck here until the war is over, you probably won't be executed."

"Yes, I do stand firmly by my innocence."

Ulfenkerki and Rowlangiv felt it in their gut that Gamald was lying. They felt in the very least he had known about the rapes and didn't act accordingly. Nonetheless, Ulfenkerki knew full well that something like that could never be proven. Ulfenkerki didn't stir the pot, as he wanted to keep the channels of communication with Gamald open, in the hopes that by chance it would help the war effort somehow.

Gamald remained stoic, but his inner self was washed with relief. "Thank you for informing me this," stated Gamald, genuinely. "My soldiers are loyal, yes, but I see that yours are equally loyal."

"You can see that from within your cell?" Ulfenkerki queried, motioning for the guard to unlock the cell door.

As the guard complied, Gamald answered, "Just by the way they talk. When your name is mentioned by one of them, it is always accompanied by a tone of respect— never revulsion. By the way, how did you ever get the moniker, the Black Bear?"

Ulfenkerki half chuckled, and said, as he exited the cell, "Apparently, I'm hairier than most."

THE WEEK PREVIOUS, Old Man Johnson had asked Will if he wanted to stay somewhere other than the Doze Inn. It'd been a comfortable few months at the Doze Inn, but Will was all for it. Who didn't like a change of scenery? So, they had packed up and moved to another inn at the Capital—one with not as clever a name, Nancy's Motel.

Both Mr. Johnson and Will always liked it when Yori stopped over. Old Man Johnson knew she was a busy lady and appreciated how she routinely made time to continue comforting Will at the loss of his mother and possibly father. Will liked her because not only was she kind and had a soothing voice, she always played games with him.

As Yori visited them that morning at Nancy's Motel, she would unveil a surprise. "Will, I have something really amazing to show you today."

"You do, Yori? What is it?"

"After you change out of your nightclothes, why don't you and Mr. Johnson meet me at the merchandise store two blocks over, and I'll show you. You know the one?"

Old Man Johnson replied, "Yes, I do."

"Excellent. See you there in half an hour."

Will was so excited that he put his pants on backwards.

With his pants resituated, he and Johnson having waited 30 minutes met Yori at the landing of the store.

Yori said to Will, "Yesterday, I came here to get some anonymous things, and in doing so I had a remarkable conversation with the owner of the store. She told me someone a while ago had purchased a toy for a child, and that the man paid extra to keep it in storage until he could pick it up. She went on to say that when the man never came back to pick it up, she became curious. She began asking people about the man, describing his features, so she could get the article to him. Apparently, the man had foolishly forgotten to supply his name.

"Now this is where I come into the story," Yori revealed.

Yori cleared her throat and continued, "Describing a person vocally isn't a very easy thing to do. So, when she'd first described the man's physical features to me, I had no idea to whom she was referring. But after she relayed a side story about the man, I pretty much knew who it was. The side story concerned an important duty the man was undertaking for Garobansurov, which would take him many miles away. To be absolutely certain I was correct about my assumption, I consulted with a few others. After this, I was positive that the person who bought the gift for their child was your dad."

"Really?" shrieked Will.

"Yup. He bought it for you and was probably going to bring it to you when he could. So, I guess that just leaves one question. Would you rather have it now, or wait until your dad comes back from his mission to give it to you himself?"

As no kid wants to wait for their gifts, Will only pretended to mull it over. He answered, "I'd rather have it now."

"Sounds good." Yori went into the store and came back out with a decent-sized bag. "We'll bring it back to the motel, and you can open the bag there, in case there are a lot of pieces. We wouldn't want any to get lost."

Yori had told the store owner that in the unlikely scenario she was wrong about Harry being the purchaser of the toy, she would personally reimburse the cost. She also made sure there were plenty in stock, just in case.

The trio began the two-block walk to Mr. Johnson and Will's room at the inn. The oldest two of the group tried their hardest to walk as fast as the enthusiastic youngest.

The three arrived at the inn and beelined into the room. With great animation, Will opened the bag, pulled out another bag, untied the rope holding the second bag together, and emptied out the metallic contents onto the bed. "I know what it is! I can make forts with these pieces."

"That looks really fun," exclaimed Yori. "I think the screws are in that little bag. You might need a screwdriver. If you do, I'll go get one. I have an extra at my house."

Will played with his dad's gift well into the night, constructing a myriad of forts. He pretended to be on important missions, just like his father, whom he missed very much. Old Man Johnson played along, always assuming the role of the antagonist in Will's playful narratives. Of course, Will had to be the protagonist, just like his father—a hero in his eyes.

IT WAS PAYDAY for the crew, but many of them were disappointed there weren't any winsome ladies nearby on which to spend their money. And even more than that, they were crestfallen by the fact there was no liquor around to purchase. Mick and Dave sensed the despondency while divvying out the stipends. Perhaps, they would get lucky, and by the end of the day, they'd come across some booze and/or women.

A small amount of luck did arrive for those desiring alcohol, as a scout had reported a town abundant in intoxicants was near. However, it first had to be conquered. The scout conveyed the town was held by only a dozen Molisian soldiers—it wouldn't be an overly challenging assault.

Mick and Dave halted the march. Dave articulated to the platoon, "We'll wait until the cover of darkness to make our move. I don't want to lose a single soldier on this raid."

"We'll approach from all sides of town in the dark," communicated Mick, while sharpening his sword. "There is plenty of time left in the day for half the soldiers to sneak the long way around to the other side of town. The Molisians will no doubt have sentries, with whom we'll have to deal."

Dave declared, "I'll take half the platoon to the other side of town and get into position a mile from town's edge. Actually, it'd be a better stratagem to have four teams. This way we can encircle town and flank from superior positions."

"Good idea, Leopard," said Mick. "I'll take a team to one side. Gus can lead a team, and Vern can head the fourth team. Each team will consist of 30 soldiers. The tricky part for the four groups will be in the timing of the advance into town. It all needs to be performed simultaneously."

"Somebody should really invent a precise time keeping device."

"Wouldn't that be the day, Dave." Having completed sharpening his sword, Mick scrutinized the rest of his battle equipment, and said, "We'll all wait until the sun disappears completely under the horizon, count to a thousand, and begin the advancement."

"Why a thousand?"

"Because it's as high as you can count."

The pair laughed a good one and went to tell the plan to Gus and Vern, who were honored to lead detachments for the first time. Further details of the plan were also discussed, including particulars concerning what to do if they were spotted by Molisian scouts.

Before separating, Mick, Dave, Gus, and Vern would enjoy a laugh from a miscalculation by Gus.

While putting on his breast armor, Gus had realized he needed to adjust it. He'd also realized he needed to tie his shoe. After taking off his armor and sloppily setting it on a rock, he straightaway tied his shoe. To the amusement of the three watching, the armor had fallen off the rock and tumbled all the way down a hill.

Gus returned to the group after having retrieved his armor and joined in on the laughter.

The relieving of pre-battle tension through a laugh goes a *long* way. Mick and Dave knew this and knew it well.

Before the sun stole away into the night, each squad formed and began getting battle-ready. For many of the troops, it would be their first battle. Luckily, it wasn't supposed to be an exceedingly difficult one. It was advantageous to start with an easy battle, as this allowed the novices to soak it all in before things got truly dangerous.

Not many experiences in life could lay claim to as many different emotions as the moments before battle. Perhaps, the only experience able to claim more was falling in love during the moments before battle. If that ever happens to you, take note, for you may never feel more alive again.

Mick and his company had the longest walk to get into battle position, so they dawdled nary a second. Gus could've taken more time negotiating with his armor and shoelace, since he and his squad were basically staying put. Vern, Dave, and their teams were to occupy the wing positions. Fully equipped, they departed for their respective places.

All four teams were now ready and waiting to strike. The teams opposite each other were two miles apart, the teams at each other's corners were much closer—you can do the trigonometry if you choose.

As most wise people would expect, the sky grew darker as the sun approached the horizon. When the sun disappeared completely, each of the leaders began counting to a thousand. None arrived to a thousand at the same time as anyone else, but it was close enough. No plan was ever entirely perfect.

Lamplight from within the small town guided their way. From all sides, the four teams closed in on the soon-to-be-once-again Garobansurovian town—like all four winds together in a grand, unified scheme.

They each dealt with things along the way as they saw fit and met up in town, all still alive.

Stained by different degrees of blood, Gus, Vern, Mick, and Dave crouched behind a wall in the still of the night and discussed the next course of action.

"What happened to you?"

Dave quietly replied to Vern's inquiry, "Just a little overkill. I must've hit his jugular, poor guy. I ran up to one of their scouts in the darkness, and my sword got the best of him."

"We confronted a scout along the way as well, but our engagement was a much cleaner affair," remarked Gus. "We got him in the temple with an arrow."

Mick added, "Our prowl into town was scout-free, but we did encounter a pair of slow-running soldiers just now. Judging by where they were trying to run, I know where the rest are." Mick pointed to the largest house in town. "They're in that house. They're not in the tavern. I guess they could be in both."

"Where is the bar, I haven't seen it?" voiced Gus.

"It's not a large one," replied Dave. "It's on the south side. Vern and I will take our teams there, while you and Mick go to the house to administer eradication. I think we'll just get in each other's way, if we all deal with the marks together."

"Good thinking, Dave," said Mick.

The quartet of team leaders linked up with their respective squads and moved silently to their targets.

Dave, Vern, and their 60-some soldiers went south, creeping from building to building. Upon reaching the tavern's vicinity, they all hid behind two nearby houses. Dave snuck to the front window of the bar, peered inside, and saw nothing but darkness.

Having slipped back by Vern, Dave commented, "It's blacker than Ulfenkerki's back hair in there. It could still be dangerous, though. We'll rush in as fast as we can, not permitting them much of a chance to figure out what's going on. I suppose it could be a trap, and they have a hundred soldiers in there waiting in the darkness to ambush us."

"You think so?"

"I really don't. We'll know immediately upon entering if that's the case. If we're faced with that much of an outnumbering, we'll retreat back to Mick and Gus's teams."

Dave told the soldiers the scoop, dropped his shield, and grabbed a torch. With the torch in one hand and his sword in the other, he silently led the way into the bar. The light from his torch flickered, as memories of similar dangerous situations seeped unconsciously into his mind. He redirected his thoughts and assessed the scene as fast as he could.

The bar was empty.

There were a couple other back rooms of the building to check, a task which Dave wanted performed quickly. Liquor bottles strewn on the floor everywhere stifled forward motion. Any chance to check the rooms quietly was lost due to the clanging sounds of everyone's feet striking bottles.

The back rooms were also empty. The coast was clear.

With the tension eased, the soldiers searched the bar for any remaining intoxicants, a failed attempt.

Vern said to Dave, "Should we hurry up and join Mick and Gus's teams? Maybe we can catch up with the action there."

"You're unequivocally welcome to try, but I'm virtually positive any action there is already over."

"You're right. I'm sure it is too."

At the same time that Dave, his torch, and his sword had led the way into the bar, Mick endeavored to unlock the door of the house for a stealthy assault. After failing a few times, Leon stepped forward, confident he could succeed. "I know a thing or two about lock-mechanisms."

Leon put his money where his mouth was and came through for the team, as the door clicked open. Mick was pleased.

Lamplight filled the house, so no torch bearers were necessary to proceed. The lower level of the house was empty, but they immediately realized the upper level wasn't. They could hear the creaking of floorboards caused by the pacing of Molisian soldiers.

They began entering the building, but the lower level's floorboards were just as loud as the upper's. Immediately, arrows flew down the stairs at them. One had missed Gus's ears by an inch.

Mick acted quickly and shouted up the stairs, "Surrender now, or we'll burn you out!"

A faceless voice shouted back, "We will surrender. We're coming down now."

"Lay your weapons on the floor before coming down."

The weapons clanked on the floor, and ten disgruntled Molisian soldiers came down the stairs with their hands in the air."

Mick addressed the Molisians, "The first to tell me where you're hiding your liquor supply will not go thirsty tonight."

Simultaneously, two of them quickly replied, "It's in the cubby hole under the stairs."

Once their response was confirmed, Mick handed them both a livery. The rest got their hands tied together.

Mick would try questioning them later, but this usually proved to be useless, as Molisians tended to be stubborn.

Half the booze got divided up amongst Gus and Mick's squads, the other half was saved for Dave and Vern's—it was undeniably a sufficient amount. It ended up being a fine payday, as they'd gotten their liquor, and they'd gotten it for free.

CHAPTER 14

WITH A BLANK stare and much difficulty, Harry Schultz shoved a potato morsel down his throat. His ability to eat was lamentably disappearing. Whatever was ailing him was hitting a crescendo. The place that seemed like haven at first was fast becoming a prison. He'd hoped that by resting up in the comfort of human habitation, he'd get better—that wasn't the case.

Time was going by unbelievably slowly. Suffering the passage of time was one of very few things a prison couldn't keep from a prisoner.

At this point, he only had the energy to leave the house once a day, which was mainly spent going to the well to get water. He was no doubt dying.

After the painful ingestion of food, Harry stood up from his spot of misery and slowly began moving his feet. The first few steps were always the worst. Since he was certain it'd be one of his last days alive, Harry resolved to witness the beauty of nature for perhaps one final time.

After getting his water and bringing it to the house, he managed to limp to the grove of sloping trees he liked so much. He sat on the mossy rock and tried to absorb as much fresh air as possible.

Feeling contrite, he was enveloped by thoughts. His information regarding the western front would never reach the King, though he took solace in knowing he tried his hardest.

His mind reverted to his beloved family. He missed them very much and was positive they missed him equally. Just then, he realized that he would never be able to bring his son the toy he had purchased. He was looking forward to watching Will build forts pretending to be one of Garobansurov's heroes. He had hoped one day they could be heroes together—a fleeting dream. Harry wasn't sure if the store owner was even still holding onto the toy for him, as it was such a long time ago.

Thinking he'd miss all the treasured moments of his son growing up and his wife's loving embrace, a tear rolled down his face.

Sitting on the rock, Harry made a point to make it until sunset. In his mind sunsets were one of life's most beautiful sights. He couldn't help but feel it was going to be his last one. Opportunely for him, it would be one of the greatest sunsets Mother Nature had ever fashioned. Every color imaginable began flashing across the sky— twice as many colors as usual. For the briefest of moments, the show allowed him to transcend the gloom lingering woefully in his heart.

Harry couldn't force himself to leave his spot until he witnessed every aspect of the sunset. It was pitch black before he convinced himself it was completely over. He rose from his perch, took note of the butt print in the rock's moss, and touched a few of the tilted trees, which were surprisingly cold already.

The darkness coupled with the lethargy made it difficult for him to make it back to the house. He stumbled on every hump of grass, stick, dirt clump, and rock in his path. He was able to remain upright for all but three stumbles.

Finally, Harry reached the house and crashed onto the floor, sadly spilling his only water all over the uncomfortable floorboards.

DAVE AND MICK decided to sojourn in the village they'd just flawlessly liberated, waiting on new information from the scouts. This way they could make the best possible decision on how to proceed. The soldiers didn't mind, as they had commandeered all the comfortable, civilized beds in town. Plus, there was even some liquor leftover.

It wasn't much of a town, so there wasn't a whole lot to do. Most of the soldiers spent their time smoking, playing cards, and talking stupid. Since the vapid tavern wasn't overly pleasing on the eyes, or any other body part, none decided to spend much time there. Unproductively, most of the squadron squandered away time from within the various houses. Mick spent his time exploring the countryside, while Dave frequently practiced his swordsmanship, exhibiting a proclivity for perfectionism in finesse.

By nightfall, the day after the victory, a scout appeared, and reported, "There is a town near here, a sister town to this one—almost exactly the same in size and appearance. It's guarded by ten Molisians. I spent some time studying their idiosyncrasies, so when I reported to you, you had the best opportunity for an easy offensive."

Dave commented, "Good thinking."

"It will be an easy incursion, since I know exactly where their sentries post up. Pretty nonsensical positioning, if you asked me."

"They're lazy about it, eh?"

"That they are. They don't even exit town to stand watch. If you were to defeat all the sentries, only a handful of soldiers would remain. And they would probably be in the tavern, which has a front and back door. These two doors present a perfect situation in which to surround them."

"Excellent work, young man." voiced Mick. "We'll assault the village in the morning."

Dave said to the scout, "There's a bunch of ale left. Have at it."

"That'll hit the spot," returned the scout, inches away from licking his lips.

Hoots from the dependable morning owl arrived on schedule, and Mick and Dave rallied the troops for the expectedly easy sortie.

None of the soldiers were disappointed in parting from the drab town, even though it was one within their own beloved country. Perhaps, if they were to run into any of its regular inhabitants, they'd suggest livening the place up a bit. Something as small as planting a few more trees would go a long way.

The march wasn't going to be long, for the sister village was only a few miles northwest. Along the way, Dave said to Mick, "I don't plan on getting too careless with this attack, seeing as though it'll just be an easy one."

"Anything can happen."

"Maybe we can overwhelm them with arrows. Half our soldiers are secondarily armed with bows."

"It's possible," replied Mick, as he instinctively reached around his pack to make sure his own bow was still intact. With relief, he felt his bow strapped to the back of his backpack, along with his quiver of arrows. "I do have some Thorncat arrows in tow, which I've always wanted to try out in battle."

"It would've been nice to try some out at the Capital skirmish."

"Indeed."

"We'll do this raid in daylight, maybe?" suggested Dave. "I know not thirty seconds ago I had said I didn't want to get careless, seeing as that surprise attacks under the cover of darkness are statistically superior. But I think we can handle this one with our hands tied behind our backs."

"I agree. Or wait. What if our scout is lying and switched sides? It's not like he's been onboard very long. Or maybe he was never on our side to begin with. Do you remember where we got him?"

"I don't. But I'll make it easy. I'll run ahead to town and look. Besides, I need to get a good run in. I've been slacking in the endurance department a bit lately."

"Thanks, buddy."

Dave ran off at the horizon and returned to his conversation with Mick a couple hours later. "Our scout supplied us with reliable information. He wasn't kidding about how badly positioned the guards are. Half the time, they're unwisely patrolling out in the open. Plus, their view of anything distant is usually obstructed."

"We'll go with your plan then and attack these idiots in the light," stated Mick.

Flash forward a few hours, and Dave and Mick's squadron was near the town they intended to emancipate from the Molisians. Having separated into halves, each team began inconspicuously moving towards different enemy sentry positions. Those with bows trickled to the front lines. Stealth was no stranger to this group.

When Molisian sentries were in range, the Garobansurovians aimed and unleashed their arrows. Being rained upon by lethality, the Molisians crouched and hid as best they could. Some died, some survived.

All the sentries who'd survived the arrows surrendered.

Those who hadn't been posted on guard duty during the arrow storm could hear arrows pinging against buildings. Upon quick investigation, they immediately came out of the tavern, holding white bar rags resembling flags high in the air.

It'd been the easiest northern town liberation yet. Though, the prisoner head count was fast becoming a little too great for comfort.

Mick fastened his bow back to his pack, and said to Dave, "I just realized I don't even know the name of this town. Technically, I didn't even know the name of the last one."

"I think they both start with a *th* sound. *Thert* and *Thorp*, or something like that," Dave responded.

"That sounds about right. I have the topography and general physical features of Garobansurov stored in my memory bank, but not all the proper nouns."

"Neither do I. There sure are a lot of them to remember."

Mick digressed, "The Thorncat arrows were a thrill. I could tell they had quite a bit more zing than regular arrows. I'm going to go see if I can find the ones I fired. I'd love to be able to reuse them."

"Hopefully, they're still structurally intact."

"Yup."

As expected, the soldiers went straight to the tavern to see if any booze was left. Dave followed, as Mick went to search for his arrows.

Once Dave entered the tavern, he was glad to see the troops had discovered a substantial amount of liquor and that it'd been fairly allocated. He was offered some, but he only partook in a single mugful.

Dave sat by Gus amongst the tavern's commotion, and uttered, "Do you hear that, Gus? It's a high-pitched shrieking sound."

After listening for a few seconds, Gus replied, "I think it's coming from over there."

Dave and Gus walked behind the bar and listened again. They heard it and tried to narrow in on the sound.

"It's coming from over there," Dave noted curiously, and pointed. "Oh, it's just the wind howling through a vent."

Gus admitted, "I was hoping for something a little more exciting than wind through a vent."

"Aren't we all, my good man? Aren't we all?"

Mick walked into the tavern and told Dave he'd located most of his Thorncat arrows, and that most of them were still in good enough shape to reuse. Mick smiled at this, and then he enjoyed a beer.

As one could see at first glance, Thorp was definitely a more dynamic town than Thert. Unlike the case with Thert, someone at some point in Thorp actually gave some serious consideration to its landscaping. They both were on the same river, but in Thorp you could actually see it, because much of the brush lining the banks had been kept trim. Nearby grass had also been manicured with precision. Trees were plentiful—a wide variety of shapes, sizes and species. There was a giant rock formation on the edge of town towering above all the houses. But the highlight of Thorp no doubt was the magnificent stone sculpture situated alongside the town square's grand firepit. It depicted an ominous mythical creature of some sort, emblazoned by the words *Artist Unknown*.

Mick and Dave informed the crew to make themselves comfortable, as they would now be waiting in Thorp for further scouting reports. And of course, the crew was asked to try and not break anything. Why go through the trouble of recapturing a town, only to see it end up in ruin?

As was the case in Thert, there were just enough beds in Thorp for everyone in the squad. Conveniently, everybody's tents stayed neatly bound.

Due to his inquisitive nature, Leon had discovered something extremely valuable for the soldiers. He searched out Mick and Dave, and said, "I found something. I figured I'd show you guys first before anyone else."

"What do we have?"

"Follow me, I'll show you."

Leon led Mick and Dave to the lofty rock formation on the edge of town. "This bush here isn't actually alive. I noticed it earlier and thought something was fishy about it. I gave it a kick, and it rolled away, just like I'm about to do now."

Kicking the bush aside revealed a small cavern in the formation. "The cavern is pretty astounding," voiced Leon, "but what exactly is going to interest you most is what lies within."

Barely enough room for the three, they inched themselves into the half-dark hollow.

Seeing to what Leon was referring, Dave blurted, "A liquor still, I believe."

"That it is," replied Leon. "The Molisians must've been brewing a supply while here. It's pretty fresh."

"There is quite a bit here too," brought up Mick.

"I bet they covered it up with the bush to conceal it not only from enemies but from their friends in Thert," observed Leon. "It'd leave more for themselves."

"Right," pronounced Dave. "Since they're so close to one another, I'm sure they'd frequented each other's villages out of sheer boredom. When it comes to Molisians and their inebriants, sharing isn't always caring."

"Morale will be high today," postulated Mick. "And as for you, Leon, you have exhibited commendable loyalty here by telling us, as opposed to keeping the booze for yourself, where you could've made a small fortune by selling it to the troops. Furthermore, there was the time in Thert when you valuably stepped forward to unlock the door in the heat of battle. As I'm sure Dave concurs, you deserve a promotion and correspondingly a pay increase."

Dave nodded in agreement.

"I appreciate that, you guys. I'm glad I can help."

"We'll even let you have the honor of informing the soldiers about your find," noted Dave. "They will love you for it."

"Thank you," replied Leon. "Today will be a good day." He left the grotto to notify the soldiers of the good news.

Still staring at the still, Mick uttered to Dave, "A good day, yes, but hopefully no more battles present themselves today."

"Good point. They will be staggeringly drunk by the end of the night. Though, I'm sure we'll be fine."

"Probably," simply put Mick.

Mick and Dave tasted the moonshine, declared it a most potent concoction, and vacated the crevice.

Later, subsequent climbing a nearby hill and seeing there were no approaching armies, Dave told himself the drunken army would be safe. To be absolutely sure, though, he posted sentries on the hill he'd climbed and on another smaller hill a mile away.

The soldiers had a merry time. Many expressed their gratitude to Leon for discovering the hidden still. As expected, Leon made many friends that day, or as he called them, *allies*.

When it was all said and done, Mick and Dave were relieved that there hadn't been too many scuffles. That much liquor could've been a disaster. The only squabble involved a dispute at a poker table—a common occurrence for soldiers at war. They even managed to refrain from putting a single blemish on the town's statue, as they all liked the fearsome stone creature.

Mick and Dave stayed awake longer than usual that night, but not as long as the hardiest drinkers of the crew.

Most of the happy members of Mick and Dave's army woke up late the next day, some even way past noon. Hawk and Leopard didn't mind it too much, since they basically planned to hang around leisurely that day again, waiting for scouting reports. Ulfenkerki would've had them doing calisthenics and drills all day—a general's frame of mind being different than that of a temporary military leader's.

JASON THORNCAT stood high on one of the guard towers of the Capital's east end. It was a platform holding a certain significance for him. It was where he first saw *her*—a woman he once loved wholeheartedly, long ago. Jason and his memories intertwined, like colorful leaves dancing atop an autumn-tinged pond on a breezy day.

He recalled many years ago he had visited the Capital for a non-military purpose. A purpose which'd escaped his memory really, and one not important to this tale.

For no real reason, he exited one of the city's shops in a daze. But his trance instantly disappeared upon laying eyes on the most amazing sight he ever saw. An unignorably beguiling lady was gliding gracefully down the street in a glamorous summer garment. Her name was Amber, and she fit that dress more perfectly than the stars fit the night sky.

Jason was so stripped of his senses at the sight of the enchanting woman that he nearly tripped down the shop's stairs. Unfortunately, while focusing on regaining his balance, he'd lost sight of the girl. Uncharacteristically for him, he panicked. He couldn't bear the thought of allowing such a hypnotically beautiful person escape from his life forever.

In his trepidation, he managed the briefest of moments for clarity. He spotted a guard tower a hundred feet frontward. From atop this guard tower he could achieve a better view of the crowd into which she'd blended. The problem was at that point in his life he wasn't exactly granted access to every military apparatus—in essence, a mere child in the eyes of the Garobansurovian Army. Young at heart, and mind flooded with passion, he cared not about passage denial.

On a mission of urgency, he began sprinting forward towards the guardtower. Along the way, he thought of what exactly he'd say if he were approached by a dutiful guard. And approached he certainly would be.

Jason was relieved when the door leading into the tower wasn't locked. But as soon as he made it halfway up, an intimidatingly stoic soldier stepped in his way, and announced, "Tours are Saturdays and Sundays only, noon to 5:00."

Hoping his preconceived plan would work, Jason replied to his elder, "I'm not interested in the tour, but what I am interested in is the strange object that plummeted from the sky and landed atop this guard tower. It seemed magical how it floated down in a geometric pattern, almost as if it were driven by some spiritual being."

Taken aback by the story, the guard voiced, "I'm intrigued. I have to see this. What did the object look like?"

Jason hurried through the innards to the top of the tower with the soldier, and said, "It looked beautiful. A beauty, the likes of which I have never before seen in my life. I must see it before it escapes from my life forever."

"I see you really got attached to it rather quickly."

"Some things just have that effect. It completely mesmerized me."

The two emerged into the open air of the tower's topside. Jason looked around feverously, pretending to look for an object, but was instead searching the crowd below for the girl of his dreams.

The guard looked dumbfounded. "There's nothing up here but dirt, pebbles, grass growing in the wall-cracks, and the blood stains of ancient battles."

In an attempt to stall, Jason uttered, "Maybe in the time it took us to get up here, it transferred somewhere else, perhaps somewhere down to the ground."

The two peered over the edge to the scene below, but the guard lost interest quickly, and communicated, "It seems you're seeing chimeras today."

"I suppose my fantasy may turn out to be an impossibility, something too good to be true, but I'm not about to give up hope yet."

The soldier shook his head. "I wish you well in your quest, but for now I must ask you to vacate the guard tower."

"Will do, sir."

Jason rushed down the stairs, leaping over as many of the steps as his legs would allow, like a flat stone skipped across the water. His heart was racing, as from atop the tower he had seen in which direction she went. She, who could turn out to be merely a mirage, for a single person couldn't possibly radiate such beauty.

Jason ran into the crowd in desperate pursuit, trying his best to not step on any toes. Subsequent running blindly for three minutes, he finally caught a glimpse of the woman who so easily captured his heart. He zigzagged through the crowd for what seemed an eternity. At last, he could see her silhouette directly in front of him—a vision of true perfection.

Exuding a confidence Jason had never before been able to manifest, he took a deep breath and approached the young woman. "Hi, I'm Jason."

"Hello Jason. I'm Amber."

"I guess to be honest, the only reason I've confronted you now is that I think you're breathtakingly beautiful, and I couldn't resist risking the embarrassment of telling you."

"Well, thank you," replied Amber, breaking a smile.

"As it turns out, I'm only a little embarrassed."

"That's good. Full-on embarrassment can get to be quite troublesome."

"That might happen yet; the conversation isn't over."

Amber chuckled. "I'll pray you do well here then."

"Thank you, I'll probably need all the help I can get in the moments to come."

"You're doing well so far," Amber professed, failing at blush suppression.

"May I walk you to wherever it is you're heading?"

"Sure. I'm on my way to my sister's. We'll more than likely talk about guys who have risked embarrassment by approaching us today."

"I bet it won't be easy to top your side of the dialogue."

"Perhaps," replied Amber, beaming gorgeously. "We'll see who else approaches me before I get there."

Jason chuckled. "Well, if someone else does, I hope I've been the most impressive."

"Maybe. I'll have to let you know."

"When might you share this information?"

"Oh, I don't know. When do you think would be a good time for me to share it with you?"

"I'm thinking over dinner tonight at your favorite restaurant." Hoping Amber wouldn't turn him down, Jason was struck by nervousness. At that point in his life, he hadn't exactly laid claim to excessive practice in asking out women.

"Are you sure you could handle it, if in fact it turns out you weren't the most interesting man who'd approached me today?"

"I believe so, mainly because I would have been the one to procure the date for the evening."

"Then, I suppose I better think of what my favorite restaurant is."

After deliberating for a moment, Amber disclosed her favorite, as Jason's heart discreetly jumped for joy.

Memories sometimes never lose their luster, Jason said to himself, as he peered down from the same tower (to which he now had unlimited access) he'd spotted Amber so long ago. He thought nostalgically about that wonderful evening at her favorite restaurant and all succeeding wonderful evenings they'd spent together. It was an unbelievable time of his life that he wouldn't trade for the world. Unfortunately, Amber was now only a memory.

Jason smiled as he looked to where he spotted Amber many years ago, for now in that exact spot walking towards him was another beautiful lady, one he loved virtually as much, but platonically. Yori Rothlin was stunning and Jason's best friend.

Jason rushed down from the tower, yet again; and yet again, successfully asked an amazing woman to dinner.

After changing clothes, Jason and Yori sat face-to-face in the Winter's Clutch restaurant. It was the favorite restaurant of many people, including coincidentally both Amber and Yori. It had a winter theme, as its ambiance was bolstered by striking artwork depicting snow and ice scenes, a monstrous stone hearth, candles galore, and waitresses in winter dresses. Even the floor resembled ice, though it was just an illusion.

Adorned by one of her own favorite winter dresses, Yori stated, "Is it just me, or does is seem cold in here, due to all the winter decor?"

"I think many people feel the same way."

"I like the feeling. It kind of takes you away."

"That it does," responded Jason.

"I'm glad you had some time to yourself this evening to do this. I know you all have been busy lately keeping the Molisian prisoners in line. They are quite the rowdy bunch."

"That they are. We've had to thwart half a dozen escape attempts already. Good thing we've stopped them all so far. Most of the Molisians, however, are behaving well and doing commendable work with the city beautification."

"I agree with that. The Capital has never looked finer."

Jason and Yori began eating their respective meals, which'd been brought to them by one of the winter-clad waitresses. "Pretty wasn't she?"

Jason instinctively gave the backside of the blue-dressed waitress a second look, and replied, "Very much so, Yori. How's *your* love life been as of late?"

"Pretty much non-existent, like always. You're actually the only one with the courage to ask me to dinner it seems."

"Call me old-fashioned."

Yori sighed. "Or maybe I'm just not that attractive."

Jason shook his head and rolled his eyes. "Yori, Yori, Yori, now that I know isn't the case. Your figure is top ten at the Capital, or so I'm told."

"You're hilarious." Yori giggled. "Having said that, there is this one guy I run into on occasion near the castle. We exchange small talk and slight flirtations. I wish he'd ask me out, but he never does. And I'm not the sort to do it myself."

"Who is it? Maybe I can have a friendly discussion with him and light a motivational fire under his butt."

"You would do that for me, wouldn't you," said Yori, chuckling. "I'm pretty sure that would scare him away entirely, be that as it may."

"Well, if you change your mind, you know where to find me."

"Yeah, I do," emitted Yori, "but while you're there tending to military affairs, you're not usually dressed as nice as you are now."

"A man has to clean up nice every once in a while." Jason brushed an imaginary spec off his attire for whimsical affect.

"Do it more often, maybe you'll catch the eye of someone."

"Maybe I will."

After meals were completed and the bill was paid, Jason and Yori left the comforts of the dinner table behind in exchange for the comforts of the fireplace. Jason tossed in a few of the logs that'd been piled up beside and lit the bundle. A roaring fire was a convenience Winter's Clutch patrons loved dearly.

The fire crackled in unrecognizable patterns, as Jason noted, "I was thinking. I get to take some time off in a couple of weeks, do you think you could take some time off too?"

"It's a possibility. What do you have in mind?"

"Remember last year, when we were in Swyrove, and you told us that story about the drought and the guy who had a large seed collection, which he used in an attempt to regrow a forest? And how only one seemingly magical tree lived and played parent to a new generation of trees, resultantly ending the drought?"

"Yup, I do. The most amazing part of the story is that 400 years later the tree is still alive. To my knowledge, it survives to this day."

"Ever since you told the tale, I've wanted to venture to it. I would love it if you could accompany me there?"

Before she could reply, Yori jumped slightly, because the fire popped. It was probably an air or water pocket in one of the logs that'd burst, she figured. "I would enjoy that thoroughly. I will indeed try my hardest to obtain some time off. I think Rowlangiv will comply."

"Excellent!" proclaimed Jason. "Good thing none of the embers that shot out during that fire eruption landed on you."

"Yes, good thing. I'd hate to ruin my official Winter's Clutch dress. Anyhow, I'm pretty sure I can locate someone who can tell us exactly how to get there. I know a few people inclined to knowing those sorts of things."

"You are undoubtedly a social butterfly."

"True. Flutter, flutter. Also, I'm wondering if maybe Old Man Johnson and Will would like to come too. I know they've been itching to get out and do something enjoyable."

"I bet they would really delight in tagging along."

"I'll ask them as soon as I'm certain I can get the time off."

"Sounds like a sensational time," said Jason, stirring the fire for the fun of it.

"That it does."

Yori and Jason sat alongside the fire, talking pleasantly, until all the logs Jason had initially thrown in were reduced to nothing more than flameless coals. The coals glowed and pulsated, sure to mesmerize the next group of folks to sit by the fireplace.

THE OTHERWISE UNIMPORTANT village of Thorp had thus far been good to Mick and Dave's battalion: no one had died or gotten injured in conquering it, the scenery had been thoroughly enjoyed, the weather had been cooperating, and last but not least there'd been plenty of booze to go around. All in all, things in Thorp were in order, even though the soldiers could sense there was plenty of battling yet to come.

All the soldiers recognized that Mick and Dave wouldn't begin heading back to the Capital until every northern Garobansurovian town was reclaimed. They were stubborn leaders but wisely meticulous. If a single northern town remained in the hands of the Molisians, lives of northern Garobansurov's inhabitants would be at stake.

"Good thing the liquor supply is dwindling," Dave mentioned to Mick, as the two walked through a civilian compatriot's house, looking for anything that might help in the war effort. King Rowlangiv had granted them autonomy for such things. "Otherwise, we'd have to cut them off tonight, in case we march to battle tomorrow."

"It's possible we will march, true. A scout or two should return at some point tonight, or at least hopefully by morning."

"If a scout doesn't report in by tomorrow, we must mobilize anyways, as one can't rule out the notion that they may've gotten killed."

"Right," agreed Mick. "No point in needlessly waiting."

"Also, if that's the case, we'll have to deploy a new batch of scouts."

"Let's hope it's not," reciprocated Mick, cautiously trying to open an unbudging basement door.

"Don't bust or unhinge it. But I guess that goes without saying."

To their surprise, the door popped open without incident. Not knowing what to expect, they descended the rickety stairs and entered the damp basement.

After panning the room with candles, they discovered nothing of use. The Molisians had more than likely already grabbed everything useful.

Having switched gears entirely, Mick and Dave began rounds, making sure all the soldiers had what they needed, not that they were provided much of anything lavish. Mick and Dave did their best. The soldiers rarely complained.

Mick immersed himself into a circle of ten hanging out in front of Thorp's only shop. "Did they leave any of the shop's stock alone?" Mick asked the group.

"Not really," answered a semi-drunk soldier. "All the men's clothes were taken, even the women's for some reason. The food is definitely gone. There may be an impractical item or two in there."

"How unfortunate," returned Mick. "How are you guys? Do you need anything, supplies and whatnot?"

"Other than needing the obvious, no, we're pretty much good."

"Just think of it this way," presented Mick, "with all the money you're saving by drinking free moonshine, you'll have superfluous funds for women when we get back to the Capital."

"That's a good way of looking at it, sir."

Mick added, "And if you're not the prostitute type, and you've no desire to extend your contract when it expires next year, you can always use your gold as a down payment for a house. There's no denying the fact that respectable women like a guy with a nice house."

"Very true."

Meanwhile, Dave held conference with those gathered at the mythical creature statue—the drunkest crew of the lot. "How are you guys doing?" raised Dave.

The soldier nearest Dave replied, "Not bad. Just relishing the last of the liquor."

"I implore you, savor every drop, and sleep at your own will," uttered Dave. "But tomorrow, we march—clearheadedly."

"Not a problem, boss."

Leon, who was nestled amidst the crowd, stepped closer to Dave, and voiced, "Were there any new scouting reports?"

"Not as of now, but if none surface tomorrow, we're going to assume they've been eliminated."

"Right. They've certainly been gone awhile. More than one should have reported back by now."

"Our sentiments exactly. Other than that, is there anything else you guys want to know or need?"

Leon looked around to his cohorts, and replied, "Nope. I think we're pretty good here. With Brutus watching our backs, nothing can go wrong."

Dave chuckled. "You named the statue Brutus, eh. It's a fitting name, authoritatively rugged. Well, enjoy the rest of the moonshine. See you all later."

Still smiling, Dave headed to the next group of soldiers within his line of sight.

Chapter 15

THE EVER-PERSEVERANT Anna was still trapped in the lifeless domain of her garbage chute, a hellscape lacking in every aspect of scenery.

Her understanding of human nature, by this point, was considerably diminished. She just couldn't fathom how her fellow man could occupy a single building under their own free will for so long—it just wasn't physically possible. No matter how hard she tried, she couldn't formulate their motivation. It mustn't be a guy thing, as she was certain the men she knew directly would never hang out in the same tavern for weeks on end without budging. Ultimately, she deduced it must be a Molisian thing.

Even though she would always be beautiful, Anna had drastically lost weight, having become the living embodiment of famine. If a person stared too long, they probably would've seen her bones protruding. Luckily, it was food not water that'd become scarce. Without water, she would've died weeks ago. There was a fair amount trickling into her cavity, forming grimy pools. Plentiful at one point, the food (nothing more than refuse) just ran out.

Even though I'm deficient in physical energy, at least I'm not deprived of mental energy. Without it, I would've lost my mind eons ago. Still possessing the mental capacity to play the math game Grandpa taught me has surely been the thing keeping me sane. I think if I get out of here, I'm going to teach the game to every single person with whom I come in contact. Who knows? Maybe it can keep someone else from becoming deranged.

I'm glad there are thousands and thousands of pebbles and plenty of space down here, so that I'm able to keep my old games intact. Being able to look at them in reverence has been my truest joy. I couldn't picture a greater joy existing in such a dark and dreary world. Although, with my games everywhere, it is difficult to move around down here. It was easier to get around when I wasn't keeping my games intact, long ago, but that wasn't nearly as satisfying. It's my art.

Anna's realm truly was a picture of organized, mathematical chaos. Perfect patterns of pebbles were strewn everywhere—on the ground, on ledges, on every surface. If one were to witness it, they'd certainly be impressed by it. The sheer scale of it was truly something to behold, especially if one understood the pebbles represented parts of mathematical equations. It was sincerely a grand tapestry.

Someday, I should really ask the builders of the tavern why they decided to install such a large garbage chute. Technically, it could compromise the structural integrity of the building. But I guess it has stood the test of time, so they must've known what they were doing. Enough thinking about engineering, a topic in which I know nothing about. I'll pass my time now by doing something I know a little more about: listening to drunken soldiers. I sure have had a lot of practice lately.

The Molisian Anna labeled *The Leader* stated, "I was wondering if maybe we should all join up with one of the neighboring villages. Some have many more soldiers than we do. If the Garobansurovians do finally send a force to reclaim their villages, it will most likely be sizable. We don't exactly have a large enough crew here to hold our town against such a force."

Upon the realization of what exactly she just heard, Anna's heart began to race. Perhaps, salvation was within her midst. She inched a little closer to the hatch as to not miss a single word.

The one labeled *Most Annoying* replied, "This is my town, and I don't want to abandon it. It may take years for a battalion to come this far north."

Least Annoying remarked, "I concur; we haven't defended it this long to desert it now. Eventually, people from Molisia will trickle into our town. We can then run our town any way we want. We will be its government."

"That's a nice dream," noted *The Leader*, "but I think if we stay, we're just going to end up dead. What if I go to one of the larger Molisian-occupied towns and merely ask for reinforcements?"

To Anna's dismay, the Molisians agreed to let *The Leader* journey to the next town for more soldiers. At first, they were hesitant, as they didn't want to share power with the other soldiers when Molisian civilians started filtering in. But they did in the end see things *The*

Leader's way. Anna was heartbroken they weren't ditching town, therefore presenting her the opportunity to escape. She was so close to being free.

She sank back into her abysmal hole and prayed one day she would finally catch a break. Anna pled that at the very least she wouldn't die of starvation: one of the most painful ways to go.

MICK WOKE UP early, feeling exploratory. Dave woke, feeling less ambitious, so he decided to stay behind and guard the gold while Mick ventured off.

At first, Mick's mission didn't take him too far away, as he only planned to probe locally.

Upon rechecking houses for war supplies, Mick had come across a parchment, which mentioned the existence and whereabouts of nearby ruins. Garobansurov was old and filled with ruins, so it didn't surprise him in the slightest. He hoped the ruins were linked to the curious statue in the middle of town. His mission instantly grew in scale.

After a mile walk, Mick came across the stone ruins revealed in the parchment. They were unlike any he saw before, architecturally. They were mostly underground, covered by time. Since the ruins were largely buried, there wasn't a way to get in—at least not one clearly visible. He had a few hours to kill, so he decided to put forth an honest attempt at getting inside—knowing many before him had tried and failed. He postulated that maybe someone had found a way in and covered the entrance back up. But something like that was unlikely, as a person looking for relics usually just grabs what they find and leaves.

Mick's imagination was in top form that day. He pictured what the ruins had looked like in their entirety back when the ancient peoples who'd built them were still using them. It could've been tens of thousands of years ago when the culture was at its prime—maybe even hundreds of thousands. It was a mystery most captivating.

Having already circled the ruins a hundred times, Mick was impressed that so far he'd been able to stave off dizziness.

Eventually, Mick gave up hope on finding a way into the structure, but he was sure to inform Dave about the existence and whereabouts of the ruins when he returned to the village. Maybe Dave would venture there and find the entrance. Sometimes a new approach was all it took.

Dave was intrigued, for he adored antiquity just as copiously as Mick. Without delay, he headed straight to Mick's find. This time, Mick was the one who stayed behind.

He realized Mick had probably searched every nook and cranny of the main structure, so to go at it from a different perspective, he decided to root around for barely discernible outlying structures. Perhaps, these would've been overlooked by past explorers, including Mick.

He took a geometric approach, spiraling away from the hub of the main ruin in his search. He figured this way he could cover the most ground in the shortest amount of time. Plus, it'd ensure the least amount of double-backing and repeat coverage as possible. He set up guide stones along the way to guarantee his spiral was proportionate.

His ingenuity paid off, for an hour into his search he found something he thought very well could've been missed by everyone before him. At a glance, the point of interest he'd found appeared to be nothing more than four boulders lying next to each other comprising a diamond pattern. Weathering had transformed the manmade erection into a vision of pure nature. He was positive his discovery was artificial, because when he squinted in just the right way what he saw was no doubt the vestige of a building—an unorthodox looking one to be sure. The best part was the fact there was a void in the middle of the rocks, just large enough through which a body could squeeze. It was a good thing he brought a torch.

Before giving the cavity any attention, Dave scratched around on the rocks to see if the removal of dirt and moss would reveal pictographs. He did find a few curious markings, but they were overall inconclusive.

Dave ignited his torch and peered into the cavity but saw only dirt and stone.

Dearly hoping that what was to come wasn't dangerous, he gritted his teeth and began descending into the darkness. Fortunately, he'd been up-to-date on his aerobic conditioning, otherwise he may've not had the physique to fit in the first place. Hesitantly, he slid down further and further, making sure along the way he wasn't entering a place out from which he could not climb.

The shaft ended up supplying 15 feet of difficult slithering—not exactly the easiest way to start a morning.

Having reached an open area, Dave held up his torch to project his light the furthest possible. Immediately, something caught his eye. It caught his eye even before the architecture itself did. "Finally, pictographs!"

The artistic hieroglyphs were surprisingly vivid and distinguishable. Dave identified a mural depicting five people, though, all of whom were very odd. The five looked to be performing normal, everyday tasks, such as hunting and farming, but their bodies were strangely contorted while doing it. Their frames exhibited an unnatural twist.

Dave pondered for a while. How could contorting your body in such a manner be even remotely beneficial? He positioned his own body in the way illustrated in the mural and became uncomfortable in the matter of only a few dozen seconds. He was perplexed.

He came out of his reverie and to the realization that he'd supply the matter additional contemplation later.

Full of optimism, Dave began to explore the rest of the realm. The layout of the building was artistically captivating, designs so unlike any other Garobansurovian ruin he'd ever visited. It was as if nothing had been created from a mold—everything was original.

However, the sector Dave had discovered wasn't all that large. Furthermore, there were no other conduits leading elsewhere. He noted there was probably more to the structure that he couldn't reach, because of how far he was from the surface's core ruin. One thing Dave didn't see was anything resembling the mythical creature statue in the middle of Thorp. Maybe they were entirely different cultures, he thought.

Having become aware that he saw all there was to see, Dave began walking towards the channel to the surface. But with this new perspective, he caught a glimpse of an object mostly buried in the sand glimmering in the light of his torch. He bent over, brushed away the sand clutching the object, and picked it up. Removing it revealed another. To his astonishment, they were figurines, and they both displayed the same contorted body positioning conveyed in the mural. Better yet, they appeared to be solid gold. To be sure they were gold, he would have to perform a simple test using a certain readily available chemical agent. The appendages of the statuettes were surprisingly intact. It was a remarkable find.

Having pocketed the relics, he began ascending the shaft. Negotiating the shaft was a much harder task going up than it was going down. The true power of gravity was sometimes realized in the unlikeliest of situations.

Having reached the surface, Dave brushed himself off. He admired both the satellite ruin and the core ruin one last time before heading back to town.

Along the way back, he thought maybe there'd be a new scouting report ready and waiting.

Having arrived into town, Dave located Mick, and to him said, "I found a way into the ruin. There was a hidden outlying structure with a shaft leading into the bowels. I'm certain I didn't see all of the underground temple, though. I had explored every nook and cranny I could."

"How did I miss it?"

"Because the outlying building at the surface didn't bear resemblance to a building at all. Weathering had transformed it into something more closely resembling boulders. But if you viewed it from just the right angle while using your imagination, you could see that it was indeed a manmade structure."

"Astonishing! What did you see inside?" Mick asked.

"For starters, there was a mural delineating five people performing normal tasks, but the peculiar part was all five were executing these tasks with their bodies bent into an abnormal contorted position." Dave showed Mick the position with his own body. "I couldn't rationalize why exactly someone would do it."

"Interesting," Mick noted and proceeded to ignite his own brain. "Maybe it's a religious thing. Perhaps long ago, one of them, or many of them concurrently, saw what they perceived to be a deity situated in the contorted position. So, throughout time, they all strived for emulation, thinking it would bring them closer to their God."

"That's a compelling hypothesis. I came up with another one. It's quite possible that their bone structure may've just been that much different than ours. We are talking about a considerable leap back into time here. But I do like your theory better." Dave reached into his pocket and pulled out his discoveries. "Here's proof that their unconventional posture truly was a significant part of their lives." Dave handed Mick the statuettes. "I found these in the ruin."

While examining, Mick voiced, "Astonishing. Their bearing is just as you described. Have you performed the gold test?"

"Nope."

"I think we can locate the proper cosmetics here in town for the test, as there were plenty of women living here before the Molisians took over."

"That's what I was thinking."

"What else was in the ruin?" asked Mick, as the two started to search houses for the ingredients needed to confirm the figurines were indeed made from gold.

"A unique artistic display waited around every corner. Truly, a person experiences an entirely different world when immersed in the realm of the ancients."

"I can't disagree with that. When we retire from adventuring, we really should take the time to excavate some of the ruins we'd come across throughout the years," commented Mick.

"I think one of us said that before," Dave put forth. "Recently, even."

"That's possible."

"The conduit leading to the underground was rather difficult to ascend—dangerous one might say. Even though I made it out, and the artistry within was worth seeing, I wouldn't recommend for you to go check it out. A cave-in could occur at any moment."

"I'll heed your advice, Dave."

"So, I take it there haven't been any new scouting reports?"

"Unfortunately, no, but the good news is I found what we need for the gold test," Mick cried out, as Dave was in the other room of the house.

"Excellent.

Mick smeared a dab of the cosmetic onto his wrist, then, he lightly rubbed the contorted relic onto the smudge. After a few seconds, he said, "Magnificent find, my friend, the cosmetic turned green! It's the indication of pure gold. I'll check the other one, but I'm sure if one is gold, the duplicate is as well."

"More than likely."

"Yup, the second statuette is gold too," communicated Mick, having witnessed the second dab turn green.

"They are probably worth a fortune," emitted Dave. "Hopefully in the future, we can think of some way to use them."

"With any luck, it's for something important."

"Exactly," responded Dave, as the two exited their compatriot's home.

Hawk and Leopard made way towards a group of soldiers and heard a shout. "Mick, Dave!"

Mick and Dave approached the soldier who'd shouted. "Yes?"

"A scout returned. I think he is waiting for you on the east side of town somewhere."

"Thanks."

Walking eastward, Mick said to Dave, "I'm a bit relieved we'll be getting a new scouting report. Going at things with fresh information is far better than going at them without it."

"You really reached deep into the barrel of philosophy with that proclamation, Mick."

Mick laughed at Dave's humorous jab good and long. "Theorizing on the nature of humanity is my thing, Dave. You should know that by now."

"Indeed, I do."

Dave and Mick found the scout easily. To the scout, Dave said, "Good to see you. What news?"

"What do you already know?"

"Since you're the first to report in quite a while, we hardly know anything."

With a surprised expression, the scout admitted, "I didn't think I'd arrive before the others. They'll probably be here soon too. We met up a couple days ago and shared data. Before we split up, they all stated they were on their way to find you to submit their reports. I had one last checkpoint to see to."

"We'll keep an eye out for them."

The scout began his report. "Judging by how many soldiers I can see here at a glance, things aren't looking good. There are four more towns in northern Garobansurov for you to retake. Two won't be difficult, each held by a force of around a dozen. The other two won't be as easy to reclaim. Of the four, the nearest is twenty miles north. It's defended by a crew a hundred strong. The city that'll be the most challenging to engage is Yernoke, which is presently occupied by two hundred Molisians. How many soldiers do you have exactly? A little over a hundred, I'm guessing."

"A hundred twenty-five."

"You have your work cut out for you then. Plus, to make matters worse, the company at Yernoke boasts a formidable archer contingent. Thankfully, the other towns are void-ranged weapons, or at least in significance. Luckily, none possess war machines."

"Is there anything else?" Mick asked the scout.

"That's all I have. Or wait, one more thing: None of the towns are walled towns, including Yernoke. A capable archer division coupled with a wall on which for them to stand would've spelt disaster."

"That's true. Well, good work. Too bad you weren't here sooner; you could've partaken in the discovery of the still. Moonshine once flowed abundantly here, though it's pretty much since been exhausted."

"That is unfortunate."

"There might be a drink or two left somewhere," said Dave. "Good luck finding it, and thanks again for the good work."

After the scout walked off, Mick and Dave talked of battle in the privacy of a nearby grove of trees. "Sounds pretty daunting, Dave. Do you think we can do it?"

"We can definitely defeat three of the four remaining towns. The one guarded by two hundred seems terribly challenging, even if we could sneak in."

"You aren't kidding. I don't know how we're going to pull that one off. One thing I do know is the only chance we have of complete success is to make sure we wipe out as many of them as possible separately, before they can team up."

"Right," concurred Dave. "Three hundred and twenty-four Molisian soldiers against our squad would be suicide for us."

"So, first thing in the morning, we mobilize, aiming to strike the closest town first, the one guarded by one hundred. Do you happen to know the name of it?"

"I don't."

"If we can make it through that without many casualties, in addition to the smaller confrontations, maybe we'd stand a chance at Yernoke. Conceiving some sort of battle advantage for Yernoke would also pay dividends. Whatever that advantage may be, who knows? As of now, I have no idea."

"Neither do I. We'll at least conquer the three towns we know we can conquer. Afterwards, if reclaiming Yernoke isn't feasible, I say we head back to the Capital, and embarrassingly report the incompletion to Rowlangiv. As calamitous as it sounds, I'd rather do that than attempt an impossible fight and die."

"I agree, that would be best. At least if that were to happen, we'd be able to soften the blow to Rowlangiv by returning with half his gold."

"Indeed. Since our immediate engagement is twenty miles away, I think we can be there and take military action on the day after tomorrow."

"In the perfect world," noted Mick, "we get there before the Molisians realize we're coming and are able to strengthen their fortifications."

"That, or before they decide to flee and join forces with those at Yernoke."

"Right. So, either way, we walk fast and keep from drawing attention to ourselves."

While Mick contemplated past, present, and future events, Dave began to melodically sing the phrase, "So far so good."

Post contemplation and singing, Dave and Mick told the officers the plan, who, in turn, told the rest. Some of the soldiers were disappointed leisure time was over, but they knew it was only inevitable.

Having been told about the first target, the soldiers were pretty confident they could easily slay the one hundred-soldier force. Even though it'd be a fairly even match-up, they radiated confidence in their survival, as they'd all heard the stories. The accounts of large forces being defeated at the lone hands of Mick and Dave were all true. The black needles were beginning to become legendary.

Thorp was now a little messier, since Mick and Dave's crew had arrived. Though, it'd certainly be overlooked, since the Garobansurovian villagers will be beyond overjoyed to move back into their town. Time spent performing a little extra tidying wouldn't coerce the slightest bit of anger out of the villagers. Besides, the Molisian occupiers had generated a far greater mess than anything Thraiker and Ghrere's squad had created.

Mick and Dave ordered a quick cleanup in the morning but didn't expect much.

Leaving the luxuries of Thorp behind, every member of the battalion slid on their game face. The easy twenty-mile march began, a mere walk in the park, thanks in part to the obliging terrain. Mick and Dave planned to cover 60 percent of the distance the first day and 40 percent the next. They intended a relaxed second day to save energy for battle, as a taxing walk sapped leg strength needed to swing heavy weapons.

The group had been on the road for half the day, when the lead group spotted something peculiar looming over the distant tree line.

After a short discussion amongst themselves, one member of the lead group went back to speak to Mick and Dave. To Mick and Dave, he said, "I was amongst the group walking point, and we noticed an interesting structure nearby. We figured we'd let the two of you know, in case you wanted to check it out for the heck of it. I really have no idea what it is. It just looks extremely out of the ordinary."

Dave replied, "How far away is it approximately?"

"I'd say about 400 or 500 yards."

"Are you telling us this," voiced Mick, "because you were hoping we'd want to see it, and as a result, you would see it too?"

"That's a possibility."

"Human nature." Mick chuckled. "I suppose it's not too far out of the way for a gander. Lead us there, my good man."

Most of the soldiers made guesses at the identity of the monolith. But upon approaching it, they realized they weren't even close with their speculations.

"It must've taken a lifetime to construct," a soldier of the lead group stated.

Another from the lead group emitted, "For strictly aesthetic purposes it seems, someone or *someones* had piled together hundreds of thousands of rocks. It's so high that it towers well over the tree line."

"I couldn't even throw a stone over it," added another.

Having been walking in the rear, Mick and Dave finally arrived at the giant pile of rocks. Mick said to Dave, "You'd think more people would know about this."

"You're right. I've never heard anyone mentioning this before. This is spectacular."

Mick circularly walked the ridge of the pile, while Dave stood still and admired.

When the two met back up, curiosity compelled them to initiate a search for a dwelling, a possible residence of the creator or creators. The forest nearby seemed the best bet for their exploration, they believed.

Upon breaking the plane of the forest, Dave pointed and commented to Mick, "Over there. That is the most beautiful grove of trees of the area. I know if I were to build a house, it'd be amidst the area's most visually pleasing setting. And that grove of trees is indisputably it."

"I would do the same thing. And to zero in a little further, I bet the home is nestled in that brush over there. From within their home, a person could see both the tree grove and their rocky creation."

"Definitely, as why build something so impressive without being able to see it from your home? Most likely, the house will be just on the other side of those shrubs."

After 100 paces, Mick blurted, "Yup, it's there. A quaint cottage with a window facing the rock mountain. A fantastic morning view."

"It seems like the person could've built a larger house with the available stones but opted to use more on the pile instead."

"Looks like it.

The pair approached the door of the cottage and knocked.

A lady answered, "Hello, gentlemen."

"I'm Mick and this is Dave. We were astounded by the rock creation and were driven here to learn a bit more about it. Is it of your making?"

"I'm Amethyst. My husband and I made it in the course of 20 years. He has since passed, though."

"Beautiful name, Amethyst," voiced Dave. "I'm sorry to hear about your husband."

"We won't trouble you too long, we are in a hurry ourselves," said Mick. "We are actually in route to recapture the towns conquered by the Molisians. Our battalion is looking at your rock pile as we speak."

"Thank you, my mom found a large amethyst once and named me after it. I hope you're successful in your mission. I had an incident a few weeks ago with the Molisians. They forced their way into my house, recklessly scavenging for booze. And I'm sure if either I was younger or they were older, they would've had their way with me."

"How terrible."

"They did find some liquor, but it didn't matter much to me, because I had no intention of ever drinking it. It was my husband's and a decade old—it'd probably gone bad."

"That's good then," emitted Dave. "I guess the only question I have for you is how come your monumental rock pile isn't known worldwide? Nobody in our squad had ever heard of its existence. It's quite the sight to behold, and I'm sure many folks would like to see it, even pay you to see it."

"Good question. The locals know about it and have seen it, due to word of mouth. Though, most travelers up to this year couldn't physically see it, therefore news of it didn't spread. We had a tempestuous windstorm earlier this spring, which toppled many of the large trees and their large crowns veiling it from the only road."

"That makes sense. We did see it from the road."

Mick commented, "Your pile will now have more visitors, but luckily your house is pretty hard to spot. It's actually surprising that the Molisians discovered it."

Wielding her broom, Amethyst stopped a spider from getting into her home via the doorway, and proclaimed, "You've got to love multi-functional brooms. I'm sure the Molisians tailed me, as they appeared shortly after I had returned from a walk."

"More than likely," responded Dave. "Well, it truly is an inspiring work of art, and I thank you and your husband for building it. If we have anything to say about it, the Molisians will not be bothering you anymore. Goodbye, Amethyst."

"You're welcome, good luck, and farewell."

After the door was closed, Mick uttered to Dave, "Out of curiosity, let's check out the fallen trees that once obscured the view of the rock pile. I'm sure they too were notably massive."

"We might as well. It is along the way."

They linked up with the squad, who were loitering near the rock pile. Some had climbed halfway up for the fun of it.

They resumed the march but stopped to gaze at the aforementioned fallen trees.

"That must be them," voiced Dave. "Monstrous oaks lie lifelessly."

"That's definitely them, as they fit the description, having fallen not long ago. Part of a recent leaf crop still clings to their limbs."

"Indeed, it does," returned Dave. "I always hate seeing instances where when one tree falls it takes another with it."

"I can't say I anthropomorphize as much, you softie," said Mick, grinning.

"My heart is bigger."

"If you say so, Whaleheart."

Forward progress commenced, as the duo continued to embrace a flexible plan.

The second half of the day's walk was less eventful than the first. The only point of note was having come across a stream teaming with spawning fish. The concentration of colorful trout presented an easy replenishing of the protein supply.

As they had prearranged, 60 percent of the two-day trip's mileage was covered during the first leg. They halted the march in a locale perfect for tents.

CHAPTER 16

POST SETTING UP camp, Mick and Dave sat around the campfire with Gus and Vern. All were animated.

Across an hour-old fire, Mick asked Vern, "What's the most remarkable thing you accomplished in your youth? Taming big-breasted beauties don't count."

Vern replied, "How about little-breasted ones?"

Gus spit out his food, laughing. He confessed, "I've certainly had my share of those."

"I think we all have," blurted Vern, as the quartet's laughter grew louder than the frogs of the nearby swamp.

Vern pondered for a moment and responded seriously to Mick's question:

"Flash backward in time a little more than a decade. I was in some town with Father, the name of which I've since forgotten—the *town,* not Father.

"Dad instructed me to wait on the street and do homework while he went and did a delivery. Desiring to utilize my free time in a way more enjoyable than what Dad had requested of me, I began searching for some other boys my age. I wanted to play a sport of some kind. The town must've been loaded with lazy youth, for I never did happen upon anyone interested in breaking a sweat. I ended up just walking around aimlessly but would eventually cross paths with diabolical folks.

"As was customary for me when nature called, I peed behind a bush, instead of tediously searching out an outhouse. I stood there, doing my business, hidden, while two people walked past me. I overheard them speaking:"

> "If we're going to steal the religious articles from the church across the street, we're going to need a bag in which to conceal them. Otherwise, as we attempt our getaway, one of the parishioners might recognize the stolen items and alert the authorities."
>
> "Wait here, I'll run to get one."

"I had to think quickly. I knew without a weapon I couldn't stop them with force. I also knew there wasn't anyone nearby, whom I could immediately ask for help. If I waited until after the crime was committed to get help, the would-be thieves would certainly get away.

"Like a bolt from the blue, it hit me. I knew what I had to do, so I did it.

"After deploying my plan, I watched from afar. I watched them run out of the church with their loot. I tried to tail them, but they were too quick. I immediately proceeded to the authorities and told them what had transpired and what I did to help.

"Ten minutes after the robbery, my dad was done with his delivery and searched me out. He asked me if I'd done my schoolwork, to which I replied, 'I worked so hard I ran out of ink.'

"On our way out of town, the lawmen rushed up to us, and said to my father, 'You, sir, have an inarguably upright son. He's solely responsible for stopping thieves from stealing priceless religious artifacts from our beloved church.'

"I wish Father would've listened to them and respected me more at the time. He didn't even want to listen to how I saved the day. I wish I would've gotten a reward too, but I suppose virtue is its own reward."

Vern sat back in his chair, seemingly done with his story.

Across an hour-and-ten-minute-old fire, Mick vocalized to Vern, "Well!"

"Well what?" Vern stared blankly at Mick for a moment, and then laughed. "I guess you want to know how I stopped them, eh?"

"Obviously."

Vern continued the telling:

"After the peeing behind the bush escapade, I took advantage of my sneaking prowess and traversed the long way around to the backdoor of the church. I knew I didn't have much time, so adhering to my plan, I began quickly.

"I jogged past the pews and went to the front of the church, where I searched for the articles that would most likely be stolen. Like I had told father, I began using up my ink. I strategically placed the ink in discreet spots on the articles, so that when the thieves would touch it, they'd get ink on their hands. I didn't apply too much though, since I didn't want them to realize it was a trap. I didn't have much ink, but I did use it all. I knew it was hard to wash off of skin but much easier to wash off metallic surfaces—nothing valuable would get ruined. The ink stays on a person's skin for a couple days. I knew this because I had in the past inadvertently spilt some on myself.

"I quickly looked out the back door to make sure the thieves weren't already upon me. Having not seen them out the door, I vacated the premises undetected and found a place to hide.

"After they committed the crime, I tailed them for a bit, then went straight to the authorities to tell them everything that'd occurred.

"A few years ago, I met someone who was present when the thieves were apprehended, so I can now tell that part of the story too, which goes as thus.

"I guess it was a jam-packed tavern when law enforcement arrived. The town only had three law agents on the payroll permanently, so for a dangerous job like that they conscripted a couple more. Five formidable dutymen stood at the tavern's exits, pressuring everyone within to present their hands. Some didn't want to. But as soon as it was communicated that a robbery had taken place at the church, the innocent folks—many being members of the esteemed place of worship—helped law enforcement with forcing everyone to show their hands.

"One by one, each suspect was checked. The guilty two had no idea what was going on and presented their hands with no objection. When the ink was noticed on their hands, they were apprehended, but not without trying to escape in dramatic fashion. They didn't get very far.

"I guess they sat in prison for a year for their stunt."

After Vern concluded his story, he added, "I know my narrative had no blood or conventional heroics, but it was the most remarkable thing I've done so far. Maybe in the battles to come I can change that."

"It was an admirable deed, my friend," emitted Mick. "An irrefutably good plan."

"We're going to need a lot of equally astute plans in the days to come, I'm thinking," voiced Dave.

"That we will," agreed Mick, "especially at Yernoke."

The quartet exchanged yarns until the fire became three-hours-old. It no longer radiated much heat. They contemplated throwing on more wood but decided not to. Gus doused the fire, and they all went to bed.

At the crack of dawn, the battalion marched onward, but not before a couple more of Mick and Dave's scouts found camp. The good news was they confirmed everything the first scout had said. Conflicting reports would've been devastating.

A few hours into the march, Leon walked up to Dave, and said, "There's an old catapult in a depression just ahead. It may still be usable. It's embedded into the soil it seems."

"We'll check it out. Thanks, Leon."

"I'll show you where it is."

Leon led Dave to the old war machine, and the latter commented, "It doesn't look too dilapidated. Let's see if the armament works."

Dave and Leon studied its mechanics for a bit, which were self-explanatory enough. They proceeded to arm it. Using a few sticks as the payload, they loaded the bucket. They made sure nothing was in the flight path—even though only sticks were about to get launched, getting hit in the face by them could still hurt.

Just before springing the weapon, Dave said to Leon, "Sticks will meet more air resistance than standard catapult ammunition, so they probably won't go too far."

The catapult was set to action. It flung the sticks a solid 80 yards.

So, what do you think," voiced Leon, "maybe triple that distance for a stone?"

"Sounds about right. If we decide to lug this thing around, we'll have to perform a bunch of tests to see its exact capabilities. We might not even be able to free it from this mud."

Mick walked up to Dave and Leon at the catapult, and mentioned, "I heard it unleash its wrath. It works, eh?"

"It does," returned Dave, "but over time it has gotten itself pretty buried. The wheels and maybe the axles may've been ripped to shreds under all the weight of the mud."

"True. It got left here for a reason."

"Only one way to know. Let's get it out of here," uttered Dave. "We stand to gain much reward by adding a working catapult to our arsenal this late in the game."

"Affirmative," concurred Mick, inspecting the catapult's undercarriage. "Having it now would be very advantageous, whereas, having it when we first started our mission would've been a nightmare."

"Definitely."

A pulling team was quickly assembled. Twenty of the strongest soldiers—Mick, Dave, Leon, Gus, and Vern included—grabbed onto the sturdy rope that Dave had attached to the catapult's frame. Through a coordinated effort, they all began to wrench. With a considerable amount of inharmonious grunting—enough to scare away the songbirds—the war machine was successfully yanked out of its greasy resting place. They dragged it to the nearest dry ground they could find.

"One of the wheels is broken," stated Dave, "but I think we can fix it in an acceptable amount of time. If I remember correctly, one of our soldiers was a wheelwright for a time."

"I think you're right, Dave. I'll go get him."

It took longer than hoped, but with the wheelwright's expertise, the wheel was fixed within two hours.

Still having a handful of miles to cover before the destination, the squadron was underway—a ton heavier, but more formidable. None of the soldiers minded their turns at lugging the old, dirty catapult, in view of the fact they knew that by possessing it they stood a better chance at victory.

Many thousands of trees, a stream, and a few frog ponds later, the crew drew close to the Molisian-held town, their destination. Mick, Dave, the officers, and all those with an agile mind started to consider the intricacies of the upcoming battle.

Mick and Dave talked seriously as they walked. "We won't be able to execute a night raid, Dave."

"True. We would surely be spotted, seeing as that it's not exactly difficult for at least one of a hundred soldiers to distinguish at least one of a hundred and twenty-five—even in the dark."

"Not all will have their eyes open, but I'm sure enough will be open to spot us. I'm wondering if we should risk collateral damage by using the catapult and its 250-yard range."

"Good question, Mick. I don't think we'll have the answer until we know with what exactly we're dealing."

"Let's go on ahead and scout ourselves?"

"Yes. While we're alone near the future battlefield, we can also hide the gold, so we're not bringing it with into battle."

"Good idea."

Exuding swiftness of foot, Hawk and Leopard jogged the mile and a half to the mark.

Hiding behind a tree situated on a hill overlooking a town full of enemies, Mick performed a head count. "Dave, I've only seen thirty Molisian soldiers so far; many are probably indoors."

"At least we finally have a challenge."

"True, but to be honest, I'd rather not be challenged and say we had a challenge, than be challenged and have some say we weren't all that challenged."

Dave had to bite his lip in order to prevent himself from bursting out with revealing laughter. "You need to write these all down."

"Better yet, I should have a guy following me around for that."

"As long as it's not me, more power to you."

"Back to the task at hand, I have a plan."

"You always do, Mick."

Mick relayed his plan, as the pair jogged back to the squad—a shorter jog than the previous, since the battalion had remained mobile. Dave liked the plan, and the two told it to the officers. Confidence and spirits were high all around.

They tried as best they could at stealth during the approach, but 125 soldiers and a catapult tended to draw much attention.

As expected, the Molisians opted to refrain from meeting Mick and Dave's army in the field. Instead, they intelligently utilized the buildings for heightened defensive positioning. Mick and Dave would've done the same thing. But what the Molisians didn't know was that Mick's plan involved an uncharacteristic taste of reckless abandon. It was an action Mick and Dave could afford, due to their high standing with the King.

On a cool, overcast day, with fear seeping into hearts and minds, adrenaline radiated so profusely it could practically be seen, heard, and smelled. The furious tendrils of battle began to outstretch, as the fire of death loomed, yearning for fuel and oxygen.

Instructing the catapult team and pointing, Mick said, "Annihilate those buildings there, there, there, there, there, there, there, and there. Leave the rest. Those eight buildings to which I pointed are invaluable and can be easily rebuilt. The rest are either historic, important, or— my favorite—*historically important*. I know we are here to liberate the northern towns, trying our best to keep them intact for the civilians, but sometimes in life you have to pick your battles. Don't worry, Dave and I will take full responsibility for the loss of the buildings."

Mick scratched his chin and pondered for a moment before continuing his instruction to the catapult team. "All in all, hopefully we can bring their headcount down a bit. But I'm mainly ordering the elimination of the eight buildings to reduce their number of hiding opportunities. The less chances they have for an ambush when we enter town, the better. Also, we'll want to charge into town under the cover of catapult fire. This is to take focus away from any archers they may have. They'll be edgy having to launch their arrows as giant stones hurtle ominously towards them. So, when that happens, try not aiming too close to us. After the infantry is entirely in town, stop the barrage and join us."

While Mick addressed the catapult operators and spotters, Dave spoke with the rest, exhibiting nary a trace of uncertainty. "Like always, our plan is meant to prevent as many casualties for us as possible. Potentially, we have a much more challenging battle ahead at Yernoke, so we're going to need as many of you operable for that as possible. By chance, do any of you happen to know the name of this town we're about to attack?"

"Horilhun," shouted someone from the back.

"Thanks." Dave waved at the helpful individual in the back, and resumed his directive, "Before charging into town, we will be destroying twenty-five percent of the buildings—the expendable ones—by catapult. The reason for this is so they'll be less buildings in which the Molisians can take refuge. We'll also be running into battle as catapult fire flies overhead. So, pay attention to that, as we wouldn't want any of your beautiful faces smashed in with a stone."

"Some more beautiful than others, am I right!" shouted one of the burly soldiers (Big Ben), who in return enjoyed a laugh from the crowd.

"None as gorgeous as yours, Big Ben," responded Dave, before recommencing the rally speech. "For the most part, our battle strategy will be flexible once we enter town. So, watch me, Mick, and the other officers for sudden changes and try to keep up. Anyone with a ranged weapon, please keep firing as we run into town. The more cover you provide, the better. And anyone who kills two or more enemies in this battle will get a bonus on payday. You'll need someone to corroborate your claim, and remember if the numbers don't add up, I'll assume too many are lying, and I'll take the offer off the table. Sound fair?"

The mass cheered. Dave took it as a yes.

The catapult was wheeled to the location containing the most usable payload stones while also being within firing range of town. The entire battalion got together, rounded up stones, and brought them to the catapult. Once a huge pile surfaced, the catapult operators began launching, as the infantry started to psyche themselves out for the charge.

Mick and Dave watched the catapult in action, and studied the enemy from afar, hoping to gain further knowledge. They learned that of the eight buildings they wanted destroyed, two contained hiding Molisians, who scurried out like exposed mice, though they weren't able to tell if any Molisian casualties resulted from the catapult onslaught—they could only hope. The most valuable information Mick and Dave ascertained from their study was in fact to which buildings the scurrying Molisians fell back. They put the vital intel to memory and corralled the infantry for the charge.

Hawk and Leopard ordered those with shields to the anterior to repel arrows during the head-on rush. Dave and Mick both possessed shields, so they too would be part of the vanguard—proud to lead the way.

Mick addressed the infantry one last time before the run into town, "They stole our town. Get indignant and take it back! Eyes of ire! Weapons on fire!"

Protecting heads and hearts with shields, Mick and Dave vehemently lead their team into the arena as catapult fire flew overhead. The squad followed loyally—not a single deserter in the lot. Arrows rained upon Mick and Dave as they ran, but they were well-acquainted with the dance of avoidance. Practice had taught them to how to move at speed and on balance.

Having felt a twinge, Dave said to Mick, "An arrow just deflected off my hip."

"It probably ricocheted off your hipbone."

"Luckily, it hit there and not eight inches over in the *sensitive area*."

"That would've hurt," voiced Mick, as an arrow bounced off his shield with a clang.

"You can say that again."

"Fifty yards left to close the gap. Almost there."

As soon as Dave and Mick entered town, they targeted the archers—the stupid ones who didn't have enough sense to break for cover. Easy defeats, upon which Mick had already tallied two kills—enough for the bonus, had he been under his own command.

With all the Molisian archers either dead or having retreated, the rest of Dave and Mick's company easily made it into town, minus the three unfortunate souls who'd succumbed to the arrow onslaught. The catapult team arrived a few minutes later.

Mick and Dave knew they had a fair advantage in numbers, so they took a few moments to gather composure. They were glad at this point to not see any Molisians fleeing, a retreat that would've probably taken them to Yernoke, making the anticipated battle there more difficult.

To help them plan, both Mick and Dave visualized what *they* would do if they were in the Molisians' shoes. Hiding in the wooden buildings wasn't the best bet—a lesson learned at the battle at the Capital. There weren't many, but there were some stone structures inside which to take refuge.

"I would relinquish the town, if I were them, as we have a six-to-five advantage, given scouting reports were correct," Dave communicated to Mick. "Mathematically speaking, they are all going to die, while twenty of us live."

"I am surprised they haven't yet abandoned. It makes me think they've formulated a plan, as I know I don't engage superior forces without a plan."

"Maybe they have a trap somewhere."

"That's possible."

Mick and Dave ordered the officers to come near, so they could quickly converse. "Dave and I think they have a trap set up somewhere. We need your input as to where and what it could possibly be."

Vern noted, "Maybe there's a pitfall trap somewhere."

Dave responded, "That could be. We'll definitely keep our eyes open for one. For argument's sake, let's pretend they have a better plan."

"Gus suggested, "Some sort of machine maybe."

"Possibly."

Leon spoke next. "They could have constructed some sort of incendiary device."

"Let's hope not," declared Mick. "That's not a very pleasant way to die."

"There aren't very many tall buildings in town, from where they could drop rocks on us, but we'll pay attention it, along with all your submissions," voiced Ghrere. "Thanks for the counsel."

"I think many of them are just hiding within the imposing stone building on the east side, waiting to fling arrows at us when we approach," added Mick. "I witnessed a few of the archers drawing back to it."

"Should we charge it, you think?" asked Gus.

"That may also be where they placed a trap in expectation of us running at them," stated Mick. "However, I'd hate to go the long way around, allowing them the opportunity to bombard us with even more arrows.”

“How vital is this structure in question within which they’re possibly hiding? Maybe we can demolish it by catapult?” vocalized Leon.

Mick answered, “It’s a vestige of an ancient civilization, so the epitome of historic. It would be optimum to leave it standing. I could be wrong, but I’m sure the villagers and the rest of Garobansurov would miss it.”

“Leaving the building intact,” uttered Dave, “perhaps, we could perfectly place a few catapult shots right where traps may be positioned in hopes of detonating them.”

Mick scratched his chin, an action to which he’d grown quite accustomed over the years. “You know, Dave, that’s not a bad idea at all—risky, but not bad. Let’s do it. We’ll clear the small buildings nearby, while the catapult operators run back and set your idea to motion.”

“Sounds good,” said Dave. “Thanks again, guys, for your pointers. Leon, find a safe place to watch and see if our catapult projectiles set anything off, while we assault the nearby premises. Focus on the choke points.”

“Will do.”

“Get back to us as soon as soon as you learn something, because if the catapults eliminate their booby trap—or traps, it’d be best for us to act quickly.”

“Gotcha,” responded Leon, before leaving the company of the officers to eye up potential spying perches.

The catapult team began their task, as Mick and Dave rallied the troops for the first of the building raids.

Gears of adrenalin having switched, a team of 30 systematically flowed through a two-story house, swords coiled. However, it turned out to be devoid Molisians—along with the second building they searched. The third ended up being protected by a couple Molisian soldiers. Though, it was security that left much to be desired, as the pair was drunk and passed out in the basement. They were bound and added to the prisoner lot. "Onto the next building," voiced a soldier.

The impact of the stones shot from the catapult hitting the ground could be heard by everyone in and near town. The thumps were loud and deep.

Mick and Dave were about to lead the team into the fourth and final building of the vicinity, when Leon presented himself for report. "Their traps are incendiary. One of the rocks landed just right and sparked some sort of canister holding oil. I'm guessing there are dozens of canisters containing flammable substances concealed by the thick grass in front of the building. Many Molisians are definitely in the building too. I saw heads popping out occasionally."

Dave asked, "Did any of our projectiles cause irreparable damage to any of the buildings?"

"Only one hit a building. Nothing more than a grazing—easily fixable. I don't think we were done firing, though. I came here as soon as I discovered their scheme."

"Excellent work, Leon," aired Mick. "We'll have to think of a way around these defenses."

Mick, Dave, and the assault team hurriedly cleared the building in front of which they were standing. "Yet another building bereft opposition," declared Gus.

Post-assault, Mick conveyed to Dave, "They probably scattered the flammable canisters where they intend to make their last stand."

"True. What if we light their fires before they do?"

"Great idea, Dave. Though, the question is, is there anyone among us proficient enough with a bow to do that?"

"You or I could do it."

"Probably, but a risky endeavor to be sure."

"Honestly, I've always wanted to shoot flaming arrows for a purpose," admitted Dave. "There's something almost poetic about it."

"A pyromaniac poet. Knock yourself out. But be cautious; they'll see you trying to set off their traps and stop at nothing to bring you down before you do."

"I got this," claimed Dave, confidently. "I'll unravel their plot."

Dave had to gather more arrows for his project, as currently his quiver wasn't exactly crammed full of them, especially of the kind he needed. He required arrows with the wherewithal to hold tinder. His search wasn't overly difficult, as between all the soldiers of the battalion countless arrows of many shapes and sizes were owned.

After Dave procured all the right arrows, he and Gus transformed the arrowheads into what was required to carry a flame.

Dave lit a punk, which he'd use to ignite the arrowheads one-by-one, and strapped on his quiver full of modified arrows. Having grabbed his bow, he got into position 40 yards from the trap field. Since he knew he'd be shot at aggressively by the enemy, Dave resolved to perform quickly—even aim quickly. He knew he would be especially vulnerable when releasing the arrows.

Posted behind a thick tree, Dave picked out the first target and lit an arrow with the punk. With a tenacious grip on the bow with left hand, he drew back the burning arrow with his right, aimed, and released quickly.

His first shot landed in the grass, failing to light any traps. It burned the grass slightly but eventually went out. If the grass had been dead and dry, it could've possibly caught fire, but no such luck. Dave tried again and successfully lit one of the canisters, which in turn lit a few more.

Feeling the heat from the blaze, Dave backed up a hair and continued. After lighting all the close targets, he began the more challenging task of lighting the faraway ones. Unfortunately, his arrow supply was dwindling.

Dave failed to light any canisters with his first three attempts at the distant targets. He now only had three arrows left. An arrow whizzed past his face—*close call.* Dangerously, he emerged from behind the tree and desperately aimed longer than normal. Despite another arrow whizzing past, his risk paid off, as a far canister was lit, taking another two with it.

He made note to enjoy his last two arrows, for who knows when he'd ever be given another opportunity to cross poetry with fire. Of his two final arrows, one hit its mark. Dave didn't think all the canisters were kindled, but he was confident that enough had exploded to allow reasonably safe passage for the squad.

Having executed his mission to the best of his ability, Dave sprinted back to the crew using the safest route he could find.

"Dave, your eyebrows are singed," Gus noticed.

"I guess I didn't even feel it happen, though the fire was certainly hot!"

"Well, did you relish your poetic pyromania?" inquired Mick.

"For sure," replied Dave, "especially the last two launches. Those, I tried to make memorable."

"I plan to make the next ten minutes memorable," proclaimed Mick. "I'm going to slice through their ranks like lightning through a tree." Gus, Vern, Dave, and Leon—who were all nearby—chuckled. "In a moment, the fires will be nearly out, then, I'll begin my memory creation."

"And I'll be glad to be a part of that memory," let out Vern. "Bring on the adversary."

"The battlefield is well-defined," specified Dave. "And I think, judging by Mick's current intensity level, the battle will be short."

Mick laughed, and said, "Short and sweet. The fires have dwindled enough now. I think we can pass through."

"Don't forget to block arrows, guys," said Dave, exchanging bow for black-needle.

Followed by the soldiers, including the catapult team, Mick and Dave charged the Molisian brigade at full force through the smoldering fires. Arrows were plentiful, especially from the Molisian side, since they reaped static positioning. Both Mick and Dave deflected a handful of arrows during the headlong charge.

Sadly, two Garobansurovian soldiers didn't make it through the arrow-storm.

Upon reaching the Molisian force hiding amongst the ancient building, Mick performed a quick headcount and realized the scouts were a little off. But that was a good thing. Mick couldn't help but wonder why the scouts' estimations were high. He shrugged off the thought and executed a well-delivered sword swing—beginning the memory creation.

Dave was no fool, he knew fighting alongside Mick would prevent a large number of adversaries from reaching his blind side. Mick knew the same about Dave. The pair really were quite the team. Gus and Vern, by that stage of the collaboration, knew the advantage as well, making a point to stay near Mick and Dave during a fight. In their own rights, they were also a formidable fighting tandem. A few others, such as Leon and Silas, also wisely fought within the vicinity of Mick and Dave.

Wearing the Quintaga armor in its entirety, Dave advanced on a Molisian wielding a funny-looking sword. It seemed to be handmade, but unfortunately for him, poorly handmade. Dave's black needle sliced the blade sheer off the grip. Thinking about all the time that'd probably gone into its creation, Dave felt sorry for the guy and his homemade sword. But he did what had to be done. There was no time for person-to-person diplomacy. Dave exhaled and moved onto the next challenger.

Meanwhile, Dave's trusty partner, Mick, faced a contender who seemed to outweigh him by 100 pounds. Mick would've had a harder time defeating the oaf had the Molisian chosen an actual war axe for a weapon. Instead, the giant of a man had selected to use a dull, wood-chopping axe. All Mick had to do to win the confrontation was drive his sword with one hand and block the axe with his shield in the other. If the axe was sharp, maybe it would've penetrated the shield, but the dull axe that it was practically bounced off. Mick's sword drove home, right into the Molisian's neck. In lieu of hesitation, Mick sized up the next target, sliding his sword out from the neck of a corpse.

Gus, Vern, and the rest of the officers were faring well, still alive and energetic.

Dave wiped the blood off his sword onto the opponent he'd just killed. Ironically, it was the opponent's own blood. Wiping off blood in the heat of battle wasn't usually something Dave did, but he had a moment to spare, as he didn't want to lose Mick's backside by wandering off.

Mick defeated his adversary, and together he and Dave searched the throng for fresh prey—and of course, the opportunists followed.

Having been witness to Dave grooming his sword, Mick glanced at it, and said, "I like your shiny sword."

Dave chuckled.

Mick looked around and noticed the battle was already half over. The Molisian lines were being decimated, though the pre-battle estimation of how long the fight would take was a bit off. It seemed he would be making 15 minutes' worth of memories, instead of ten.

He also saw that much of the fighting was occurring inside the ancient building, while some was transpiring amongst the smoldering fires.

Realizing the battle was going well, and that not too many compatriots had fallen, Dave sighed relief. He surged some adrenalin for the closing stretch, as the final phase of the battle for Horilhun began.

Dave committed to a rendezvous with a Molisian enemy clenching a mace. Dave caught himself looking twice at his opponent's weapon, because maces were a rare sight.

The engagement with the mace wielder was Dave's longest of the battle, since, as it turned out, there was justification for him using such an uncommon weapon— he was uncommonly proficient with it.

Since maces were by no means inexpensive to construct, Dave made mental note of where it landed— underneath its former keeper. Upon completion of the battle, Dave would retrieve the mace, as he was certain someone in the battalion would want it.

Mick sidestepped an incoming lunge and followed with a power swing. He missed, barely. Mick's opponent was just about to counter the power swing but was stabbed in the back by an attentive Vern. "Good timing, Vern."

Vern replied, "He looked angry."

Through a series of fluid stabs to a hairy face, Leon killed his second opponent, glad to be getting the bonus. He would end up defeating three Molisians in total.

Mick stared down what he was hoping to be one of his final adversaries of the encounter. He relinquished the stare-down and rushed in, led by black needle's keen edge. Blow-by-blow, Mick incrementally depleted the Molisian soldier's sands of time.

Subsequent Dave's victory in his confrontation with the mace wielder, he searched the field for the next opponent. Through the nearly invisible haze of heat waves, he spotted what would probably be his last adversary of the battle. Dave had witnessed the Molisian defeating one of the pleasanter soldiers he'd recruited for the battalion and darted in with a vengeance.

The two combatants exchanged multiple attacks and blocks. Both became drenched in sweat and determination.

In the heat of battle, Dave came up with a scheme. He eyed up the area directly behind his enemy, pretending an ally was coming to his aid. The Molisian took notice of Dave's eyes and glanced to the same spot. Dave saw the averted eyes and sprung the trap with one giant swing to the head. He connected just enough to follow through with a few jabs. Dave's last rival fell to the ground clutching his bleeding neck.

Mick's last opposer would turn out to be his easiest. He took advantage of a turned back and whipped a cantaloupe-sized rock at the Molisian's head. Needless to say, the guy fought and died while in quite the stupor.

Mick and Dave scanned the scene of victory, a military success that most would've considered a convincing defeat.

"I'd say we triumphed commandingly, having only lost minimal soldiers. The black needles' blades certainly took pleasure in swiftness today," Mick said to Dave, pleased.

"I see all of our officers survived."

"Excellent. How many dirt naps in total did you distribute, Dave?"

"Five, including the archer on the way in."

"I supplied five and a half—the half representing my last one there—my rock, not I, pretty much won that fight."

"It seems the rock wanted to try a hand at earning the bonus," jested Dave. "I'm curious to see who all will be getting it."

"Let's go find out," blurted Mick, enthusiastically. "Mathematically, it can't be over thirty-four, since you, I, and the rock killed eleven of the eighty."

"Taking the math a step further, considering those who defeated only one, in addition to those besides us with multiple kills, the bonus should go to less than twenty."

"Good point. Hopefully, we aren't confronted with liars."

Mick and Dave began corralling their soldiers, many having been bloodied by the battle. A few were too injured to move fast, but Mick, Dave, and a few others helped them join in.

When everyone was gathered, Dave announced, "That couldn't have gone much better, militarily. Lamentably, we'd lost a few brave men and women, they having strayed too close to the horizon of death. However, the freedom for which they fought and gave their lives is now sturdier for all of Garobansurov. You all fought with great skill, teamwork, and honor. Mick and I are glad to have fought this battle with you. Now for the fun part: acknowledging those among you who earned the bonus. Step forward if you slew two or more Molisians today."

A couple dozen congregated in front of Mick and Dave.

Seeing how many there were, Mick whispered to Dave, "A few more than expected, but not much more."

Dave quietly replied, "We'll just chalk it up as unintentional human error. A few of them could've thought they mortally wounded someone, but in actuality, the Molisian in question rose to fight again."

"Right. Anyone can make that mistake."

The private, muffled conversation between the pair ceased. Mick addressed those beaming converged before him, "Excellent work soldiers. You fought well. We'll hand over your reward as soon as we transport the rest of our gear into town."

With a taste of spectacle, Dave proclaimed, "Let's hear it for these ace warriors!" After the crowd ended the round of applause, Dave continued, "Our next course of action will be the easy task of lugging all the equipment and catapult into town, as we'll be making Horilhun our base of operations. According to the scouts there are three more towns to capture—one of them, Yernoke, is guarded by a force larger than our own. Though, I promise, if Mick and I feel we can't win at Yernoke without sustaining heavy casualties, we won't engage. We want to stay alive just as much as you. It's going to require great planning, no doubt. In the meantime, make yourself at home here, drink all the booze you can find. Like always, no looting anything but booze. We'll stay here for at least one night. We'll let you know if it'll be more. Once again, commendable weapons-manship everyone. If that's a real word."

With the establishment of the new base, the seeds of total victory in the north were now sewn. Having penetrated as far north as they had, Mick and Dave were beginning to see the light. They may just yet make it out of the King's mission without too much hardship.

CHAPTER 17

WHILE ALL THE MILITARY and personal impedimenta was being dragged into town, Mick went to collect the gold from the hiding spot. It was a nerve-wracking affair, due to the possibility of it not being there.

Phew, it's here. I think during the next battle I'll just leave the gold in either my or Dave's tent. Leaving it in the countryside is just too risky.

Mick and Dave selected their base within the base: one of the small homes on the west side.

"I'm surprised during the battle we didn't notice the large pond nearby," Dave mentioned to Mick, while unloading gear. "You'd think we would've heard its large quantity of loud geese."

"Right, you'd think. Did you know most birds mate for life?"

"I can't say I previously had a firm handle on that bit of info. That's intriguing. Unfortunately, I don't think most people mate for life."

"True. From what I've gathered, most Icytryxans do though."

"Yup, I've gathered that as well."

Horilhun was the second-largest town in northern Garobansurov, behind only Yernoke, which was why the Molisians had defended it so valiantly. Horilhun maintained a substantial populace for the reason that not long ago it was home to a goldmine. When the mine had run dry, many of its employees moved on to find other work—most to Yernoke to work the mine there. Those who'd stayed behind had no need to search for further work, as they'd already struck it rich. Some of the soldiers of Mick and Dave's company knew this story well and searched all through the mine for any riches that may've been left behind, as Mick and Dave had informed them that any gold found therein could be kept. The entrance to the mine was very near the ancient building around which the battle had been centered. Though, all that was found of value was booze stockpiled by the Molisians.

There were two taverns, the largest of which was fancied by Mick and Dave's unit, as it was clearly the sort that much time and resources had been spent on its construction. It was pleasant on the eyes, ornamented by wooden beams larger than most of the soldiers had ever seen. The other tavern was not as grand, more than likely having catered to those of the mining era requiring a less costly evening. Grunts needed to wind down as well.

Dave saw to making sure all the fuel canisters near the battlefield were disposed of, as accidents could happen. But before doing that, he retrieved the prized mace from underneath the Molisian with whom he'd exchanged blows.

Dave met up with Mick nearby and showed him the mace.

After executing a few swings, pretending to smash in a skull, Mick commented, "It's an exquisite weapon. Any ideas what you want to do with this exemplary specimen?"

"Probably get it into the hands of someone who can do the most damage with it. Any suggestions as to who that may be?"

"I'd think one of those receiving the bonus. In fact, I'm about to go pay that now."

"Good idea," returned Dave. "First, we'll ask who among them is proficient with a mace. Then, of that lot, we'll narrow it down even further to those exceeding two kills. Finally, I'll give the meticulously crafted mace to the person who comes up with the best way of using it in the next battle—creativity is key."

"That'll be interesting. I'll summon the gold, while you corral its recipients. I'll meet you there."

Subsequent Mick and Dave parting, Dave gathered together all the soldiers who'd receive the bonus. To them he said, "Mick will be here shortly with your gold incentive, but in the meantime, I ask who among you is competent with a mace?" Half of the gathered two dozen raised their hands. "And of you who have their hands raised, who would like to use an intricately fashioned mace as your primary weapon?" Nobody put their hand down. "Now, who among you had three or more kills during the last battle?" Half lowered their hands, leaving six individuals, including Vern and Leon.

Mick returned with the gold coins and handed them out accordingly. The 24 soldiers were very pleased, as they ran their coins through their fingers, watching them glimmer in the sunlight.

Dave continued his mace address, "Now for the fun part. You six, if you choose to, can explain to Mick and I the way you intend to use the mace during the next battle. The mace will then be given to whoever of you six illustrates the most optimal way of using it. Mick and I will judge." Dave reached into the crotch of a tree, grabbed the cleverly hidden mace, and presented it to the six hopefuls.

The six soldiers expressed great admiration for the mace and how very interested they were in participating in the contest.

The group receiving the golden bonus disbanded, except for Mick, Dave, and the six contenders, who convened in a nearby home. One-by-one, each competitor was escorted into a private room to deliver their narration. Each went into detail describing maneuvers they would perform, gruesome deaths they would generate, and specific strategies they would deploy—all in all, pretty conventional mace usage. Only one—the winner—hadn't rambled on with predictability. He delineated how in the course of the next battle he'd utilize the mace to gain that which was coveted militarily, all the while aiming to fight as little as possible. Mick and Dave loved the philosophy of it—fight smarter, not harder—and deservingly handed the mace to Leon. The others were disappointed but glad to have been given the chance. The runner-up, a nice fellow named Rhyod, was especially gracious in defeat, as was Vern.

The soldiers spent the rest of the night in revelry. Mick and Dave knew it was practically the best way to keep them happy—they had fought well and earned their confiscated booze.

Hawk and Leopard spent their time—like they always did immediately after reclaiming a town—searching for paraphernalia that could help in the battles to come. Their search was more fruitful than that of the last town, having found a stockpile of arrows. They would make a point to salvage the ones from the battlefield as well. There were also many weapons still clutched by the dead Molisians, but not many would be commandeered, since the soldiers had already seized prime weapons from previous battles. Along with the arrows, Mick and Dave also procured an enormous amount of food—better food than what they had. The cook got to work straightaway.

The fresh morning air lured Mick and Dave out of their tents and to duty. They began devising the plan for the next town storming.

"There are three Molisian-held towns remaining— three last targets," Mick said to Dave, as the two stood by the goose pond. "Which town shall we go after first?"

"I'd say the closest. As long as it isn't Yernoke yet."

"Right. That one needs a lot more planning than what we can do today."

"Before we strategize any further, we might as well go ask the scouts which town is next in succession and what they know about it."

"Good idea," stated Mick, a couple minutes prior to having successfully summoned the scouts.

The next town down the road was fittingly named Deepwood, which the scouts relayed was deep in the woods. Other aspects of Deepwood were also concisely provided.

In no time, Thraiker and Ghrere learned what they needed to know, dismissed the scouts, and resumed their planning. "Since our next mark is defended by only a dozen Molisians according to the reports, the assault should be pretty straightforward—straightforward on paper at least."

"Right, Dave. Nevertheless, we should still march at full force."

"I concur. But after that, I think we should come back to Horilhun, where the troops have room to breathe."

"No arguments here." Mick tabled, "If we leave now without the catapult, we can cover the ten miles to Deepwood in a day and fight in tonight's darkness."

"The soldiers aren't going to like the short notice, but it is what it is."

"Yup. They're going to have to get by with nothing but our soothing voices and perpetual charm as motivation." Mick chuckled, then digressed. "Although it's unlikely, we should be on guard at all times for the force at Yernoke, as they might decide to attack *us,* instead of the other way around. But I highly doubt they'd want to surrender the defensive advantage they gain by occupying town."

"Let's hope they do. We'd stand a much better chance of winning in the field, even though they outnumber us two to one."

"Daunting, when you boil it down mathematically like that."

"True," vocalized Dave, having took a deep breath. "We might as well start telling the squad the bad news. The time to mobilize is upon us."

The troops rallied through about as much friction as Mick and Dave had expected. Some were hungover, but that's to be expected, and some were glad to be moving things along. They couldn't wait to spend their pay at the Capital and knew they'd head there once all of northern Garobansurov was liberated.

Leaving the catapult and its dependable performance behind, the battalion began the march to Deepwood. Heavy gear was left behind as well. The plan was to return to the base of Horilhun after Deepwood. It was possible the gear and catapult would be stolen before they got back, but Mick and Dave figured the chances of this were ridiculously low.

Greased by morning energy, the first few miles of the march practically flew right by, despite the uneven topography.

As the name suggested, Deepwood was surrounded by a vast, mostly virgin forest; the fringe of which Mick, Dave, and the crew reached by midafternoon. Named by the ancients, the forest was dubbed Starless Forest, due to how hard it was to see the stars from within. Most of northern Garobansurov was forested, sitting comfortably beneath the Baustics, but that which surrounded Deepwood was particularly dense. It lacked in anything considered a field or even field-like. Without the path, it would've taken most people weeks to get from one end of Starless Forest to the other. Unless one had visited it personally, only someone with a vivid imagination could picture how congested the forest floor was, as impassable shrubbery and fallen trees were strewn everywhere.

It was said that the path from Horilhun to Deepwood took a team of 50 laborers three years to construct—an endeavor considered a waste of time by many, due to how infrequently it was utilized. But to those who had used it, it was deemed a godsend.

Technically, the platoon was glad to be marching in the cool, shady respite of the forest, since it was a rather warm day. They didn't even mind the bugs.

The soldiers noticed the path conveniently meandered around rocks, gullies, high spots, and especially impenetrable greenery. Every once in a while, they saw places where the path-crew had transferred dirt from high ground to low ground, which had been done to limit switchbacks. The soldiers figured the massive logs lining the path in parallel fashion were also placed by the path-crew. These giant log monstrosities were a sight in themselves, having once lived longer than four human life-ages.

On many instances, a merry crew was a slow-moving crew, dawdling and partaking in countless wasteful endeavors. But this was not the case for Mick and Dave's. They were content and expeditious, trekking through the beautiful Starless.

They'd covered the distance to Deepwood in no time and established a base half a mile from town. A handful of tents, hammocks, and resting pads served as a place for rejuvenation before the imminent battle. Fresh legs were vital for optimum performance.

Having finished pitching his tent, Mick said to Dave, "It will no doubt be risky keeping the gold in one of our tents during the battle. Thievery is and always will be ever present in every walk of life. But I suppose wherever we end up stowing it will pose much risk."

"The team has proven to be trustworthy so far."

"True. They are a pretty solid group. But… It usually takes a case of deceit before one can realize who is deceitful. So essentially, it's not easy knowing who is corrupt before you're faced with their corruption."

"Definitely. We'll just have to keep our eyes open and keep on keeping on," returned Dave. "As soon as the blackness of night arrives, we'll assault?"

"Sounds good," returned Mick, as he chucked his armor into the tent from a distance in a show of theatrics. "As long as we're not surprised when we do our surprising. I'll be happy."

"Was that toss some kind of symbolism?" Dave chuckled.

"It very well could've been."

"But, yeah, being a step behind while thinking you're a step ahead is always a possibility."

Gus and Vern walked up to Mick and Dave. "Next time, Mick, let's see if you can land your armor in your tent from even further back," said Gus.

"I might just try that."

Vern inquired, "So what's the game plan, my good men?"

"We attack at dark," replied Mick. "I was just about to go ahead and scout the town to see if there are any additional tactics we could implement."

"Excellent," stated Vern. "This should be an easy one."

"Yes, in theory," replied Mick.

"As long as there aren't any unexpected events," added Gus.

"Occasionally facing unexpected events is regrettably an inevitability," voiced Dave.

"Too true," agreed Gus.

Leon joined the party, and said, "Will we be having an officer's meeting before this battle?"

Mick answered, "I don't think so. I was just about to go scout the town, but the plan basically is to attack at dark."

"I like that. My new mace and I will be ready," asserted Leon.

"I'll go ready the night-sword," mentioned Dave.

"You have a sword specifically for nighttime use?" asked Gus, astonished.

Dave smiled and chuckled. "No, I just figured it'd sound awesome."

"It did, buddy." Through a laugh and a good-humored elbowing, Gus emitted, "The path to hilarity leads right to you, Dave."

"It has to go somewhere," reciprocated Dave.

Gus inserted, "*Black needle* does also suggest nighttime use."

"Indeed, it does."

Mick left the jovial company of Dave, Gus, Vern, and Leon to perform the scouting. He stuck to the shadows on his way to Deepwood, having remembered to augment his clothes with camouflaging leaves. He had no desire to be easily recognizable.

Because he traveled slow, having strived for silence, it'd taken Mick an entire 20 minutes to cover the half-mile to Deepwood. At the edge of town, he found a large tree surrounded by clusters of smaller ones, a barrier behind which he could stand and study unnoticed. He watched for about an hour before taking up another 20 minutes to sneak back to base.

Mick searched out Dave to tell him what he saw while scouting. "It seems the previous reports were right. I only saw about a half-dozen soldiers meandering around town. I'm sure there were additional soldiers nestled inside the tavern and other buildings. I didn't see any strategic defensive placements. Although, let's try not to be overconfident. I'd say a conventional blitz attack should suffice."

"Sounds doable. Did you notice any archers or guards?"

"I saw one guy with a poor-quality bow strapped to his back, and another pretending to stand guard. They both spent more time napping than they did being vigilant. The guy with the bow was stationed on the highest rooftop in town. I'm surprised he didn't tumble off."

"They must not know some of the other northern towns had already been reconquered," stated Dave.

"A huge advantage for us, to be sure."

"A good ole dash'n'stab," uttered Dave, producing a quick grin.

Battle time approached, and the troops prepared for the hike through the dark. Both Mick and Dave decided on light armor for speed and stealth. The sky was on their side that evening, as there was only a quarter moon's worth of detrimental illumination.

Mick made sure the gold was in a secure spot in his tent. He emerged with his sword and joined Dave in rallying the soldiers.

Just like Mick on his scouting mission earlier, the whole team began creeping virtually soundlessly through the forest to Deepwood. As a guiding beacon, the fires of town shimmered between the trees. Mick and Dave's company would've been spotted walking through the wood by a more attentive adversary, but thankfully their opponent was anything but that.

Once the leaders reached the forest edge abutting town, they halted for regrouping. It took nearly five minutes—longer than expected—for every soldier to trickle into the assembly at the tree line. Nevertheless, they all appeared ready and willing for battle.

The sky presented good news. A wisp of clouds breezed in, completely covering the quarter moon and its revealing light. "The perfect time for action."

Having flanked the town, as was standard procedure, they advanced as quickly and inconspicuously as they could.

Donning their light armor, Mick and Dave tiptoed up to a building and peered around it. Having spotted two Molisians, Mick and Dave popped out from the building's backside and charged. The two Molisians didn't stand a chance, for as soon as Mick and Dave had engaged, ten other Garobansurovian soldiers followed suit. The two Molisians quickly realized that facing that many and emerging victorious was too much to ask of anyone. They laid down their arms, hoping to survive as prisoners. It was a wise decision.

The huge patch of clouds moved on, but it was too late for the light of the moon to matter.

The odds suggested that the bulk of the Molisians were hanging out in the tavern, so Mick and Dave beelined towards it. They were fairly sure which was the tavern, since northern Garobansurovian taverns were easy to distinguish amongst a group of buildings, as they were typically the largest. Plus, taverns of mountainous climate zones almost always served warm meals to cold souls, which usually added to their size.

Candles could be seen glowing in the tavern windows, as Mick and Dave led the bulk of their troops towards the front door. The rest of the battalion infiltrated the other parts of Deepwood.

Having wasted no time peering into the window, Dave kicked in the door, and he, Mick, and their team began storming in. Mick and Dave rushed in faster than the fell swoop of an eagle. Immediately, they were confronted by nine startled Molisians. Since none of the nine showed any signs of surrendering, Mick, Dave, and their band got right to work.

Mick ran at a soldier, who for some reason was laughing with what was indisputably the continent's most annoying laugh. Mick couldn't wait to put an end to the laughter. He began with a decoy, a one-handed sword swing, which he followed with a pivot and a swing by his other arm's elbow. The connection had quickly put an end to the annoying laugh for the time being.

Dave picked out an adversary and took notice of his opponent's fear and unwillingness to forfeit. Dave charged and fluidly weaved his black needle into flesh. Having seen enough of his own blood, the Molisian's fear turned into acceptance, the realization that he'd never be an important figurehead amongst his people. He died knowing he tried.

Mick finished off his opponent, having precisely placed his sword tip into his opposer's sinus cavity. The continent's most annoying laughter would be no more. A new titleholder would have to be chosen.

Mick turned around and noticed there were basically no further enemies left for him to engage. The remaining Molisians already had three or four Garobansurovians draped over them.

Just as Mick sighed relief, he was surprisingly stuck with an arrow. He was overwhelmed by shock. It took a few seconds for him to gather composure. He was relieved to see the arrow hadn't hit a critical part of his body. It'd lodged in his back, only embedding in muscle. Having a strong back really came in handy more times than what one would've thought.

Mick ripped out the arrow, realized the bleeding was manageable, and scanned the scene to ascertain from where the arrow had come. After having concluded that every threat within the bar was neutralized, he swiveled his hips to look out the tavern's front window. He gasped, seeing that his team was trapped. A new Molisian force had come out of nowhere. And to make matters worse, it consisted of skilled marksmen, expertly firing arrows into the bar from the street.

Still grimacing from the arrow wound, Mick said to Dave, "We're surrounded by new hostiles. Though, not all of our battalion is here in the tavern, the rest should be out there somewhere."

Out of habit, Dave took a peek out the broken window for affirmation. Narrowly missed by an arrow, he replied, "Maybe this squad of archers shot them all down from some strategic vantage point that we missed."

"I hope not. It would be much easier for us to escape, if we had two battle fronts with which to attack this new threat."

"It would also be easier, if there was a back door," said Dave. "But there isn't."

Gus joined the conversation. "We can't just smash open our own back door either, because all the walls, besides the front, are reinforced with immovable stones."

Dave added, "There's enough wood here that it's imperative we escape as fast as possible, before they decide to burn us down."

"True. We outnumber them," mentioned Mick, "so I don't think it'll be too arduous to sprint through the front entranceway and overtake them. Though, we need a sound plan, as I think we've already lost too many soldiers."

Gus blurted, "I have a proposal, which by no means lacks creativity. Vern and I could bust a hole through the wooden roof and fling all these beer mugs lying about at them for distraction, while you make your move out the door." Gus pointed. "We can create a platform on that balcony over there to get closer to the roof. It's a desperate plan, I know, but I think it'll work."

"What are you going to use to bust your hole?" asked Dave. "It's not exactly a delicate roof."

"My fists. These babies are solid iron." Gus laughed. "Just kidding. I'll use the shovel sitting beside the fireplace."

"It might work," remarked Dave, "assuming it's sturdy. Some shovels are junk and break way too easily."

"True. Only one way to find out," said Gus, as he and Vern started their task. They had no intentions of taking longer than a couple minutes to get through the roof.

Many arrows were flying into the broken windows. Mick, Dave, and their crew tried to stay low and behind barricades and shields. Leon came up with a brilliant idea of rolling all the empty beer barrels towards the door to supply more cover. Eventually, they'd have to jump over them to get out the door, but it was a small price to pay for the supplementary protection.

Gus and Vern dawdled nary a second in ripping a hole through the roof. They'd gotten it done even quicker than they'd anticipated, as the shovel had held firm. A light beam now penetrated the tavern, kissing the floor.

The pair crawled down from the balcony, and using crates they gathered together all the mugs and everything else in the tavern with substantial mass. With their hefty crateloads, Gus and Vern got into position and began their bombardment. They knew none of their airborne mugs would actually kill an adversary, but a distraction was all they needed.

Timed perfectly with the onset of the mug throwing, Mick and Dave began making haste towards the door, followed by the rest. Holding shields in front of their faces and hearts, they jumped the barrels. Mick could feel the pain of his back injury as he leapt, but it wasn't enough to slow him down. It'd take more than a hole in the back to do that.

Once Mick and Dave's crew made it out the door, they began sprinting as fast as they could at the enemy contingent. As they ran, still covering their vitals with shields, many arrows struck their legs, wounds they'd have to worry about later.

Dave lowered his shield in confrontation with his first foe and began working his sword as hard as he physically knew how. Two metallic blades clashed wildly. When he realized his opponent was tired and no longer capable of swinging his sword effectively, Dave quickly glanced around to see with how many Molisians they were dealing. He perceived a couple dozen at most.

Mick took off running at a stand-alone adversary. For some reason, the Molisian was standing ten feet away from the rest. At no point in his life would Mick ever learn why the Molisian was doing such a peculiar thing. The lone warrior threw down his bow, switched to his sword, and coiled up in preparation to strike Mick. Mick couldn't help but laugh to himself when he saw the guy get hit in the face with a beer mug.

Dave supplied eternal rest to his winded opponent and moved on to assist a fellow compatriot with an opposer. Two on one battles were fun, as long as you weren't the one.

Mick took advantage of his enemy being stunned by a beer mug and drew blood with his very first sword flourish. However, the Molisian displayed some ability. It took Mick much time to notice any slowing in his quarry. By the time Mick was able to slay his man, the battle was practically over.

Mick walked up to Dave, and said, "We lost two soldiers, I see. One was by melee and the other by arrow. I'm thinking we also lost all those who didn't accompany us into the bar."

"Right," replied Dave, wiping a mixture of dirt and blood off his sword into the tallest grass within his vicinity. "They were probably cherry picked."

"Hopefully not."

"I wonder why this batch of enemies hadn't been teamed up with the one in the bar."

"Good question, Leopard. The answer to which I don't think we'll ever learn. Or wait, we may be able to find out, since we do have prisoners to question."

"Correct. Though, before we do that, we might as well go inform Gus and Vern the fight is over, so they can stop flinging mugs. Maybe we can save a few mugs from annihilation for the crew's victory drinking tonight."

Before entering the bar, Mick and Dave noticed the mugs had stopped flying out of the hole. "I guess we don't have to tell them."

"True, Mick. Let's go congratulate Gus and Vern on their mug-throwing, nonetheless."

Dave and Mick stepped back over the barrels but were confronted by a sight they didn't expect at all. Their most loyal crew members, as well as a few others, were fighting each other, seemingly to the death. Mick and Dave immediately rushed in to stop the brawl, which wasn't an easy task by any stretch of the imagination.

Mick shouted, "What is the meaning of this? Gus, Vern, Leon, you are officers, our trusted friends! Explain this treachery!"

They all started speaking at once, so Dave instructed Leon to expatiate first.

Leon spat blood and began. "It all started like this: My friends and I were on our way to help you in assaulting the archers. We would've been the last three out the tavern door, but on the way out, something caught our attention. We'd looked up at Gus and Vern, as they were throwing mugs, and saw a pouch lying a few feet from them. It caught our attention because it was lying on its side with gold coins spilling out. I realized it was more coins than what they could've possibly accumulated up to this point. So therefore, I put two and two together and concluded they had stolen your gold, Mick and Dave, the very gold you were using to pay us all. These two thieves must've gone back and grabbed it, while we were all making the march through the woods. So, in light of this, my friends and I confronted them about it. Ultimately, it was a foolish decision on our part, because Gus and Vern out of their guilt promptly attacked us. They are great fighters, and the two of them nearly defeated the three of us. Good thing you walked in when you did, otherwise, there'd be more dead people than there already are. And there's the proof of the treachery right there." Leon pointed to Vern's hand. "He's still got the gold in his hand."

Mick and Dave saw the gold in Vern's hand, though, it was in a different pouch than the one within which they'd been storing it. They could tell it was the same amount of coins that they had left behind in the tent.

Dave took the gold from Vern's hand, and said, "Now for your side of the story, Gus, Vern. Let's hear it."

Vern cleared his throat and began. "As you know, Gus and I were heaving the mugs out of the hatch. We weren't able to see when the battle had stopped, but we were able to hear when it did, as there was an abrupt disappearance of the sounds characteristically found at a battle. We halted the throwing and immediately observed that Leon and his cohorts weren't outside helping you in the fight. Instead, it appeared they were hiding in the corner. We confronted them about it. We asked them why they weren't outside helping you. They proceeded to fabricate some story about needing to tend to wounds. Suspicious, I asked to see the wounds. They pointed out some minor abrasions, and while I was inspecting, I noticed Leon was holding a pouch—a different one than the one you two had been toting.

"Normally, I don't think very fast, but at that moment I did, as a thought seeped into my mind that a scheme of betrayal had conceivably unfolded. I thought everything just seemed too incredulous, and that it was possible that the mysterious pouch was in fact full of the King's gold, stolen by Leon and his cronies. I threw caution to the wind and reached for the pouch to feel what was inside. Upon realizing that what I felt did indeed feel like gold, I tried to rip the pouch from Leon's hands. He wasn't having any of it, so he and his squad started to attack us. We could've killed them immediately, as Gus and I are twice the swordsmen as they. But we wanted to keep them alive, so you could punish them how you saw fit. A few moments before you came in to stop the fight, I was able to wrestle the gold from Leon's grasp, which was why it was in my hand when you came into the scene."

Rebutting, Leon pronounced, "If all that is true, then why didn't you just go and quickly retrieve Mick and Dave, instead of fighting us. Why risk Mick and Dave having to decide between your words and ours."

Vern hesitated in his response, enough for Dave to say, "Good point, why didn't you?"

Gus saw that Vern was freezing and couldn't come up with an organic, valid response. He could see the look of downright panic in his friend's eyes. Gus was just about to speak in an attempt to save their confidence, maybe their freedom, when he began to hear an unexpected voice emanating from an unexpected place.

"I know who did it. I know who stole the gold," said the voice.

In stark wonder, the group turned and stared at what seemed like an apparition.

CHAPTER 18

VERY MUCH RESEMBLING a corpse, Harry lay motionless in his corner. He knew it would only be a matter of moments before his time was up. He wished he had the energy to see his grove of slanted trees one last time. He frantically visualized all his favorite memories of his son and wife. He hoped they were okay and would live much longer than he. He hoped Will would grow into a fine Garobansurovian man, serving the King with as much pride as he had.

Defeated, Harry curled up into an even tighter ball atop the cold, hard, wooden floor.

He scanned the scene as if it were the last sight he'd ever see, for all he knew, it would be. But in that scan, he spotted something he had yet to notice in all the long days previous. It was as if his desperate state allowed him to see with a type of focus he'd previously never been able to wield. Across the room—ironically not far from the parallelogram cast on the floor that he'd observed many times before—he spied an opening in the floorboards just wide enough to be considered unnatural. Maybe it was a trapdoor.

For a moment, the new discovery brightened his spirits, but the euphoria quickly faded. *What benefit could a trapdoor provide for my abysmal state, really?*

Harry decided that with his last ounce of strength he would crawl over to his discovery to see if it was indeed something noteworthy. One last hoorah to take him into the next world.

He took a few deep breaths, as deep as his fragile lungs would allow, and wiggled himself across the room. Glad the effort didn't kill him, he stared at the gap in the otherwise gapless floorboards. He shook out the sore in his crawling arm and stuck his finger in the gap for inspection. Harry pried with his finger and was shocked to feel movement. It was a trapdoor!

Fighting through the pain his entire body was in from lying on the floor the past few days, he leveraged open the door. Thankfully, there was just enough daylight left to illuminate the space below. He could tell it wasn't a very large space, but large enough for someone to have performed something secretive within.

Harry lowered himself into the dusty cavity, but not without discharging a shriek of agony.

Once his feet touched ground, he focused his eyes to the available light. He pivoted his head away from the crude ladder and onto what lay hidden, obscured for years. It was a lab, a science lab of some sort.

Having inched closer, Harry could see there were scientific instruments strewn on tables, along with all sorts of chemicals contained within tubes, flasks, bottles, and jars of all shapes and sizes. Though, he had no idea what any of the chemicals were, as none were labeled. Plus, he knew nothing of elements and alloys. He'd always wanted to know more about chemistry, among other sciences. *I've never had much time for study—always such devotion to country*, he proudly thought to himself.

Although his sight had been slowly deteriorating, he inspected the rest of the dimly lit hollow as best he could but found nothing else remarkable. He took a moment to ponder what may've happened down there, so many years ago. There weren't exactly many chemists in Garobansurov, so anything that had transpired was probably interesting.

His energy, much like his recent luck, ran out, for his legs gave way and he plummeted to the ground.

He eventually realized he hadn't at that moment tumble to his death.

After gathering composure, Harry resolved to do what he could to get himself back to vertical. He grabbed onto the side of the table for stability and slowly pulled himself to his feet. But while he had forced himself up, he'd felt something peculiar underneath the table.

After regaining equilibrium, he reached back under the table to inspect its underside more thoroughly. He discovered a hidden compartment, which concealed another substance-filled bottle. But this one was different. This one was labeled.

He realized there was a single word written on the bottle, but he couldn't read it, because it was covered in dust. First, he blew on the bottle, but got nowhere. Next, he wiped it with his shirt and was now able to discern the lone word. The word was *ante*. What could *ante* mean? Harry sifted through his vocabulary to make out words with the prefix, suffix, or base word *ante*. He started with proper nouns, but nothing from his memory came to mind. He knew of a lake labeled *Antol* lake, but that wasn't a match.

His mind began to hurt from having so many words run through his mind at once. Grinding through his vocabulary wasn't paying off. What is it that could possibly have a reason for being hidden under a table so discreetly?

He slumped, but in doing so, *it* hit him like a bee sting. He realized that what he was holding was exactly what he needed most: *antidote*. But his hope quickly faded, because he realized that in the correct spelling of antidote an *i* proceeded the *ant*, not an *e*, as the bottle said *ante*.

However, he had nothing to lose. It was possible that whoever labeled it got lazy with the spelling and had mistakenly inserted an *e* into it. He determined to swallow a mouthful.

While running the concoction down his throat, he thought that there was probably enough left in the bottle to cure a handful of people, if it was indeed an antidote. *Hopefully, it's the antidote for what's ailing me. Why wouldn't anyone take it with them upon departure? It's an enigma to be sure.*

After a little more consideration, Harry gained a slight sense of positivity. He'd logicized that whoever once lived there would've been subjected to the same venomous beasts that attacked him, and that these folks would've also needed an antidote. It was a good reason for optimism.

He hoped the optimism would help him survive a touch longer.

He'd calculated that if the elixir were coincidentally exactly what he needed, it'd take effect in 12 hours, as he'd heard this about other well-known medicines. To survive the night and the 12 hours would be his last push, the final act of a convincingly righteous and true life.

The air of night settled upon the desert, summoning all that is nocturnal.

Either there were plenty of doves in the afterlife, or there were more of them greeting Harry that morning than normal, three to be exact. Typically, he would've been lucky to hear one. Nonetheless, it was a welcoming sound. After glancing around, he realized he'd survived the night. It was just a strange day for doves.

He also noticed his eyesight was much clearer than the day before.

Standing wasn't as much of a process either. It felt so good to stand without cringing. His heart fluttered due to these new developments. Walking was still difficult, but at least he could now do it without having to bite his lip and pray for balance during every step.

Harry went to pick up the elixir bottle that still lay undisturbed near to where he slept. He stared at the plainness of it and the letters there upon. *Could it be true? Could this really be the antidote?* He immediately clung to the bottle as if it were worth his own weight in gold.

Finally, Harry set the bottle in a most secure place. One where he knew the bottle wouldn't roll to the ground and shatter, get stepped on, have something fall on it, or be carried away by an animal.

To his delight, as the day progressed, he was able to walk increasingly better. And by dusk, he was able to once again limp out to the grove of slanted trees he loved so much. There, he thanked the heavens for what seemed to be a miracle.

A few days went by, and he became well enough to start planning his attempt at returning to the Capital to finish his mission. And after that, he would see his family. Though, it was still a long trek to his family after the Capital.

Just before the much-anticipated exit from the housing compound, Harry grabbed the life-saving antidote from its secure resting place; for he, unlike its creator, had the utmost intention of bringing it with wherever he went.

For a moment, he pondered. What possible reason could the chemist who created it have for leaving it behind? Leaving it to forever hide under the table beneath the secret trap door. If it were accidentally left behind, it wouldn't have been placed in such a hidden locale. It would've been resting on some platform in plain sight. It was obviously placed where it was with the intention of it staying a secret.

In the end, the only logical conclusion Harry devised was that the chemist wasn't a very moral person—someone evil who didn't care whether his traveling companions, or anyone else with whom they'd come in contact, lived or died.

What other unscrupulous deeds could the inventor of this antidote be unleashing, as I prepare to give getting out of the desert a shot?

"EXCUSE ME?" blurted Dave to the apparition, the unhealthily skinny woman who'd appeared unexpectedly.

The lady cleared her throat, and replied, "I heard the whole ordeal. I know precisely who the thieves are and precisely who the noble souls are."

Mick swallowed hard, and stated, "Your help is certainly welcomed. Judging by your appearance, it seems like you have quite the story to tell."

"I do," returned the lady, "if you have the time. The story is a long one."

"This is important," said Mick, "so go ahead and orate. Would you like something to drink first? You look pretty rough around the edges."

"Yes, I am rather parched. Fresh water would be excellent." Dave extended his canteen, and after taking a long gulp, she began. "I used to work at this bar, this restaurant, and my name is Anna. I was working when it all happened. The Molisians came out of nowhere and assaulted town. Idiosyncratic of Molisian raiding parties, they raped and murdered innocents during the attack. Many of the victims were my friends."

"Instead of being another casualty, I thought and acted quickly. Just before the aggressors entered my building, having seen everyone before me fail at running away, I crawled down into the garbage chute, the one behind the bar. The owner of the establishment thought he had a brilliant idea by making an overly large garbage chute, so that way he and his employees didn't have to waste time lugging garbage outside. Most of us had just thought he was lazy. Though, my opinion of his idea has since changed."

"When I initially crawled down, I had only envisioned myself having to stay in the stench for a day, maybe two, tops. I figured the soldiers would raid the village, take whatever they wanted, rape whomever they wanted, and move on. I've never been so wrong. Their leader must've decided the village had some sort of strategic value for their cause. So, a regiment stayed behind, and unfortunately for me, they stayed in the tavern the whole time. If they would've left town for even five minutes, I would've attempted an escape. No such luck. I have no idea why they thought this place was so astonishing. I've worked here for a long time; it really isn't that great."

"I bade my time, having no idea if they'd find me. They were close a few times. The scarier moments, however, were the ones where I almost lost my sanity. By no stretch of the imagination is it easy being trapped in a hole for months. I spent a lot of my time playing a game with pebbles that my grandfather had taught me. I also spent a fair amount of time listening in to the soldiers' conversations, though their dialogue wasn't exactly a grand, artistic expression of thought, so I wasn't able to do that for very long. On a few occasions, I learned of their plans, but it was never anything helpful for me or any escape I might've attempted.

"I ate next to nothing, as most of the available edibles were too moldy for digestion. I drank the water seeping in through the walls. It must've been somewhat sterile, or else I'm sure I would've gotten sicker than I had.

"Occasionally, some of them would go out on a booze raid, but a chunk of them would always remain behind. And to add my irritation, the guy with the annoying laugh always stayed behind. As soon as I'm finished with my recitation, I'm going to guess which one of the dead had the annoying laugh and kick him in the face. It'll be revenge for an annoyance that felt like an eternity.

"One day, I was surprised to hear the soldiers in a commotion. It was a different kind of commotion than the normal drunken revelry I know so well. This kind was more organized and serious.

"I immediately got into listening position. It didn't take long for me to understand what was happening." Anna paused for dramatic effect. "'Twas the greatest understanding for which I could've hoped—they were under attack. It was about time the King sent a force to reclaim town. I guess it was possible Garobansurov had fallen and along with it King Rowlangiv. But I had the feeling that wasn't the case. I don't know why I felt that, I just did.

"Legitimately enthralled, I slumped back into my hole and let things above unfold.

"Music to my ears, I relished every cry of death from those I recognized. Over time, I had been able to distinguish everyone by their voices. I know for a fact the one with the annoying laugh died, as I heard his death-shriek plain as day.

"I resolved to attempt an escape. My plan was to adapt to whatever happened above.

"Though, as you'd expect, I was ultimately overjoyed to hear that your force defeated the Molisians, who unknowingly had me trapped for so long.

"I was especially surprised to hear who the leaders of your party were: Knowing Circle recipients, Mick Thraiker and Dave Ghrere. I became excited for the meeting."

"I was just about to climb out, but then I heard something which compelled me to wait. I heard talk of treason. I needed to stay veiled in order to learn more. And as I hoped, they did reveal more.

"When the bulk of the force had rushed outside to face the new batch of Molisians, I got close to the surface and listened as best I could. I'd heard the discussion between both parties and the resulting melee. I wanted to rush out and help the good guys, but I refrained, because I knew I was too weak to help. And more significantly, I knew that if the traitors won the fight, they'd surely kill me, the witness, as well.

"Even though it was uncomfortable to lay low, I let things play out. But to my extreme elation, events took a turn for the better, as the battle outside had been won and more of you came back in.

"Finally, after I don't even know how many months of torture in my prison, after learning more about myself than I ever thought possible, I emerged from the abyss to an air so fresh I nearly cried, though I probably will shortly."

"But first things first. The group who'd stolen the money out of the tent just after your army began the assault is standing right there, the leader being the one clutching the fancy mace." Anna pointed straight at Leon and his cohorts. "The two who threw mugs out the roof exposed the plot and did their best to intervene in the name of justice," said Anna, looking at Gus and Vern. "You two are unquestionably great allies to the King and all of Garobansurov. I thank you."

Upon Anna's conclusion, Leon became enraged and stepped forward to speak. "That is a lie! Gus and Vern found this woman in the streets during the battle, and probably paid her to come in here and make up a story. She's undoubtedly very talented, perhaps a bard, and was able to conjure the story on the spot in order to suit her benefactors. I demand her testimony be stricken."

Anna produced a surprising chuckle, and said, "You want me to prove my story is true, to prove I spent months of agony confined to the bowels of a garbage chute? Ha. I will do just that. Follow me."

Staking claim to extreme intrigue, Dave and Mick followed Anna to the chute. The three of them descended into the darkness. As one would imagine, it took a few moments for Mick and Dave to get used to the smell. Once their eyes adjusted, Dave began to light a torch.

While Dave fumbled with the torch, Anna spoke. "You'd be surprised how accustomed to minimal light your eyes can become over time. I hope my new handy skill never dissipates. So, I told you about the game my grandfather taught me, and how I had spent most my time down here playing it, right?"

"Yup, you did," replied Mick.

"The condensed version of the rules goes as thus: Each separate pod of stones consists of multiple, perfect mathematical equations. And each stone represents a number or an operator depending on its size. The vertical rows align mathematically with the horizontal rows of each pod. For each equation of the pod, I'd taken out an expression—including operators—but left the other, so I could fill in the blanks later. When I solved each pod, I would just leave it undisturbed and move on to the next. After time, they became quite artful to me. You'll see what I mean as soon as Dave has that torch lit."

"Almost got it," voiced Dave. "I should've brought a candle to light it, instead of this clumsy flint and steel."

Dave produced the necessary spark, and the torch set ablaze, illuminating Anna's realm. Mick and Dave gasped, awestruck at the sight. Hundreds of individual game-pods stretched out across the space, all in near-perfect geometric patterns, all twinkling like stars in the half-light. Most were on the ground, but there were some atop various debris piles.

"Go ahead and check my math," asserted Anna. "You'll see that every horizontal and vertical row form a perfect equation."

It took a bit for Mick and Dave to become acquainted with what pebble size correlated with what number, but after a while, they were able to see that Anna was right: mathematical perfection.

"More artful than any painting I've ever seen," exclaimed Mick. "A true sight to behold."

"I can no doubt see why you left each one up. They're definitely mesmerizing," noted Dave. "The display is undeniably representative of a long, grueling period of time. I profess this adamantly."

The three emerged from the chute, and the first thing Dave did was quickly but gracefully strip the reward-mace from Leon's unexpecting grasp.

"Having peered through the lens of proof," proclaimed Dave, "Mick and I have determined Anna's story to be true. Leon, you and your cohorts have been judged the traitors. You will be brought before the King for final judgement and punishment."

Leon shouted, "How can you be so certain with just the testimony of one lady?"

Mick replied with unwavering confidence, "When it comes to disputing one party's word against another's, there's nothing better than the arrival of an impartial eyewitness."

Leon shrunk.

Without ceremony, Dave bestowed the exceptionally crafted mace upon the soldier, Rhyod, who was the runner-up in the mace contest. Dave couldn't help but notice a certain irony, and said to Leon, "You should've adhered better to the focal point you'd laid out in the contest. You should've fought smarter, not harder."

Ecstatically, Rhyod grasped the weapon, as gracious in victory as he had been in defeat.

Mick announced to the soldiers currently in the bar, "We'll stay the rest of the day and night here in Deepwood. The same rules apply, loot only booze, smoke, and war supplies."

The bar emptied of all but a few. Mick said to Gus and Vern, "Now to address the two of you. What you did here today could've only been done by those with the highest of honor. Garobansurov is proud to call you her own. You two are first-class citizens and Dave and I are extremely grateful to have you with us."

Gus asked, "What exactly was it that you saw down in the chute that made you see the truth?"

"All the while Anna was imprisoned, to pass the time, she played a game consisting of various sizes of pebbles. Each size represented a different number. An unimaginable amount of stone mathematical equations line the world below us. We'd performed the calculations and established that they were all indeed perfect equations. Though it may seem impossible to believe, the pods of pebbles make an otherwise insipid place appear quite beguiling. She was clearly confined to the chute for a very long period of time and would have absolutely no reason to fabricate her testimony."

"Sounds fascinating," returned Gus. "I think I'm going to check it out myself."

"The torch is sitting next to the chute," stated Dave. "Though, don't try relighting it with flint and steel while down there. Long story."

"Gotcha."

Mick voiced, "I remember in your story, Anna, you'd mentioned a soldier with an annoying, tormenting laugh. I remember how you wanted to find him and understandably kick him in the face."

"That I did."

"You won't have to look very hard. I know exactly which one it is, as I'd encountered him and his annoying laugh in battle. He's the one against the wall with a gaping hole in his sinus cavity."

Anna walked up to the corpse, stared, but only pretended to kick. He'd suffered enough. Afterwards, she said to Mick and Dave, "There's a town relatively nearby they always talked about. Apparently, it's being guarded by a lot more soldiers than you encountered here."

"Yes, Yernoke. We may attempt an assault there too, contingent upon certain things."

"I can help," noted Anna. "I've seen firsthand of what these Molisian villains are capable. I yearn for my country to be rid of them."

"What do you propose?" Mick perked up.

"I know the countryside well, and where pockets of Garobansurovian survivors and would-be soldiers would hold up. Additionally, I've always had a way with words and could probably convince many of them to come aid in your mission."

"Coincidentally," returned Mick, "a recruiting specialist is exactly for what we've been searching."

"Excellent! I'm glad to be of service."

Vern overheard the conversation and spoke. "With Mick and Dave's permission, I'll accompany you, Anna, through the countryside in case there are any other Molisians skulking about. I'm sure Gus will want in on the action too. I'll ask him as soon as he emerges from the chute. It's the least we could do for what you did for us."

"I've never declined bodyguards before, so why stop now?" answered Anna. "Though technically, you'll be my first."

Dave voiced, "Yes, it's an excellent idea. If we are to invade Yernoke, we'll need to do it with additional soldiers."

"Even though we're temporarily abandoning the catapult and other gear, we'll post up here while you're away," proclaimed Mick. "We'll also reclaim the small village fifteen miles from here. According to the scouts, only a meager Molisian contingent resides therein. Only this village and Yernoke remain for us to reconquer."

"That'll work out splendidly," stated Anna. "I'm figuring on a forty-five-mile loop myself, maybe five days' worth of enlisting. I'm guessing both our endeavors will take roughly the same amount of time."

"We'll supply Gus and Vern with some gold, so that way you can pay signing bonuses upon signature. And if new soldiers want to fight just out of revenge and patriotism, all the better," communicated Dave.

Gus returned from the chute, and Vern asked his question. Gus didn't hesitate a second to express his eager commitment to guard Anna as she recruited.

The three of them left for the mission, but not until after Anna stuffed herself with food and human interaction. Mick, Dave, and their squad provided perfect conduits for conversation. Anna's frailty vanished, her life heightened by new friendships.

Dave shackled and confined Leon and his crew, who would all be brought before the King.

Dave said to Leon, "I just remembered something. The lady at the Infertile Zone, Lois, said you'd survived the poison of the beasts, whereas the others did not. I am curious. I wonder at the truth behind that situation."

Unmoving and voiceless, Leon stared back with cold eyes.

Meanwhile, Mick spearheaded the burying of the deceased, both Molisian and Garobansurovian. The task took Mick and his crew the rest of the day, because the ground was unexpectedly hard. The gravestones ended up being simple, but no less punctuated by heartfelt sentiment.

Having gotten nothing out of Leon, Dave spent the rest of the daylight hours repairing the hole Gus and Vern had created in the roof of the tavern. It was an easy fix, as he'd conveniently found all the necessary materials and equipment in a nearby shed.

Sitting beside their tents at sunrise, Mick and Dave began planning the invasion of the next town. Since the assault wasn't supposed to be complicated, they decided to approach with stealth, as opposed to with brute force.

"We need to decide which soldiers will accompany us. It's obvious which ones are the most talented with weapons," Dave said to Mick.

"It is, but we must also take into account that not all of our weapon aficionados are apt for stealth."

"Very true. Furthermore, some soldiers are better at battling nocturnally than others. I don't know if it's better night vision, better balance, better awareness, or whatnot, but such a trait is unarguably important."

Mick returned, "I agree. I'll get the parchment and quill, and we'll begin picking those most suitable."

Dave and Mick proceeded to compile their list of accompanying soldiers. After a couple hours, they decided a 30-person force would sneak up on a reported 16 Molisians. Eight were proficient with weapons, seven with stealth, six with fighting in the dark, and nine with all three categories, including Mick and Dave.

Mick and Dave corralled the troops and told them the plan. All of those selected were honored to have been picked for the incursion. They would be set to depart in the morning.

Mick and Dave spent their evening at a part of Deepwood that'd previously caught their eyes: a man-made water feature that seemed to defy the laws of physics. They sat and watched the crystal-clear water flow deceptively endlessly from one side of the feature to the other. At first, they didn't know how the illusion was achieved, as there was no power source in sight.

Eventually, they discovered the water source was a spring, but it took longer to ascertain why the water seemed to disappear into thin air.

"I'm half-tempted to dig a hole next to it to probe where the water is going," Dave admitted, deluged by inquisitiveness. "It's not probable the water is seeping into the ground that fast naturally."

"I'm not going to stop you and your probing," Mick reported back.

"I have a better plan."

"I'm all ears."

Dave looked around, and said, "I'm going to inspect all the buildings nearby. Maybe one of them has a flume of some sort for water flow, forming a connection from the building to the water feature."

"It's possible. I've seen aqueducts in stranger places. I'll check the east buildings, and you can check the west ones if you want."

"Sounds good."

Mick scrutinized the nearest eastern house, finding nothing to aid in the solving of the enigma. He was just about to start the inspection of the second house, when Dave approached.

"Come with me, you've got to see this."

Mick followed Dave to the first house Dave checked and into a well-concealed basement. "Well, ain't that a sight!" blurted Mick.

"The basement door was veiled by a tapestry, which may've been why the Molisians weren't able to find it and ransack the place."

Mick looked closer, and voiced, "I bet with this pool being so deep, it could support many fish. Maybe it was used for aquaculture."

"I think if that was the case, it would smell more like fish down here."

"You're right. It, like the one outside, must be a purely aesthetic water feature."

Dave guided Mick to a certain wall. "Here's the channel in the dirt funneling the water from the outside fountain to this one.

"The stones are stacked perfectly—pure ingenuity," vocalized Mick in awe. "I'm guessing the pool is at least ten feet deep."

"It's massive enough to allow adequate evaporation and ground seepage for the prevention of overfill."

"Massive is an understatement. I bet the homeowners, our Garobansurovian countrymen, sit down here relaxingly at night, entranced by the sights and sounds. I know I would."

"Yes, it is a rather peaceful marvel of engineering. Actually, there's no reason for me not to sleep down here by it, tonight."

"Excellent plan, Dave. No reason for me not to either."

Having gathered their sleeping bags, some snacks, and a sense of whimsy, Dave and Mick set their plan to action. They would end up relishing their night in the basement completely.

Their intrinsic quest for enjoyment would never diminish, even when wedged within the distracting clutches of war.

After their extremely comfortable poolside sleep, Mick and Dave were in good spirits. Mick announced, "Let's get this shindig rolling."

"Time to poke the beast," returned Dave.

"Time to disrupt surface tension."

The pair exited the basement just as full of excitement as they had entered it.

The chosen 28 soldiers were ready to go when Mick and Dave approached, even after having found a sizable amount of liquor the night previous, and even after having enjoyed an equally sizable amount of drunkenness. There were no rookie drinkers in that bunch.

Dave addressed the assemblage, "Given optimal circumstances, this should be the penultimate battle before the respite of the Capital. Let's get in, recover our town, and get out. Those of you who don't possess a bow, borrow one from someone. If it's lost in battle, we'll reimburse."

Mick added, "No one dies."

The assault party took heed of Mick and Dave's words and departed Deepwood optimistically, ready for strategized action. The rest of Mick and Dave's company were given instruction to stay healthy and in shape, as arduous conflict loomed. None of them altogether minded not being picked for the attack, since there was leftover booze. Those who did get picked didn't mind either, for they would receive a bonus.

418

CHAPTER 19

I T TOOK A WHILE for them to get through the deep wood that, as one would guess, surrounded Deepwood, but once they did, traveling was swift. They covered three-fourths of the distance in one day and made camp in a concealed locale next to a bog. Luckily, it wasn't mosquito season.

They made sure all the tents were hidden. If any rambling Molisians were to spot them, all notions of a surprise attack would be foiled. In such an occurrence, there'd certainly be deaths in the offensive. Fortunately, the bog itself supplied ample cover, as thick shrubbery abounded. They reinforced the disguise by placing sticks and greenery around the tents. Moreover, a giant log of concealment lay half-dead on the periphery of the encampment. It seemed out of place, almost magical, as swamps hardly ever harbored such massive trees.

Having heard one of the soldiers had stepped knee-deep into quicksand, Dave was intrigued and went to check out where it'd occurred. Quicksand had always fascinated Dave. In his youth, he'd managed to save his friend from quicksand, but not without having spent hours scrutinizing the pit. At the time, he'd wanted to understand why his friend wasn't able to foresee the doom. But it was to no avail, as he was never able to figure out why quicksand was so adept at camouflage. Though over the years, Dave had learned there were many different kinds of quicksand, and that it came in many different shapes, sizes, colors, and viscosities. Mick was interested in it too, but not like Dave. He remained at camp and played cards, while Dave investigated.

In due course, Dave joined the cardtable and said, "I deduced that our guy got lucky. The quicksand is far deeper and more treacherous in other parts of the marsh."

"Hopefully, nobody sleepwalks tonight, and wanders into those parts unknowingly," noted Mick. "Hopefully, I don't."

"Same here," returned Dave. "However, I do have a proclivity for it, as I had sleepwalked last week. But at least I didn't end up outside my tent."

"I'd have to say," Mick declared, "sleepwalking into quicksand would not be a pleasant way to die."

After the quicksand conversation dissolved into the vastness of the marsh, one of the cardplaying soldiers voiced, "The frogs are certainly out in full force tonight. I love listening to them."

"Gotta love frogs!" Mick blurted in animation, as he raised the bet, wielding four jacks. He shrunk, having realized his enthusiasm could've been understood as a tell. Luckily for him, no one was paying attention, and he won the hand, becoming 18 gitis richer.

The party continued their game for a couple hours further and enjoyed a good night's sleep. Most of the battalion had slept deeply on both ends of the night, as the frog lullabies did not disappoint.

At daybreak, Mick and Dave rallied the troops. Camp was taken down and cautious walking resumed. There weren't exactly vast swaths of countryside to cover before reaching the destination, but there was an annoying headwind.

Having successfully sidestepped windburn, they got within a mile of town and stopped the march. Mick separated from the group and went on ahead to scout— a task he typically enjoyed.

Subsequent being gone an hour, Mick returned and spoke to Dave. "It's a small town, only being guarded by around ten Molisians. We won't wait until nightfall to attack, I have a better plan. There's a large rock formation overlooking town—basalt, which I was very surprised to see they weren't using to their own advantage. Idiots. Luckily, you had instructed everyone to grab a bow before we left. We can all hide behind the formation until a bulk of the Molisians are within sight, then, we can sneak out onto the ledge and shoot down as many as we can. It's a tactic needing the visibility of daytime hours."

Dave was pleased with the plan and eyed up his archery equipment propped up nearby. "If we can bring down at least half with our preemptive arrow-cascade, I think the remaining few will surrender without a fight."

"Oh great, more prisoners. But I suppose it's better than less teammates."

Dave added, "We should've brought the best archers and atlytl wielders on this mission, but some things just can't be forecasted."

Mick stated, "Although we've no Icytryxans, a sizable portion of our crew consists of reasonably skilled long-range fighters. So, all is well."

"A little luck is going our way."

Mick put forward, "I think it'd be in our best interest to assault as soon as possible, as I think the wind may pick up even more and coerce our arrows off-target."

"Good. I was actually in the mood to shoot off a few arrows."

"Splendid. You managing to hit one will greatly increase our odds of success."

Dave pondered his chances. "From how far away do you estimate we'll have to launch?"

"Fifty yards, downhill."

Dave scratched his chin. "I'd say there's about a fifty-fifty chance I'll bring down my first target."

"I like those chances." With enthusiasm coursing through his veins, Mick slapped his buddy on the back. "Ready, old friend?"

"Time to ride the wind," Dave returned.

The 28, plus Dave, started following Mick to the planned launch platform. It wouldn't be a long walk.

Technically, the basalt formation they'd use as their platform began protruding the planet's surface a quarter mile from town. While they walked, Mick and Dave scrutinized the ancient rock outcrop for signs of life, as many different species used its crevices to live. It was something the pair did more times than not when confronted by rocky bluffs.

The squad reached Mick's destination and halted.

Mick snuck out onto the ledge and hid behind it's only tree, an unimpressive specimen barely thick enough to conceal a body. He watched the town below for the most opportune time to begin the offensive. At first, there were only three Molisians within firing range—not optimum. He would end up spying for a long time.

When there were finally seven Molisians standing out in the open, Mick signaled for the team to creep out onto the rock shelf. Without delay, the team began tiptoeing to their marks, aiming to glide as fluidly as they could.

Dave got into position and singled out his target, zeroing in on an adversary standing straight ahead. Common sense dictated to refrain from cross-firing, as the closer the target, the easier the shot, normally.

With strategic patience, Mick watched the team, waiting for everyone to be ready. He could tell when they'd be ready by the fixation in their eyes. When every eye was a picture of pure focus, he gave the signal to launch.

Arrows began sailing quietly through the air.

At the sound of arrows striking buildings, most of the Molisians panicked. Some even foolishly ran closer to Mick and Dave's crew, which made for easier shots.

Dave had narrowly missed with his first shot, though he connected on his second.

One of the seven Molisians, a veteran, had intelligently crouched into a ball while running away. He would never be seen again. The rest weren't as cunning and were stuck with arrows.

In one fell swoop, Mick and Dave's team had immobilized or killed six of the town's ten Molisian soldiers.

Mick ordered, "Sweep through town as quickly as possible. Maybe we can catch a couple before they withdraw to Yernoke."

The team got off their rocky precipice and started searching for the remaining enemies. There weren't many buildings to search, as it was a small town. They only found one. The rest had more than likely fled when they saw the arrow cascade.

The lone captive was pissed that he decided to take a nap when he did. He was questioned by Mick and Dave in the town's only two-story home.

After basic introductions, Mick asked the unarmed Molisian, "I know why your army is here, but why are you, personally, here?"

The Molisian P.O.W. realized escape was impossible. He grasped that his captors were experts with their swords, since at the moment they weren't even bothering with constraints. He replied, "The same reason you're here."

Dave returned, "And that would be?"

"Because we're bored with where we were."

Mick and Dave chuckled. "I can't argue with that logic," professed Dave. "Do you care to be more specific?"

"Sure, but before I do, do either of you know what that thumping sound is?"

Mick responded, "We're under an oak tree. Acorns are hitting the roof."

"I wouldn't have guessed that. I never was a very observant person." The Molisian smiled. "I'm here attempting to claim your land through legal warfare, because I lost my farm to a creditor, became homeless, and would rather be at war than continue living alone in the woods, eating the same thing that's hitting the roof."

"Don't worry," asserted Mick, "we have no intentions of killing you. You don't have to plead a case for the legality of your actions. War is war—unless you personally committed criminal acts along the way?"

"What would you consider criminal?"

"Murdering and raping innocents."

"So not looting?" inquired the captive.

"Nope," answered Dave. "We can overlook that. Who doesn't participate in a little looting now and then? You can't follow every rule thrown at you, otherwise they'll always be someone taking advantage of you. Unless you're Icytryxan, in which case there'd be no rules with which to begin."

The man looked dumbfounded. "What's an Icytryxan?"

"Oh wow, you've been isolated in this little town for far too long," stated Dave. "They are a race of people poles apart from our own, who live on an island archipelago far to the south. They're helping us in this war, and they're a large reason why your army failed at taking the Capital. They have innate qualities which allow them to live their lives free from politics, lies, money, and other such illogical mind frames. Which is why I said, *unless you're Icytryxan.* They make no rules, for rules are not required, as they're moral without mandate."

Mick added, "The way we are as a race has its advantages too, though."

The Molisian reflected, "They don't tell me anything, I guess. I would love to meet one of these folks."

"You will. They're still at the Capital, which is where we will be bringing you prisoners when our mission in the north is complete. The King is just. He'll treat you well."

"How many other prisoners do you have?"

"A few dozen or so," replied Mick.

"Alright. You won't get any trouble from me. I'm just glad to stay alive. Are the female *Icytryxa-dingers,* or however you pronounce it, cute?"

"Very."

"In that case, haul me to the Capital all you want." The Molisian glowed acceptance.

Mick and Dave shot a few more war-related questions at the cooperative prisoner but gained nothing but inconsequential answers.

Acorns continued to fall on the rooftop, drawing in squirrels far and wide.

Mick and Dave decided on behalf of their crew to make camp in town, as opposed to starting the trek back to Deepwood. Besides, they had some time to kill before Anna, Gus, and Vern were expected to return with, what they hoped, new recruits. No invasion of Yernoke would materialize before that.

Mick and Dave wanted to discuss Gus and Vern, two outstanding soldiers who deserved praise, as they had time and time again proven their worth. To sit comfortably for the discussion, Mick kicked a branch off of a chair. Dave lay in the grass.

Before bringing up the topic of Gus and Vern, Dave stated, "It sure is a cozy looking cabin behind you, Mick."

"There's no denying Garobansurovians have quite the knack for constructing quaint homes."

"Quite right, you'll get no denial from me." Recentering his attention, Dave declared, "I wish there were a way to show Gus and Vern how much we value their loyalty. The mere conveyance of words doesn't seem enough. And we can't bestow the King's coins for something like this, as it wouldn't seem personal."

"You're right."

After a pause in dialogue, Dave jumped up from the grass and exclaimed, "I got it! For their unwavering loyalty in the Leon affair, I know what they deserve: *the contorted relics*. The value of those golden statuettes I found in the ruins is immeasurable. This is half because they're solid gold, and half because they no doubt have great antiquity value."

"Yes! Collectors and historians would love to get their hands on such artifacts. That is an excellent idea, Dave. Should we hold a ceremony of sorts, or just hand over the relics with minimal pageantry?"

"I would advocate nothing extremely ostentatious, but just handing them over seems pretty dull. Something in-between the two would get my vote."

Mick proposed, "Since they're not slated to be back for a couple days, let's spend some time thinking how exactly we'll go at it."

"Good idea."

ACCOMPANIED BY a rapidly recruited 30 soldiers, Anna, Gus, and Vern had one more hotspot to attempt before returning. On nothing more than a deer trail, the three walked together, leading the pack. They were headed towards an encampment that Anna knew about. She knew it was where many men went to get away from their wives for hunting. She thought maybe a large group had escaped to the locale when the Molisians had invaded.

Gus commented, "Anna, you're really proving to be as good with persuasion as you had said you were. You have an astounding gift with people."

"Well, thank you, Gus. I like people, so I guess they like me in return. That's all I know. Or wait, I know one more thing, and that is life is much better not being trapped in a pit."

Gus and Vern chuckled. "I could imagine."

"The encampment is around the next corner I think, although technically I've never been there myself," stated Anna. "There were always a particular handful of bar patrons who'd talk about it and explain in boring detail where it was located. I listened to them drone on, obviously for tips—a disinterested waitress is a poor waitress. The encampment is situated near the intersection of this trail and a creek valley."

Vern emitted, "Things are getting wet'n'greasy—a good place for a hunting encampment."

"True," replied Anna.

The trio rounded a corner and crested a ridge. They didn't have eyes on the encampment yet, but they did on a creek valley. Plus, their trail was starting to widen, which was a sign of consistent usage.

After traversing a quarter mile through the valley, Gus pointed, and said, "Right there, in that grove of old trees is exactly where I would put an encampment."

"Definitely," agreed Anna. "There's a certain beauty and mysticism in being surrounded by ancient trees. And those are certainly ancient. Great age for any living thing is rare."

"It's also rare for non-living things," added Vern. "I'd bet my sword there are far more young stars in the night sky than there are old ones. If only it were possible to know their ages. It would be interesting to see a graph depicting the age of every star in the sky."

Gus shot back, "Yes, it would. I love graphs. The world needs more of them."

"To the limbs, trunks, leaves, and charm of old trees we go," sang Anna. "What will we find? My friends and I would certainly like to know."

Right around the time Anna got to the fourth verse of her song, they uncovered the encampment—exactly where they thought it would be. It was 100 feet away from a creek and practically the same size as they'd been picturing it. With smoke billowing out of their chimneys, a dozen makeshift huts huddled together.

To keep things less intimidating, Gus instructed all the new recruits to wait behind, while he, Vern, and Anna made introductions. They could see 20 people amongst the huts and assumed more were inside.

Gus and Vern followed Anna underneath the enticing umbrella of the ancient trees. She uttered, "Cedars and hemlocks."

". . . and a few overwhelmed birches," added Vern.

Escorted by a flexible plan, Anna approached the individuals who most looked like they wanted to be approached. "Hi, I'm Anna. Pleased to make your acquaintance. To my left is Gus and to my right is Vern."

"I'm Mort and this is Ken," the tallest of the pair said nervously, not knowing if he was confronted by fellow Garobansurovians or adversarial Molisians.

"Nice to meet you," stated Anna, as she went to shake hands.

Just then, someone who'd recognized Anna came out of the woodwork. "Anna! Many said you were dead! They said you were snagged in Deepwood."

"Nope, I survived. Long story. I'll tell you about that later. It's great to see you, Orphis."

"Yes, same to you. Gertrude, Brian, and Victor are here as well."

"Excellent, I can't wait to see them," professed Anna. "The group waiting behind on the periphery are new recruits for the war effort. You'll get a kick out of this, Orphis, I'm carrying out official business for Mick Thraiker and Dave Ghrere."

"The Knowing Circle recipients!"

"Yes, the very same. And they are on official business for the King himself."

"From waitress to lady of importance. Something drastic must've happened to you, Anna, indeed."

"It did. But for now, I must ask for the allowance of our new recruits to sojourn in your encampment for a bit. I also ask of you to get everyone of your group together, so I can speak with them all."

"I'm guessing you want to deliver a recruitment speech," Orphis said, light-heartedly.

Anna chuckled. "You've always known me well, like the time a decade ago when we were all in church, and I sprinted out the door in the middle of the sermon. Only you knew that I wouldn't just run out for no reason."

"That's right, I followed you. If it weren't for your keen eye in noticing the burning home, the Newberry kids probably wouldn't have been saved."

"Exactly," returned Anna. "The fact that you know me well and followed me created two avenues of help for the kids, instead of just one."

Orphis stated, "Apparently, I choose wisely whom to know well."

"That you do."

Orphis looked to Mort and Ken who were still standing beside him. He wanted to give them the opportunity to speak in opposition to Anna's request if by chance they were opposed. Seeing they weren't, Orphis decreed, "I will personally vouch for you, Anna, and those you've deemed trustworthy. My sponsorship should be enough to permit your stopover."

"Thank you so much, Orphis. That means a lot."

"You're welcome. And I'll let everyone know right away you wish to speak."

Every member of the encampment honored Orphis' backing of Anna and her party. There being no objections, the new recruits filtered in, doubling the local population.

Each new soldier of Mick and Dave's battalion had their own traveling tent—a necessary item for such a station. The tents were set up immediate the preexisting structures of the encampment to maximize concealment.

Gus and Vern made a lap to see if they recognized anyone, but to no avail. They proceeded to make themselves at home. They would enjoy the luxury of their tents being close to a creek and fish much of the time.

As promised, Orphis assembled the community for Anna's speech.

Anna stood in front of the assemblage and began with a preamble detailing her story in the garbage chute.

Everyone was astonished. They never would've imagined a person could possess such patience.

Once the preliminary account was complete, she began the recruitment aspect. "Yes, you all have stayed alive, evading the Molisians in this cleverly disguised encampment, outlasting many of your countrymen. But that won't last forever, if Mick and Dave aren't successful in taking back the entire north. If you're not found by the enemy first, you will unavoidably face winter, where surviving will be much more difficult. Even if this upcoming winter is mild, sooner or later, an unforgiving winter will inevitably be upon you. The law of averages never fails. Instead of fighting unconquerable winters, you might as well fight the real enemy alongside proven battle-maneuverers. There was a reason King Rowlangiv sent Mick and Dave to recapture the north: Their resume is undeniably impressive. When I emerged from the chute, I witnessed firsthand how they operated masterfully under pressure. It was decision making as best as I've ever witnessed. They win battles, it's a fact. They secured the east last year, now, they just need a few more brave soldiers to secure the north."

Anna took a deep breath and resumed, "I understand many of you aren't soldiers, having never in your life swung a sword while one is being swung back at you, though it's easier than you think when you're going into battle with a strategic advantage. Transcendent tactics— which the Knowing Circle recipients exude in multitudes—is equivalent to outnumbering an opponent, sometimes three-to-one in an open field. There's one more major battle in the north left: Yernoke. They will outnumber us there, true, but not by much if you join. And I promise, Mick and Dave will not go into the battle without *knowing* they can win.

"The time is now. You won't ever have a better chance to fight and regain your homes. Mick and Dave's battalion have already secured half a dozen northern Garobansurov towns. They've encapsulated pure efficiency in assault missions. Amongst them they boast archers, superior armor and weaponry, and certain warriors who've defeated multiple opponents per conflict. And that isn't even including Mick and Dave themselves, who at Fort Gravividon slew fifty each in one fell swoop.

"Don't end up like me, constrained to a cell, suffering endlessly, waiting to die. Fight to get paid generously, but more importantly, *fight for your freedom*, and *fight for those you love*."

The crowd was silent upon Anna's conclusion. They talked amongst themselves, as Anna waited patiently.

"Do we have to sign anything to join you?" asked a gentleman standing in front.

Anna replied to the man loud enough so the rest could hear, "I have contracts with me, yes, and the official wax seal from the King. To get paid like the rest, you'll have to sign. However, you can make your own terms if you wish, obviously getting paid less for signing for a shorter stint. You can also sign nothing and fight for nothing but honor."

Immediately following Anna's answer, a man from the back shouted, "I like it. I want to fight!"

The rest of the crowd snowballed enthusiasm. Anna was pleased.

Anna found a table for her and her paperwork, where most of the encampment joined in to discuss the specifics. In the end, she managed to get 15 to sign and five more to fight just to get their houses back.

After all questions were answered and signing bonuses divvied out, Anna joined Gus and Vern—who'd helped in drawing up contracts—at their cozy place by the creek. Fishing poles were in full operation.

"Not bad, guys. We'll be bringing 50 new soldiers back to Mick and Dave. I think they'll be pleased."

"Yes, I'm sure Mick and Dave will be ecstatic," agreed Vern. "You are very good at recruitment, a true way with people. Commendable. It seems as if it was destiny that we were there when we were to save you from your prison. Have you given any thought to coming to the Capital with us when this is all over? Your ability to secure enlistees would be an attribute our army generals and even Rowlangiv himself would value very highly. The importance of your service to Garobansurov would be immeasurable."

Anna pondered for a moment. "I'd be lying if I said these last few days spent recruiting hadn't supplied me with a great sense of pride and accomplishment, although I have family and friends in the north, whom I cherish dearly. Accompanying you to the Capital would certainly be something I'd have to think about long and hard. It was a good question, Vern. We shall see."

"I know I personally would like you to join us," asserted Gus. "You're an enjoyable, charismatic person, Anna."

"Well, thank you, Gus. You two have been great traveling companions as well."

"Pleasure time is almost over, unfortunately," stated Vern, having just checked his fishing line. "No fish. In the morning, we must head back to Deepwood, and after that, to war."

"Yes, war is a wretched circumstance," Anna voiced, "but one that is unavoidable."

The three friends spent a few more hours of comradery at creekside, talking artfully, before going to bed with ease.

The morning dew arrived, adding to the locale's natural beauty.

Those who'd slept in tents woke to tent walls saturated with dew. Touching a wet tent with one's foot in the morning was, more often than not, an uncomfortable feeling. But it wasn't the end of the world.

Completely rejuvenated, Gus, Vern, and Anna met up just outside their tents.

"Another fine day. The weather has definitely been cooperating with us," commented Vern, through giant, muscle-relaxing stretches. "Just have to get the kinks out."

Anna placed her breakfast over the previous evening's fire, which only needed a little fuel to resume its blaze. "Are you guys hankering breakfast too?" After Gus and Vern each responded with a yes, she tripled the amount of eggs and tack over the fire.

While consuming their meal, the three discussed the quickest and most efficient route back to Deepwood. It would be an easy debate, as all three would be in agreement.

"Yes, the rock-strewn path is the shortest as the crow flies," said Gus, "but constantly watching one's footing in an effort to avoid rocks is overly demanding."

"Ain't that the truth?" Anna emitted.

As it would save time and energy in the end, they decided on the slightly longer but much easier route, the one devoid millions of half-buried rocks. It would lead them past Lake Yarenhall, then wind through the deep forest surrounding Deepwood.

Anna's friend, Orphis, had chosen to fight, resolute in reclaiming his home. He'd risen early to make sure all his things were in order.

All the new recruits from the encampment linked up with the group previously recruited by Anna. Together, the eager, vociferous lot departed the majesty of the tree-concealed encampment. Some from the encampment had stayed behind, clinging to hope that they'd survive the long, cold harshness to come.

The return trek was mostly hazardless. The only problem they encountered occurred at Lake Yarenhall. A skirmish resulted when one of the new recruits learned that another slept with his girlfriend a while back. Skillfully, Anna smoothed it over. She was good at these things. Maybe it was her comforting voice, maybe it was the words she chose, who knows? Some mysteries weren't meant to be solved.

Once the squad reached the thick forest before Deepwood, their marching formation changed. The trail was thin, so the pack stretched out, forming more of a line than a blob. Conversations dwindled.

Finally, after a scenic trek through the wilderness, Anna, Gus, Vern, and their accompaniment reached Deepwood and the rest of the battalion. Conversations regained momentum.

Gus, Vern, and Anna immediately noticed the bar/restaurant in town, the same in which Anna had been trapped, was different. It'd received a remodeling and was now 50 percent larger. The three took a moment to enjoy the smell of the fresh wood and peered inside the building. They noticed virtually everyone was inside. They also noticed Mick and Dave were standing in front of the crowd and behind a table. Atop the table sat a curious bundle, covered by a velvety cloth. Anna, Gus, and Vern went inside, momentarily leaving the new soldiers behind.

Dave caught eye of the new arrivals and announced, "How many recruits have you brought, Anna?"

Anna shouted back, "Fifty."

Astonished at such a large number, Dave cried out to Anna, "Impressive. Can you instruct them all to squeeze in here? They can prop themselves against a wall or stand wherever there's room. We have something important to present."

"Most certainly."

Anna's recruits filed into the newly-remodeled establishment, and all found a place to stand. Elbow room there was naught.

Mick began orating to the crowd. "We'd figured the owners of this place wouldn't mind us enlarging it, as hardly anyone refuses an increase in value to their property. It's top-grade cedar we milled ourselves. We'd needed to create a venue large enough for this ceremony of sorts. Needless to say, we didn't go big enough, as we had no idea that so many new soldiers would be joining us. Bravo, Anna."

Dave was handed the figurative baton. "Mick and I felt this occasion necessary because of the heroics of a certain pair of individuals amongst you. Without the loyalty, ingenuity, and downright selflessness of these two, our total endeavor would've surely fallen apart. The King would've been out-and-out dejected. We thought for a long while on exactly what we could do in repayment of such a deed."

"Finally, it struck me. Some time ago, I found hidden underground ruins, the entrance to which was quite concealed. I'm sure I was the first to enter and explore it for thousands of years. It was real awe-inspiring stuff. Therein, I discovered the hieroglyphs of an ancient race, a people about whom I've never heard nor read. The strange thing is they all had peculiar postures. Unnatural to us, their postures were contorted. It could've been a religious thing, who knows. After getting my fill of the perplexing cavern and the inexplicability within, I began working my way out. But as I headed towards the light of the exit, I spotted something half-buried and glimmering. I unearthed the curious objects and put them in my pockets. I've been toting them ever since. As you can guess, these astonishing artifacts are underneath the velvet cloth in front of me."

Mick took over in the deliverance. "When Leon and his cohorts decided on treason, they had no idea they'd be outmatched. Gus and Vern, you two have earned the highest respect a commander can bestow, the kind of respect that simply can't go unrewarded. May this serve as a reminder to you all that loyalty to the King will never go unnoticed." Mick unveiled the deserved, contorted relics for the crowd to see. "They are solid gold and as old as anyone could imagine. Gus, Vern, step forward to receive your just reward for dutifully foiling the dastardly."

Humbly, Gus and Vern walked to the front and picked up the relics from the table. Applause formed, and they both smiled. Neither had ever seen such exquisite artwork, or unusual artwork, or valuable artwork.

"We would risk our lives again for you two, Mick, Dave, even without reward," proclaimed Gus. "Thank you so much for this honor."

Vern added, "Yes, without hesitation. Only the two of you have ever given us a fighting chance to prove our worth. For that and these statues, I earnestly thank you."

Taking advantage of the spotlight, Gus cracked a joke, "Judging by the aroma, we are all going to partake in a feast in our honor too, eh?"

"You got that right!" returned Dave, amongst the laughter of the crowd. "Let the feasting begin."

Almost everyone started forming a line to grab their share of the incredible feast. Those who hadn't were not yet hungry enough to wait in a line. To prepare the food that all were about to eat, Mick and Dave had uncharacteristically slaved in the kitchen half the day.

While the line took shape, Mick, Dave, Gus, and Vern stood around the table that'd held the relics to talk.

Mick pointed out, "Dave and I found a lot of the food along the route back from our last battle. If someone hadn't picked it from the gardens while it was still fresh, it most likely would've spoiled by the time the homeowners returned. Some of the meat was from our normal stock. But most of it was from a nearby farmer graciously giving us a couple dozen chickens. He was surprised they were even still alive, having been away from his home and the abandoned poultry for some time. He said either the Molisians or predators should've found them. They are resilient specimens, no doubt. He donated them to us in gratitude for us making the north safe again."

"That worked out well," noted Gus. "Maybe by eating this hardy fowl, their inextinguishable spirits will infuse into us."

"I never knew you to be the spiritual type, Gus," Dave voiced, as he handed overflowing beer mugs to Gus and Vern.

"I'm usually not," admitted Gus. "Maybe theses relics have some sort of magical hold over me, not unlike these frothy beverages."

Dave looked at the froth and chuckled. "We haven't noticed the relics having any sort of unexplainable power. But maybe they do. In a world that hasn't seen any sort of magic in tens of thousands of years, maybe these relics are the return."

"If anything, your swords are the return of magic," postulated Vern. "The wooden hilts of the black needle swords sticking to a hand like a spiderweb to a plant is as close to magic as I've ever known."

"Someday, we'll learn if that is true," commented Mick. "We ever continue that search."

"Well, let's toast to that search." Vern said, as he raised his beverage high. "To the sword quest, and to our mission."

The mugs clanged and the four called out in unison, "To the sword quest and to the mission!"

Nothing magical would ever be discovered about the relics, but Gus and Vern would cherish them until the day they died. They would never seek an appraisal, nor wonder upon their monetary value. Receiving the relics would be the greatest honor they'd ever experience.

Mick, Dave, Gus, and Vern eventually sat to partake of the appetizing bounty. Every soldier of the battalion filled their stomachs with food and drink. A person couldn't possibly cram more revelry into that tavern than what was crammed into it that night.

Things got more serious the next day, however.

Mick and Dave held an officers' meeting in the morning to discuss Yernoke. But before the meeting, they paid Anna a visit. They'd given her tons of praise at the ceremony for her superb recruiting, but they felt the need for just a little more. There were also other things to discuss.

After pleasantries and praise, Dave got to business. "We need you, Anna. The King needs you. Garobansurov needs you. Our allies, the Icytryxans, need you. It was fate, the way our paths collided. Your ability to recruit soldiers is truly something to behold."

"I always did make good conversation," followed Anna, "but I think it was my time of solitude in the garbage chute that transformed me into someone who values conversation from every angle. And in this, I feel I can better see the way others view the world."

"Yes," Mick put forth, "I can perceive how that would grant an exceptional recruiting acumen."

"Definitely. You certainly wield an acuity for persuasion," communicated Dave. "So, Mick and I, on behalf of King Rowlangiv, would present you with a contract of the highest quality for your continued services. After whatever happens at Yernoke, Mick, I, and the rest of the contingent will head back south to the Capital. This is where someone with your talent would shine the brightest. You would be paid well by Mick and me but probably better by the King. Other benefits would include the immediate granting of an officer position, immunity from actual battle if you wish, and the full-on enjoyment of Mick's and my company."

"You should've just led with that last perk, you could've saved us all some time." Anna spewed giggles.

Dave and Mick joined in with chuckles of their own. "We'll keep that in consideration for next time."

"At first, I was hesitant in continuing with the army, as I've family and friends here in the north, whom I'd miss dearly if I were to leave," said Anna. "But then, I realized I may have no family and friends left if the Molisians were to win this war. I'd never be able to live with myself if I knew I could've helped but didn't."

"It's the same with Dave and me. We'll draw up the formal contract after the officers' meeting," stated Mick, "which you may now attend, since you are one."

"Sounds great," Anna returned. "I'll put on my game face."

"You two go on ahead to the meeting," insisted Dave, "I'll be there shortly. My skin is playing host to a nuisance, I've a sliver that needs attending. It's been killing me."

"Okay, see you there. Good luck with your removal."

Dave searched out a tool he could utilize for the extraction, while Mick and Anna walked towards the pre-designated place for the meeting. The sliver was more perseverant than Dave had anticipated, but he was eventually successful, and he too headed for the meeting.

Mick and Anna arrived at the barn chosen for the meeting, where half the officers were already waiting. Mick told those present about Anna's new station in the squad. They were all glad to be gaining a masterful recruiter.

When the rest of the officers and Dave showed up, Mick began the meeting. "This is a very important get-together. We'll now decide if we'll march to Yernoke, risking depletion of the squad, or if we'll head back to the Capital and present the King with a sizable addition to the army."

Dave added, "There are an estimated 250 to 300 Molisians defending Yernoke, whereas we now possess 180, a noticeable, disadvantageous difference. Plus, those garrisoned at Yernoke are no inept force, they have proven that by capturing it in the first place. Yernoke is easily defendable, due to its guard towers and spread-out nature, a layout which serves well in preventing surprise night attacks. If we are to proceed, we will need a brilliant, elaborate plan."

"Each segment of six-to-nine buildings houses a guard tower. There's an estimated dozen towers in total. We can't be certain all the towers will have sentries posted, but we can be certain the majority will, and that they'll be armed with bows. There's a pond in the middle of town and a swamp on the south end. Also, there's no outer wall due to the city's huge diameter. We have a catapult at our disposal, but we must not try to destroy all the homes in town," Mick detailed.

"Drawing them out in the open for a toe-to-toe fight would be inconceivable, since they enjoy the greater headcount," discussed Dave. "Even though we may win such an encounter on the field, due to the superior swordcraft of a few among us, we must refrain. The sacrifice would be too high. Do any of you know anything about Yernoke that may be helpful for our circumstance?"

Anna stated, "The bases of the archer towers are metallic, so there'd be no chance of burning them down inconspicuously. The top portions are wood, but due to the skinny framework and overall layout, they're unlikely to catch fire by flaming arrow. This would explain why they've stood for so long."

"Yes," returned Dave, "the Yernoke towers are of legend. I'd hate to be the one to destroy them."

Another newer officer, Jeffrey, spoke next. "I've been to Yernoke relatively recently—before the takeover—and one thing I noticed that may be of assistance is that none of the homes have basements. The groundwater is too high."

"That is helpful, Jeffrey. At least we now know they won't be hiding in basements," noted Mick, which would end up being the last thing he'd say in 25 minutes. The meeting went on, and as everyone discussed far-fetched strategies, he pondered.

Finally, Mick devised a scheme he thought worthy. He explained it in detail to Dave and the trusted officers. After the concise explanation, he asked, "What do you all think? Dave? I believe this is the way to capture Yernoke, while ensuring much of our battalion stays alive."

Dave replied, "Other than the blisters our feet will succumb, I do feel it's an astute plan. I'm totally behind it."

After hearing the officers speak in favor of his stratagem—including Gus and Vern—Mick announced, "So it is decided, we will assault Yernoke. Afterwards, as we march back to the Capital in victory, we'll relish the thought that all of the north has been secured. Rowlangiv will be utterly pleased."

"It'll definitely make the return journey much more agreeable, seeing as though our blistered feet will hurt the whole way," voiced Dave, through a chuckle. "It truly is a great plan; let's begin the preparations forthwith."

"The operation commences," declared Mick.

Mick and Dave laid out to the officers what battle preparations they wanted each to undertake, and all left the morning meeting with something to do.

In the coming days, every member of Mick and Dave's battalion helped with the requirements of Mick's plan. It took two entire days of physical labor for the assembly phase, but it was time, energy, and sweat well spent.

With constructions finished, the entire company finally left Deepwood. Not part of Mick's plan, due to its cumbersome nature, the catapult would continue to be left where it was. Maybe when the villagers started trickling back, they'd find use for it.

The walk from Deepwood to Yernoke took most travelers three to four days, depending on urgency. Mick and Dave were shooting for closer to three.

Atypical of a stroll through northern Garobansurov, they marched all day through unremarkable beauty.

They ended up stopping for evening camp on the banks of Black River, which unlike its name suggested, displayed a brownish hue. Sometimes it seemed black due to an illusion brought forth by unconventional lighting, as its steep embankments tended to block the sun. Technically, it was a river so isolated that nobody paid it much attention.

Mick said to Dave, as the two sat relaxing their legs, "We've got a pretty active camp tonight. To the left, I see Anna and a handful of soldiers at target practice; across the river, I see Gus, Vern, and Jetaz catching many fish; and to the right, I see a murder of crows increasing in size."

"Active indeed," replied Dave. "It seems Gus, Vern, and Jetaz are catching enough fish to feed the entire camp. And the murder."

"The river is teaming with finned vertebrates this evening."

"Truly. And judging by Anna's enthusiasm with that bow, it seems she's intending to fight in the battle."

Mick looked to the left. "I wish she wouldn't—an acquisition too valuable to risk losing. But it undoubtedly is her decision."

"She's got spunk."

"That she has," Mick agreed. "She's been hitting center-target pretty consistently, I've been noticing."

"Spunk and a steady hand," acknowledged Dave, as the murder continued to swell.

Gus, Vern, and war-axe wielder Jetaz ended up feeding many stomachs with their catch. In three hours' time, each had caught 25 bass measuring an average of 18 inches. Anna added a plump pheasant to the pot, which she spotted just before it'd gone airborne. It was convenient she had a bow in her hand at that moment.

Peaceful starlight reflected off tents, as peaceful soldiers slept within. Though, as destined, the arrival of the sun ruined both peacefulnesses.

Situationally immune to the exertion-induced fatigue that would slow many folks, the troop labored through steep hills without losing momentum. Their labor paid off, as they ended up covering the amount of ground Mick and Dave had hoped for the second day. They were all proud to have worked as hard as they had.

Camp that night wasn't as bustling as the night previous; everyone was tired from the strenuous traverse. Due to aching muscles, and the soothing howls of overactive animals in the distance, most slept for many hours, including Mick and Dave.

If their morning calculations were correct, Mick and Dave would be at the final camp, their pre-battle base, by nightfall. It would be situated far enough away from Yernoke that no one from there could find them, but not so far as to hinder all the preparations that still needed to be done. Teams of soldiers would have to trek to Yernoke inconspicuously to prep the field, per Mick's plan, before any fighting could commence.

Calculations were spot on, as at the conclusion of the third leg of walking, just before nightfall, the squad reached final camp. They found a suitable spot two and a half miles from Yernoke. Navigating around camp would be difficult in the dense thicket, but it'd provide the perfect veil, absolute secrecy being vital to Mick's plan.

Mick and Dave knew it wasn't exactly going to be a horde versus a horde, heaping piles of bodies, deep pools of blood kind of a battle. There was a time and a place for such a showing, but this wasn't going to be it.

Once tents were erected, Mick and Dave spoke to a fraction, one-third to be exact, of the battalion. Mick announced, "At the crack of dawn, we will begin to warily setup the battlefield near Yernoke. It will more than likely take every hour of tomorrow's daylight, leading up to a nighttime battle."

Dave voiced, "Pay attention to your surroundings, it'll be easy here to get lost. Whatever you do, don't yell out if you do get lost. It's better you stay lost for the time being, than to alert the Molisians of our whereabouts. Sleep well, for many of you will be waking with the sun."

"So, as a reminder, don't stray away from camp and don't light any fires," added Mick. "Although, I'm sure you all already know that. I'll go into the specifics of battle prep tomorrow."

After Mick and Dave were done addressing the first one-third, they went on to the next and said pretty much the same thing. After that, they concluded with the final third.

Almost everyone went to bed early, not for the same reason as the night before, but because of boredom. There wasn't really much for a person to do when they couldn't stray away from their tent, make a fire, or get loud.

CHAPTER 20

CUSTOMARILY, Yori Rothlin visited Will and Old Man Johnson on weekends, when she had the largest amount of free time, as being the King's favorite advisor was busy work. However, it was now Wednesday for her visit. There was something important she wanted to discuss with them.

"Hello, guys," Yori said, just after entering the room. "How was school today, Will?"

"Hello, Yori. It was okay."

"So, I came by today to ask you something."

Will perked up. "You did?"

"Yup. I met up with our friend, Jason, last night, and we decided it was time for a vacation. We resolved to go on a trip to see a fabled tree that has been said once saved the country from drought. It's very old and very legendary. I had to ask many people, but I now know exactly how to get there. After we agreed to go on the trip, Jason and I came up with the idea of asking the two of you if you wanted to come? It'll be a week-long adventure, and you'll probably miss a bunch of school, which will be okay; I know the King."

Will immediately shot his caretaker, Old Man Johnson, wordless expression, asking him if it was okay to go. Being big-hearted, Mr. Johnson couldn't refuse the request. Instantly, Will was energized by elation.

Glad they both agreed to come, Yori said, "We'll leave in two days. Remember though, we might not find the mythical tree, because I've heard the trail leading to it is quite indiscernible. Regardless, we will have a fun trip together. Who knows what will be in store for us?"

Yori stayed for another hour and took leave, ecstatic to have made a young child happy, a brave lad who'd seemingly lost his whole family. It was a burden no kid should've had to face.

NOT FAR FROM the scene depicting Yori radiating content, General Ulfenkerki met up with King Rowlangiv at the castle for discussion. It was bound to be a reciprocation of words fit for leaders.

Ulfenkerki emitted, "One wouldn't expect it, but it seems as if Gamald is a man of his word. His troops are almost finished rebuilding town and have gotten to this point without much incident."

"Yup," returned Rowlangiv. "Our decision on that has turned out to be the correct one. I just wish we could turn them to our side."

"Yeah, having Gamald's army transform into Garobansurov citizens would be beneficial. It's too bad they are wicked at heart and lazy overall. It's quite obvious that if we were to grant them citizenship, they would act the part only to turn around and betray us. They'd run amuck, relay falsehoods, and disobey the laws. They're too used to their old way of life. It's partly genetics too, I'm sure. Nope, they will remain prisoners until the war is over and, if we win, be escorted back from whence they came."

"Which doesn't seem like is going to be any time soon," added the King. "Have you been communicating with Gamald much lately?"

"Sparsely. He seems content just biding his time. He has no interest in speeding the war along. I'm certain he has a scheme up his sleeve, but I'd be damned if I could figure out what it is. He's as clever as we've always assumed."

"Oh well." Rowlangiv sighed. "At least the Capital's alcohol supply is holding up long enough for them to be nearly finished with the building projects. We would've been lost without it."

"And our town would still look like a battlefield."

"Too true. This war, as does any, has sure depleted our resources."

"War certainly is unavoidably draining. On a different note, how long before the ships embark on the information gathering mission to Riftolen?" asked Ulfenkerki.

"In a week or two, General," replied Rowlangiv. "I just wish it weren't such a costly and dangerous procedure. Nobody wants to set afloat on the waters of war. It can only be assumed the sea abutting Riftolen is dyed with blood."

"Who knows, maybe we'll get lucky, and one of the information runners we sent will return before the ships have to set sail."

"It is possible. But it's been quite some time now.

"Unknown occurrences at our westernmost city, Riftolen—Mick and Dave and their risky quest to take back the north, a scheming Gamald and the other prisoners—all things that have been preventing me from getting a full night's sleep. It's been a long couple of weeks. This war needs to end, and in a positive way." The King took a few deep breaths.

"What doesn't help is the fact we've no diplomatic relations with Molisia, either with the nobles of the north or the lowborn of the south."

Rowlangiv chewed on Ulfenkerki's words for a while before responding to his general. "In the past, we've failed at every act of statesmanship we've attempted with Molisia. We need a new angle, but I have no idea what that could be. All we can do is continue to formulate and, in doing so, refrain from politicizing our country any more than it already is."

"I agree, sir," returned Ulfenkerki. "On a personal note, I just got my new sword."

"Ah, the one Tim Warmane had been fashioning for you. Is it incorporated with apparent magical powers, like the ones he made for Mick and Dave?"

Ulfenkerki chuckled in his normal unpracticed way. "Don't I wish. Though, I do always keep my eyes open for black needle pine trees, when I'm in an area of a forest exuding a mystical feeling."

"Which parts of a forest normally do that?" asked Rowlangiv.

"I couldn't really respond with an exact mathematical equation, but generally any area that strikes me as being dissimilar from the norm."

"Intriguing. I need to get out more. I haven't seen a locale like that since…" The King trailed off in rumination. "since before the war."

"Right, you should get out more. It's good for your health."

ENDOWED WITH THE kind of sleep only fresh air can provide, the kind the King desperately needed, Mick and Dave woke before the sun even considered poking its nose above the horizon. The level of darkness was only exceeded by the level of stillness, as the duo sat in front of their tents. They were both anxious, as there was a lot to do that day. Hopefully, it'd be a productive and calamity-free day.

Dave whispered to Mick, "How many trips do you estimate we'll have to make to the battlefield for prepping today?"

Mick thought on Dave's question for a moment, and replied, "I think you and I will only make one full trip. We'll stay in the vicinity of the battlefield all day, directing everyone with the setup. Somebody will have to trek a little to meet up with incoming groups to guide them, as navigating the terrain will prove to be rather difficult."

"So, should we tote our swords and full battle armor right away this morning?"

"Yes, that's more than likely what will happen. It'd be wise not to wear out our legs too much before the battle," hypothesized Mick. "Gus and Vern can dispatch everything here at base camp, instructing who to come by us at the battlefield with what gear and when. Only a small contingent at a time should come by us to avoid spooking the Molisians, since we'll be so close to the confines of Yernoke. As soon as Gus and Vern are out of their tents, we'll relay these details to them. I'm guessing they'll be out shortly, as I see movement within their tents now."

"That there is."

Two minutes after the rustling of Gus and Vern's tents, the pair emerged, noticeably groggy.

"Ready for a long day?"

Replying to Dave with sincerity but without enthusiasm, Gus voiced, "As ready as I'll ever be."

"Excellent. A little early for you, eh?" communicated Mick. "We're going to have you two be in charge here at base camp, as Dave and I will be in the swamp all day. You will be the dispatchers, directing who to come where with what gear and when."

"The four w's," noticed Vern.

"Yup," emitted Mick. "Who, where, what, when."

Mick and Dave explained every facet of the plan to Gus and Vern and what exactly they needed to do. Gus and Vern understood clearly and told Mick and Dave they would have no problem accomplishing things from their end. Mick and Dave had utmost confidence basecamp would run smoothly.

"Next time we see you, the fighting will be soon to commence, so have a good battle, Gus, Vern, if we don't talk to you beforehand, things may get wicked in battle," Dave uttered.

"You too," replied Vern. "If things get wicked, it's because I made them so."

"That's the Vern I know and love!" blurted Dave.

Mick and Dave gathered together the soldiers that would be making the first trip to the anticipated battlefield. They also collected the first batch of battle paraphernalia needed for Mick's plan.

With the sun now having finally poked its nose above the horizon, the small group began the little under two-and-a-half-mile walk to the outskirts of Yernoke. Free from recoil, each member of the team strenuously lugged a sizable load.

The way to Yernoke taken by most was by easily-travelable road. Dave and Mick's way, however, was nowhere near as easily-travelable or kind to the body. They had to be as unobtrusive as possible, sticking to a route presenting no chance for a wandering Molisian to spot them. Being surrounded by thick terrain conducive to concealment made for tricky navigation, so they needed to pay close attention to where they were at all times. Anna walked along halfway, so she knew the right path and could guide the coming groups to the halfway point. Either Mick or Dave would then meet up with the new group and lead them the rest of the way to the destination.

Post trudging through thick underbrush for many thousands of steps, Mick, Dave, and the first group finally reached their target.

Staring into the uninviting swamp that lay before them, Dave sighed and stated, "I'm afraid, folks, this is when the blisters come to the party."

Mick and a few others chuckled but dreaded the honesty of Dave's statement.

The group set to work immediately. They knew there was plenty to do in a limited amount of time, a wide array of tasks to complete in many different locations. As they worked, they made sure to refrain from anything that'd draw attention. Staying unnoticed by the Molisians was imperative. Besides Mick and Dave—who made sure to appreciate the experience—the soldiers had never before evoked such a degree of awareness. Likewise, most of them had never before gotten so wet and dirty.

The initial batch went back to base camp when everything they could do was accomplished. A new group replacing the old came with fresh supplies, Mick having met Anna at the halfway point for the first switch off.

So far so good.

Throughout the day, four different batches of soldiers would come, and each would work just shy of four hours without a wince. The last group would stay for the battle and be joined by the other groups.

By the end, Mick and Dave were confident in what they'd prepared for the upcoming assault. They were glad the entire setup operation had stayed discreet. Though, Dave wasn't as gleeful about his newly formed blisters.

Chapter 21

MICK, DAVE, AND THE last prep crew waited a couple hours for the rest of the battalion to join them for the battle. They decided they'd initiate the attack a couple hours after sunset. They felt this'd be advantageous, as it gave more of a chance for the Molisians to be either drunk and staggering or asleep.

When the last of the soldiers had trickled in, Mick and Dave walked amongst the crowd, telling them that whoever made multiple kills would receive a bonus. It was a proven motivational method.

Before they all proceeded with the offensive, Mick and Dave gave a motivational speech. Traditionally, it was something they did every time they led a squad into a substantial battle. Time was of the essence, so they weren't overly verbose.

Standing in front of everyone, Dave began in eloquent fashion. "We stand at the fringe of a swamp, at the very fringe of critical conflict, embedded with a sense of self dignity. These trespassers have stolen our homes, our land, our way of life. We won't stand idly by."

Mick continued, "We won't allow these foreigners to reap what our countrymen and we have worked so hard to sow. We are more powerful than the soldiers before us, far more skilled with weapons. Our strategy is superior, our minds the instrument through which victory will be claimed. Their numbers advantage will diminish at the opening stages of our assault and become altogether obliterated in no time at all."

Dave resumed, "You all know the plan and what exactly needs to be done. There is no force stronger in the universe than one that sticks together as a team. And there is no team that sticks together better than we. We will rout the Molisians from northern Garobansurov, once and for all."

The soldiers knew better than to loudly show they were moved by the speech, still, they each found creative yet inaudible ways to express motivation. Mick and Dave clearly saw the expressions and were proud. They were proud seeing the troops stoked to such potent intensity. They were proud in the highly competent squadron they'd formed.

The Garobansurovians were ready, their minds were focused. In 30 minutes, it would begin. Everyone knew exactly what they needed to do. Those designated for the scattered swamp installations were prepared. The team hand-picked for the initial attack wave was poised. The defensive team was set. The lone medic was composed.

Each contingent added up to a sum greater than all its parts.

The soldiers were adrenalized. Aided by Mick's solid plan, they showed minimal fear in going up against a force superior in number.

In the half hour leading up to battle, Mick and Dave made sure what armor they'd decided to don was in tip-top order. They'd opted for light armor, due to the imminent swamp crossings. Being heavy in a swamp was a condition nobody would choose willingly.

With five minutes left to go, they both ran their swords one final time through a sharpener.

"Almost time to roll," Mick declared.

Mick, Dave, Gus, Vern, and 46 other soldiers formed the team that would assault town through the benefit of surprise. Basically, they would strive to kill as many as they could while unseen, and when seen, they'd attempt to lure the Molisians into the trap. The rest of Mick and Dave's squadron would be waiting in the swamp to spring the trap, stationed strategically within the many defensive positions they'd constructed that day.

The wild creatures of the swamp born attentive were amply aware something drastic was about to happen, unlike the Molisians at Yernoke.

Mick and Dave knew sacrifices would have to be made for victory, so they stole a moment for reflection. They took deep breaths in preparation of destiny.

"Time to roll," Mick proclaimed, as he, Dave, and the other 48 members of the assault team officially began the offensive. Their blisters were about to receive blisters of their own.

Throughout the day, during prep work, Mick and Dave gauged the best possible route to take into town through the swamp. It was the one that keep them the most hidden, while keeping from them an overly arduous trek. A whole slew of things they didn't foresee were unveiled as they traveled the dark, mysterious swamp. But so far there was nothing that led Mick and Dave to believe they'd chosen the wrong route.

After a half hour of wetness, unexpected wildlife, and unstable footing, they could finally see the periphery of Yernoke. With their feet on solid ground, the truly dangerous territory had now been breached.

All 50 hid behind the nearest building. The pond which emptied into the swamp lay ahead.

Mick whispered to those nearby, "In retrospect, we should've waited a little longer to begin. There are more still awake than I thought there'd be. I can see the tavern is still bustling. Let's try to avoid that section."

Dave communicated, "You all know what to do. Split up, and when the Molisians become aware of what's going on meet at the rendezvous point for the next stage to begin. Try to kill as many as you can in secrecy."

"For as long as possible, avoid the guard towers, the tavern, and any other locale densely populated with sleepless individuals," added Mick. "Also steer clear of the homes situated on the knoll on the other side of town. It'd be a good place for them to have placed additional snipers."

"Hopefully, we can remain stealthy for at least 10 to 15 minutes. Split into pairs or trios, good luck, and see you soon at the rendezvous point," Dave concluded, knowing nothing vital was left unsaid.

Both Mick and Dave had a plethora of experience in covert missions, so they separated, each accompanied by soldiers less knowledgeable in sneaking. Gus and Vern also split up and hooked up with the less experienced. This wasn't particularly because they had a propensity for slyness of foot, but because they were generally bad asses at heart.

The stage was set, the curtain rose, and the performers leaned in.

Dave and his partner, Albert, sprinted in the shadows to a house 100 feet away from the nearest guard tower. They couldn't distinguish the silhouettes of guards watching from the tower, so they figured their own silhouettes were equally hard to distinguish. It also may've been an empty tower.

The front door of the house was locked, so they tried the side door, which they learned was also locked. The side door was the one more concealed from the guard tower, so that's where they'd decided to put their focus. Neither Dave nor Albert were experts at lockpicking, but since there was no other way to get in quietly, they tried. Dave slid his knife into the slot, and after a bit of jimmying, he found himself being successful. The door slid open, luckily without a creak.

Before moving in, Dave cupped his ear with his hand and listened against the door. He heard no voices, no movement, or no snoring. No anything. So, the pair proceeded to go in and search the house, Dave going one way, and Albert the other.

In the matter of 20 seconds, they deduced the house was empty.

Being in an unoccupied building, Dave was able to speak in a normal voice. "There are definitely signs of recent activity—half-eaten food not yet moldy, dust-free surfaces. I bet the soldiers who've chosen to lodge here are currently at the tavern."

"More than likely."

"I wonder what valuables they have stored that would require them to lock the doors. No time to wonder, though. Moreover, there's no time to wait for them. We must move on to the next building."

"Right behind you, Dave."

Mick and his partner, Mary—Mary Steelback to some—found an unlocked building a considerable distance away from any guard tower. They progressed into the building cautiously and heard what sounded like a bed squeaking. Mick and Mary soon learned it was indeed someone in a bed making the sound. Instead of slaying the Molisian in the bed right then and there, he decided to first scan the rest of the house for others. Before Mick began his scan, he posted Mary next to the sleeping man. She and her sword would spring into action at the first sign of arousal.

Mick tiptoed through the rest of the practically pitch-black house and found no other targets. He returned to Mary, and the two of them eliminated the enemy with precision. They wasted no time advancing to the next building.

Gus was accompanied by two other soldiers. The three of them hadn't been as stealthy as Mick or Dave's team, but they were successful. Nowhere near gingerly, the team pried open the door of a home with a giant war-axe and blitzed in. They caught a soldier off guard that didn't have the time to grab a weapon or yell out before his demise.

Vern's team of three was like Dave's in that they'd entered an unoccupied building for their first incursion. For their next target, since they'd have to move in closer to a guard tower, they'd slow things down.

Indelibly infused by the ability to plan ahead, Dave hesitated a few moments before going to the next building. In his hesitation, he carefully scanned for any aural or visual signs that the assault team had been spotted. Having uncovered none, he and Albert peered into the windows of the nearest home. After perceiving only darkness, they tried all the doors, as was routine. They, again, were all locked. And, again, they'd attempt to pick the lock most hidden from the nearest guard tower.

Subsequent an effective pick, Dave made mental note to inform the residents of Yernoke, should he happen to come across any in the future, to install better lock mechanisms in their doors.

The duo crept inside and came to the startling realization that there were two Molisian soldiers awake in the dark. They couldn't ascertain what exactly it was they were doing in the dark, but it didn't matter. The sight triggered Dave's reflexes, and he began to sneak forward with Albert close behind. As Dave advanced, he heard commotion outdoors, but he couldn't let it affect him; he and Albert needed to worry about the moment.

When they got close enough to hear the Molisians breath, Dave and Albert initiated their pounce.

In pure coincidence, back when Dave had surveyed the cityscape for warning signs, Mick was doing the same.

He also determined it was still clear to enter another building.

Conveniently, Mick and Mary Steelback found another house with an unlocked door, moreover, a door that was propped wide open.

Steelback was a moniker given to her because she once took an arrow to the back, but for some unexplained reason it'd bounced off entirely. At the time, she was wearing no armor, no protective device whatsoever. Those who witnessed it were rather impressed.

Along with a rigid back, Mary was also known to be quick with a blade, hence why she was chosen for the assault team, a real asset.

Inside the house with the open door, the pair performed an inconspicuous and thorough search. Unlike their first run-through, the second was devoid adversaries. Having no one to stab, Mick and Steelback made for the egress, but as soon as they exited the door they heard yelling.

Mick stood still to listen carefully.

Just before pointing, Mick turned to Mary, and said, "The yelling is coming from that guard tower eighty paces away. The team has been spotted. Time to make haste to the rendezvous point."

"Right beside you," Mary communicated, while quickly sheathing her sword.

As Mick ran towards the rendezvous point, he was glad to see Gus and his crew alive and with the same trajectory. Though, there were no signs of Dave, Vern, and their teams.

A stone's throw away from Mick and company, a clay ashtray flew violently at Dave's head. Dave expected it was the only weapon within the Molisian soldier's reach. Dave avoided the projectile and sunk his sword deep into the thrower.

Ashes were now everywhere.

The Molisian nearest Albert wielded a weapon more deadly than an ashtray, but one equally unconventional: a fire poker. Stoking the fire was probably what the Molisian was doing last. Albert's sword and the fire poker clanged together violently. But eventually the flimsy poker was overpowered by the sheer weight of the sword. Albert finished off his adversary with a precise neck slice.

Dave stuck his head out the door to figure out what the commotion was he'd heard at the onset of the engagement. It didn't take long for him to determine the vanguard raid was over and that it was time for stage two of the battle.

The pair began running through the shadows to the assembly point. Dave and Albert spotted Vern and his troupe ahead and sprinted to catch up, neither bothering to look back to see if they were being chased. However, they did heed the steep embankment of the community pond, as tumbling down would spell certain demise.

A torrent of arrows originating from the towers flew overhead, as Dave and Albert caught up with Vern's crew. Together, they would survive the gauntlet before the rendezvous point.

By the time the cluster of Dave, Vern, and their teams had arrived at the assembling locale, half the assault team was already present, including Mick, Gus, and their parties.

Mick said to Dave, "As I'm sure you're aware, we have to wait until the rest of our squad gets here before escaping into the swamp. Otherwise, we won't be able to lure in the Molisians."

"Right," agreed Dave. "We also have to make sure enough of the enemy is around to see it."

"Exactly. We need them to think with their impulse brains and follow us into the swamp, instead of wising up by organizing and waiting until a solid plan is conceived. A mass is more likely to foolishly chase us into the swamp."

"True," voiced Dave, as an arrow whizzed by. "Smart individuals after seeing us go into the swamp would halt out of a healthy fear of the dark and strategize in lieu of mindlessly pursuing."

Mick added, "The more Molisians that see us go into the swamp, the better."

"I concur. Let's hope more of our team arrives."

A few moments were spent in safety, before Mick blurted, "I'm going to peer around this hulking building in front of us to see what's going on."

"I'll cover you," put forth Dave, instinctively checking his sword for debris.

Peering around the building, Mick saw a few good things and a few not so good things. Highlighting the good, 18 members of their platoon were heading their way. And highlighting the not so good, their countrymen were being pursued by a horde of Molisians. The chase was too close for comfort.

Mick and Dave would've jumped out from behind the building in support, swords a-blazing, but they determined it wouldn't have helped anything. Instead, they made it known to their team they were headed in the right direction. "Over here, over here!"

Those being chased heard Mick's guiding cries, started sprinting, and successfully closed the gap. Mick performed a quick head count and was pleased 45 altogether had made it.

The pivotal moment had arisen. Would the Molisians follow them into the swamp, or would they halt and strategize? Only fate knew.

Over half of the Garobansurovians funneled straight into the swamp. Additionally, as was part of the plan, another two handfuls began to go around the swamp, one to the left and one to the right. It was a device to separate the Molisians, leading them to separate defensive stations.

The designated actors comprised of Mick, Dave, Gus, and Vern would perform the dangerous task of going into the swamp last and putting on a show for the Molisians. It would be an exposition of enticement to make the Molisians think their opposer's operation was more fly-by-night than it really was.

The bulk of Mick and Dave's team had disappeared visually into the swamp, but they could still be heard. When the Molisian stampede rounded the large, obstructive building in front of the rendezvous point, they could hear water splashing and twigs breaking.

The stampede's appearance was Mick, Dave, Gus, and Vern's cue. As arrows screamed at them, the quartet entered the swamp, pretending to stumble on various imaginary obstacles—they were in essence *bait*. Dave even went as far as to trip ungracefully into the water. The Molisians couldn't help but fall for the ruse and continue the pursuit into the swamp, cowards compelled to prey upon the seemingly weak.

By the time Mick, Dave, Gus, and Vern were deploying their subterfuge, the whole of the Molisian force stationed at Yernoke was awake and aware what was going on. Each and every one of them would eventually trickle into the swamp, minus the 50 that'd been killed during the initial assault.

Most of the Molisians followed Mick, Dave, Gus, and Vern into the heart of the swamp, but some trailed the individuals escaping the swamp's edges. It was just what Mick's stratagem beckoned.

With foes hot on their tail, Mick, Dave, Gus, and Vern realized they no longer had to keep up the charade of clumsiness, as the plan had worked. They could tell there was an overwhelming amount of Molisians in the morass. The Molisians were in the Garobansurovians domain now. The trap was set.

Knowing the best route to take, having been in the swamp all day, Mick and Dave eluded the chasing Molisians for quite some time. However, with such a large group of chasers, some were bound to be at the pinnacle of speed and close the gap.

Mick and Dave found themselves engaged in armed conflict five minutes into the swamp.

"It's too bad we didn't make it one more minute," said Mick quickly to Dave. "That's how near we are to the first defensive installation."

The pair of Molisians gifted with the ability to close gaps quickly in swamps, unfortunately for them, weren't equally gifted in swordplay. Mick and Dave annihilated them upon confrontation. Although, the brawl had taken long enough for other Molisians to catch up.

Gus and Vern were 40 strides ahead of Mick and Dave, when the first clash in the swamp took place. They were ahead because Mick and Dave had gotten a little carried away with their acting performances. It wasn't often Mick and Dave got to be showmen.

Having heard the clanging of swords to the rear, Gus shouted to Vern, "They caught Mick and Dave. We must go back to help!"

"Right behind you."

By the time Mick and Dave were facing the second batch of gap-closers, Gus and Vern were at their sides. The four tried their best to eliminate their Molisian opponents in swiftness, so they could resume to the nearby defensive site, where help awaited.

"We're winning," noticed Gus, "but I can hear an overwhelming amount of Molisians closing in."

The four began executing risky but panic-free maneuvers for the means of quickening the skirmish. It worked, and they were on their way.

Darkness swelled when Mick, Dave, Gus, and Vern approached the first defensive station, as they'd entered a thicker part of the swamp. Sight was limited, but it was a strategic limitation, as Mick and Dave had the terrain memorized while the Molisians didn't. Because of the low visibility, the Molisians wouldn't be able to see the defensive installation.

By this time, the Molisian soldiers of Yernoke were fairly widespread in the swamp. Even though it was stupid for them to have followed into the swamp in the first place, they weren't complete fools by trying to wade through the deepest parts of it.

As if on a leash, Mick and Dave walked their pursuers straight to the elevated defensive station, where archers and a single atlytl wielder waited nervously. If one were to listen carefully enough, they could hear the elderly Silas of the nomads grinding his teeth.

It would've been too dark to effectively aim arrows and atlytl projectiles, so those of the defensive station lit and threw light bombs. Even with the light from the light bombs, it'd still take a quick-thinking, long-range specialist to distinguish friend from foe.

"All it takes is one imperfect face recognition, and we're done for," said Mick.

"Good thing our incredible good looks make us so easily recognizable," returned Dave.

The four shared a laugh—a good way to calm nerves.

Arrows began flickering against the small amount of light emitted by the light bombs. It was an undeniably eerie sight.

In the matter of moments, the first defensive station saw complete success. Four Molisians had been killed, having received the benefit of dying with honor. No matter how their cause was viewed, one risking their life for what they believed was honorable.

Mick, Dave, Gus, and Vern continued onto the next defensive installation, but unfortunately, unlike at the first, they'd have to draw swords.

Weapons clashed, as the brawl grew towards an unescapable intensity. Blood mixed with swamp water, layered in unignorable gore.

Once arrows were just as likely to kill allies, Mick shouted up to those in the defensive blind, "Come join us with your melee weapons. You're of more use to us down here now."

The four soldiers of the blind complied, and the skirmish became 8 versus 11. Mick and Dave were confident, despite being outnumbered.

Mick fought from atop a cedar root for balance and footing, since the unstable peat of the swamp would supply neither. Dave found and fought from a tamarack root. Gus and Vern didn't care from where they fought, as long as they had someone to fight. However, unluckily for Gus and Vern, they each only got to fight one Molisian at that point of the battle, since Mick and Dave slew more than their fair share.

On through the swamp the four proceeded. The long-range specialists stayed behind at their defensive station to cherry-pick stragglers.

Motion was everywhere. Minus the time a tornado had gone through, the unnamed swamp had never before seen such action in its over 10,000 years of existence.

As like many swamps, it was once a lake, one rich with history. Long ago, the lake was the site of a great battle. There wasn't a soul alive who knew why this battle took place, they just knew that it took place. Occasionally, someone hunting in the swamp would stumble upon the boats, bones, and weapons of warriors who'd fought in the ancient lake battle. The peat of the swamp was an excellent preservative, having kept the evidence remarkably intact throughout the millennia.

The story of the lake and of its battle went deep.

Mick, Dave, Gus, and Vern came to their third defensive installation, which was different than the first two in that it wasn't manned by long-range specialists—short-range ones lay hidden within. When the pursuers came through, those hidden revealed themselves through surprise attack.

The Molisians were thunderstruck at the arrival of the new soldiers. Mick's plan was working splendidly.

A couple more defensive stations were visited by the Garobansurovian quartet, each one ended up serving its purpose. In fact, all the defensive stations of the swamp but two would end up being successful.

Having reached the end of the swamp, Mick, Dave, Gus, and Vern took deep breaths. They spotted many of their countrymen assembled on dry ground, unorganized. It was inevitable that with such an intricate plan disorganization would ensue at some point.

Striving to reorganize, Mick and Dave gathered together everyone within eyeshot. A hundred soldiers formed an encirclement without delay.

Mick instructed, "Any minute now, what's left of the Molisian regiment will emerge from the swamp. I'd be greatly surprised if that force were still greater in number than we, as I've seen many dead Molisians settle into the muck. Once we defeat those who emerge, we can go back and secure Yernoke. However, if none emerge in a few minutes, they are more than likely attempting to go back through the swamp, back to Yernoke to regroup. We can't let that happen, as there are too many battle advantages for the squad occupying town. If in a few minutes the surviving Molisians don't appear, we must run around the swamp to Yernoke. It's a longer trek than going through the swamp, but because of the traction supplied by the dry ground, I'm sure we can beat most of them back to town."

Dave added, "There are probably additional members of our team in the swamp, stranded for various reasons. We'll keep our eyes open for them. But we won't have much time to wait for them. They will eventually know what's going on and search us out."

Having finished addressing the squad as a whole, Mick and Dave began conversation with Gus and Vern.

"Now we wait for things to unfold," stated Dave. "Excellent work in there, Gus, Vern. I was also glad to have seen how effective Silas was with his atlytl. I'm glad we took a chance on him. And I especially got a thrill out of that spin move you performed at the fourth defensive pod, Vern. It was truly something to behold."

"It was a spur-of-the-moment sort of thing," stated Vern. "I needed all the momentum I could get at that point."

"I missed seeing it," said Mick, in disappointment.

"Me too, unfortunately" voiced Gus.

"Too bad; it was as pretty as a picture," Dave noted.

"If only more of the women I bring back to my place were as pretty as a picture," blurted Vern, tailed by an eruption of laughter from the group.

"The lady you encountered in the town with the restaurant on the lake was as pretty as a picture," accredited Gus.

"Ah yes, Justine," Vern reminisced. "She was as pretty as a picture, indeed. If I do recall, we all had beautiful women that unforgettable evening."

"We did," stated Mick. "Lovely Lisa. Her lips were as red as the chair in her living room."

"Verona," added Dave, with a silly smile. "Vivacious Verona and her vibrant bedchamber. Good times, if I do say so myself."

"I'd hate to break up our stroll down memory lane, but it seems like the Molisians began making their way back to Yernoke," communicated Mick. "I think we would've seen some by now."

Dave put forth, "We'll give them a couple more minutes, then, we'll make the dash to Yernoke?"

"I concur," returned Mick, "a couple more minutes should suffice."

"A couple more minutes of memory lane for us then," voiced Vern.

Enthusiastically, the quartet talked more of Casil, of its restaurant on the lake, and of its excellent women. One couldn't have asked for a better two-minute discussion.

With the waiting now over, Mick sounded off to all the gathered Garobansurovian soldiers, "It's clear the Molisians went back to Yernoke, or at least are trying to. We will move at speed and hopefully beat most of them there. Travel lightly, or you'll get winded. We'll reap the benefit of outnumbering them when we get there, I'd bet my life. We are the soldiers of the King, ones who'd walk beside him through any adversity. But in this case, we'll be running."

The soldiers were inspired and quickly got prepared. In no time they were all off and running. It was a two-mile run around the swamp, as opposed to one mile going directly through it. Mick and Dave anticipated the strong runners, including themselves, would complete the course in under 15 minutes, whereas the majority of the squad would do so between 20 and 25. There would be no time to wait for the slow; the faster they got to Yernoke, the better. Mick and Dave knew that if enemy archers were to get into the towers before they did, they'd be doomed.

Not entirely realizing the coincidence of how many times they shared similar feelings, Mick and Dave felt close to accomplishing their King-appointed task. With each passing stride, any fears they had of losing their lives in Garobansurov's north were slid further into their pockets. Their main concern now was keeping their soldiers, their friends, alive.

Of course, anything could happen in battle.

Mid-run, Dave said to Mick, "My body feels light as a feather today. I swear we are nearing Garobansurov's land-speed record."

Mick chuckled, spat, and reciprocated, "I've been too busy watching for arrows coming out of the swamp to notice how fast we're going."

"Trust me, it's pretty fast, especially since we're weighed down by weapons."

"Outstanding. I think we'll be able to see the edge of town, after rounding this next bend to the right."

"Bummer," uttered Dave. "I was enjoying this run."

Mick chuckled again.

Chapter 22

AS DAVE, MICK, AND their battalion began rounding their right turn, possibly towards victory, Harry Shultz began rounding one to the left. He hoped his rounding would unveil a victory of his own. A feeling deep within the pit of his stomach was telling him that just around the corner was the end of the desert, salvation.

He had been staggering for many days, looking for the way out. The good news was that the mysterious antidote he'd discovered in the hidden room was continuing to make him feel better. In that regard, he was out of the woods. Now, if only he could get out of the desert.

The reason Harry thought he was about to reach desert's edge was that he'd been following a dry river bed for many miles, and even though his knowledge of geology was limited, he had the feeling the bed would eventually lead to water. The appearance of water meant the desert was about to lose the battle against other planetary biomes. He would be happy with any other biome.

Harry mused, *What is it that lay hidden behind this giant rock I'm rounding? Alas, trees! Groves and groves of trees! There's water, no doubt.*

He could tally it as wisdom: dry, primeval riverbeds sometimes do lead to water. After a week of roaming the desert, carrying far less water than he wished he could carry, Harry had finally found his way out. Now, if only he knew where he was. He did at least know he was still safely within Garobansurov, since he was aware maps showed that the desert was surrounded by his home country on all sides.

Harry ran his hands across dozens of trees, a complex feeling one would never truly realize they'd miss until it was gone.

His next mission was to attain more drinking water. He was knowledgeable in many water-syphoning tricks, so he had utmost confidence he'd be successful. Harry aimed for the thickest stand of trees in his field of vision. Since he was on high ground, there were a few from which to choose. He selected one that wasn't exactly a rainforest, but it looked promising.

Having entered the three-acre span of various evergreen species, Harry got busy. First, he searched for standing or running water, but his hunt was to no avail. That would've been too easy. Next, he looked for soil containing the slightest bit of moisture, for if he found that, he could try digging a hole, a natural reservoir.

He spent an hour digging holes but failed in procuring a water source this way. After that failure, he constructed a few overnight evaporation catches and attached them to trees. But this wouldn't supply the amount of water he required. If he'd had more material for the catches, it would have, but materials were limited in such locales.

Harry sat on a rock and pondered. He thought only of water.

Eventually, he got sick of thinking of water and fell asleep.

The next morning, he woke up and drank all the water he'd collected in his evaporation catches, which totaled half a cupful. It was nowhere near enough, but it quenched his thirst, nevertheless.

Brimming with morning energy, he decided to check one of the other thinner, less promising groves of trees for water.

Sometimes fortune struck when one least expected it.

After roaming the new grove for only five minutes, Harry came upon the smallest trickle creek you could imagine. Size was of no importance, as it was more than enough water to satisfy his needs. The creek emerged from the east and flowed to the west and was as clear as the day.

For shits and giggles, he searched out the creek's source. He found that the water emerged from an area that no doubt contained springs. It was a pretty little area Harry thought.

He refilled all his containers with the heavenly tasting fluid, stretched a bit, and began following his newfound creek. He had no idea where it would take him—probably nowhere near where his information and he had to go—but wherever it did take him, it'd be better than the desert. "Stupid desert."

ANNA REACHED THE outskirts of Yernoke, running in the lead pack along with Mick and Dave, proving to herself she was still in tip-top shape. She may've even been able to win another bet if one were to be presented.

Dave began investigating the edge of town, while Mick spoke to the lead pack, which consisted of the battalion's five fastest runners that day and more than likely every day. "It's imperative we press our advantage and not wait for the rest. It's vital we infiltrate Yernoke immediately and occupy the archer towers before the Molisians do. It might be dangerous business, but it needs to be done."

"We know what we signed up for," voiced Anna enthusiastically, as she stretched her quads in a way that somehow seemed like she knew the absolute best way to stretch, like she'd performed post-run stretches 1,000 times before. Which she had. "Let's go occupy!"

"I like that attitude," admired Mick. "Follow me."

By the time Mick and Dave were done assessing the situation and ready to go into Yernoke for the second time that evening, Gus and Vern caught up with the lead pack. The seven—the vanguard—proceeded with eyes wide open.

As they entered Yernoke, Dave looked back to make sure there was another group of runners behind that could see them entering Yernoke. Dave hoped all the runners could see someone ahead entering town, so they too knew to enter.

The seven set a course, beelining to the nearest row of archer towers. "One person per tower!" shouted Mick.

A hundred strides into Yernoke, Mick and Dave were glad to see it wasn't overrun by Molisians. However, after 100 more, they observed a Molisian contingent coming out of the swamp and heading straight at them. A foray would undoubtedly ensue, the victors would claim the towers.

On the not-so-bright side, Mick and Dave's seven would be outnumbered by five. On the bright side, four of Mick and Dave's seven were the best fighters of the battalion and quite possibly of all Garobansurov. Anna was one of the battalion's least gifted with a sword, but fortunately her companions knew it and would protect their valuable recruiter. Though, she wouldn't need much protecting, as she was almost as intelligent in battle as she was with social confrontations.

Before Mick reached for his sword, he loosed an arrow into the pack of a dozen Molisians, having no idea if it would connect.

Dave tried to outrun the Molisian pack to the top of a tower, but failed, having been confronted by an adversarial pair in front of the tower's ladder. The two were foolishly thinking they could defeat the one, a master.

Dave used the tower as a shield for his left side, so he didn't fall prey to any flanking maneuvers. Faster than a meteorite flashing through the sky, he defeated the first adversary. Through a series of calculated sword jabs and slashes, Dave slew the second Molisian guarding the way to the top of the tower.

With the way now clear, Dave ascended the tower, intending to put his bow to good use. During the climb, Dave mumbled, "I should really have acquired a better bow by now."

Mick had a firm grasp on his black needle sword, aiming to fight alongside Gus and Vern, so the three of them could help Anna. Together, the quartet faced the bulk of the Molisians, while the other two members of the lead pack battled for supremacy over archer tower entrances. Unfortunately, one of the two died in the struggle but took his opponent to death with him.

The other Garobansurovian fighting for an archer tower, Eddie, succeeded and climbed the tower. In separate towers, he and Dave were in excellent positions for long-range fighting. They waited patiently for their time to strike.

Agile of mind, Mick noticed Dave and Eddie had secured archer towers. By a flick of the head, Mick signaled Gus and Vern to drag the fight towards the towers, so Dave and Eddie had clean shots. The Molisians had no idea what was going on, since it was all happening so quickly.

In the mere matter of 30 seconds, two Molisians had been immobilized by arrow and another two by sword. Gus, Vern, and Mick were swinging their swords so precisely that their allies' ears, noses, and fingers were being missed by sheer inches. Close proximity teamwork had certainly been on display that night.

When two more Molisians ran out of blood, the last of the bunch had no other option than to surrender. For the time being, they'd be kept in a secure area. Luckily, Mick had discovered chains and shackles quickly, otherwise, the keeping of prisoners could've gotten messy and/or complicated.

By the time the chaining was complete, a dozen more of Mick and Dave's runners had arrived. They all went straight into the towers, while Mick stayed at ground level.

When 20 more Garobansurov soldiers filtered into town, Mick gathered them together, establishing a ground force. He led them to advantageous ambush positions near the swamp. Here, Mick and his newly formed force waited for more Molisians to show their faces.

Here and there, Molisians emerged from the swamp, but only two had the courage to storm the town. It was later ascertained that one had recently lost his wife in the war, and the other was just nuts. The rest of the Molisians who'd made it back into town immediately surrendered. In addition, 50 of the Molisian soldiers fled, thinking, *Screw it, I'm going home.* Most were just glad to have safely found their way out of the dark, mystical swamp.

Having realized no further Molisian soldiers were presenting themselves, Mick relaxed his muscles. He sheathed his sword, went over by Dave—still in his tower—and shouted up, "The north is secure! Mission accomplished!"

Before climbing down from the tower, Dave shouted down, "That worked out well!"

Mick and Dave were especially pleased that most of their squad survived the battle. The duo knew the King was probably hoping more soldiers would be returning with them. But Thraiker and Ghrere were confident he would still be happy with what he was getting. Maybe they'd find more recruits throughout the march back, since they now reaped the benefit of having procured a recruiting specialist. Mick and Dave took solace in the fact the King would be ecstatic to learn the north was now safe once again.

The sun finally decided to enrich Yernoke with some light. To most, it'd seemed dark for a long time.

Most of the battalion was too tired to celebrate the victory with hour-upon-hour of merriment. Slogging through a swamp all night was unquestionably taxing. The majority just went to bed, ironically in many of the same beds the Molisians had been sleeping a few hours previous.

But there were always those prone to post-battle revelry, no matter the circumstances. Gus and Vern had fit that description perfectly. Anna normally wasn't affixed by such a label, but this time was different, as she was undergoing an emotional high, having fought in her first battle. She was quite certain it would also be her last, as she'd wreaked most of her vengeance against the Molisians in that one skirmish. The rest she would wreak through her recruiting. She ganged up with Gus, Vern, and a dozen other rabble rousers at the tavern. They all drank, sang songs with cheerful lyrics, and made memories they were certain they'd never forget.

Mick and Dave would stay awake for a few hours to make absolute certain no further Molisians returned to Yernoke. They made an appearance at the tavern for the festivities, then went somewhere more relaxing to wind down.

Sitting in extremely comfortable chairs overlooking the community pond, Mick said to Dave, "I'm glad this phase of our life is over, the tiptoeing on the precipice of leadership complete. Yes, it was an important part of our walk of life, but I'm looking forward to the next stage and the next precipice."

"Same here. I learned a lot about people and leading them, but I can't wait to get back to the Capital and start something anew."

"Whatever that may be," supplemented Mick.

"Indeed, whatever that may be. Which could be anything," noted Dave, as he readjusted in his chair, so his eyes could penetrate the depths of space. The greedy sun had not yet stolen all the stars.

AT THE SAME crack of dawn, Jason, Yori, Will, and Old Man Johnson left the Capital and began their trip to see the fabled tree. Yori had been given halfway decent directions and a crude map, so she was confident they'd find their way. They were all overflowing with the kind of excitement that only the commencement of a new journey could provide. Will was especially saturated by many levels of rapture. Jason and Yori were delighted to be doing something recreational for a change, as free time for them hardly ever revealed itself. Old Man Johnson was exuberant just seeing everyone else so full of life.

Fog had condensed on most surfaces, a rather lovely sight for their opening walk.

Jason looked to the bright, blue sky and said to his walking partners, "Hopefully, good weather and good walking conditions, hand in hand, are bestowed upon us during our quest."

"I'm fine with a little rain," reciprocated Yori, "but I could go without one of those all day rains we had a few weeks ago."

"Mother nature got it out of the way for us, so all is well," revealed Old Man Johnson.

"Excellent," Yori returned.

"The weather usually isn't much to worry about, it's bandits who present the biggest hazard," Jason stated.

"I brought my trusty throwing stars," Yori mentioned, "so, outlaws pose no risk."

"Yes, we're in good hands indeed," declared Jason.

"I brought a weapon too," Will emitted enthusiastically, "my knife."

"Definitely in good hands," expressed Jason.

"I brought a weapon too," Old Man Johnson let be known.

Jason kicked a branch out of the path, and asked, "Which one? One from your collection?"

"Nope." Mr. Johnson received a quizzical look from Jason. "My mind," answered the old-timer.

"Ahh, the best weapon of all," proclaimed Jason Thorncat, "inexhaustible, always available, unbreakable, and in many cases un-dullable."

"Is *un-dullable* even a word?" Yori chuckled. "I know *indelible* is. But, yes, if it's not, then it should be."

"And I coined it," Jason stated with pride. "An extraordinary day, to be sure."

The jovial quartet put eight miles in the first day. Since vacations were few and far between for Jason and

Yori, they would spare no expense for nightly accommodations along the way. Inns weren't exactly plentiful in the countryside, so on days when none were available, they planned on paying country folk for a place to sleep. It was a common practice in Garobansurov. They didn't even lug their tents along. They did, however, plan the trip's first leg around the fact there was an inn along the way eight miles from the Capital. It was a quaint inn in a quaint town.

"I've never had occasion to stop here in Farjorn," professed Yori.

"I have once or twice," emitted Jason, "with army squads, having never stayed very long. It's a good place to secure provisions, necessities that may've been forgotten but then remembered." Jason scratched his chin, looked to his left, then to his right. "The inn is over here."

Disappointment stayed clear, for there were rooms at the inn available. Jason had tried his hardest to pay full price, but the proprietor wasn't having any of it. The man had a knack for patriotism and remembering faces, knowing full too well Jason's high standing in the army. He wouldn't even let Old Man Johnson pay full price for his and Will's room. Yori would share a room with Jason but not a bed.

The rooms were lovely they declared—simple, yet artful. They knew they'd sleep well.

After the four had gone to eat at Farjorn's only restaurant, they sat in Jason and Yori's room to play cards, tell jokes, and share stories—right up until their eyelids became too heavy.

In the morning, they shared a small conversation about how comfortable the blankets were, broke fast, and resumed trekking.

They walked a mile more than the day previous, probably attributable to the downhill course.

No inn was available for the second night of their trip, so Yori was unleashed to work her charm on homeowners to gain sleeping arrangements.

The first farmhouse they tried was an unsuccessful endeavor, due to there being no rooms available. The couple that owned the home had eight kids—no need to say more.

At the second farmhouse, Yori's charm successfully earned them lodging for the night. Jason was especially pleased to pay a fair price, having not been recognized again, not that he didn't fully appreciate the courtesy extended by the innkeeper in Farjorn.

They woke early and started again.

They weren't exactly sure how many days of walking it'd take them to get to their destination, but they were fairly sure it'd be at least a few more, and that they'd relish every step.

THE DAY AFTER Mick, Dave, and their squad reclaimed Yernoke in the name of the King, Mick and Dave decided the trip all the way back to the Capital would begin on the morrow. It had the makings of being a long walk, but a pleasant one, since they'd taken every possible stronghold in the north away from the Molisians. They had no reason to believe it wouldn't be a safe walk south.

Permission was given to the soldiers to enjoy the day, and that they could consume all the alcohol they wanted. The Molisians had been brewing a good supply of their own, so there was plenty available. Like always, they were not to break or steal anything, to which they complied with no argument.

The highlight of the day occurred in the afternoon, when the battle bonuses were divvied out.

First, the soldiers were given their regular weekly pay, cherished coins that were really starting to accrue for most. Almost every soldier had a solid plan as to on what they were going to spend their coins once arriving to the Capital. Some were even going to use it as a down payment for a house, as there were plenty of homes available, to be sure.

After each soldier received their proper weekly pay, Dave addressed the crowd, explaining who was getting what bonus, "For starters, bonuses will be given to the crew that outran everyone else around the swamp, bravely partaking in the battle for the archer towers. Gold coin bonuses will also be handed out to those accomplishing two or more kills throughout the entirety of the conflict. And last but not least, golden bonuses will be given to a couple soldiers, who in the heat of battle daringly carried their compatriots too injured to walk out of the swamp. You know who you are."

When the formality of the bonuses was finished, most proceeded to get drunk, including Mick and Dave. All thru the day, sounds of revelry rippled into the wilderness surrounding Yernoke.

By that stage of the campaign, many solid human bonds had been forged. As a rule of thumb, there weren't many who could've spent much time with those they despised.

With the exception of no one, the soldiers of Mick and Dave's battalion ended up having a fine day.

The morning sun brought with it more of a mindset for seriousness. The squad woke, totally focused on a quick journey back to the Capital.

Standing in front of the house in which they'd slept the night before, Dave and Mick were almost ready for the departure of Yernoke.

Dave cracked his neck, and said to Mick, "There are many miles between Yernoke and the Capital."

"But in theory, without having to reclaim towns along the way, the trip back will be multitudes shorter than the trip here," replied Mick.

"True. Plus, we'll save time by not having to wipe the blood off our swords so frequently."

Mick chuckled. "Yes, there's that too."

The pair checked the house to make sure they weren't forgetting anything. On his way out the door, Dave voiced, "Looks good. Are we ready to hit the road?"

"As ready as we'll ever be."

Mick and Dave joined the already gathered mass of soldiers standing by the tavern anxiously waiting for departure. Mick scanned the crowd to see how many were missing yet and figured a couple dozen. He gave a shout to hurry the stragglers along.

After everyone had finished trickling in, Mick proclaimed, "All are present. It's time to initiate this fun-filled march back to the Capital."

They all left Yernoke, full of energy and full of life.

Walking was the battalion's only mission, which they'd performed perfectly for many days.

Seven days to be exact was when they were finally struck by something to slow their march, not that it was slowed much. It was the point when many of the soldiers who hadn't signed contracts—fighting strictly for the security of the north—would part ways with the bulk of the squad. Camp was set up, where a farewell affair would transpire—nothing extravagant, just a little something for remembrance. Goodbyes were said, and most had a drink or two, it being the first indulgence of the sort since leaving Yernoke. The experience was emotionally heightened, as many had finally come to the realization that they'd truly been part of a winning team—like the old adage: *You don't know what you've got until it's gone.*

The departing few left camp enough time before sunset to reach their destination by dark, leaving behind a group saddened by loss. Camp faded into a joyless murmur after the numbers depletion, but by the time morning came, they were again enthusiastic, anxious to get moving.

Nothing of note happened for a few days, other than Gus grasping he was now stronger than a year before. But immediately following this awareness, he registered the notion that perhaps it was just in his head, and that maybe the multiple days of walking were making him think too much.

On the tenth day since leaving Yernoke, the battalion finally came across a caravan of folks returning to their northern homes. It was a jovial trek whose time had come and made possible only by the bravery of Mick and

Dave's band. News had spread far and wide of the battalion's successes; the caravan was proof.

Both parties made the chance encounter an excuse to take a break from walking. During the sojourn, many members of the caravan voiced earnest thanks to Mick, Dave, and their crew for liberating their homes and hometowns.

Mick met a lady amongst the caravan named Gretchen. The two talked for a bit within the shade of a spruce tree.

"To which one of our lovely northern towns will you be returning, Gretchen?" asked Mick.

"At first, I was going to stay at a friend's, who is also among us and returning home. But that was before we met up with you, and I learned you'd already secured Yernoke. So, I'll be heading home to Yernoke, but not before a short and enjoyable stay with my friend at her house."

"I hope your house in Yernoke hasn't been too defiled by the Molisians."

"It's not the house worrying me, it's my bar. I own the tavern in town there."

"You'll be pleased to know," said Mick, "that not only is the tavern still in one piece, it happens to be relatively unharmed. The Molisians must've really liked it and didn't want to cause it any damage. My squad fancied it as well. It's a fine establishment."

Relief rushed over Gretchen. "I am so happy to hear that. My husband's grandfather having built it, the tavern has been handed down through the generations. My husband passed away a few years ago, him having bequeathed it to me. At the time, I could've sold the tavern for a handsome sum, but it's too sentimental to me, as it'd meant so much to my late husband and his family. I've served drinks with an authentic smile ever since."

"And I'm sure the townsfolk appreciate it," declared Mick.

"I was devastated the day the Molisians ransacked town and forced us to flee. But escaping with my life was the wise decision. Things really do sometimes work out in the end. Well, it's not the end yet. The war still rages on, but I'm still very pleased for the moment."

"Yes," said Mick, "it was the wise decision. It could've been worse. You'll have to talk with a soldier we have among us. She worked at the tavern in Deepwood and wasn't as lucky when the Molisians appeared. She was never given the opportunity to flee, as she was coerced into hiding in a garbage chute the whole while Deepwood was occupied by the Molisians. The ordeal lasted many months for her. She was only able to escape when we attacked. Her name is Anna—wonderful lady. She's our chief recruiter now."

"Now that's a story I would like to hear," Gretchen avowed.

"It is quite the story. I'll introduce you to her."

"I would appreciate that, Mick."

"Not a problem at all. I think I last saw her over that way." Mick pointed.

As Mick endeavored to lead Gretchen to Anna, she said to him, "Under similar circumstances, I would've been doomed, since my tavern has no garbage chute in which to hide."

"It isn't something you see most having."

"Nope. Old taverns had them—I mean *really old*. I never knew Deepwood's tavern had one. Up until now, I would never have wanted one in my bar, but now that I know how handy they are, maybe I'd reconsider."

Mick chuckled. "Yup, they have their benefits apparently."

Mick spotted Anna picking berries, delectable morsels which were clearly abundant of the area.

With Gretchen at his side, Mick approached Anna. He threw a few berries in her basket that he quickly grabbed along the way and said, "Blackberries I presume?"

"The one and only," Anna returned.

"Anna, I'd like you to meet Gretchen," Mick announced. "I partly informed her of your recent and tragic story in Deepwood's tavern. She was intrigued, especially since she's the owner of Yernoke's tavern."

Anna put her basket down and shook Gretchen's hand. "I heard a woman owned the tavern in Yernoke. I mistakenly pictured the woman to be really old for some reason. I was obviously wrong. It's a pleasure to meet you."

"Your visions were half-right, as I'm older than I look," Gretchen admitted.

The pair chuckled. They would get along splendidly.

Anna began giving Gretchen the long version of her story, which would last until it was time for the two parties—soldiers of the battalion and civilians of the caravan—to go their separate ways.

Mick vacated Anna and Gretchen soon after he introduced them and took advantage of the stopover by initiating a hunt in the nearby grove of trees. Meat replenishment wasn't vital at the time, but he figured it was still a wise thing to do. His aim would end up being true, as he'd add 20 pounds of succulence to the meat cache.

While Mick was spending his time hunting and enjoying the woods, Dave was helping the camp cook prepare meals for all those who wanted them. And believe, you, me, there were many hungry bellies.

The meetup—the welcomed contrast to laboriously walking—concluded, and both groups resumed their respective journeys. Virtually everyone involved relished in a lively time.

Chapter 23

ONE WOULD THINK the opposite, but in the preceding days, Jason, Yori, Will, and Old Man Johnson's exhilarations had grown by degrees. They were truly enjoying each other's company. It was as if the path they were on was specifically designed with the four of them in mind.

If calculations were correct, they were to reach their destination on the morrow.

Just about to conclude the day's walking, their minds started to focus on the nightly stopover.

Jason announced, "It would be nice to find a home at which to sleep tonight equipped with a swimming pool in the basement."

Yori and Old Man Johnson chuckled, the latter commented, "Yeah, Mick and Dave told me you guys were blessed with one while in Swyrove. That must have been quite the experience."

"Indeed, it was. The whole thing was unforgettable," Yori voiced.

"That it most certainly was," agreed Jason.

"Although I highly doubt there's a pool in the basement, there's a farm off in the distance we could try for lodging," said Yori.

"You're currently in point, lovely lady, lead the way," Old Man Johnson emitted.

The quartet navigated to the farmhouse, and through Yori's charm, they successfully procured a place to sleep. Unfortunately, there was no basement swimming pool at the homestead. However, there was something nearly as enjoyable—hosts Gary and Gertrude, with charisma and the willingness to learn Fantysy-escape.

A perfect-sized table for the playing of board games resided in the well-kept basement of the farmhouse. It was a six-legged mahogany mammoth occasionally used for family get togethers. Surrounded by perfect lighting and walls of stone, all six would play a basic version of the Icytryxan pastime well into the night.

Halfway through the game, conversation switched from current events to the quartet's point of destination. Jason said to Gary and Gertrude, "None of us have been to the tree of legend, but we've heard stories. We've heard that it almost single-handedly ended a drought a long time ago, and it's still alive, having outlasted its own offspring."

Gertrude spoke. "Yes, they are very engaging stories. As to their trueness, I can't personally attest. But I've always believed them to be true. I know the tree exists, as I'd visited it many years ago. It was still vigorous and definitely looked as old as the stories suggest."

Gary added, "A couple years ago, I'd heard from some travelers that it still survives. So, the odds are favorable that it's still reasonably healthy now."

Hearing the words of their hosts regarding the tree brought spirit to Jason, Yori, Will, and Old Man Johnson. It was an extravagance of which they didn't need much more, since it was already hovering at maximum capacity.

Due to the late hour that everyone went to bed, the trekkers departed later in the morning than they desired. Though, they still expected to make it to the fabled tree that day. It would just be closer to nightfall as opposed to mid-afternoon.

THE RIVER HE was following twisted and turned as frequently *as airborne dust particles*, Harry thought. He wasn't even sure he was entirely gaining ground. He was sure, nonetheless, he had no idea where he was. There was no one to ask and no signs of life in the slightest. But being around water and no longer exhibiting sickness symptoms had him very optimistic. He'd even been able to obtain food from out of the river.

At midday, however, Harry became worried, as off in the distance, huge barricading rock formations loomed. Normally, it wouldn't have been overly arduous to circumnavigate such obstructions, but he certainly didn't want to lose sight of his guiding river. The terrain was unquestionably the sort where one could easily get turned around.

Harry observed, *Where there are rock formations, there are waterfalls. Sticking to the river is sometimes an improbability when waterfalls are involved.*

Sure enough, he soon perceived the roaring sounds of waterfalls.

Ten minutes after he heard them, he saw them. An impassable series of three waterfalls stood before him. He would have to go around, as the rocks of the area were sky-high and unscalable, just like he dreaded. The good news, though, was that he spotted a tall tree in the distance, conveniently near the river, that he could keep in his line of sight as he navigated around the rock limitation.

He began the indirect route, but immediately noticed the going would be slow. There were sharp, annoying stones strewn everywhere to go along with the uneven topography.

Harry was nearing half an hour on his demanding trek around the massive tower to the sky, when he discovered a small cave. Out of sheer curiosity, and human nature, he peered inside. Straightaway, the unmistakable smell of earth—one of his top three favorite scents—wafted over him. He poked inside but realized ten feet in was about all his body would be able to manage, as it wasn't exactly a large crevice.

He stole one last smell of earth from the darkness, recalibrated, and moved on. Once out of the cave, he made sure to immediately spot the top of the tree he'd been following.

Harry continued rounding the lofty rock and passed the apex of his detour. He was now basically heading straight to the tree and back to the river. Smooth sailing ahead, he thought, given no surprises.

Three thousand steps subsequent the cave, the guiding tree and the river was before him. But these weren't the only agreeable sights before him. Their silhouettes reflecting in the river, he could see a group of people in the distance. Finally, he could ask someone where exactly in Garobansurov he was. As Harry walked towards the group, his mind raced.

Am I on the eastern side of the desert? Hopefully, as this is the nearest side to the Capital. Or perhaps, I'm on the southern side, closest the ocean? The north side of the desert is where I'd begun this whole ordeal. If that's the case, I'd be distressingly losing ground. And for the love of God, hopefully I'm not on the west side, the side furthest from my destination.

When he approached the group, due to a certain unexpectedness, he no longer cared on what side of the desert he was.

THE CONSTITUENTS of Mick and Dave's battalion who cared to be knowledgeable on where they were located in the world knew their journey back to the Capital was roughly at its halfway point. Spirits were still high, as on certain occasions, it took a long time for the thrill of victory to wear off. And they had succeeded in many.

At the nightly camp, having just finished performing the monetary count, Mick said to Dave, "The coins are relatively numerous yet. And that's even taking into consideration there are still a few more paydays to divvy out. Hopefully, the King will have good use for the coins when we return to him what's left."

"I would think so," Dave voiced, closing his tent door. "I think Rowlangiv will be pleased, especially with the additions to the army and the north being completely secured."

"Quite right. I know I am pleased with our results. Yes, it could've gone better, we could've amassed more soldiers, but all in all, I've been sleeping pretty well at night."

"Same here. Changing the subject, I hope our homes are still intact. We've certainly been away awhile."

"Indeed, we have, Leopard. Maybe our unknown neighbor is at their house, as we are not at ours'."

Dave chuckled. "That seems to be how it works. One day, we'll finally discover their identity."

Swathed in evenfall, Gus, Vern, and Anna joined Mick and Dave in front of their tents for cards and humorous stories, one of the most common and finer ways to spend an evening, no doubt.

THEY WERE DRAWING near the objective of their journey, a hunch conceived by them all. Yori, Jason, Will, and Old Man Johnson were growing more anxious with every step, as most were touched by excitement when expecting to see something new. But even knowing their target was near, they couldn't help but stop to investigate an interesting locale they'd spotted from the path.

"You don't normally see earthen ravines as defined as this," Jason said, surrounded by walls of earth on three sides.

"It would've been the perfect place to build a house in primordial days," Yori noted. "The earthen barriers would supply the perfect protection from would-be animal attacks."

"True," voiced Old Man Johnson, "there were some pretty ferocious creatures back then, according to legend."

"Maybe the evidence of there being a dwelling of some sort here at one time has since been buried," Yori suggested.

Will grew in enthusiasm. "We could dig and find out." Will wasted no time, aggressively beginning to dig with his hands.

The rest of the party didn't quite share Will's enthusiasm but humored him by digging alongside. However, as opposed to Will, they utilized nearby flat rocks as makeshift shovels, not being in the mood for the annoying, unnatural feeling of mud-encrusted hands.

After spending 20 minutes breaking up ground—finding nothing but dirt, pebbles, decaying twigs, and earthworms—they discontinued the endeavor.

"It's possible something might be buried far below, maybe even hundreds of feet under the surface," Jason commented. "But I'm afraid these crude tools would be ineffectual for such a monumental undertaking."

Will was disappointed they didn't find anything intriguing, but he understood and appreciated the good-hearted attempt.

Will took his eyes off the dig site. Children sometimes being oblivious to such matters, Will didn't mind his crusty, mud-laden hands as he walked away. The rest shook their heads and smiled.

The quartet left the ravine behind and resumed walking the trail.

Finally, they arrived at their unmistakable objective and noticed the ancient tree was still alive. It touched a higher part of the sky than they ever imagined.

Jason said, "We are not alone. There is someone else desiring to admire the living relic."

"Actually," Yori interjected, "he seems to be more interested in us. He's heading directly towards us."

"Well, we might as well offer introductions," Jason remarked.

Smiles in tow, the four of them walked towards the man and were greatly surprised when Will started to run to the man. But in the matter of moments, upon hearing the word that Will yelled in elation, the three understood Will's actions.

"Dad!" Will jumped into his father's arms, in a reunion overflowing with emotion no less than any other. "What are you doing here, Dad?"

Through tears, Harry replied, "I lost my way, but now I am found. What are you doing here, and who are those people you're with?" Though, immediately after Harry finished his sentence, he recognized one of his son's traveling companions. "The taller man I can see is Jason Thorncat."

Will answered, "The shorter man is known as Old Man Johnson. He's the one who's been looking after me. The nice lady is Yori. She works with the King."

Jason, Yori, and Old Man Johnson, having covered the distance slower than Will, reached Will and Harry.

Jason was extremely happy at the confrontation, as he knew instantly that Harry was one of the lost messengers.

Harry spoke. "I nearly died in the desert, poisoned by one of its creatures. I'd been stranded at an old, abandoned compound and have been lost for a long time. I have no idea where I am now even."

Yori noted, "We are in the presence of the *legendary tree,* said to have stopped an ancient drought. We departed the Capital on a journey to see it. We're on a vacation of sorts."

"Is that what this is?" Harry returned. "I've been taking advantage of its great height for a while now, using it as a guide mark to circumnavigate a rocky obstacle. It's a lovely tree, indeed. So, are we near the Capital then?"

"Relatively, yes," Jason responded, "compared to how far you've already traveled. But before we continue this conversation, there is something I'm afraid I must tell you."

Harry could sense the change in Jason's demeanor and braced himself. "Go ahead."

"The reason your son is accompanying us is because your wife passed away. He was found wandering aimlessly through the countryside. Old Man Johnson has graciously been his caretaker ever since. Mick Thraiker and Dave Ghrere were the ones who discovered him and escorted him safely to the Capital."

Clearly devastated, Harry sat on a nearby rock, as tears began welling up. All vibrant colors dimmed to grey. He remained silent on his rock, trying his hardest to think of every memory he possessed of his wife, believing the more he remembered at that moment the more that'd be preserved.

Will saw his father in pain and wanted to comfort him, so he came up with the idea of sitting in his lap.

Sitting lovingly in his father's lap, Will's plan worked.

Harry gathered himself, stood up with a new disposition, and said, "I suppose the King is still waiting on the report from Riftolen?"

"Yes," Jason replied, "we'd almost given up hope the information would ever arrive. We had already begun talks of alternative methods for acquiring the data."

"I'm glad I'm available now and can provide," Harry dutifully stated.

"Definitely," remarked Yori. "It'll save us a lot of gitis. The alternative methods weren't cheap by any stretch of the imagination."

"The information is for the King," Jason emitted, "we'll let him be the first to hear it."

"Alright, sir. I was honored to have embarked on this mission for him."

"He sensed your honor, Harry, I can most certainly tell you that."

Color was starting to seep back into Harry's world. "So, now I'd like to avert my attention to you, Old Man Johnson. Do people really call you that? That's rich. Anyhow, I can't thank you enough for what you've been doing for my son."

"It's been my pleasure. He's a well-behaved young lad. We've had a marvelous time. And, yes, they do. I don't mind, as it implies wisdom." Johnson released a slight laugh.

"That it does," agreed Harry. "Tell me all about your marvelous time, I beg of you."

Old Man Johnson went into detail on all the adventures he and Will shared. The youngster helped in the telling, while Jason and Yori went to admire the ancient tree of Calamity's End—or so they started calling it.

Staring up into the tree's grand crown, Jason said to Yori, "It certainly looks its age, so many gnarls and forks. The ravines in the bark are so deep one could get stranded in them."

"It looks strong, like it'll stand another hundred years."

"Let's hope so. Well worth the trip."

"Yup." Yori suggested, "Let's make camp in the shade of the majestic living legend."

"Sounds great, but are you referring to the tree or Old Man Johnson? I'd be fine with both."

Old Man Johnson overheard Jason's comical witticism and busted out laughing.

Since the five of them didn't have tents along, they constructed small, makeshift shelters under the tree for sleeping. Afterwards, they each found a rock or stump on which to sit. Along with wonderful company and the coolness of the tree's underside, they enjoyed a churning river and a towering mountain in the distance.

Yori told Harry about her finding the toy at the store meant for Will, and that it was given to him. Harry was grateful. They clued Harry in on everything that'd transpired on their part of the world since he'd been gone, including Will's discoverers' mission to reclaim the north.

They all ended up going fishing and tree climbing, except Old Man Johnson, who had no desire for the latter.

They spent one night at their camp under the tree, before starting the trek back to the Capital. They would've spent two, but it was urgent Harry's information reached the King's ears.

The trip Will determined was the best of his life—his entire life.

THE MAJORITY OF Mick and Dave's battalion had sore feet—some having never healed properly from the swamp escapade. But they all took solace in knowing the Capital was now only within a couple weeks' walk. Mick had assured them once they reached the Capital they would be granted appropriate respite.

They stopped next to a pristine lake for the night. As being a relentless lifelong pursuit, it was in Mick and Dave's nature to search out the loveliest places to pitch camp. Easy access to the lake was provided in the form of a prominent sand or pebble beach. Some soldiers would set their tents away from the lake, while others would set theirs right on the beach. Those on the beach would face difficulty on occasion of rain, but only a fool would degrade the proverb stating, *No guts, no glory.*

Of course, Mick and Dave plopped their tents right on the beach.

It was getting late in the year, so the water temperature wasn't suitable for a swim, but the crew partook in various other lake activities. Mick spent an hour combing the beach for artifacts, while Dave enveloped himself in the variety of heightened contemplation that only the cool, refreshing air wafting off a lake could provide. They were productive endeavors for both.

At sunset, Mick and Dave joined the group of soldiers whose tents had been set up nearest them. Discussion was loaded with hilarity, quips, wisdom, and respect.

Curious about the war, one of the soldiers asked Mick and Dave, "Where do you think the next battle will transpire?"

Sitting comfortably, rolling beach pebbles under his toes, Dave replied, "Since we just secured the north, and the eastern front remains safe—last to my knowledge— the west is basically all that remains, which includes Garobansurov's second largest city: Riftolen. However, the west is no doubt isolated from the Capital, as it's separated by many miles and a desert. News is scarce concerning that part of the country. But despite the obscurity, to answer your question, my guess would be somewhere in the west."

The young soldier asked one more question about the war: "When we get to the Capital, if soldiers were immediately required in the west, would we here make that long trip?"

Dave answered, "I can promise King Rowlangiv and General Ulfenkerki would allow sufficient rest between extended traverses. It's widely noted that they both operate on empathy."

Mick put in, "Throughout the history of Garobansurov, only on a handful of times has an army marched from the Capital all the way to Riftolen. Usually, the western armies comprised of western enlistees are adequate."

"And on occasion," Dave added, "soldiers have been shipped from the southern side of the continent to Riftolen. Though, I do know the crown doesn't currently possess enough ships for such a grand undertaking."

Mick and Dave could see the young soldier was soaking in the information like a sponge. The soldier was glad he inquired, as knowing was better than ignorance.

Topics drifted away from battle, the last one of the night being the science behind wave-created patterns in beach sand. They wondered why exactly the patterns took the shape they did. There was no denying the fact that the subject matter discussed by inebriated/merry soldiers could sure be inventive. Many theories were presented, but since nobody stayed awake long enough to conclusively prove their hypothesis, the case remained open.

And it remains open to this day.

AS THE WARMTH of the season waned, the fivesome drew closer to the Capital. The newest member of the party, Harry Shultz, was a man ecstatic to be a part.

Yori said, midstride, "One more night of sleeping and half a day of traveling tomorrow, I figure, and we'll be back."

"Then it's down to business again," stated Jason, a clear tone of disappointment in his voice.

"I must confess, you all make excellent traveling companions," declared Harry.

"I agree," emitted Old Man Johnson. "It's too bad the trip has to end. But I suppose all good things do."

"We have one more night of fun ahead, though," Yori said, cheerfully. "It was a marvelous idea to take a slightly different route back, because now we get to stay at a different inn. Whose idea was it again? I forgot."

"I think it was mine," announced Mr. Johnson.

"An excellent idea, indeed," aired Yori. "On top of that, I know just where we'll be going. It's not exactly an inn—well, it sort of is. A family of whom I'm aware took an ancient tavern they had in their possession and converted its main space into a couple of rooms to rent out to travelers. I've never been there myself, but I hear the architecture is intriguing because of its age."

"It sounds like a marvelous experience for our last night of vacation," imparted Jason.

Yori didn't know exactly where the inn was located, but she knew approximately. When they arrived at the general vicinity, she took her best guess. She began leading the group to an obviously old building atop a small hill, surrounded by a field dominated by spires of purple flowers. Even the flower species looked ancient.

As they took the path up the hill through the flowers, Old Man Johnson said, "It's fun to imagine how long and how many people it took to create the depression shown in this path."

"You're right, it is," replied Harry. "It's a pretty well-worn, deep depression—so many foot strikes."

Will felt the urge to stray from the path and run playfully through the flower field. Nobody stopped him; they just smiled.

Having finished the ascension of the small hill, Yori knocked on the door of what looked to be the building's living quarters. She said to the lady who answered, "Hello there. My name is Yori. Forgive me if I'm wrong, but is this the place with rooms for rent?"

"It is, my dear. You're in luck, both rooms are vacant. And please, call my Beatrice."

"Good news to be sure, Beatrice. I've also heard this building was once a tavern, long ago?"

"That it certainly was. Hillcrest Tavern was what it was last called. Follow me, all of you, and I'll tell you about it along the way." They all listened in as they walked around to the other side, except Will, who was still running aimlessly through the field. "This establishment has been in my family for countless generations. Though, the last beer was poured way before my time. My husband and I thought the place too beautiful to sit idly by, growing in deterioration as the years pass. We figured by making an investment in preservation and adding rooms for passersby, we could extend its life. We have since been returned that investment, and then some. Plus, there's been no indication the building has reached its final years."

The group stood, admiring the cedar woodwork. Prior to following Beatrice inside, Yori stated, "It's incomprehensible how the building has remained intact and functionable for so long."

Having left the door open for Will, Old Man Johnson quipped, "Funny, I was thinking the same thing about myself."

The party chuckled, as old man jests never got old, especially in Garobansurov.

Will saw that everyone had gone inside and hustled to catch up.

"I'll give you the grand tour," Beatrice extended. "One of the rooms is on the left side of the hallway, and the other is on the right. They're pretty much identical. However, the art is different, and the furs are different species."

"I love the stillness and the lighting. But what I love most is the air of antiquity. It feels aged, no doubt," commented Yori.

The group checked out the rooms. Then, Beatrice presented the rest of the tour. "At the end of the hallway resides a common room. It serves as a good way for tenants to get to know each other, if they so choose, as more times than not, strangers to each other occupy the opposing rooms. Throughout the years, many different activities have taken place within the common room. To name a few: card and board games, drinking and drinking contests, storytelling, armwrestling matches, fights, and spontaneous displays of sexual exhibitionism. All in all, the area has seen its share of use, especially in winter."

"I'm sure we'll put it to good use, tonight," declared Jason. "This is the last night of our vacation, we intend to make the best of it."

"Have at it," Beatrice emitted. "There's also a scenic, half-mile path leading down the north side of the hill. It'll take you past a meandering stream and the vestiges of a few old buildings that weren't as sturdily built as this one. I recommend it, given your legs aren't already too sore from having traveled so far."

"Much appreciation to you and your info. We'll probably give the path a whirl," said Yori. "And please, you and your husband, come join us tonight in the common room, if you wish. I'm sure we'll end up playing a game of some sort and telling a story or two. But I doubt we'll do any of the other activities you'd mentioned, especially the spontaneous exhibitionism."

Beatrice chuckled. "Well thank you, we may take you up on that."

After paying the reasonable rooms' fee and 45 minutes of winding down in the rooms, Yori, Jason, Harry, and Will walked the path Beatrice suggested, while Johnson took a nap.

They would not be disappointed, especially he in his nap.

The stream to which Beatrice referred was crystal clear and picturesque, and the building remnants surely tickled the imagination. Will spent half the walk on his father's shoulders, both of them enjoying the moment and a bond never severed.

Just like the nature walk, the evening—the grand finale of the trip—would end up being nothing short of entertaining. In fact, enjoyment herself would grab them all by the wrists and escort them though a good time.

A collection of games had been stashed away within a chest in the corner of the common room. One game in particular looked awfully inviting, due to its apparent complexity. The party, including Beatrice and her husband, planned to play it well into the night.

The playing of the game was heightened by the interesting creaks and moans of the building. They learned the sounds, for some reason, were only made at night.

Beatrice postulated, "It has something to do with the expanding and contracting of the basal stonework. The stones cool off in the night air and settle, I believe."

Moving a piece on the gameboard, Jason said, "That definitely makes sense. Another thing I tend to notice more at night, as I'm lying in a tent alongside the rapids of a river, are the sounds the rapids make. It's as if the rocks of the rapids are nocturnal, rolling around and audibly hitting each other exclusively when the sun goes down. I rather enjoy nighttime at the riverside."

"I've also noticed," Old Man Johnson voiced, "how sometimes at night after a certain sort of rainfall—I never could figure out exactly which sort—all the animals of a vast forest will come alive. One night I could identify over 50 species communicating to each other, whereas normally, you'd only hear five to ten nocturnals. It's a rather interesting phenomenon, I've always thought."

"As I lay helplessly dying in the desert one night," Harry said, "I noticed I could hear more of the desert animals calling out than normal. It wasn't 50 species—as you'd picked out that night, Mr. Johnson—but it was enough out of the ordinary for me to take note. It wasn't raining nor was there anything abnormal about the weather that I could tell. The whole thing was undeniably eerie."

"Yeah, it could be anything unexplainable causing the curiosity," Old Man Johnson stated. "Interesting stuff indeed."

"It kind of makes me at this moment want to listen more attentively to the animals outside," Yori admitted.

"Me too," Beatrice added.

For the heck of it, just before the conclusion of the game, the whole of the party went outside to count how many animal species they could hear. They only heard six, the least common being a heron, and determined it wasn't a night of distinct interest. But they did determine it was a night to remember, nevertheless.

Beatrice's husband ended up winning the game, not that he was particularly practiced at it, having only played it twice before. Either great luck or great strategy had met him that night. He was congratulated by all.

After the relic of a game was packed neatly into the box and put back into the chest, everyone retired to their respective beds.

Before leaving for the Capital in the morning, Yori and the others promised Beatrice they'd spread the word of her inn's magnificence. Beatrice became elated upon their pledges.

The final segment of the trip seemed like a short walk to them, even though it really wasn't. This was because they had no desire for the trip to end. Time flew by fast when you were having fun, or so certain wise men had said.

They reached the Capital by mid-afternoon—back to the grind. Old Man Johnson took Will to their old room, as the rest had important business. Yori and Jason corralled General Ulfenkerki, and together with Harry the four of them went straight to the castle and to the King.

Standing firm, the King was staring out a window of one of the castle's eastern rooms, when Jason, Yori, Ulfenkerki, and Harry approached. Rowlangiv turned around and immediately recognized Harry. Along with being an equitable King, he also had the intelligence to remember important faces. "Now that's a sight for sore eyes!"

"I finally made it back," Harry replied respectfully, as he made a point to tell himself to try and not speak over his King.

"Better late than never," Rowlangiv uttered, clearly glad to see Harry. "I bet you have one heck of a story to tell. And I'm guessing, since Yori and Jason are here standing with you, that you ran into them somewhere out in the wilderness, while they were on their trip?"

Jason communicated, "That he did. Coincidentally, our chance meeting occurred at the very point of our destination, Harry having no idea where he was at the time."

Harry, Jason, and Yori orated to Rowlangiv the details of the meeting, Harry's chance encounter with his son, and the rest of the trip. Afterwards, Harry divulged the entire account of his trip back from the west: of the deaths of the other messengers; of getting attacked by wild, poisonous beasts; of getting lost in the desert; of nearly dying at the compound in the middle of nowhere; and of the miraculous antidote hidden within a secret room.

After the discourse, he presented to Rowlangiv the saving bottle marked *ante*.

Rowlangiv inspected the bottle, and asked, "Do you mind if I show this to our chemists for analyzing? They may be able to duplicate it and potentially save lives."

"Not at all, sir. Go ahead and keep it. I have no further use for it. I'd actually kept it for that very reason."

"Thank you," returned the King. "That really was quite the experience to have befallen you. I'm glad you pulled through."

"Thanks, sir."

"We may as well shoot straight to your official report of the west now, Harry," emitted Rowlangiv. "I'm dying to hear it."

Harry had known exactly what he was going to say in his report, all except the first sentence, which he'd adlib. He took a deep breath and began. "I regret to inform that the General standing in this room is the only one left alive in Garobansurov. Generals Dalarginta and Wiotweisten had perished in small skirmishes seven and nine months ago, respectively. Fortunately, their charges didn't buckle under the losses. Lieutenants Ayena and Destroyer—a moniker—had risen to the call, maintaining the forces protecting the west and Riftolen. Ayena commands the army defending Riftolen, while Destroyer and his army range the countryside and nearby villages. Each army was 500 head strong at last count.

"All the ships of Riftolen were laid to waste by the Molisian Navy. Yet, the defensive batteries of Riftolen were strong enough to prevent the Molisian Navy from successfully conquering the city. It truly was an epic land-to-sea battle. In an effort to conserve what ships they had left, the Molisians fled. From that point on, they only reappeared for reconnaissance. It was estimated they had five large sailing ships designed specifically for war and half a dozen cruisers remaining. Who knows how many more they've built in the time I've been making my trip here.

"The folks of Riftolen were in the process of shipbuilding; but as you know, without copious funds, civilians aren't exactly highly motivated. The soldiers were helping with the construction, but even with their assistance, ships weren't turning out at speed. I'm guessing the two ships they were working on when I left are probably now finished. They were a couple of real beauties last I laid eyes. But they certainly didn't have the firepower to clear Garobansurovian seas of the Molisian threat.

"Riftolen's preservation lies balancing atop the thin edge of the wedge.

"And to add to the precarious situation, scouts reported that Molisian soldiers were amassing at the northwest border—not in an extreme amount, but enough to raise alarm.

"Upon my departure of Riftolen, its mayor—Reed Shawler—communicated to me and the other messengers to ask you, King Rowlangiv, for reinforcements. Reed completely understood if it was something that wasn't at all possible, as he was aware war had been occurring on all fronts. He sent his best regards. His last words to me, spoken in what I perceived as utter sincerity, were, *Long reign King Rowlangiv.*

"I received a chance to talk with many of Riftolen's inhabitants, and it was the consensus that faith in the Crown was still intact, a Garobansurovian people loyal through and through."

When Harry finished delivering his report, King Rowlangiv took a second to ponder, looked to Ulfenkerki, and said, "I guess it could be worse."

"True, sir," the General replied.

"Including what we already have, we couldn't possibly build enough additional ships to overpower what the enemy potentially brandishes," noted Rowlangiv. "Maybe in a year, we could, but that would be too late, I'm afraid. Things are escalating everywhere rather quickly. If we possessed the proper funds for motivation, it'd be possible to assist Riftolen. But the treasury has been scraped pretty dry as of late."

"And I'm certain the Molisian prisoners wouldn't help build the very devices used to fight against their countrymen," Ulfenkerki added. "Not without being paid handsomely, anyway."

"I earnestly desire to assist Riftolen—our left hand of defense—but I don't know if anything we could do would help." Rowlangiv sighed heavily. "Marching a force there would take far too long, and if we sailed soldiers aboard an insufficient amount of boats, they'd fall victim to their navy."

Ulfenkerki looked out the window to think. He noticed a rock with an abnormal amount of moss—an observation having no real bearing on anything important. He turned from the rock and refocused.

A few minutes elapsed, and the General finally spoke. "Perhaps, sir, we could begin construction on a fleet, and maybe a cache of wealth for speedier shipbuilding will miraculously appear at some point along the way. If it doesn't, even if we don't utilize them to ferry soldiers to Riftolen, having the extra vessels couldn't hurt. Those of my charge—and most likely the Icytryxans— won't mind a little extra physical labor to pass the time."

Jason augmented, "I know I personally wouldn't object. Sore muscles and I are old friends."

Rowlangiv smiled at Jason and his wit, then turned back to Ulfenkerki. "It's undeniably a course of action that holds water, General. I would have no idea from where such a pile of gold, precious gems, or any other valuable trading commodities would appear in order to make the plan entirely successful, but I do like it. My decision is thus: The General's plan will commence and as soon as possible. I'll see if I can allocate any funds from elsewhere to the cause, but as you're all aware, war requirements have already been siphoning the treasury considerably. Nevertheless, let's get the ball rolling. Yori, you can go ahead and start informing everybody of the General's plan, and that it's to begin immediately."

"Right away, sir," Yori responded, knowing exactly what her first few moves would be. Yori knew the steps of heralding the King's decisions as perfectly as most knew the backs of their hands.

Before the conference concluded, the King solemnly emitted, "Harry, what you did for Garobansurov, the sacrifices you made, the hardships you endured, will never go forgotten. I thank you from the bottom of my heart. I'm truly sorry about your wife. Please enjoy this time with your son. And if there's ever anything you need from the Crown, feel free to ask, and I'll see that it's fulfilled."

"It's been my honor, sir," Harry uttered, tall and proud.

The room emptied quickly, as everyone but Harry had important business to attend to.

Harry went to the inn where Will and Old Man Johnson were staying. He walked up to the front desk and paid two weeks' worth for the room adjacent Old Man Johnson's. He knew eventually he and his son would travel back home, but not before he recuperated. The mission had been extremely strenuous, and a sojourn was what his mind, body, and heart utterly desired.

For two weeks, Harry, Will, and Old Man Johnson enjoyed each other's company. They saw the sights of the Capital, ate whatever they wanted, and played a myriad of games. It was sort of a way for Old Man Johnson to say goodbye to Will, because he knew Will and Harry would eventually leave for home. All the time Mr. Johnson had spent taking care of Will made him grow quite fond of the boy. He would surely miss him.

CHAPTER 24

WHILE HARRY, WILL, and Johnson enjoyed their two weeks, along with the Crown's shipbuilding initiative seeing two weeks' worth of progression, Mick and Dave's battalion walked hard. They covered much ground.

"It seems as if the dew drops on those trees are so evenly spaced that the hand of God dipped them into a lake," Dave noted to Mick, walking with most of his weight on his right leg. He'd suffered a pulled left hamstring the day previous.

"It is a rather beautiful sight, almost as much as the Capital will be when we finally lay eyes upon her this afternoon," Mick replied.

"We've been away for quite some time. I wonder how much of it has changed."

"There undoubtedly was substantial damage from the battle," Mick commented, as he moved a branch perfect for tripping out of the path. "I'm curious how much has been repaired."

"We'll soon find out, only one river fording to go," voiced Dave, sidestepping animal scat, an awareness of mind which seemed others before him had lacked.

"Yup. It's been a long, perilous undertaking, one in which we've cheated death many times."

"And one in which he has done the same to us," Dave tagged on.

"Mister Grim Reaper: the most powerful of all equalizers."

Having walked efficiently for the better part of the day, together with there being no mishaps in crossing the river, the company could finally see the great walls and multistory buildings of the Capital in the distance. Twenty minutes later, two hours before sunset, they approached the main gate. *Mission: Officially accomplished.*

Mick and Dave shot to the head of the column, so the guards at the gate would see them and know the incoming formation was friend, not foe. With a wave of the hand, the front gate was opened. Including the additional recruits Anna skillfully obtained along the way: 150 new soldiers for Ulfenkerki began filing into town.

"Don't spend your coins all in one place," Dave comically shouted to the soldiers, soldiers who'd so faithfully followed him and Mick through thick and thin. "First, we'll introduce you to the General and possibly others, then, you'll be free to enjoy the city. Being your commanding officers has been Mick's and my pleasure. Minus the obvious few— the traitors—you have all been outstating soldiers. Who knows, we may battle alongside you again, as the war with Molisia shows no signs of termination."

The squad let their appreciation for Mick and Dave be known.

Mick and Dave led their battalion through town towards the army barracks, drawing much attention from the city folk along the way. New faces always tended to draw attention, no matter the circumstances.

When they neared the barracks, Mick and Dave noticed Ulfenkerki, Jason, and a couple other officers were already standing out front to greet them. Apparently, news of their return had traveled faster than they.

Followed by Jason and two other officers, General Ulfenkerki started walking forward to close the gap. The General shook Mick and Dave's hands, and said, "Thraiker, Ghrere, welcome back to the Capital, and with an entourage, no less."

"General, good to see you," said Mick. "They're a hardy, victorious entourage, worthy soldiers eager to serve their king."

"Magnificent," Ulfenkerki reciprocated. "So, you were successful in reclaiming the north?"

"Every northern town and stronghold, large and small, has been stripped from Molisian control, I'm proud to announce," proclaimed Dave, "thanks to the outstanding valor of these fine men and women standing before you."

"Well I'll be damned!" the General emitted, in melodic fashion. "Extraordinary accomplishment if ever there was one. You two certainly are the yardstick by which achievement is measured. Your soldiers' legs must be weary from a long, grueling march." Ulfenkerki looked to the officer standing next to Jason, and instructed, "Have them go ahead and unwind."

The officer complied, wasting no time in showing the soldiers to the barracks.

"I have all their signed and sealed contracts in my backpack," Mick reported to the General.

"We'll file those away later," noted Ulfenkerki, "but for now, let's go inform Rowlangiv of the superlative news."

"Yes," said Dave, "good idea."

The group proceeded into the castle, and thanks to information provided by an attentive guard, they found Rowlangiv without much effort. The King had been exercising in the recreation room of the lower level and hadn't yet heard about Mick and Dave's return.

Having relinquished what he was doing, a relieved monarch flashed his guests a genial grin. "I love a surprise, probably one of the top 20 aspects of life. It's been an exceptionally bounteous couple of weeks, everyone is showing up; first, Harry, now, the two of you." Rowlangiv embraced his friends. "Ecstatic to see you, truly."

"Never disenchanting to see you either, sir," returned Mick Thraiker.

Dave added, "Who knew you possessed such finesse with a fist; you were really showing that punching dummy some dexterous maneuvers."

"It only looked that way; it's immobile and doesn't return blows," Rowlangiv remarked in joking tone.

The group chuckled, not to patronize the King, but because he was genuinely a funny person when occasion called for it. After the chuckle, Mick and Dave set down their heavy backpacks and weaponry. Ulfenkerki, Jason, and the other officer also lightened their loads.

Ulfenkerki emitted, "I must say, sir, over the years you've certainly been exhibiting improvement in the pugilistic arts."

"I try to stay committed," replied Rowlangiv. "Speaking of improvement, has there been any in our war standing, Mick, Dave?"

Mick answered, "I'm pleased to inform the north is now completely secure. We reclaimed in your name every town and stronghold between here and the border. The Baustic mountains and its foothills have never been so peaceful. The town of Yernoke was the most difficult to regain, but as we speak, its Garobansurovian flag waves high in the sky. Plus, we enlisted 150 new soldiers for the army, who are now getting settled in the barracks. We also picked up a master recruiter along the way, a beautiful young lady attached to a heck of a story."

"I look forward to hearing it," stated the King. "And now, I'll share our news. A couple weeks ago, one of the long distance messengers returned—ironically, the father of the boy you found wandering the countryside—and gave us a full report of everything transpiring in the west. Because of this report, I decided to initiate a plan, one conceived by the General. It consists of building ships to transport soldiers to assist Riftolen. However, the plan has a stipulation. We don't have the funds or manpower to build enough warships in a reasonable amount of time to be successful. But the General suggested we start building them anyway, and maybe miraculously a pile of money would fall from the sky. It's a long shot, but Riftolen is in dire straits, and we have to attempt something."

With his mouth practically stretching from one end of the room to the other, Dave revealed a toothy smile. "I don't know about falling from the sky, but perhaps sprouting from the ground would suffice?" Dave reached to the ground, into his backpack, and pulled out a sack. "We only required half the gold coins you gave us for the mission, sire, here's the other half. Hopefully, it's adequate to succeed at Riftolen." Dave extended the sack to the King.

Rowlangiv was flabbergasted. Astounded by the immense weight of the sack, he was overjoyed that he'd begun the General's plan a couple weeks ago. "I don't know how you two do it so consistently, but you saved us once again. This will definitely be enough to construct a fleet quickly enough to sail to Riftolen with confidence. Sprouting from the ground, indeed."

Ulfenkerki declared, "I love it when a plan comes together."

"Let's hope the Molisians haven't been equally blessed by ground sprouts," voiced the King. "Although, I won't worry about it. I've utmost confidence we can make safe the western sea. How did you two accomplish so much with so little?"

Mick answered, "With superb soldiers, solid strategy, loyalty to a fault from a certain duo, and a little luck."

"Well, let's hear all about it," Rowlangiv uttered enthusiastically.

Mick discoursed on the whole of the mission. He told of every town, every battle, every person of significance, Anna's story of being trapped in her underground prison, Leon's deceit, Gus and Vern's faithful actions, and a little comic relief. He was so detailed he even included some of the romantic encounters.

After the expatiation, Ulfenkerki spoke with resolute disposition. "Anna will be my new lead recruiter. The stalwarts, Gus and Vern, will be immediately installed into permanent officer positions. I've come to believe the value of these three to be immeasurable."

"Dave and I firmly stand beside that statement. Anna, Gus, and Vern have qualities unparalleled."

"There was a certain part of your story, Mick, that especially caught my attention," said the King. "You said this traitor, Leon, was part of a caravan now settled in the Infertile Zone."

"Correct. He's now imprisoned here at the Capital."

"You mentioned he survived being poisoned by a creature, whereas his traveling companions did not. Curious. Just two weeks ago, I was given this." Rowlangiv reached into the pocket of a jacket lying nearby and presented to Mick and Dave the bottle found by Harry labeled *ante*. "I was going to bring it to our chemical engineers after I was done with the dummy beating."

Dave perused the bottle and began saying the four letters aloud, "A-N-T-E."

"Apparently," said the King, "whoever wrote on the bottle and inserted the chemical within, didn't know how to spell antidote. The contents of the bottle saved Harry's life, as he too was bitten by poisonous beasts. Inches from death, he drank this antidote and survived." The

King told the whole of Harry's ordeal to Mick and Dave. Afterwards, Dave relayed exactly what Lois had told them about the day the creatures attacked and of her group's relocation to the Infertile Zone. The stories took up a half hour of their lives. Though, it was time well spent, for intrigue was thicker than the walls of the castle.

"It's uncanny how everything lines up so seamlessly," noted the King. "It appears Leon, the hobby chemist, conceived this antidote, and for reasons unbeknownst left it behind without sharing it with the other poison victims, leaving them to die. He may be a murderer along with being a traitor. Once evil, always evil."

"We can question Leon," stated Mick, "but he's no idiot. I doubt he'll give anything away. Our conjecture isn't proof enough to convict him of murder."

Rowlangiv responded, "True."

Leon would be interrogated by many people for many moons, but he'd never confess to them nor let further evidence slip. Nobody but one would ever learn definitively if he let his compatriots die and why. Most who were familiar with the story were suspicious, while some were certain of his guilt, regardless. He would keep his guilt hidden nearly to his death.

The antidote would eventually be replicated and save many lives throughout history. Leon would never receive credit for his discovery, a small price to pay for murder.

Leon and his cohorts, for their treasonous acts, were kept in the Capital's prison for fifteen years. The day before Leon died—a few decades after being let out of prison—he confessed his guilt to his wife. He also confessed to her why he didn't share the antidote with the others. His lack of compassion was because the two who needed the antidote were his childhood enemies. It was a rivalry most would've disregarded by adulthood, but not Leon, he never forgot. And he never regretted any of it once.

The dialogue in the castle concerning the Leon matter reached its conclusion. All but one went from the recreation wing to a comfortable drawing room, one flight up, for further discussion.

Mick, Dave, Jason, Ulfenkerki, and Rowlangiv talked in great detail regarding the optimization of the gold coins Mick and Dave returned. A foundation for efficient shipbuilding needed to be laid out. In these intricate blueprints, much of Garobansurov and its people would be utilized at some point or another.

"In my assessment," said Ulfenkerki, "we should be ready to sail for Riftolen in under six months."

"I was thinking similarly," noted the King. "By then, we should have enough ships constructed to haul a sizable force; a staunch, powerful contingent consisting of both Garobansurovian and Icytryxan troops."

"Precisely," emitted Ulfenkerki.

"Thraiker, Ghrere," Rowlangiv raised, "will you be accompanying us to Riftolen? You by no means should feel obligated, as you've already proven your loyalty to Garobansurov, ten times over. Your value to the furthering of our freedom has been immeasurable. The choice of whether or not to come is completely up to you. I'll be sailing to Riftolen with the troops, and of course I'd feel safer knowing you'd be at my side."

"As would I," added the General.

Jason jumped in. "And I must say that without question you'd make the long sea voyage more bearable. Who knows, we may again hook into another fish so immense that landing it takes the combined efforts of the three of us."

Mick chuckled. "Yeah, that was indeed quite the experience on our way to Swyrove."

Dave phrased, "We will be heading back to Chalatore soon, and all I can say for now is that we'll think it over while we're there."

"So, don't count us out," Mick attached.

"Fair enough," produced Rowlangiv. "If you decide to accompany us, shoot to be back to the Capital within five and three-quarters months to be safe. We may not depart until six months from now, but you never know."

"Very well, sir," said Dave.

For a couple hours, the group lounged in the relaxing room with red-tinged upholstery. They discussed more of Mick and Dave's mission, Capital incidences, the Icytryxis/Garobansurov relationship, and the excursion to the fabled tree.

After the agreeable meeting with Rowlangiv and company, Mick and Dave were finally afforded the opportunity to see how Old Man Johnson was doing. The pair had learned easy enough where he was staying.

Mick knocked on the door of Johnson's room, and bellowed, "You in there, old friend?"

Having recognized the voice immediately, Johnson opened the door as quickly as his old bones allowed. "I was starting to wonder if your mission this time around was going to last longer than the Icytryxis one."

"Nope, a few weeks shorter," replied Dave.

"It's good to see you two survived yet another bout of danger. Come inside, tell me all about it."

Mick and Dave made themselves at home in Mr. Johnson's room, and the three started discoursing on their escapades. Since Harry and Will were occupying the room next door, Will could hear and recognize their voices. He burst into the room, happy to see Mick and Dave again. Old Man Johnson introduced Harry to Mick and Dave, and the three fast became friends. Harry earnestly thanked Mick and Dave for helping Will reach the safety of the Capital.

Post pleasantries, Mick clued in Harry on Leon and whatnot. Harry was astonished, learning of the antidote's origin and the treachery therein.

Five separate voices echoed in Mr. Johnson's room for hours.

By the end of evening, Mick, Dave, and Old Man Johnson resolved to begin their trek back home to Chalatore in two days' time. Also, since it was along the way, Harry decided he and Will would travel with them. The more the merrier.

Mick and Dave flipped a coin. The winner, Dave, slept on the second bed of Old Man Johnson's room; the loser, Mick, the floor.

Since it was now Mick and Dave's last full day at the Capital—at least it would be for a while—they were determined to see as many friends as possible. They'd start with one of their best, a beautiful man whose time had been cut short, Thyxer, laid to rest at the Capital. Traditionally, he would've been buried with his Icytryxan ancestors back on Swyrove, but such a feat would've been too physically arduous. In fact, the Icytryxan army had begun a new tradition of burying their fallen soldiers *side-by-side* with Garobansurov's, as in Mick and Dave's speech on Swyrove. The fallen few of both armies were buried side-by-side, promoting brotherhood in death as well as in life. The sentiment was beloved by all.

The cemetery was centrally located, a mere few hundred yards from the castle; a well-maintained, well-landscaped locale. Syryx and Yusyta joined Mick and Dave in the lovely morning visit. They all contemplated in reverence on their many fond memories of Thyxer. They also paid their respects to all the other fallen veterans buried at the cemetery.

Afterwards, the quartet decided to eat breakfast together at a nearby restaurant, one specializing in early risers.

At a mammoth of a table, Syryx professed, "I cherish the exact place they put him. The tree he lies underneath is undeniably breathtaking."

"Thyxer will enjoy many cool mornings, thanks to its abundant shade," Yusyta added.

"I know the person in charge of the cemetery's landscaping," produced Dave. "She has 50 years' experience in the landscaping arts. The King himself chose her for the position."

"It certainly shows," vocalized Syryx. "The setting is gorgeous."

Mick asked, "Yusyta, when's the next time you plan to visit Alfonso? As you're aware, we're leaving for Chalatore in 24 hours; it's always pleasurable having you accompany us home, while you journey to Dourinuset. Harry and Will are coming too, so along with Old Man Johnson it'd be six in total."

"Sounds frolicsome. I hadn't planned on going again for a couple weeks, but maybe I can advantageously rearrange a few things. I'll get back to you about it by tomorrow morning."

"Excellent!" returned Thraiker. "I hope you do. The trek would be the peak of many peaks."

After somehow managing to gulp her entire beverage gracefully, Syryx lobbed out to Mick and Dave, "Please tell Yusyta and I all about the north: the people you'd met, the diverse environments you'd encountered, and the amazing things you'd seen. I want to hear all the fascinating details."

"We will gladly do so," reciprocated Dave. He and Mick began taking turns, speaking candidly of their northern excursion.

The four ended up being at the restaurant for two hours, loving each other's company and talking up a storm.

Subsequent the get together with Syryx and Yusyta, Dave and Mick paid others a visit. Tim Warmane and Gregg Hogarty were on that list, friends whose words never disappointed. They also visited a few other soldiers and civilians, telling them all they would be leaving on the morrow but intended to return at some point.

Late afternoon rolled around, and along with it, their day's last rendezvous. Hawk and Leopard met Yori and Jason on the main thoroughfare for an evening of drinks and exuberance. Despite the early hour for drinking, congestion had already manifested, as the Capital showed no signs of losing vitality. As many would say, prosperity, even during wartime, was the sign of an exceptional King.

Their first stop was a certain tavern, having breezed in not because it had inviting flare, but because all except Jason had never been there before. Here, Yori finally heard all the details of Mick and Dave's northern mission.

"An absolutely captivating oration, guys. I was utterly absorbed by the telling." Yori articulated, "I had previously heard some of the things concerning your mission, but from people who weren't there. Without a doubt, those who'd participated in an ordeal are those who can best describe it."

"I like how you said that," expressed Dave. "It rolled right off your tongue."

"On occasion," cracked Yori, "eloquence will reveal itself in the unlikeliest of places."

The four chuckled and prepared to leave their first stop of the evening.

At the second tavern, Yori and Jason talked of their trip to Calamity's End to an extremely interested audience of two. Mick and Dave resolved to visit the ancient tree themselves one day.

Having departed the second tavern, the four began walking down a lantern-lit boulevard, a thoroughfare full of animation.

Jason asked Mick, Dave, and Yori, "Since we're nearby, do the three of you care to patronize the rowdiest place in town? I'm in the mood for a little excitement."

"I'm game, if you two are," answered Yori.

"I see no reason to refrain," posed Dave.

"Lead the way," Mick announced. "It's our last night at the Capital for a while; we might as well make the best of it."

Their chosen path would not let them down.

Mick, Dave, and Jason woke up the next morning on the semi-comfortable grass of a public park, Yori having somehow managed to make it home. The guys sat up, looked at each other, and laughed, having recalled the wild circumstances that'd brought them there.

"Who knew a quartet could have that much liveliness?" uttered Jason.

"You can say that again," agreed Dave.

After a good-humored reminiscing of the previous night's fun-loving activities, they all stood up and shook hands, bidding farewell.

Jason declared, "You guys really did perform marvelously in the north. True grit. Have a good trip back to Chalatore."

"Thanks, Jason," returned Mick. "It should be enjoyable; we'll have plenty of excellent company for it."

"That you will," stated Jason. "Will, Harry, and Old Man Johnson truly are that."

Dave jumped in, "Yusyta might be coming too now."

"Well then, your trek will be utmost pleasurable. I'm jealous."

Dave voiced, "The homestretch, the last 80 miles, will be just Old Man Johnson, Mick, and I."

"Nice. It goes without saying, but stay safe," emitted Jason, "and I do hope you join us on the Riftolen expedition."

"Stay safe yourself, old friend," let out Dave.

Mick added, "If you see us again before you depart for Riftolen, it means we're coming."

"I'll keep my eyes open for you," Jason concluded.

After parting with their childhood friend, Mick and Dave called upon another childhood friend. Old Man Johnson was in his room at the inn finishing up with his packing, when the duo appeared. Mick and Dave also had to pack, but it'd be an easy task, as they hadn't unloaded much from their backpacks since returning from the mission in the north.

Old Man Johnson said, "I got word this morning that Yusyta will indeed be accompanying us."

"Wonderful," emitted Dave.

Harry and Will were set to go, followed shortly by the rest. Along with their gear, the five grabbed their senses of adventure and left the inn.

At the pre-designated place, they met up with Yusyta, and together the six began to walk. Mick and Dave were headed to their homes on the pond just outside Chalatore. Old Man Johnson was steering to his cabin near Chalatore. Will and Harry were headed to their farm northwest of Chalatore. And Yusyta was headed to the hilltop Dourinuset Monastery to visit her husband, Alfonso.

High spirited, all six girted up their loins and left the Capital behind.

Chapter 25

TWO HUNDRED YARDS distance from the Capital, Old Man Johnson turned around to view it. He was certain he'd never again lay eyes upon Garobansurov's most magnificent city. "I'm satisfied in knowing I made the absolute best of my last venture there." He blissfully pondered all the great people he'd met and places he'd seen therein. He consolidated his thoughts to a level of conclusiveness that his life truly had been vast.

A dozen days and nights had elapsed. They'd been enjoying the trip as much as they'd anticipated, but the highlight of the trip was soon to occur.

Like many evenings before, the six began to make their nightly camp along the banks of a river.

Harry scoped the lengths of the river, ascertaining if there were any deep spots, a worried father making sure nothing too dangerous was present for an occasionally inattentive son.

Unlike every river scrutiny before on that trip, he found a part unusually deep. Puzzled by the discovery, and driven by curiosity, he further examined the area, trying to figure out why exactly the area was so deep and wide.

He found the answer downstream, then went to get the rest, so they too could see his remarkable discovery.

Having everyone's undivided attention, Harry announced, "I had to move aside a lot of brush and dirt to get at it, but as you can see, a primordial dam lies before you."

"That is amazing," exclaimed Dave. "I've been through these parts dozens of times and had no idea this was here."

"Probably because of all the debris that was concealing it," Harry reasoned. "I'd surveyed the area closely, because I was curious about the river's deep locus, for which I'm positive the dam is responsible."

"Right," agreed Mick. "Even though a structure is no longer impacting a body of water, its influence can still be perceived countless years succeeding its demise."

"It looks to be hundreds, maybe thousands, of years old," voiced Yusyta. "Very interesting."

"The reason for the dam being constructed at this exact spot could've been a myriad of things," communicated Harry. "Maybe it powered a waterwheel, which turned a mill for grinding or sawing. Though, I don't see any vestiges of a waterwheel or mill lying around."

"Powering a wheel is a likely reason," vocalized Yusyta. "Less likely, the dam could've been set into place to create a recreational area, a leisure scene for swimming and lounging."

"Possibly."

"Let's make our thirteenth nightly camp right here," Will suggested eagerly, a smile running across his face.

They all fancied Will's proposal and moved their already half-setup tents to the area adjacent the eight-foot-tall dam remnants.

Since it may've been his last chance to do so, Old Man Johnson went fishing with Will. During the pair's bittersweet moment, the rest performed a plethora of activities, including scanning for other signs of past inhabitants that'd stood the test of time. They did find some, but none as grandiose as the dam itself, nor did they find any conclusive evidence supplying an answer to the question of why the dam had been erected in the first place.

As it turned out, the deep water harbored many fish. The pair had caught enough to supply hearty platters for everyone. After supper, they went fishing again but this time practiced catch and release. They endeavored to catch the biggest fish ever.

A larger than normal campfire had been assembled, which fit alongside a larger-than-normal wind. Together, the two acts of nature composed music for the six.

Fire towering before her, Yusyta emitted, "I must've swallowed a pine needle while gathering firewood. I can't seem to extinguish this bitter pine taste from my mouth."

"I've been there before," Mick noted.

"Just once, I'd like an evergreen needle to leave a pleasant taste lingering in my mouth." Yusyta chuckled.

Old Man Johnson laughed and digressed, "Here's something I find interesting for you all to consider. It's funny how sometimes when you hear wind blowing in distant trees, you can count to a certain number, and hear it again in the canopy above. And sometimes when you hear it in the same distant trees, and carry out the same count, you don't hear it again at all. Wind mustn't be too fond of patterns."

"Very true, my good man. In fact, much of nature doesn't seem to be governed by patterns," Mick added.

"Intriguing, indeed." Dave declared, "There's always beauty in the woods, you just have to know how to look."

"Isn't that the truth?" Harry voiced.

Dave asked Harry and Will, "I'm not sure if you've ever heard, but are you familiar with Yusyta's love story, and why exactly she's going to Dourinuset Monastery?"

"I just know her husband is there, and that she's on her way to visit him," replied Harry. "I can't say I've heard their love story."

"Well, in that case, Harry, Will," Yusyta jumped in, "I will tell you the entire story. Mick and Dave are even in it."

"That we are," said Dave. "It truly is quite the romantic tale."

"And maybe by airing it, I can get this taste out of mouth," wished Yusyta.

Surrounded by gusty winds, in front of an immense fire, Yusyta began sharing her and Alfonso's story to Harry and Will—the kind that anyone could tell was 100 percent true. Mick, Dave, and Old Man Johnson were already acquainted with every detail, but they listened in as if they weren't, for it was one of those timeless narrations to which a person could listen over and over again—especially when told by Yusyta. She was such an adept storyteller.

The story blended with the wind and fire so harmoniously it was clear the *three* were supposed to make music together all along.

Harry and Will had certainly been enthralled by Yusyta's hour-long story and thanked her for sharing it. If Yusyta told the story 10,000 times, she'd still want to tell it 10,000 more.

Afterwards, topics bobbled from one to another, like a pair of loons bouncing from one fishless pond to the next. In the end, all the topics they'd discussed were declared entertaining.

The group confessed to having a thoroughly mesmerizing time next to the ancient dam and went to bed smiling and smelling of smoke.

A few days of efficient walking later, they arrived at the dreaded fork in the road where Yusyta would separate.

"Enjoy the climb up the hill to Dourinuset, Yusyta," Dave insisted, full of heart.

Mick added, "Say hello to Alfonso and the rest for us."

"I'll certainly do both," Yusyta returned. "I had an amazing time accompanying you all on this trek. I hope to repeat it someday. Safe travels to all of you on your journeys home."

The whole of the party expressed their earnest appreciation of her company and bade their lovely Icytryxan friend farewell.

Post hugs, Yusyta walked to the left, while the rest walked to the right. When separated by 50 feet, all six turned around for one final wave goodbye.

Saddened by the diminishing, Mick, Dave, Harry, Will, and Johnson continued walking, and couldn't help but notice they were now strictly a party of males. They took pleasure during the next few days but were certainly unenthusiastic about Yusyta's absence.

Three days after Yusyta's departure, another dreaded fork approached. This one was for Will and Harry, who would travel a couple days to the north to their farm.

"We're not far from where we discovered Will wandering the countryside," Mick stated.

"Just over that hill," Dave said, as he pointed.

"I can't express enough gratitude to all of you for what you've done for us," Harry put forth. "Such selflessness is a rarity these days."

Once the fork lay beneath their feet, Old Man Johnson gave Will a great hug, and said, "I'm going to miss you, little buddy. We had a lot of amazing times together, which I'll never forget. I wish the best for you and your father."

"I'll never forget them either," Will said with a frown.

Harry voiced, "I'm sure we'll see each other again."

Final heartfelt goodbyes were exchanged by all. Father and son walked off into the distance, as Old Man Johnson felt sorrow creep over.

However, the sadness wasn't eternal, for in the span of the rest of Old Man Johnson's life, under the power of aged legs, he trekked to see his little buddy twice, as it was a trip much shorter than the one to the Capital. Plus, Will made the journey to see him thrice. All five instances were utterly joyful reunions, high watermarks for an old man in the twilight of his life.

The venturing party had now dwindled to how it began many months previous, encompassing the initial trio of Mick, Dave, and Old Man Johnson. But it wouldn't remain so for very long.

The day subsequent Harry and Will's parting, three days' walk yet from Chalatore, the trio chanced upon a man needing assistance.

"Hello, good sirs," a stranger sitting uncomfortably at the side of the road said to Mick, Dave, and Johnson.

"Same to you," voiced Dave.

"My name is Joe. I'd hate to trouble you, but you wouldn't happen to have any extra food, would you? I had plenty with which to finish my amble home, but I clumsily tripped at the least opportune time, and my once adequate supply tumbled irretrievably into the depths of a lake. I mean really, what are the odds of that?"

"A pretty unlikely occurrence, indeed," replied Mick. "But as luck would have it, we possess a surplus of sustenance and would be happy to oblige."

"Thank you, outstanding gentlemen."

While Mick pulled bundles of fish, bread, and assorted vegetables out of his pack, Dave asked Joe, "Which way are you headed?"

Looking over his shoulder and pointing, Joe replied, "that direction."

"Us too. We would enjoy your company, until our paths diverge, if you'd like? The more the merrier."

"Sounds lovely. I'll take you up on that offer."

Mick handed the friendly newcomer the bundles, and after Joe quickly satisfied his empty stomach, the foursome resumed walking.

Mick inquired, "So, Joe, what brings you out into the majestic Garobansurovian countryside?"

"I guess you could boil it down to my powerful long-term memory."

Mick, Dave, and Johnson were puzzled, but only for a moment, as they suspected Joe would elaborate.

"I have an uncanny ability to memorize every single detail of every locale I visit. This faculty of mine feeds an addiction, one which compels me to see as many different places as possible. It's been an obsession since childhood."

"That brings up an interesting question: Is the witnessing of beauty relative? Not exactly an easy question for anyone to answer." Mick released his hold on deep thought and asked Joe, "So, your brain releases endorphins through the memorization?"

"Yes, that sounds about right. I'm constantly traveling, constantly endeavoring to find places I've never been."

"That sounds like a pretty fulfilling life, if you asked me," noted Dave.

"I've no complaints. I've experienced much," returned Joe. "I'm finally going home now, after a six-month stint on the road."

"Where do you call home?" asked Dave.

Joe went on to say he lived on an isolated pond, for which he supplied an unmistakable oral description.

The quartet would trip together for the next three days, all going home to Chalatore. Mick and Dave each walked with a little more spring in their step, happy in finally having met the owner of the only other abode on their unnamed pond, almost large enough to be considered a lake.

About the Author

NICHOLAS WUDTKE, minimalist, naturalist, and ponderer of philosophy, is rarely seen doing otherwise than sitting on a rock or fallen tree somewhere in the still of Wisconsin's vast Chequamegon-Nicolet National Forest, writing. Nicholas is the father of two sons, one who passed away at a young age due to complications of severe brain damage. Nicholas spent the best years of his life caring for this child, whom he named Lifeson, and his current epic fantasy series is being written in honor of him.

Nicholas enjoys trail running, backpacking, bonsai trees, fossil hunting, and last but not least, listening to favorite rock band Rush, his inspiration, insisting one can come nowhere even close to experiencing this rock power-trio enough.

NICHOLAS WUDTKE

Author of a list of novels—*The Swords: Friendships and Winds of Far-off Places*, and three installments of his seven-novel *Black Needle* series, including: (1) *Parabolic, Magnetic Key*; (2) *Blunt but Imminently Fatal Projectile*; and (3) *Deserved, Contorted Relics*, Nicholas is a free spirit, currently living in a small home surrounded by trees, a swamp, and fresh air. He cherishes his time with his son, his girlfriend, and the rest of his family and friends.

GET YOUR NEXT GREAT READ!

VISIT

WWW.NICHOLASWUDTKE.COM

TODAY!

www.ingramcontent.com/pod-product-compliance
Lightning Source LLC
Chambersburg PA
CBHW070810190726
48292CB00006B/1953